PARIS RULES

What Reviewers Say About
Jaime Maddox's Work

Bouncing

"Jaime Maddox, Jaime Maddox. She always seems to start out with these feel good lesbian romances. You're reading along, enjoying the fun and light ride, and then—BAM—you get hit with the twisty and suddenly the light ride turns into a twisty, turney awesome mess."
—Danielle Kimerer, Librarian, Reading Public Library (Reading, MA)

Deadly Medicine

"The tale ran at a good, easy pace. ...It was one of those books that it is hard to put down, so I didn't. ...Very, very well done."—*Prism Book Alliance*

Hooked

"[A] compelling, insightful and passionate romantic thriller."
—*Lesfic Tumblr*

[Maddox] did an excellent job of portraying the struggles of addiction, not the entire focus of the story, but informative just the same. ...All the characters are deep, bringing them to life with their complexities. An intricately woven story line adds credibility; life leaps from the pages."—*Lunar Rainbow Reviewz*

Visit us at www.boldstrokesbooks.com

By the Author

Agnes

The Common Thread

Bouncing

Deadly Medicine

Hooked

The Scholarship

Love Changes Everything

Paris Rules

Paris Rules

by

Jaime Maddox

2022

PARIS RULES

ISBN 13: 978-1-63679-077-0

This Trade Paperback Original Is Published By
Bold Strokes Books, Inc.
P.O. Box 249
Valley Falls, NY 12185

First Edition: January 2022

CREDITS
Editor: Shelley Thrasher
Production Design: Susan Ramundo
Cover Design By Tammy Seidick

Acknowledgments

As always, I owe my family for tolerating me when I ignore them during fits of creative genius. Carolyn, Jamison, and Max: I love you.

I am forever grateful to my dear friend Margaret, who reads my initial drafts and still talks to me afterward and gives me sound advice to make the final product much better than the first. Likewise, my editor, Shelley Thrasher, is patient with little issues like point of view, and when I change software mid-edit, and gives suggestions that make my manuscripts greater novels. I feel fortunate that the fates brought us together at BSB. Thank you, Shelley. Thanks to Tammy Seidick for this great cover. Thanks to the women of BSB who make all of this possible: Radclyffe, Sandy Lowe, Stacia Seaman, Cindy Cresap, Ruth Sternglantz, Toni Whittaker, and Carsen Taite. Finally, somewhere out there people are reading these words I string together, and I thank each of them for doing so, because if you read, I can continue to write.

Dedication

To my lovely wife Carolyn:

Twenty years ago, we flew to Paris as friends and came back to a whole new world. It's been wonderful, with traces of terrible from time to time. We've cried a little, but mostly after laughing hysterically. Now that we're older we think of the things we might have done differently, but I don't think we could have done them better. I look forward to more golf, and dinners that other people cook, and adventures on every continent. Whatever I do, as long as I'm with you, I know it will be amazing.

CHAPTER ONE

PARIS DREAMS

Nice, France
Then

Carly Becker stepped out of the large glass double doors of Le Negresco and into the balmy Mediterranean night. Before her, expensive cars jammed the Promenade des Anglais in both directions. Vacationers hurried back to hotels or, like her, out for the evening. It was just seven o'clock—plenty of time to make it to their destination in time for the sunset.

"Ready?" Pip asked as she gently rubbed Carly's elbow and then quickly returned her hand to her side.

"Yep. Just taking it all in. What a view." Past the cars and the pedestrian traffic, Carly saw only the brilliant blue waters of the Côte d'Azur. The Blue Coast.

"Do you want to stroll along the Promenade like proper French people or window-shop on this side of the street?"

"Let's cross over. We have time for a stroll, don't we?"

"Of course."

They proceeded to the crosswalk and then traversed four lanes when the light allowed, finding themselves on the paved surface of the forty-foot-wide pedestrian thoroughfare. Bikers pedaled and joggers ran, while couples walked hand in hand, enjoying the pleasant night.

For the millionth time in her young life, Carly longed for the same social acceptance heterosexual couples enjoyed. The setting inspired romance, and she wanted nothing more than to pull Pip close and kiss her, just like the man and woman ahead of them were doing.

Pip seemed to read her mind. "When we get back to the hotel…"

"Hmm. Don't we have an early morning?" Pip had planned the entire trip, and even though Carly liked to manage things, it felt nice to turn it all over to Pip and just relax.

"As a matter of fact, we do. The taxi will pick us up at seven, our train is at seven thirty, and we should be at the hotel in Paris by eleven. The concierge has our tickets, and I've ordered room service, so we have nothing at all to do in the morning."

"I'm sure we'll think of something," Carly said with a wink that made Pip blush.

"We could always catch a later train…" She allowed the sentence to dangle seductively.

"Decisions, decisions," Carly said as she balanced her hands before her, puckering her lips as if reviewing her options. "Hot sex or Paris."

"You know, we can always have sex *in* Paris. As a matter of fact, I think it's required."

Carly felt the smile explode on her face. "I don't know how we'll find the time! There's so much to do. Museums. The Eiffel Tower. Lunch at cafés along the Seine, leisurely walks along the riverbank. I want to march through the Arc de Triomphe like my grandfather did after World War II and have a picnic at the Tuileries. I want to experience it all."

Pip laughed. "You're right. We may not be able to squeeze in sex around all that touring. I'm a little worried. After the past week, I might go into withdrawal."

"It has been an unforgettable week." They'd arrived in Nice precisely seven days earlier, and Pip had played the role of tour guide since then. She'd spent the summers of her childhood in the South of France, with her French grandmother and her German husband, who shared an apartment in Nice. They'd boated to St. Tropez with one of Pip's childhood friends and spent the day on the beach before a sunset cruise. They'd made love every morning, lunched at beachside cafés, and had gourmet dinners from Cap d'Antibes to Monte Carlo. It had been blissful.

"Did you enjoy Eze?"

Carly thought of the medieval, walled town they'd visited that afternoon. Nestled on a cliff overlooking the sea, it was quaint and charming, with winding cobbled pathways leading to a statuary garden at the top. The view of Eze from the surrounding countryside was almost as spectacular as the view of the sea from the town. They'd hiked all the way from the beach at Eze Sur Mer to the top, where they'd dined on oysters, and stopped for a crepe on the way down. "Yes. This has been one of my favorite days."

"Better than Cannes?"

"Well, the shopping was better in Cannes, but Eze is special. There's something about a place so ancient. Maybe this is an American thing, this fascination with everything in Europe that's been here so long. Do you think? I mean, where can we go in the US that's more than a few hundred years old?"

"You're in the right country if you like old," Pip deadpanned. "The buildings, the art. Even the people are antiques."

Carly laughed. "I won't tell your grandparents you said that."

"Hah! They'd be the first to admit it. They're decaying by the minute."

"They're the liveliest eighty-year-olds I've ever met."

"It's the alcohol. It acts as a preservative."

Carly bit her lip. "They do drink a lot."

"Why do you think they have a driver? They're always pickled."

They reached Le Meridien and crossed the road once again, then took the elevator to the rooftop. "I'll bet two bottles of champagne are chilling, and one of them will already be uncorked."

"I hope so," Carly replied with a wink as the elevator doors opened. She adored Pip's grandparents, and they'd been generous and kind since her arrival. How could Carly find fault? And, besides, Carly thought, who was she to judge? It wasn't as if she and Pip were drinking Orangina.

They stepped into a vestibule and then around a corner, and Carly stopped as the Mediterranean once again appeared before her. It was lovely from street level and from their room at Le Negresco, but from here, ten stories above sea level, they had no obstructions to the view. They were facing north, and in the distance, Carly followed the coast—from the Monument du Centenaire in a garden of green, to the tip of Cap Ferrat, poking out into the blue water. It was simply magnificent.

"Oui, Penelope! Carly!"

Carly turned her head to find an animated octogenarian waving a champagne glass in their direction. He approached tentatively, and Carly knew his legs rather than the champagne were affecting his gait. "Bonsoir," he said and kissed the air beside both their cheeks.

"Bonsoir, Myron," Carly said.

"Bonsoir, Grandpère," Pip added.

"This way." His diction was heavily accented, and he tended to substitute a word in French or German when he couldn't come up with the correct English, but Carly found him very charming.

"Come. Genevieve awaits us." Carly marveled that the champagne remained in his frenetic hand without spilling, but it did.

Carly followed Pip, taking in the crowd on the rooftop terrace—couples and small groups—some eating, others enjoying cocktails, all with their chairs turned toward the vast sea beyond them. The clouds were sparse, and the sun, already sinking, had morphed into a shimmering ball of reds and pinks. It would be a magnificent sunset. The table Myron led them to, in front and at the end of the terrace, offered the best view in town.

Pip's grandmother was sipping her champagne when they arrived, and after the requisite kisses on the cheek, Carly sat beside Pip, facing the Mediterranean. Myron filled two glasses for them, and they toasted. "To our new friend Carly."

They touched glasses, and Carly sipped the ice-cold drink, closing her eyes to concentrate on the subtle flavor of the wine.

"It's good, yes?" Myron asked.

"Very."

"Their best bottle," he said as he turned his neck to stretch. "Viv, can you give me a pain pill?"

"Certainly, darling," she said as she reached into her bag, pulled out a gilded pillbox, and handed it to her husband.

"Getting old, ladies—it's no fun. I have so many pills now, I have to label them so I can remember what they're for."

Carly nodded sympathetically, and Pip rescued the conversation by directing it to the next leg of their journey. Paris.

All her life, Carly had heard stories from her grandfather and watched movies about the romantic city on the Seine. And in sixteen hours, she'd be there, with the woman she loved by her side. It was a dream come true. Pip, who'd been to Paris dozens of times, would serve as her guide there, too.

"Oh, you'll love the Royal. We always stay there when we're in Paris," Viv said. "Just a few minutes' walk to the Arc d' Triomphe."

Carly had talked of the war with them. They'd both been in the French Resistance, and Myron had been captured by German forces during a mission to bomb a railroad tunnel. He was presumed dead. It took him several years after the war ended to find Viv, living in America and married to Pip's grandfather. He, too, had been a soldier, and helped liberate the South of France, where Viv was in hiding— and helped mend her heart after the apparent loss of Myron. Although she'd tried for a while to acclimate, Viv never truly fit in in Scranton, Pennsylvania, and one day she abruptly stopped trying. Without taking so much as a bag of clothing, she left with her young son—Pip's father Marc—and returned to France. When he was a teenager, Marc decided he would rather live in America, and back he went. He still lived in Scranton, in a house on Nay Aug Park, with Pip's mom, Kay.

"It'll be the first thing we see," Carly said.

Myron raised his glass again. "To your grandfather, Carly. And to yours, too," he said, looking at Pip. "We'd all be speaking German if it wasn't for them."

"I'll tell him you said that," Carly replied. Her grandfather loved to talk about the war, and she'd been thinking of what she might take him back from France to celebrate the role he'd played in defeating the Nazis.

Myron gently placed his glass on the table and massaged the left side of his neck. "Are you planning two days at the Louvre, or just one?"

Shrugging, Pip sipped her wine. "We have only a week, and there's so much to see. I think just one day."

"Do you have a plan?"

Carly stared at him, puzzled, and he explained. "You'll want to see *Mona Lisa*, of course. You should go to her first. None of that making your way from gallery to gallery—you'll never see everything that way. Pick what you want to see and do that early. Then wander and enjoy."

"That sounds like good advice." Carly had heard the line to see the da Vinci masterpiece was sometimes quite long.

"We have…" He looked confused. The hand that had been rubbing his neck moved to his throat, and he gasped as he fell forward. Viv screamed, and Pip, who was seated across from him, jumped from her chair. Carly turned and yelled for the waiter. "Call an ambulance!" she demanded. His look was dismissive at first, until he gazed beyond her and saw Myron slumped across the table. Then his eyes flew open wide, and he yelled something in French that set a dozen people in motion.

Someone who professed to be a doctor rushed over, and Pip deferred to him, backing off to help Carly comfort her grandmother. Two more men came, and a woman, and within seconds, they had pulled Myron to the floor and started resuscitative measures. Carly couldn't watch the horror of it all, and when she turned, the sea that she'd so recently been admiring swam nauseatingly before her.

Flanking her, Carly and Pip ushered Viv away, to the hotel lobby, and waited what seemed like hours for the ambulance to arrive. Eons more passed before the attendants reappeared. Carly and Pip huddled around Viv, forming a protective cocoon. Like her granddaughter, Viv was petite, but unlike Pip, who played tennis every day and lifted weights to build a strong physique, Viv was frail. Even as she hugged her, Carly was careful not to hold her too tightly, for fear she would cause harm.

Images of first responders helping Myron swirled through her brain. Oxygen and IVs and CPR, just as she'd seen on *ER* on television. Instead of the scene she'd imagined, though—with paramedics running beside a stretcher, rushing Myron to the hospital—when they finally appeared, the team was quite calm. They moved slowly, carefully maneuvering their burden through the lobby of Le Meridien. When Carly looked at their passenger, she didn't see the lively man she knew, but a still form covered by a white sheet.

"Oh, fuck," she said softly as tears poured from her eyes.

Pip looked up and saw it too, then folded her grandmother in her arms, blocking the view of the stretcher transporting the remains of the man she'd loved her whole, long life. The medic noticed them and approached briskly, telling them the sad news that Carly already knew. Myron was dead.

Shuffling her feet, barely registering the surroundings, Carly helped escort Genevieve to the car and to her apartment. Pip stayed with her grandmother while the driver took Carly back to Le Negresco. Somehow, she managed to pack their bags, hastily throwing toiletries into a suitcase beside the dirty laundry, left to be sorted later. She folded the clean clothes and carefully placed them in another bag. On the bedside table she found Pip's glasses. From the drawer, she retrieved a bottle of Motrin and the small vibrator they'd used to give each other so much pleasure during their week in Nice. Just that morning, twelve short hours before, they'd made love.

How long ago that memory seemed now! How insignificant. Viv had met Myron when she was just twenty years old and had loved him for sixty years. Would she and Pip have that long? They were about the same age that Viv and Myron had been at the end of the war—twenty-five—and very much in love. They'd been dating for over a year and had moved in together the Christmas before. If Pip were on that stretcher, Carly would be devastated. After a lifetime with Myron, what must Viv be feeling now?

Suddenly tears flooded her eyes again, and she sobbed. Myron had been such a sweet man. He'd opened his home to them, and though they'd declined the invitation, preferring to have privacy at the hotel, they'd dined there and utilized his Mercedes and driver. He'd paid for every dinner and even gifted them bright Hermes scarves to welcome them to France.

Poor Pip. She'd been coming to France since she was a baby. Her dad's father was there for her through the winters in Scranton, but every summer, Pip had spent six weeks in Europe, learning French and exploring with Myron and Viv. Myron had owned a yacht then, and they'd cruised everywhere from the Canary Islands to North Africa to Israel and Italy. He wasn't related by blood, but he had no children of his own, and he'd spoiled Pip lavishly.

The porter hauled the bags on his trolley and loaded them into the car, while Carly checked out of the hotel. With a sigh, she asked the man at the desk to cancel the taxi they'd requested for the trip to the train station. They wouldn't be going to Paris in the morning. They probably wouldn't be going at all.

Chapter Two

Out of the Bunker

Lake Winola, Pennsylvania
Now

Carly felt the jab of pain behind her eyes, and even through the fog of a dense, alcohol-induced sleep, she envisioned an ice pick. It was a sobering thought, one that caused her to roll from the morning light, seeking relief.

"Oh, fuck," she murmured as she touched the woman in the bed beside her. Her mouth felt like it had been stuffed with cotton balls, and she could barely recognize the words.

Carly threw open her eyes and repeated the protest. "Fuck, fuck, fuck," she said softly, hoping not to awaken the sleeping beauty. It took her a moment to gain her bearings. She was in her guesthouse, but what day was it? And who was the naked woman? She looked young. Hopefully she was at least twenty-one, because alcohol had clearly been involved in the evening's festivities.

Struggling to recall the events of the night before, she slowly rose to a stooped position, silently congratulating herself for the wise decision to invite her date to the guesthouse, rather than her own home. It would have been much more difficult to escape from there.

With a pounding heart and a wobbly gait, she snuck from the bedroom. In the living room she found her shoes—a sensible pair of loafers—on either end of the fireplace. Her coat—a blessedly long, down-filled, stadium style—hung draped casually over the back of the couch. Another pair of shoes, heels, had been neatly placed beside the recliner, and a coat—long like hers, but red wool instead of gray—was neatly folded and lay in the seat.

The vivid red color jarred Carly's memory, and she envisioned glimpses of the girl in this room, sitting as she carefully removed her shoes while Carly had haphazardly kicked off her own. The kiss, and then the clumsy dance to the bedroom as two unsteady pairs of legs tried to navigate as a single unit. Their clothes, discarded at the bottom of the bed as they hurriedly undressed beneath the blankets in the cold room. Before that a party, at her friend Erin's house. They were celebrating her birthday. The girl was someone from Erin's office—a new dental hygienist. That was it. It all made sense now.

Her purse. What had become of that? Standing, she walked around the couch and found it on the floor beneath her coat. Thank the gods. Peeking inside, she saw her cell phone and drew it out as she pulled on the coat and zipped it. To hell with her clothes. She'd retrieve them later. Sliding her feet into her loafers, she found a name on her favorites and dialed.

"Good morning," Natasha Peterson said in a voice that sounded much too happy to suit Carly.

"Tash, I'm in trouble. I need your help," she whispered into the phone.

"What could you have possibly done already? It's only seven o'clock. On Sunday."

Ignoring the sarcasm, Carly opened the door to the cottage and stepped into the frigid morning. There, nearly kissing the house's front stoop, she found her BMW. Just beyond that, another car, a blue SUV. "Great," she said as she surveyed the car for damage. Not only had she driven when she'd had too much to drink, but her companion had as well.

"There's a woman in my bed. I need you to remove her."

"Is she alive?" Natasha asked.

"Shit! I don't know. I didn't check. But probably." What could they possibly have done that would kill her? She was barely old enough to drive. If Carly had survived the night, the girl should have, too.

"Where are you?"

"The guesthouse."

"At least you had your wits about you and didn't take her into the main house."

"That thought gives me no comfort right now. Will you help me? She's really cute. I bet if you crawled in beside her, she'd never know it wasn't you last night."

Tasha laughed. "I've been cleaning up your messes since college, but I've never shared a girl with you. I'm not going to start now."

Tasha had been Carly's first love, and twenty-five years later, they were still best friends. "Tash, please. I need you."

"It must have been some party."

While the details were unclear, Carly suspected Tasha was right. "I'm never leaving my house without you again."

Tasha roared. "That's probably wise."

"Tashy, please help me."

"You'll be fine. Go back to the main house. Just let her sleep it off, Car. When she wakes and finds you've gone, she'll be as mortified as you are, and she'll slink away. Wait—she does have a car, doesn't she? There was an ice storm last night, and I don't know if an Uber could get to the lake."

"Yeah. There's an SUV in the driveway. It must be hers," Carly said as she picked her way past the vehicle. The storm Tasha mentioned made the journey hazardous, but when she looked around, the beauty of the ice-encrusted landscape stunned her. Every surface glistened in the bright morning sun, and the world still slept, blanketed by the ice. The air was crisp and burned as it hit the back of her nose, and she pulled up her coat to shield her face. The quiet, the stillness, was profound. For a moment she was awed, but then reality once again hit her, in the form of a biting observation from her best friend.

"So you were drinking and driving." It wasn't a question. What could she say? Skating along her sidewalk, she felt miserable.

"Carly? Are you still there?"

She'd reached her front door and keyed the code into the digital pad. It beeped, and the door opened.

A sigh of relief escaped her. "I'm in the house."

"Good. You'll be fine. Just hide out upstairs in case she peeks in the windows."

"Ha, ha."

"One of these days, Carly Elizabeth Becker, you're going to get yourself into real trouble."

Still wearing her coat, but shoeless, she made her way to the kitchen and changed the subject. "Are we still on for the golf expo at Mohegan Sun today?" she asked as she filled a mug with water and put it in the microwave, then filled a glass and downed half of it. "Will the world unthaw by then?"

"Of course. Shall we do lunch?"

Carly pulled a bag of coffee and a bagel from the freezer and her French press from the cupboard. "What are you in the mood for?"

"Ooh, what's that Japanese place by the square in Wilkes-Barre? They have great sushi," Tasha said.

"Hmm. I can do Japanese," Carly replied as she opened her refrigerator and peeked inside. The options were limited. Leftover Italian from a few nights before. Chinese takeout that was even older. Yogurt in four different flavors. All the condiments a girl could wish for.

Grabbing a container of cream cheese, she put the cell phone on speaker and placed it on the counter. The microwave beeped, and she poured the water into the press while her bagel toasted and added a shot of Bailey's Irish Cream to her favorite mug.

"Did you get the email from Mountain Meadows about the women's golf league?" Tasha asked.

"When? I didn't see it," she demanded, instantly on alert. She hated missing things—feeling disconnected, out of control.

"It came in yesterday, late in the afternoon."

Carly thought back a day. She'd picked up her friend Maggie, and they'd made a stop at Cooper's Seafood in Scranton for happy hour before heading to Erin's party. She hadn't checked her email since she'd left the house at four o'clock.

Sighing, she sipped from her favorite mug. Thank Goddess for coffee. Grabbing the phone again, she walked across her kitchen and gingerly fingered the curtain on the window facing the guesthouse. The front of the blue SUV was just visible from that angle. "Fuck," she said.

"Fuck what?"

"She's still here."

Tasha laughed. "Her car is behind yours, isn't it?"

"Yeah, why?" Carly asked, defensive for reasons that were not Tasha's fault. She was upset with herself, not Tasha. But as usual, she was taking it out on her bestie.

She pulled her bagel from the toaster and slathered it with cream cheese.

"You won't be able to get your car out. Do you want me to pick you up?"

"Fuck, Tash. She can't still be here at lunchtime." Carly rubbed away the pain starting to form between her eyes.

"Have you ever slept until noon after a bender?"

Carly put her food and the phone on a tray and carried it upstairs to her bedroom. "Me? Never. You know I have an aversion to sleeping late. I'm too much of a control freak. I'm afraid of missing something when I sleep."

Tash cleared her throat. "I would say intoxication is a total loss of control, darling."

"It's just a way to relax, Tash," she retorted as she grabbed the remote and turned on the fireplace. Even though the thermostat was programmed, the room was cold, and she felt the chill despite her long coat. Above the whish of the fire, she heard her friend sigh.

"So what'd the email say?" she asked as she slipped off her coat and into her robe. She crawled beneath the covers and powered up her laptop to check for herself.

"They mentioned the expo, and the new league. But, more importantly, they released this year's schedule for the women's golf league. Opening meeting, opening night, all the makeup days and tournaments, even the banquet at the end."

"Hmm. That's a switch. Usually I'm waiting until July to plan my summer, because you never know what's happening with the league until it's almost over."

"I guess the new president listened to all the complaints."

Carly bit her bagel and sipped her coffee before she replied. Linda Frame, a highly successful realtor who was one of Carly's chief competitors, had taken the reins. "About fucking time. Linda is sharp. She'll do a good job this year."

Carly leaned back into her headboard and paused for a second, trying to find the right words to express the thoughts kicking around in her head. "I don't know, Tash. I feel sort of restless about golf. I'm not sure what it is. Maybe it's the same eighteen holes twice a week. Or maybe it's the same bunch of women. The same faces. The same drama. The same winners every year, the same women invited to play as guests of the members, the same teams for the charity tournament. It's *the same everything*. I'm just…"

"Bored. You sound bored."

She sighed, unsure. "Maybe…I've been feeling this way for months. I thought I'd perk up after a week in Florida with you and Pip, and I did. For the week I was in Florida. Now, I'm back to feeling… whatever this is."

"I'd say you need to get laid, but it sounds like you've already tried that."

"How do you know I slept with her?"

Tasha laughed. "I've met you."

"You're so sweet."

"Pick me up at one."

"If she's still here, I'm canceling. If not, I'll see you then."

Carly read the email from the club, and the hundred others she'd received since she last checked them the morning before. As the owner of a very successful real-estate agency that employed a dozen agents, she never stopped working. She answered some, deleted others, and an hour later, she searched the daily listing of open houses. It was hard to believe, but some agents actually waited to list important events like that on the day of. Thankfully, none of them worked at Becker Realty.

Sure enough, multiple open houses were scheduled for today. She pored over the list, looking for any that hadn't been there the day before, and when she found one, she jotted the address on a sticky note. She'd already assessed the others, but she wasn't familiar with this property. She'd do a drive-by with Tasha on the way to the expo. She liked to scout the competition, liked to know what neighborhoods were popular. It benefited both her buyers and sellers that she knew the market.

Closing the laptop, she got out of bed and stretched, then walked to the window. The two back bedrooms, including hers, faced the lake. She gazed out onto the snow-covered surface, smooth except for the tracks of snowmobiles. A few houses over, someone had cleared a patch the size of a softball field, and Carly had seen what looked like a skating party there the day before. This morning, though, the world beyond her window slept, perfectly still except for the winding trails of smoke escaping chimneys and dancing into the sky.

She walked to the small front bedroom and peeked around the edge of the blind. A sigh of relief escaped her lips. The SUV was gone.

Practically skipping, she headed back to her bedroom and pulled her yoga gear from the closet. Mat, stretchy pants, slim-fitting top. Seated on the bench at the bottom of her bed, she glanced in the mirror. At forty-five, she still looked good. She'd always been slim, and she'd managed to stay in shape. Much of that was due to her combination of exercise and good genetics, rather than a true effort on her behalf. She had no gray in her dark hair and no wrinkles around her chocolate eyes. Her smile was still full and bright. A bit of color remained on her cheeks from the trip to Florida. It gave her a healthy look, she realized as she slipped the shirt over her head. Probably why the teenager from the night before had seen fit to follow her home.

Why did she do such stupid things when she was drinking? She'd driven home and brought a woman half her age with her. She could have hit a tree. The woman could have been a psychopath.

Pushing play on her CD player, Carly lay back on her mat and began stretching. Enya filled the room as thoughts filled her mind. She was a lucky woman, she reminded herself. Her business was successful. She owned a beautiful home, two cars, and had the ability to eat and travel wherever she wanted. She was fortunate enough to have excellent health, a blessing quite a few people she knew didn't enjoy. A few friends had died—some from cancer, one from a crazy infection, one in an accident. The friends that remained, like Tasha and Pip, and a few others, were great people who loved her and filled her idle hours.

So why did she embarrass herself like this? What did she hope to gain from a casual hookup? The sex probably hadn't even been very good. Damn. She wished she could remember it.

And what were her friends thinking about her? It didn't bother her that Tasha knew about the girl. Tasha knew everything about her and loved her anyway. But the others who'd been at the party would have an interesting tale to tell this morning, and that pissed her off.

She had only herself to blame, though. She debated calling Erin, but she couldn't deal with that just now. More than likely, Erin would call her anyway. And Carly would dodge the call, just like she'd dodged the girl. It was just easier than having to explain something she really didn't understand herself.

Chapter Three

All-nighter

D r. Paige Waterford opened the sterile package with care, touching only the surface of the wrapping that would contact the patient's tray table and not the inside that she needed to keep clean. She swallowed the hint of anxiety that always accompanied such moments and went about her business.

"Okay, sir. I need you to bend over and hug the pillow now, just like I showed you."

The man sitting before her hesitated, and she stepped around from behind him to look him in the eye. "I did this to my niece once, and she still speaks to me. It's going to be okay."

"Is it really necessary?" he asked, stretching the word *really* into about twelve syllables.

Paige explained again why she needed to do the spinal tap. Although his CT scan was normal, a patient complaining of an explosion in the back of their head and subsequent headache had a small but not insignificant chance of a brain bleed, and sometimes the first CT scan didn't show the damage. Often, by the time symptoms made a second scan necessary, it was too late.

He produced a guttural sound that made Paige laugh, but she held his gaze. "Okay. Do it."

Walking behind him once more, she explained what she was doing as she ran her pointer finger along the bones of his spine, feeling for the space between them where she would puncture his spinal canal.

"I'm going to mark you with my fingernail now, so you'll feel some pressure." She poked him until a line appeared in the correct spot, then studied the tray. Everything was laid out, just the way Paige liked it. Organization was the key to her success.

She forgot her anxiety as her instincts kicked in, and the procedure moved very quickly from there. Betadine swabs across the back, then a sterile drape to protect the surgical field. A dollop of anesthesia beneath the skin to dull the initial sting of the three-inch-long needle. Then the insertion.

"Be very still now. You'll feel a prick at some point, but it shouldn't be too bad." Guiding the needle between the bones took a little bit of guesswork, based on a ton of experience, but she had perfected the skill. Feeling a little give when the needle pierced the covering over the spinal canal, she stopped and pulled the stylus from its center, and a drop of clear, colorless fluid appeared on the hub. "We're in!" she informed the patient, and the breath she exhaled temporarily fogged the eye shield on her mask.

"I didn't feel a thing," he said, and she smiled. She felt amazing. A spinal tap wasn't a simple procedure, but she'd done it with ease.

Using her left hand, she placed the first test tube beneath the hub and watched as it filled, drop by drop.

"The fluid looks like water. It's perfect. I have to send it to the lab, but I think it's going to be okay."

She switched tubes and filled the second.

"So what's wrong with me?"

"Sometimes it's not what's wrong that matters, but what isn't wrong. If we don't find anything serious, then there's probably nothing to find. Maybe it's just a migraine."

Pulling the needle, she applied pressure with a piece of gauze.

"So can you give me something for this damn pain, then?" he said with a laugh.

"I certainly can."

She capped four tubes and labeled them, then sealed the lot in a plastic bag before wiping the patient's back and helping him to a comfortable position on the stretcher.

"My shift ended about half an hour ago, so one of my colleagues will be coming in to give you the test results. I'm going to prepare all the paperwork and give you some medicine and a few prescriptions to go home with. Follow up with your doctor this week, okay?"

"Thank you," he said, and she squeezed his shoulder.

"You're very welcome."

She had a bounce in her step as she left the room. That was her touchdown pass. Her three-point buzzer shot. A chip-in from just off the fairway. And she'd nailed it. She'd studied and worked for most of her life to become a doctor, and at moments like this, it was all worth it. If only for a little while, she was flying high.

Back at the nurses' station, she logged in to the computer and entered orders in the e-chart, then handed the spinal fluid to the nurse. "Please deliver this to the lab. I don't want the orderly to lose the tubes again."

The nurse laughed. "No trouble. You should go get some sleep. Are you back tonight?"

She shook her head. "Thankfully, no. This was my fourth straight night, and I have a busy day ahead of me, so I don't plan to sleep until later. Maybe if I wait until tonight, my body will get back to day-shift mode."

"I don't know how you doctors do it. At least the nursing staff stays on nights, so we don't have to yo-yo back and forth."

"The yo-yoing does suck," she admitted with a smile. "But at least I'm never on call."

"What plans do you have?" she asked.

"The golf expo, at the casino."

The day-shift doctor, loitering as he waited for Paige's sign-out, jumped into their conversation.

"That sounds like a great day. Gambling and golf."

"I don't think I should gamble without sleeping. It's probably just as bad as drinking and gambling."

"That's a *good bet*," he said with a chuckle as she groaned. "Pick up some swag for me, so I know what I missed. I thought the life of an ER doctor would be grand, yet here I am, working every other weekend…"

"Just like the rest of us, Jack. Stop complaining, or I'm not sharing my lunch today." The nurse frowned at him, but Paige knew she was only teasing.

Jack turned an imaginary key across his lips and then motioned her toward the computer for sign-out. She told him about the spinal-fluid orders and two trauma patients who were waiting for routine CT scans.

"All the discharge instructions are done, so just print them when you have the reports. And that's it. How are the roads?" There had been an ice storm, and the results had shown up in the ER in ambulances all night long. Fortunately, those who'd crashed their cars hadn't been badly hurt.

"The roads are just wet at this point. You'll have an easy drive home and then to the casino. Have fun today," he said as he picked up a chart and went to work.

"Thanks," she replied. She walked through the halls outside the nursing station with the sense of relief she always felt at the end of a shift. No one had died or had significant problems. And she'd worked only an hour overtime.

After punching in the code on the door to the physicians' lounge, she escaped inside. It was an oasis, a big, bright, quiet refuge in the middle of the chaos of the ER, and she immediately felt a sense of calm. She hung her lab coat in her locker and threw her scrubs into the laundry bin, then pulled on the jeans and sweater she'd worn to work the night before. After exchanging her work clogs for Uggs, she pulled on her parka, grabbed her backpack, and headed home.

The parking lot was attached to the parking garage via a bridge, and she was happy she'd used the lot the night before, instead of a closer spot on the street. Everywhere she looked she saw evidence of the storm—wet roads, vehicles and trees encrusted with ice, and busy people scraping the windows of their cars and SUVs.

She paused to take it all in. The sun was dazzling as it reflected everywhere—off the glass tower of the hospital, the ice on the trees, the water on the road. She squinted and breathed deeply, imagined the ice flowing through her throat, into her lungs, scraping her airway, burning. She shivered and buried her nose into the collar of her coat and picked up her pace for the last few steps to the car.

Allowing her Jeep a minute to warm up, she plugged in her phone and selected her favorite playlist. It was a twenty-minute drive to her home in Clarks Summit from the hospital in Scranton, and she liked to use that time to unwind. It was hard not to brood when people died, or when patients' family members acted like asses, or the people she worked with pissed her off, so the routine helped, and she stuck to it, even when she'd enjoyed an easy night like the one that had just ended.

Humming along to Quintango, she relaxed, and the drive went quickly.

Her ringing phone interrupted her concert. Liza. Paige smiled as she pressed the phone connection on her steering wheel and said hello.

"Greetings from the frozen tundra," Liza said in her strong Brooklyn accent. "How's Scranton?"

"Thawing," she said. Her drive had been easy, the roads wet, but she worried the ice on trees might fell them, along with the fragile power lines in her community.

"As long as the roads are open, and that's a big *if,*" Liza said, "we should be at your house in forty minutes. Can I bring you anything? Dunkin'? A waffle with strawberries? A crepe with Nutella?"

Paige sighed. "I wish. But I think I'll just have time for a Pop-Tart. Don't want to be late today." She turned onto her street and into the driveway of the large contemporary she called home. Although the roads had been salted, her driveway had not, and the Jeep skidded when she braked. Letting out a breath when she stopped, she paused to look around. Her house, nestled in the trees, was an amazing ice sculpture this morning.

"What just happened?" Liza asked.

"I almost took out a small tree."

"But you didn't?"

"I did not."

"Good work."

"Thanks. Be careful in my driveway." Pressing the garage remote, she watched as the door opened. "And I'm going to be late, too, if I don't hop in the shower right now."

"Okay, bye," Liza said before abruptly hanging up.

She was laughing, as she always did with Liza. Their senses of humor were in harmony, and they had the rare ability to crack each other up. It was just one of many things about Liza she loved. It was as if they'd known each other since kindergarten, but they'd met only last fall.

The laughter quickly faded as she pulled into her garage and noticed the two parking spaces beside hers were empty.

Leaning back into the comfortable leather, she sighed. These days, life at home was much more stressful than at work.

She found the seed spreader she used for the ice-melt and pushed it to the drive, where she inched back and forth a few dozen times. The results were instantaneous, and she watched little pockets appear in the glass-like surface. Satisfied that she wouldn't break her leg the next time she left the house, she headed inside.

On the kitchen island, she found the note from her husband. He'd left, again, escaping to his fishing cabin. After reading it, she threw it into the trash. Rubbing her tired eyes, she sighed.

It was a sigh of relief, she realized. She wouldn't have to deal with his mood, arguing with him because she wanted to do something for herself. It was an argument they had frequently, whenever Paige decided to do something for her own well-being. It wasn't enough that she voiced her needs—Will wanted her to explain them. To defend herself. And for some reason, she found that a daunting demand. Most times, she just acquiesced. On the rare occasions she found the perfect words to articulate her feelings, he dismissed them, calling her silly or crazy or selfish. But she didn't feel any of those things—at least not when she was by herself, with her thoughts. She felt anxious, and sad, and restless, and she was just trying to change that attitude. To feel good about herself again. She knew she was an attractive, intelligent, successful woman. That's what her logical brain told her, but the message somehow got lost on the way to the emotional part of her brain, where she felt so screwed up.

Yet her needs were hard to suppress these days, and they kept surfacing. She knew she needed to listen to her heart, to do some things for herself. Her desire caused arguments and hard feelings at home, but she had to do it anyway. She just felt like she had no choice. If she didn't do something, she felt like she'd go off a cliff.

Today was one of those times, and she was happy he'd left, because she didn't have the energy to fight with him. They'd been fighting for years, and she was tired of it.

Forcing thoughts of him from her mind, she turned on her Keurig and headed to her bedroom, stripped off her dirty clothes, then turned on the shower. While the water warmed, she brushed her teeth and thought about the day ahead, and that quickly, her mood changed as excitement coursed through her. A new golf league was ready to launch, and she was one of the founders. Swinging Around the World, SAW for short, was coming to Scranton, and she couldn't wait. She'd make new friends and see some old ones. It was something fun and different in the middle of the run-on sentence that was winter in Northeastern Pennsylvania. More importantly, its arrival promised that the summer would be a great one, too. Golf was something she loved, and this league was something for *her.*

After showering and drying her hair, she dressed casually in jeans, a green turtleneck that complemented her blond hair and blue-green eyes, and a thick golf sweater. She completed the outfit with her favorite pair of Uggs. She really couldn't wait for golf season and its wardrobe of shorts and sleeveless shirts. She. Could. Not. Wait.

Glancing at the clock, she realized she had to hurry, and she skipped down the stairs and into her kitchen. She popped a Pop-Tart into the toaster and fixed her coffee, with one ear listening for the sound of Mallory's horn. From their Pocono home, Liza and her wife Mal practically had to drive past her house to reach the casino, so they'd offered to pick her up. And besides, carpooling gave her some extra time with two of her favorite people.

A few minutes later, a honking noise from outside her window told her that her friends had arrived, and she hurried from her kitchen, feeling happy. Alive. The best she'd felt since the last time she'd seen Liza and Mallory, two weeks earlier. She wasn't sure what it was about these two women, but she loved spending time with them. And *I'm going to have them for the entire day,* she thought as she locked the house and headed out.

The ice on the driveway had melted, and she scampered across the concrete and into the backseat of Mallory's sporty Cadillac SUV. "Hey," she said in greeting. "How are you ladies?"

"Other than a downed power line, just another day in frozen paradise," Liza replied as she blew a kiss in Paige's direction.

Paige chuckled as she buckled her seat belt. "Did you have any problem finding the house?" During the few months they'd been friends, she'd been to their Pocono house, and they'd met at restaurants, but they'd never been to hers.

"GPS," Mallory replied.

Paige sighed. "Yes. Where would we be without it?"

"Lost!" Liza said with a chuckle.

Mallory put the SUV into reverse and backed out of the driveway. As she turned, her eyes locked with Paige's.

"Doesn't that sort of make you a bad lesbian? I mean, shouldn't you be handy with a compass and a map?" Paige asked, trying to stifle her smile.

"Stereotype much?" she quipped.

Paige laughed, but the truth was, she was curious about all things lesbian. It was as if a magnet was drawing her thoughts in that direction. It had always been there, but since meeting Liza and Mallory a few months ago, it was happening more often. She adored them and really connected with them as individuals, but the fact that they were a couple appealed to her as well. Through them she had an angle into a world that simply fascinated her.

"So, you worked last night, huh?"

Paige sighed. "Yeah. Weekends and nights are part of the job."

"We could still do Dunkin'. Should we stop?"

"Hmm. I just had a cup, but maybe it's not a bad idea. If you'll join me?"

"I'm always ready for coffee," Mallory said. "I work some long nights myself, and sometimes it keeps me going."

Mallory talked about her job as she drove. After majoring in computer science in college, she'd opened her own IT company years before, and she had grown it into a successful business.

"I'm practically allergic to electronic devices," Paige confessed. "I think you must have a natural talent, like Picasso or Beethoven, to be able to fix computers."

Turning to face Paige, Liza smiled. "I've always said she was a genius."

Mallory rubbed Liza's shoulder as she pulled the car into the queue at Dunkin'. "You're so sweet, I'm going to buy you a coffee. Just so you know how much I love you."

Paige loved the way they interacted. They were the cutest couple she'd ever met.

"So tell me about the other people who'll be here today," Paige requested. Liza and Mal were members of Brooklyn SAW, and when they'd suggested Paige form a SAW league in the Scranton area, she didn't hesitate. The stories she and Mallory had shared about their golf adventures had done more than pique her interest. Paige was really excited. She would have driven to Brooklyn every week to play with them if they hadn't suggested a league here. She only hoped the women of Northeastern Pennsylvania showed enough interest to make it work.

Liza told her about friends from the Harrisburg area who would be at the expo. They'd driven in the day before and stayed overnight at the casino, so they were already there, setting up a table for the group. Two other ladies, from New Jersey, would be there as well. "You'll like everyone. They're all nice. A few are a little…competitive, but I overlook that," Liza said.

"I thought you liked competition?" Paige asked.

"Please," she said. "None of us is going on tour. It's about being out in nature, and exercising, and sharing some laughs. About going to new places and meeting new people. In twenty years, I won't remember what score I shot, but I'll remember the people I met."

"And they'll remember you," Paige said with a laugh.

"Everyone always does," Mallory said with a chuckle.

"I know you love me," Liza retorted as she rubbed Mal's shoulder, and then she turned again to face Paige.

"Who did you invite?" Mallory asked Paige.

Paige told her about all the people she'd reached out to about SAW. Her friend Linda, the realtor who'd sold Paige her house a few years back, was the champion at Mountain Meadows Country Club. Linda was the first person Paige had called about SAW, and it had been a good move. Linda was the chair of the women's league at The Meadows and had mentioned SAW in an email that went out to all the members. Quite a few women had expressed an interest. Paige hoped they'd show up, too. She'd invited her sister and her niece, ladies from her own league, people from work, and even the owner of the public course where she played.

"He offered to host the league," Paige said.

"That's great. You're really ahead of the game."

"I don't feel that way. Aside from my sister and my niece, Linda's the only one who's committed. How many do we need?"

"Each club can have a maximum of eight players each week, but we count only the top four scores. So technically speaking, you could have four players to get started. You're set."

"My sister and my niece are awful players," Paige said. "But don't tell them I said that."

"Never. But you want more people, so you don't have to play every Friday. That's hard. Weddings, vacations, work…sadly, it all interferes with golf. Most teams have around fifteen or twenty members, and they take turns. Then it's not too much of a burden each week."

Paige sighed. "Whew. That's a big ask. I'm going to hope for a few more, so we can field two teams."

"It shouldn't be a problem," Mallory said. "People love this."

They talked about the weather, and Liza suggested they plan a trip south to play golf before the season. "Maybe we can get some people together," she suggested. "Make it an outing."

"That sounds great. Someplace warm, please." Paige had visited her parents in Florida for Christmas, but she'd been able to get only four days off from work. Plus, she was visiting *them*, so she didn't really do anything except bake a few cookies and clean up after dinner. She couldn't remember the last time she'd really been away. Her niece had invited her to Paris the previous fall, but Paige hadn't been able to get the time off. Jules was a senior in high school, and the trip was a French Club activity, so it would be stress-free for Paige, but no way could she make it work with her job schedule.

She felt bad, but Jules had promised her she would have another opportunity in the fall, when she started classes at the University of Scranton. Paige looked forward to it and had been putting money aside to cover the cost. She'd been to Europe a few times and had even spent a semester in Ireland, but she'd never visited Paris. And taking her niece would be fun. She loved spending time with Jules. She was a typical teenage girl—energetic and wise and adventurous—and she made Paige feel much younger than her thirty-two years.

Yet Paige sensed that she didn't need the frantic pace of her niece, but something more relaxing. Golf at the beach might be a little crazy, too—the golf, the shopping, the parties. But she was sure she could carve out some time for herself to curl up with a book or in front of the television, to just breathe a little and de-stress. These days, life at her house was very stressful.

If she could just string together five days off, she could get away someplace warm, with Liza and Mal. The more she thought of it, the more the idea blossomed in her mind. She grew excited as she envisioned a warm sun, and a dew-kissed morning fairway, and Mallory and Liza. "Let's do it. Let's find a golf trip somewhere warm."

Liza turned, a bright smile across her face. "It seems as if the three of us are of one mind."

Paige's smile matched Liza's. "We could get into so much trouble together."

Mallory sighed. "That's what I'm afraid of."

CHAPTER FOUR

SWINGING AROUND THE WORLD

A few minutes later, Mallory pulled her car up to the valet, and they all hustled inside the casino, eager to escape the biting cold. Paige led the way. "What would you say to a steak later?" Mallory asked as she nodded toward the sign for Ruth's Chris.

Paige thought for a moment of the note from Will. No reason to rush home. "Sounds perfect."

At the entrance to the convention area, several men sat behind long tables draped with Mohegan Sun tablecloths. One handed them ID badges and issued them directions to their booth. Mallory turned to her. "I betcha I can find my way, even without a GPS."

"You're my hero," Paige said, and she wasn't really joking. She admired Mallory so much. While she wasn't incapable, Paige had never really learned any of the practical aspects of running a house. Her mother, a nurse, and her father, a pharmacist, had simply hired a series of handymen to take care of the little issues that came up from time to time, and Paige had never bothered to pay attention to their efforts. Since she'd purchased her own house, when little things went wrong, she was caught between Will's ego and the desire to get things taken care of. Usually, his ego won, and home repairs were ignored, while Paige tiptoed around the hazards, trying her best not to do any further damage.

Mallory, though, took care of all their home maintenance, and Paige marveled when she shared details of changing the air filter on her furnace or applying a coat of polyurethane to her wooden deck. The tasks were mostly small things, but lately, when something went wrong at home, Paige had started calling Mal, who was usually able to talk her through it. The feeling of accomplishment was incredible when she completed a project, and they had started talking more and more about the ideas she had for her house.

"C'mon. I'll show you the way," Mal said as they entered the exhibit hall. Colorful banners hung from fifty feet above the floor, welcoming them. Looking around, Paige couldn't see the end but noticed about six rows of exhibitors. The place was massive, but Mallory indeed found their booth, a spacious twenty-by-forty-foot area off in the far corner. She pointed to it from a hundred yards away. Paige could see the SAW banner, as well as four ladies who seemed to be hard at work arranging things.

"Could we get any farther from the action?" Liza complained.

"Remind me again how much it cost us," Mallory said. "Oh, yeah. It was free."

Paige was amazed. "It was free?"

"We're a nonprofit, and the organizers would rather give away space than have it empty. So, yeah. Free."

"This is incredible," Paige said as she felt the energy of the room. Dozens of vendors were hard at work, scurrying about, setting up tables and displays. Some were promoting clothing, some equipment, some were from country clubs and public courses. In the middle was a gigantic virtual golf course, and even after staring for a moment, Paige wasn't sure what they were selling.

"Hiya, ladies," Liza said as they arrived at their booth. "Some place you have here."

One of them laughed as she answered, turning in a circle. "We tried to spread everything out to take up room. We could still install a driving range, though, if you'd like. They're selling them a few aisles over."

Paige inspected their work. In front and to the side was a table draped with the SAW banner. On its surface, stacked into neat piles, were brochures. Sitting beside that was a clothing rack, holding women's golf gear sporting the league logo. In the rear, a laptop and projector were playing a slideshow of women golfing, gathering, talking, laughing. And on the right, the group was just finishing the assembly of the putting green. A carry bag sat beside it, and a number of putters were stored inside. A sign behind the green read, "Try your luck…Sink the most putts to win a free membership!"

"Everyone, this is our friend Paige," Mallory said, and she made introductions. Paige greeted them and asked how she could help, but it appeared they had already done all the work. She spent the next twenty minutes talking, until a loud voice interrupted her.

"Great job! The biggest booth at the expo."

She turned and found her friend Linda approaching. Relieved that someone she knew had actually showed up, Paige ran over and wrapped her arms around her. Linda was in her forties, a hair over five feet tall, and weighed less than the average newborn baby, but her fiery personality was huge. "I'm so glad to see you," Paige exclaimed.

Trying to remember the names of the four women she'd just met, Paige turned to them and introduced Linda. "This is the first member of our club." Paige beamed.

Liza corrected her. "You're the first, Paige."

"Well, I haven't actually signed up yet, so…"

Mallory handed her a piece of paper from the table, along with a pen. "Go ahead. Make it official." Paige laughed as she signed her name, then passed the paper along to Linda.

"If you pay your membership dues today, you get a 10 percent discount."

Linda nodded toward the large sign behind the putting green. "Or I could sink the most putts and win a free membership."

"Absolutely," Mallory said. "Do you want to be the first to try?"

Linda approached the golf bag beside the green and pulled out a putter. After examining it, she returned it and retrieved another. That one seemed to satisfy her, and she mimicked a putting motion. "How does this work?"

"You get ten putts. The one who sinks the most wins."

"What if there's a tie?" she asked suspiciously.

Mallory was ready with an answer. "We'll do a drawing."

Linda nodded and addressed the ball, while the rest of them watched. She nailed the first three putts before missing. "It seems like it's working okay," Liza observed.

"Am I the guinea pig?" Linda asked.

"No," one of the ladies from New Jersey admitted. "We've already tried it."

Linda sank seven of her ten putts.

"I think that could be a winner," New Jersey said. "The last time we did this, the winner had only six."

She shrugged. "I plan to join anyway, so it doesn't matter. But I invited the entire membership of the Mountain Meadows women's league, so it wouldn't surprise me if someone beats my score."

Paige was excited to hear that Linda had followed through on her promise. "Thanks, Linda. I hope some of them come. Maybe one or two will even join the league."

Linda nodded. "The roads are okay, so I think they will," she said, and told Paige what she'd done with sending out the schedule for the season ahead of time, so the ladies of the league would be able to commit to SAW if they had the notion.

Paige gave her a thumbs-up. "It seems you didn't get to be realtor of the year by accident."

Linda winked in reply. "Stick with me, kid."

An overhead announcement interrupted them. "Attention, vendors: the doors will open in thirty minutes. Thirty minutes until we tee off. Good luck and have a great round."

Paige couldn't help but smile at the corny words of encouragement. "I'm going to grab a bottle of water. Does anyone want one?" she asked. The vendor just up the concourse offering golf tours to Europe had a large cooler of water. "Wanna come?" she asked Linda.

"Absolutely. Should we wander around now, before it gets busy?" she asked.

"You know, that's not a bad idea. We probably shouldn't wander, though. We should sprint. I don't want to miss anyone at the booth." Suddenly Paige realized that Linda might not have the same idea about the day. "But, hey. If you don't want to stick around, don't feel obligated."

"Are you kidding me? I wouldn't miss it. This is going to be great fun."

"Thanks. I appreciate all you've done already."

They reached the booth with the water and introduced themselves. "We figured we'd let you practice your sales pitch in exchange for a free water," Paige said.

The man laughed. "Please, help yourself. And it's not much of a pitch." He told them about the custom golf tours he offered to some of the most exclusive courses in the world. "It's not meant for budget-oriented golfers," he said with a flick of his wrist. "I cater to people who are looking for a high-end, luxury experience."

Paige nodded politely but inwardly cringed. Will had been injured the last month of her residency, just a few weeks after they'd begun moving into their first house and before she even collected her first paycheck as a real doctor. Because he had been injured at work, he was still getting paid, but Paige wasn't sure how long that would last. With her portfolio of bills—medical-school loans, a car payment, a mortgage, and the normal costs of running her house—luxury golf vacations were not in the budget.

"I'll look this over," she said before they moved on.

"You're not dealing with that guy for golf travel. I can get you luxury at bargain prices," Linda whispered.

"Oh, yeah? I was just talking about a golf trip with Liza and Mallory."

"*Oh, yeah?* One of the ladies who plays at Mountain Meadows is a travel agent. As a matter of fact, if you're interested, we have a trip to Myrtle Beach in a few weeks. It might be too late for the airfare, but if you're willing to drive, or if you can book your own flight, I might be able to get you in. She can probably get another condo for you and your friends, and you can join us for golf. And après golf."

"Hmm," Paige murmured, thinking again that a golf getaway was just what she needed. A little time away from work, and Will, and the craziness of her life. "When is it? What's the weather like in South Carolina?"

"We're going the first week of March. And I don't know how the weather will be, but I guarantee it will be warmer than it is here." She chuckled as she patted Paige on the shoulder.

"Tropical, compared to Clarks Summit."

"Do you think you could get time off?" Linda asked. "Would Will mind you going away with the girls?"

"Yes, and yes. But, truthfully, I could use some time away from him."

Linda stopped and looked at her with an expression of concern. Since Paige had been in the throes of residency, Will had done the majority of the house hunting, with Linda finding properties, Will previewing them, and Paige touring only what he'd vetted. They'd developed a nice friendship, and Linda had actually taken them out to Mountain Meadows for a round of golf to celebrate after their offer on the house was accepted. They'd been contemplating membership—had actually submitted their application—at the time of his accident. "How's he doing?"

Paige shrugged. "Depressed. Miserable. Demanding. Controlling."

In spite of Paige's descriptors, Linda laughed. "Don't sugarcoat it for me. I can handle the truth."

Sighing, Paige turned to face her. "I worked my entire life to get to where I am, Linda. And just as I crossed the finish line, this happened. Is it so wrong that I'd like to play golf on my day off and just have a little fun in my spare time? Or to go out for a nice dinner with my sister or my niece? Or, heaven forbid, with a friend? It's like he begrudges me any happiness. Since he's sitting home, he wants me to as well. And I can't do that all the time. The things we used to do around the house—like play chess, or Scrabble, or even video games—he has no interest in anymore. He's punishing me for leaving the house by ignoring me when I'm there."

"Is he seeing a therapist?" Linda asked as she gently touched her arm. "Are you?"

She sighed, feeling defeated. "He isn't—he just flat-out refuses. But I am. I've been seeing a woman in town. She's helping me."

"Good." Linda stopped and looked at her with a penetrating gaze. "You have a right to be happy, Paige. Don't forget that. And," she hesitated before continuing, "even before the accident, Will was the boss. He wanted it his way. When I was trying to find you a house, he dismissed most of them without a second thought. Places you would have loved. I figured you trusted him, but sometimes I felt like it was his house alone, not yours collectively. I would imagine he's a beast now that he's lost control. But think about the golf trip. It'll do you a world of good."

She'd heard the same thing before—from her parents and her sister, who'd known Will very well for years. But Linda had seen only snapshots of their marriage, taken over the course of a few months. And she'd nailed their relationship. Was their pathology that obvious, or was she just that observant?

They arrived at a booth offering a free pair of golf shoes to the winner of a drawing. All they had to do was fill out a paper with their name, phone number, and email. "Are you going to supply the telemarketers with more fodder?" Paige asked.

Linda winked. "I give my junk email and work number. I never check that mail, and no one gets through my receptionist."

Paige laughed. "I'm going to do that right now. I'm setting up a junk-mail account."

"What about the phone number?"

Paige pursed her lips. "I'll use the ER director's number. I hate him."

Linda roared in response. "Remind me not to piss you off."

"I can't believe they closed!" Carly said as they pulled into the valet parking area at Mohegan Sun Pocono. "I loved their food."

"I don't think it was the quality of the food," Tasha said. "Downtown Wilkes-Barre has too many Japanese restaurants and not that much traffic."

"Well, a hotdog wasn't my fantasy."

"How about the seafood tower at Ruth's Chris? You can have all the oysters."

Carly loved that idea, and she smiled before replying. Tasha was so good to her. "Fine. But we still have to go for Japanese. Soon."

"How about Friday night before the theater?"

"Perfect."

The valet took their car, and they scampered into the casino. "Ahhh," Carly moaned as the warm air engulfed her. "It's fucking freezing outside."

They made their way to the convention center, paid their entry fee, and walked inside. Drifting out of the flow of traffic, they glanced at the brochure. "Is there anything special you'd like to see?" Tasha asked. "The event ends in two hours."

"Perfect. My indigestion from the hotdog should be subsiding by then, and you can get me those oysters," she said as she looked at the ads and the layout of the convention center. "I'd like to stop at this luxury-golf travel booth. It's close to the booth for the women's league that Linda mentioned in the email. Swing Around the World. SAW. And I'd like to enter the drawing to win a pair of golf shoes. I love that brand. I need new rain shoes."

"You don't play in the rain."

"But I play when it's wet, and I hate soggy feet. How about you? What would you like to see?"

"The travel booth sounds interesting. We can get some brochures and tell Lynn where we want to go. And I'd like to demo a new driver."

Carly tried hard to dampen the amusement in her tone. Tasha was forever trying new clubs, hoping the latest technology would help improve her lackluster performance on the course. "Really? A new driver. I'm shocked. But okay."

Tasha shot her a look. "So what if I wasn't born a natural athlete like you." She tossed her hair and stuck her nose into the air. "I have looks and brains instead."

"Hmm. I'd have a hard time choosing, but fortunately, I don't have to. Goddess gave me all three."

Their playful banter continued as they made their way from booth to booth, and Carly knew how lucky she was to have such a wonderful friend in Tasha. Not for the first time, she wished things had turned out differently between them. They really did get along fabulously, until Carly entered the sterile environment of Tasha's house, where she had to take off her shoes before leaving the vestibule and hang her coat in the closet immediately to the left of the front door. A dozen reasons, all running in the same vein, amounted to total disaster when Carly had tried to make a romance work. She had to accept it. They were better as friends.

Still, at times Carly thought it might be nice to have a lover to do things like this with. She'd had that intimacy with Tasha for a few years in college, and then with Pip for another ten, but since then, she'd been on her own. She'd dated dozens of women, but none who held her interest. None with Tasha's intelligence and wit, or Pip's sense of adventure.

She'd met Tasha at nineteen, and her two big relationships had amounted to thirteen years of her life. Half of her adult life. The other half she'd filled with friends and family. She couldn't say she was lonely, but sometimes she thought there could be so much more to life. After talking about the subject with her therapist, she'd made a plan— by the time she was fifty, she wanted to meet a woman and settle down. She'd even made a list of everything she was looking for in her future bride—and golf was at the top of the list. She had to play golf—and what better way to meet someone than by joining a league like SAW? She already knew every lesbian in a twenty-mile radius of Scranton— this move would expand her possibilities tremendously.

But she wasn't in a hurry. She still had almost five years, and if she knew one thing about herself, it was this—she knew what she wanted, and she didn't intend to compromise. Unlike her clients, who bought houses that were less than ideal and added on or knocked down walls, she knew she couldn't change someone. She'd tried that approach and failed. Now, she was older and wiser, and much more patient, even if she occasionally did stupid things like bring home drunken women half her age.

You are a work in progress, Carly, she told herself, repeating the words of her therapist.

"Here's the virtual-reality course," she noted a moment later. "I think they're hawking drivers."

"Oh, yes," Tasha said with a glee that instantly lightened Carly's mood.

Tasha rushed over and talked to one of the sales reps, and Carly stood and simply looked around. The exhibits were what she'd expected, but the energy was tremendous. It wasn't loud so much as thrumming, like a beehive, with people orbiting in every direction possible. Closing her eyes, she swallowed the air and could almost taste the excitement.

Fingering some clubs, she watched Tasha talking with the sales rep, and inside of five minutes, she had a ball on a tee and was staring down the fairway at the first hole at Banff Springs. They'd played there on a golf outing a few years earlier. The scenery was magnificent, with a stand of tall pines lining the hole and a majestic mountain in the distance. Still, Carly grimaced, waiting for the disaster, and as she anticipated, the tee shot went far right, into the trees.

After several shots with multiple drivers and the same results, Tasha thanked the salesman, and they moved along. Carly didn't say a word.

"Shut up."

"I didn't say anything."

"I know what you're thinking."

Carly didn't deny it and managed to keep her expression neutral, but finally, she cracked up.

"That's it!" Tasha replied. "I'm not sharing the oysters."

"I'm sorry. I'm shallow and insensitive. But you know this about me, so why should you let it upset you after all these years?"

Tasha ignored her. "There's the travel guy," she said instead, and they stopped to talk to him. One of their friends from Mountain Meadows had put together a ladies' trip to Myrtle Beach, and they were both planning to go. But now that she had her summer schedule, another trip—like a luxury golf vacation—might be an option. Although she wouldn't book with this guy, Carly listened for suggestions to share with her friend. She'd put something together if Carly wanted.

After talking for a few minutes, she asked for some brochures. She was getting hungry, and inpatient as well. They took the proffered pamphlets and had moved a few steps away, when Tasha gently grabbed her elbow. "There's the booth for the women's league. How about we make an appearance, then go get some dinner?"

Carly looked ahead, meaning to answer, but instead, the sight of a woman left her speechless. She was medium height and thin, with short blond hair that fell just below her ears. At the moment Carly looked, she was pushing it back behind one ear, revealing the soft angle of her jaw and the elegant lines of her neck. Her mouth was turned up in a smile as she explored the exhibit hall with her eyes, the rest of her still in spite of the activity all around her. It was the exact pose Carly had held a moment earlier, and the joy on the woman's face seemed to transfer to Carly. She felt her like a warm caress, like stepping into the sun. Ooh, she thought. What a cutie-patootie. This new league had some potential.

❖

Fatigue was beginning to set in, and Paige had been discreetly covering yawns for the past hour. Liza and Mal had mentioned dinner, and Linda and the other girls were interested as well, so she thought she might try to find a coffee to perk her up until they ate. Then, when she finally cuddled into her bed, she'd sleep for days.

Checking her watch, she realized less than an hour was left of the expo. The crowd had thinned considerably, with only a few stragglers stopping by in the last minutes, and Paige saw some of the vendors beginning to break down their exhibits. She eyed the SAW area and realized the deconstruction would be easy. Interested golfers had taken the literature they'd displayed, so all that remained were banners, the projector, some clothing, and the putting green.

In the putting contest, Linda was tied with a few other women, so it looked like they'd hold a drawing before they left. Paige couldn't believe how many women had come by to talk to her and the others about the league. Her sister Helena and her niece Jules had stopped in and said hi, and a few friends from work had as well. Some clearly weren't interested but tried the putting contest anyway. Still, she'd collected more than twenty names and email addresses, and she suspected that the majority of the women who'd signed up would follow through with the registration to secure their memberships. The day had been a smashing success.

Looking around for inspiration for her coffee, Carly spotted the hospital CEO, Natasha Peterson. She was laughing and turned to look at the woman beside her. Paige looked as well and felt the oddest of sensations. It was as if a camera were capturing the vision—slow-moving frames of the woman as she turned her head, laughed, and brushed her shoulder-length hair back from her eyes. The movie in her mind was silent as Paige's sense of hearing faded, and nothing was in focus except the woman, who suddenly caught her eye as she walked toward her.

And then, Natasha Peterson touched the woman's arm, and she shifted her gaze, and whatever had happened in that moment was gone, except for the feeling of weightlessness that caused Paige to nearly topple over.

Trying not to stare, she turned and saw Linda talking to two other women, and she took a few unsteady steps in their direction. From the corner of her eye, though, she saw Natasha and her friend, who seemed to be floating in Paige's direction.

"Paige, perfect. I'd like to introduce you to two friends of mine," she said as she pulled Paige a little closer. Reluctantly, Paige focused on the two women with Linda.

"This is Alex Dalton, the assistant pro at Mountain Meadows, and her wife, Britain Dodge."

Paige nodded hello and smiled, and they wished her luck with the league, but she could hardly register their words. She knew or, rather, she sensed Natasha Peterson was approaching—Natasha and the woman beside her.

"Sometimes I wish I hadn't become a professional golfer, because I miss out on some of the fun stuff, like this."

"And I just don't have much time right now. Good luck, though. I'm sure it'll be a big hit," Britain said.

Paige brought herself back to the moment in time to figure out what they were talking about. "No worries," Paige said. "But it's nice to see women have an opportunity in the pro shop."

Alex nodded. "It is. But this is only a hobby for me. I teach and coach a high school basketball team, so my schedule is packed during the school year. I pick up my clubs in April and put them away in September."

"It sounds like you have a busy life."

Shrugging, she looked toward her wife. "Britain is a medical student, so she's always got something going on. I need distractions to keep me out of trouble while she's saving lives."

Paige couldn't suppress her smile as she asked Britain for details and talked about her own position as an ER doctor.

"Let me give you my card. It seems we're not meant to be golfing buddies, but maybe I can set something up for you to come in and spend time with me in the ER. Whatever. Sometimes it's just nice to have an ally."

Britain's jaw flew open. "That would be fabulous."

Paige pulled a pile of business cards from her back pocket and handed one to each of them. "Are you coming to dinner?" Paige whirled her finger in a circle. "I think most of the group is heading to Ruth's Chris when we're done."

Britain and Alex turned to each other. "Up to you," Alex said.

"If we don't stay too late," she responded as she looked at Paige. "You know how it is. My schedule is crazy."

"I worked overnight last night and haven't slept yet. I do know how it is."

"Hey, ladies!" Paige heard Linda's greeting and looked up to see Natasha Peterson and her friend.

"Paige, these two would love this league. You have to tell them about it."

Paige nodded as the newcomers approached, fighting the nervous energy that suddenly filled her. "Let's talk more at dinner, okay?" Britain suggested, and Paige agreed before turning her attention to Natasha. She swallowed and smiled, calming herself, looking into the eyes of the CEO but seeing the woman next to her.

"Hello, Ms. Peterson." She greeted the hospital CEO and then turned her gaze to her friend. Piercing eyes of onyx examined her, and Paige felt the woman assessing her, determining if she was worthy. But worthy of what? Paige didn't have a moment to reflect on the question before Natasha responded.

She smiled. "Outside the hospital, it's Tasha."

Linda nodded and thumped her fingers against her forehead. "Of course. You two know each other."

"Yes, but I don't think Dr. Waterford has met Carly."

Paige again turned her attention to Tasha's companion as Tasha waved in her friend's direction. "This is my dear friend, Carly Becker."

Paige looked at the woman, as her senses dimmed again, and she smiled tightly to hide the fact that she seemed to have forgotten how to speak.

"Hi. Nice to meet you," Carly said politely, then nodded toward the putting green. "What's the score to beat?"

"Seven," Paige replied.

"How'd you do, Ace?" Carly asked as she looked at Alex, and her entire demeanor seemed to shift from reserved to playful.

"I didn't try it yet."

Paige observed as Carly focused her dark eyes on Linda. "You're not really going to let her putt, are you? She's practically on the LPGA tour."

"Oh, stop whining, Becker," Alex retorted.

Linda pointed a finger. "It's a valid question, Alex. But I'm not getting in the middle of you two." She turned toward Liza and Mallory to ask, while the rest of them migrated toward the putting green.

Alex pulled a putter from the bag and laughed. Although the grip was gray, the rest of the club, from the shaft to the head, was neon pink. "Here you go, Carly. This is perfect for you."

"What is this?" she asked, looking at Paige. "Mini golf?"

Before Paige could answer, Britain did. "What are you talking about? I love pink."

"I hate it," Carly retorted, a wounded look on her face.

By then Alex had pulled another club from the bag. "Okay. Try this one then. I'll challenge you. Loser buys drinks. We're going to Ruth's Chris when this is over."

Carly shook her head. "Are you kidding me? I'm not doing it. That's just throwing my money away."

Paige had been watching the exchange with interest and decided to interject. "Alex doesn't have time to play in SAW, Carly, so you should give it a try. You could win the membership, even if she wins the drink."

"I'll have a drink with you guys, but I'm not gambling." She nodded toward the door. "I'd have a better chance in the casino."

Tasha shook her head and grabbed the pink putter. "I'll go first, while you guys figure out what you're doing." Then she turned to them and winked. "I'll give you the read."

Taking her place on the putting mat, she missed the first five attempts. Stepping away, she handed the putter to Britain. "I think this is broken."

Britain laughed but accepted the club and had no better luck. "I think Tash is right," she quipped, offering the putter to Carly.

Carly shooed her away and grabbed another putter from the bag. Kneeling behind the green, tilting her head in an exaggerated pose, she pretended to read the putt.

"Come on, wiseass. Get on with it." Alex leaned on the pink putter as she threw out the challenge.

Carly stood and addressed the ball, then nailed seven putts.

"Top that," she said as she handed the putter to Alex.

"Game on."

After missing the first putt, Alex drained the next eight.

Carly shook her head. "See. That's why I don't gamble."

Paige stood to the side, silently observing the playful banter between the friends, inexplicably envious that she wasn't part of their circle. Four women, presumably two couples, who so clearly enjoyed each other's company. Had she ever had that with Will and their friends? They'd been companionable at one point, certainly, but she suddenly had difficulty remembering when. And she doubted they'd ever looked as happy as these four women did now.

"Well, Carly, since Alex's score doesn't count, you're tied for the lead with Linda and two others. And I think we're about done here, so we might as well pull the winner." Mallory looked from Linda to Carly. "Since half of the finalists are here."

After scribbling names on scraps of paper, Mallory placed them into a SAW baseball cap and thrust it toward Paige. "You're the president of this new league. Pick the winner."

"This must be fixed," Carly said with a laugh. "Linda knows you."

Linda protested. "Do you doubt my integrity?" she asked as she dramatically placed her hand over her heart.

"Actually, yes," Carly said dryly, and Paige had to suppress a laugh as she reached into the hat and made a show of mixing up the entries.

"Drum roll, please," she said as she purposefully looked from Carly to Linda, briefly locking both of them with her gaze before pulling a name. She looked down at the paper in her hand, then back at the women as a surge of excitement coursed through her. Once again, her eyes met Carly's, and she felt her equilibrium disturbed. "Carly Becker," she said in a soft voice that belied her emotions.

For a moment, Carly's expression was neutral as cheers and laughter erupted from the group. Then a huge smile spread from across her face. "I think I'm going to like SAW."

Paige handed Carly a certificate, something Mal had printed at home, that gave her instructions about her free membership, and then they began packing up the booth. Everyone helped, and in a few minutes, the entire exhibit was condensed into a few boxes, which they carried to a loading area and deposited into the back of someone's oversized

SUV. Then, they turned around and walked to the steak house. Liza and Mal strolled with Natasha and Carly, and Britain kept pace with Paige.

It turned out that Paige knew Britain's father, a retired cardiologist, and they explored further connections on the five-minute walk. And though Paige found her endearing, she had trouble focusing on their conversation as she saw Carly in the group ahead of her.

Paige had felt like she'd been hit by lightning when she first saw Carly, and the stunning effects came back every time she looked at her. She was totally off balance.

When they reached the entrance to the restaurant, they huddled by the door as Mal went in to announce the group, and Paige stopped a few feet from Carly. "Congrats on the putting contest," she said when their eyes met.

Carly's face turned up in a small smile. "I guess it's fate. I was thinking of joining, but now it's a no-brainer."

"That's good for me, then. I wasn't sure anyone would join."

Carly turned her head and seemed to study her for a moment, before offering a gentle nod. "Then I think you'll be pleasantly surprised."

"Okay, ladies," Mal said, interrupting them. "Our table's ready."

As the group began to move, Paige tried to stay near Carly, hoping to sit by her during dinner, but fate had other plans. Britain grabbed her arm, she hesitated, and the woman from Harrisburg stepped between them. When they arrived at their table, Carly was seated at the end, already engaged in conversation with Liza and Mal. Paige had no options but one of the end seats, as far away from Carly as she could be.

The dinner conversation was lively, and Paige found herself laughing more than she had in ages. Despite the good company, though, she found herself leaning just a little, turning her head a few degrees, searching the other end of the table for Carly. And on the few occasions she caught a glimpse of her, she felt a happiness she didn't bother questioning.

CHAPTER FIVE

TEE SHOTS

It was well before eight o'clock when Carly, balancing her coffee and briefcase, punched in the alarm code at her office the next morning. She had a closing to prepare for, and though she tried not to schedule closings on Mondays because Mondays inevitably followed weekends, the couple buying this house was from New York, and it worked out better for them to do it today. And as Carly often preached to her staff, the client is always right.

Leaving the common space dark, she made her way to the corner office and settled in behind the well-organized desk. As her laptop came to life, she pulled the bagel from her bag and took a bite, then grabbed the relevant file from a drawer.

She could have done this at home, but she frowned upon removing closing documents from the office. They contained so much confidential information that could fall into the wrong hands if her briefcase was stolen or her house burgled. It was better this way.

Besides, she didn't mind coming to the office first thing. An early riser, she'd been up with the sun and already accomplished more than most people would the entire day. She'd done her yoga and weights, walked three miles on the treadmill while reading the newspaper on her iPad, thrown a load of laundry into the washer, and set her robotic vacuum to clean the first floor of her house. Her workout had been vigorous, so she treated herself to coffee and a bagel from the shop near her office, and she felt energized, ready to face whatever came her way.

The quiet office was just the setting she needed to accomplish what she needed, and later—if someone invited her to dinner—she'd feel no guilt in leaving early. In the warm weather, her early start usually meant the day ended with a round of golf.

When she was sure the closing documents were prepared correctly, she checked her email. Junk, junk, junk, junk, and then one that caught her eye. *Welcome to SAW.* Apparently, efficiency was the rule at SAW. It had been only half a day since she'd won the putting contest and her free membership, and it had been a Sunday.

Clicking on the email, she read a rather standard greeting, then reached the interesting part. The group was having an organizational meeting at the home of the chapter president, Dr. Paige Waterford. It gave a link to click to register for the meeting.

Carly sat back in her chair and sipped her coffee as she thought of Dr. Paige Waterford. Paige. She'd caught Carly's eye from a hundred yards away, and as she got closer and had a better view, Carly was even more drawn—right up until the point when Tasha offered that friendly greeting, and Carly realized they knew each other. That would be just too uncomfortable. Carly couldn't count the women who'd cried on Tasha's shoulder when things didn't work out with Carly, but they were usually women Tasha could dodge or block on her phone or otherwise avoid. How could she do that with a doctor who worked in her hospital?

Carly's planned seduction had ended at the moment of their introduction. Still, she couldn't deny the excitement she'd felt when they'd exchanged a few words before dinner and disappointment when they'd separated at the restaurant's door. Before Carly knew what was happening, Liza had taken charge of the seating and positioned her at the end of the table, cut off from Paige. Sure, she'd enjoyed the conversation with Liza and Mallory, and thought they might become friends, but she'd shifted in her chair more than a few times, trying to catch a glimpse of the blonde at the other end of the table. She carefully crafted the questions she lobbed at Liza and Mallory, trying to learn more about Paige without tripping Tasha's alarm bells. And though she could have quizzed Tasha about Paige on the ride home, she remained purposefully silent, not wanting Tasha to know her thoughts.

She couldn't help thinking, though. A beautiful, thirty-something doctor working at Tasha's hospital—why had her best friend never mentioned her? Tasha was single, and attractive. She'd dated people from the hospital before, so it wasn't taboo. Why not Paige?

Carly sighed as she sipped her coffee. She'd barely spoken a word more than hello, and already this woman seemed like more trouble than she could possibly be worth. Carly should ignore SAW and Paige Waterford. Yet, somehow, she just couldn't do it.

Typing Paige's name into her computer, she searched for more information but didn't locate much. She found a rather generic professional profile and a review. Ha. Paige had only two stars in four reviews. One patient praised her, with a five-star tribute for making an obscure diagnosis that apparently saved her life. The other three were one stars, from patients who complained about waiting times, the smell in the bathroom, and an inability to get pain medication. Carly shrugged. Online reviews were one of her biggest worries as a small-business owner. An irate customer who posted a one-star review was like a torpedo sinking a business's reputation. But she supposed Paige, as an ER doctor, wouldn't care much. When people had emergencies, they were stuck with the doctor on duty, even if she had only two stars.

Carly found another hit, a newspaper clip from an opioid-crisis community program. Paige was quoted about the Warm Handoff Program she'd helped to organize and explained how it would help the community. That was a noble if futile cause. One of her agent's sons had battled addiction—was forever battling it. Not the kind of work Carly would want, but she supposed it was good that someone did it.

The next item she found caused her to pause. It was the record of her home purchase from almost two years ago. The property was transferred from Marvin and Sarah Steiner to William Balliet and Paige Waterford.

Interesting. Who was William Balliet? Paige had definitely pinged Carly's gaydar, and she hadn't been wearing a ring. Probably not a husband. Father? It wouldn't be the first time a woman had her father cosign a mortgage. And that made sense. Carly had sold a number of homes to physicians, and in spite of the earnings potential and typically excellent credit, many of them were just finishing their training and were strapped with debt. Few had ample cash on hand for down payments and closing costs. Some had non-spousal cosignatories on their loans, which translated to those names on the deeds to the property they purchased.

Oh, why did it matter anyway? She'd seen a million pretty women in her life and had dismissed 95 percent of them. What had Paige Waterford done to get under her skin like this?

It was inexplicable. Carly had simply been walking beside Tasha, talking, when she'd spotted Paige. And since that moment, it seemed like the universe was a little off tilt, spinning just a little faster, making her dizzy.

She just needed to stop thinking about Paige. If only she knew how.

"That's an interesting expression," a voice called from the doorway. "Is it gas?"

Carly laughed at her personal assistant.

"And if so, is it safe to enter?" Dominica hovered by the door, but without waiting for Carly's answer, she walked through, closed it behind her, and settled into the chair across the desk from Carly's.

"How was your weekend?" Carly asked Dom, the mother figure who'd been with her since she opened the agency two decades ago.

"Normal. Crazy. I met the new baby." She scrolled through pictures on her phone and handed it over for inspection.

Dominica and her husband, Mike, had four boys and a dozen grandchildren. Her grandson, Mikey, had just given them their first great-grandson, also named Michael. "Oh, Dom! He's gorgeous. What are they calling him?"

"So far it's Little Mike, but we'll see."

Carly handed back the phone, then leaned into her chair, happy for Dominica's many blessings. She was an intelligent, sophisticated, sweet woman—a true lady, with dignity and a level of sophistication that had set the tone of the office from the first moment she'd walked through the door. That was when Carly was thinking of buying the building—her first major personal real-estate purchase. Dom had asked intelligent and thoughtful questions, and she wasn't afraid to challenge the contractors who were offering bids for their services. Since then, Carly had sold Dom a share of the business, and they worked equally hard to make it successful.

They faced each other again as Dom inquired about Carly's weekend. "I went to that golf expo. The one at the casino. It was good."

"Good? Does that mean you met lots of single women?"

"Dominica! There is more to my life than just women."

"I know that. But the sole purpose of SAW, to quote you, is 'hot chicks with golf sticks.'"

Carly diverted her eyes as she sipped from her coffee, a shrug lifting her shoulders. "I may have said that."

"Yeah, so? Any candidates?"

"Candidates for what? I met a few women to play golf with, that's for sure."

"How about the nineteenth hole? Anyone to socialize with between rounds?"

Carly sipped and thought of Paige. "There's a definite possibility. She's a doctor and she plays golf."

"A doctor. I always wanted one of my boys to marry a doctor."

"Shoo," Carly said with a sweeping hand. "She works with Tasha."

"That would not be good."

"Very not good."

She shrugged. "I brought eggplant for lunch. Yours has your name on it."

Carly's mouth watered. Dominica was a great cook. "I love you, Bella. Why couldn't you be gay?"

Dominica walked away chuckling, as Carly picked up the phone and dialed her therapist, who, remarkably, answered the phone.

"Good morning, Carly."

"It is good," she lied. "But I think I need a tune-up." The thoughts of Paige had pushed her, but really, it wasn't just that. It was everything. The girl in her bed the morning before. Her drinking the night before that. This general anxiety she'd been dodging for months. She needed to figure out her mood before it became chronic.

"Is it an emergency? I can see you today," Ann Marie replied.

"I have a closing. But I can squeeze you in later," Carly said.

Ann Marie chuckled. "Carly, Carly, Carly. I'm the one squeezing here. How's four?"

Feeling better already, she agreed and disconnected the call before turning back to her computer. The email was staring at her. Pushing the thoughts of Paige aside, she thought about what SAW had to offer. Golf, which she loved. Travel. Women. It suddenly seemed like a no-brainer.

Hovering her finger over the mouse, she envisioned the stupid pink putter. She shook her head, clicked the link, and accepted the invitation to the meeting.

❖

It was almost noon when Paige opened her eyes the day after the golf expo. Rolling onto her side, she stretched and yawned, then lay quietly, listening for signs of life in the house. After a few moments, she accepted the fact that she was still alone. Damn. Why did she even care? If Will wanted to be alone, and so did she, why did it matter that he'd been the one to leave? Reaching out from beneath the thick down comforter, she retrieved her phone from the table beside her bed and dialed Helena's number. "Hello, my beautiful sister," Helena greeted her.

"Good morning. How are you?" she said through a yawn.

"You have the life, sis. Sleeping 'til noon like a college kid."

"Oh, yeah," she said sarcastically. "I'm the envy of women across the globe."

She heard Helena pause. "Would you like to meet for lunch?" She sounded exasperated, and Paige wasn't sure if that frustration was her own or directed at Paige. Helena, who was in the habit of running the world, was never quite satisfied with how Paige managed things, including her life.

"I was hoping you'd ask," she replied as she stretched.

"State Street in an hour?"

"See you there," Paige said and disconnected the call.

Snuggling back under the covers, she closed her eyes and tried not to think of Will. When had things gone so wrong? If she wanted to be lazy, she could blame the accident. He'd fallen through the ceiling of a burning house and shattered his pelvis, and the nearly two years since had been a hell of surgeries and rehab and pain for him. And it had been a different hell for her—managing the house, working, juggling appointments, trying to keep him from getting addicted to medication that made him feel better. Handling his moods—depression, anger, despair. And her own moods, as well. Her own life had changed radically, too, and she'd never had time to process her feelings about finishing residency and moving on to the next leg of her journey. And she was still trying to figure that out—what was the next step for her?

Before his accident, they'd been planning to have a child. At least Paige had. Will already had a son and wasn't eager to commit to another, but it had been a deal breaker for Paige. Sometimes, she thought he'd been lying about a baby the whole time, just to get her to marry him. As if she'd change her mind about something like that.

Since the accident, though, all the talk of a baby had stopped. All talk in general had stopped.

Their relationship had suffered as much as they each had individually. But the problems had been there before the accident, and the broken pelvis had just made them worse. The stress of his injury brought to the surface the issues that had started brewing at the beginning.

Trying to redirect her thoughts, she turned to her phone and played some relaxing music as she began her meditation. She started on a beach, with her toes sinking into the sand. She envisioned the sun warming her and could hear the surf and smell the salty air. And then she drifted, suspended in a moment—the moment she first saw Carly Becker the night before.

She could still picture Carly's piercing eyes as they studied her, taking everything in. She had been mesmerized, and her mouth went dry again just at the thought of her. It was as if Carly had an energy field around her, and it had zapped Paige. It was inexplicable, but she was certain of one thing—she wanted to get to know Carly. Please join SAW, she said quietly. Please join. She'd won the free membership, right? Carly would join. If not, Paige had her email. She'd find an excuse to reach out to her. She didn't know what she'd say, but she had to see her again. It was as if Carly Becker, simply by casting her gaze upon her, had cast some sort of a spell as well.

When she had arrived home at eight the night before and practically dove into a bath of bubbles, it wasn't Will, or her friends, or the new golf league on her mind, but Carly Becker. And Tasha Peterson, too.

She had never considered the possibility that the hospital CEO might be gay, but after seeing the personal exchanges with Carly throughout dinner, she had no doubt in her mind that they were lovers. Their intimacy was obvious, even to a straight girl like Paige. The idea unsettled her, and she wasn't sure why.

She had pulled up Becker Realty on her phone, disappointed at how little information about Carly she could glean from her company's website. She'd founded the agency more than twenty years ago and now had ten associates working for her. There was information about awards and charitable endeavors, and of course there were homes for sale, but other than the briefest of bios, she learned very little about Carly herself. She'd lived in Northeast Pennsylvania her entire life and graduated from Paige's alma mater, the University of Scranton. Shortly after that, she formed her company and quickly added associates to grow the business.

An internet search of Carly's name provided more information, but not much. A few pictures were related to her business and a charity golf tournament, but not enough to satisfy her curiosity. Yet why did it matter? What was it about a woman she'd met for a moment that had her so curious?

An hour later she walked into the State Street Grill in Clarks Summit to find her sister seated at a prime table.

"You live five minutes away. How could I get here first?"

"You had clothes on when we spoke earlier, and I didn't."

"Oh. Yikes. Didn't Mommy warn you about the dangers of sleeping naked? Diseases and such."

"I'm a doctor, Lena. You can't scare me."

"Still. Frostbite."

"It *is* fucking cold."

"Why didn't you move to Florida with Mom and Dad after residency? Then I'd have no reason to stay here."

"Because you're here. You and my beautiful niece. Why would I want to be anywhere else?"

Lena smiled. "Touché."

"How is my niece, by the way? I didn't get more than a peck on the cheek at the golf expo."

"She's excited. She's been checking out her college classes online. And," she paused for the drama of it, "she found the date of the U's fall-break Paris trip."

Paige nodded. She'd known it was coming and had been saving her money, picking up an extra shift here and there to cover the vacation.

"You're going to break her heart if you don't take her," she said with a stern look. Before Paige could reply, she continued. "I know you've been carrying a big financial burden, sis. If it's the money, I'll pay for her. Hell, I'll pay for you, too. She just wants to spend time with you."

Paige sighed. "I'm sorry it didn't work out last fall. It was just bad timing. If I know the date ahead of time, I'll request it off."

"Okay. But the offer to pay stands. Do you think you'll be able to get the time off in October?"

Nodding, Paige chewed her lip. "I'll be able to get time off, and I'm paying. It's her graduation present."

"Perfect. That's settled." After pulling out her phone, Lena began typing. "I'm sending the date to you now. Add it to your calendar."

"Yes, General."

"Stop it."

Paige laughed.

"How'd it go yesterday? It seemed like it was a success."

She could hardly contain her excitement as she shared all the details with Helena. "And thanks for signing up. I know you don't love golf. We had so many people, I'll let you off the hook and tell you it's no longer necessary for you to participate if you don't really want to."

Lena shrugged. "Open your menu. Or do you know what you want? I have to get back to the office, so we should order," she said as she flagged down the waitress.

She took their orders, and Helena continued as if they hadn't been interrupted. "Jules seems to be looking forward to golfing. There's not a soul her age, but I think she wants to spend time with you and me, so it's the perfect opportunity."

Paige smiled. "Thank you," she said, and spent the next ten minutes telling Lena about the league. Always Paige's biggest supporter, she'd signed up without even knowing what she was getting herself into.

The waitress arrived with their food, and they dug in. Between bites, they continued to talk. "Did you get the welcome email?"

Lena nodded. "Yes."

"Great. Did you RSVP to the meeting?"

She nodded. "Saturday at your house?"

"Yes."

"I had to decline. I have a work thing. What will you do with Will?"

She wasn't sad that her sister couldn't make it but not happy either. Having Lena there could go either way—she might chat people up and make them feel comfortable, or she might tell them where to sit and tick them off. But the turnout at the expo had been great, and she was sure the league was going to take off. "It's fine. I think I'll have a good turnout. And who knows about Will? I'm not sure he'll even be home by then."

Lena looked confused. "What? Where is he?"

"He went to the cabin."

"What do you mean *he went to the cabin?* You haven't seen him in days because you just worked a gazillion hours in a row, and now he's gone?"

She dredged her French fry in ketchup and then bit the end as she shrugged, averting her eyes from her sister's angry gaze. Fisting her burger with both hands, she took a big bite to buy time as Helena continued her tirade.

"First of all, it's freezing outside, so it's too cold to fish, and there's no television reception, and no Wi-Fi, so what the fuck is he doing up there by himself? And second of all, why isn't he home with you?"

She thought of a flippant response, because sometimes Helena's protective attitude needed defusing. But she simply didn't have the energy, and out of nowhere, tears stung her eyes.

"I don't know. Sometimes I wonder if we ever really had anything in common, or we just tried really hard to make something out of nothing. Since the accident, there's nothing."

"Is it him, or is it you?"

She studied Helena for a moment, trying to divine the meaning of her question. In typical Helena fashion, she jumped right back in before Paige could respond.

"I mean, seriously, Paige—I can't believe there's any substance to this relationship anymore. I understood it when you were an inexperienced college student, and he was the big hotshot medic and fireman. Strong and handsome and a hero. And a pretty smart cookie, too. You told me he really taught you so much back then. But while you were working your ass off—what was he doing? Fishing? Riding his quad?"

She raised her eyebrows in response.

"C'mon. You know I'm right. Did he ever sacrifice his lifestyle to accommodate the demands of your schedule? Heaven forbid he should miss poker night with the guys. Did he do a thing around the apartment—cook, clean, throw in a load of laundry? I remember one day I was talking to you on the phone, on your day off, after you'd just worked a thirty-six-hour shift, and you were at the grocery store. You told me there was no food in the house. And where was he? Off with his buddies somewhere."

She could have told Helena that she enjoyed the mindless tasks like folding laundry and shopping for groceries, because they filled time and helped her relax. But that wasn't the point. She thought about the couple she'd met the day before, Alex and Britain. Britain was in medical school, and Alex had taken a second job at the golf course. Yet as much as they'd struggled financially during Paige's residency, Will had never seemed motivated to help their situation by working any harder. Ambition didn't course through his veins, that was certain. She routinely picked up extra shifts to make extra money, but Will had always preferred to spend his time off playing. As much as he made, he spent.

Not that she blamed him. His job as a paramedic and fireman was stressful, and he needed to decompress when he could, just as she did. But she accomplished things while de-stressing—like laundry and groceries—and he didn't. Was she resentful? Maybe. Or maybe Helena was right. Will had been attractive when she was a starry-eyed kid learning from the guy with all the experience. And maybe the reverse was true, too. He'd liked being her mentor. Now, maybe they were bored with each other. Maybe he had grown resentful of her success. And maybe she was full of shit. She wasn't sure, but she sure wasn't happy anymore.

"I don't know. Maybe you're right," she admitted. "I guess I could blame a lot of things. Does it matter?" she asked with a shrug. "The question is how do we fix it?"

They both took a bite of their food before Helena answered. "You're a doctor, so you know the answer to that. You need a diagnosis in order to figure out the cure, right?"

Paige couldn't help but smile at her sister's analogy. "Right."

"You need to think about this, the diagnosis, in order to find the cure." She paused and chewed, then nailed Paige with her gaze. "If you want to find the cure."

"Hmm," she said. What did she really want? The question had preoccupied her thoughts lately, but no matter how much time she spent on it, the answer didn't come. She wished she understood it all. Her questions just brought more questions, though, and never answers. She knew only that she was unhappy and didn't know why. Certainly, she had moments of happiness, like the night before. Time she spent with Liza and Mal. The moments were fleeting though. Nothing sustaining.

She had no diagnosis. And no cure.

Chapter Six

Off Broadway

"You're going to love this show, Jules," Paige predicted as the waiter placed a plate before her. They were at a Thai restaurant, a few blocks from the Scranton Cultural Center, where the curtain was about to go up on the traveling production of *Chicago*. She looked at her sister and niece, sitting across from and beside her, and thought no one would have guessed their relationship. In contrast to Paige's fair complexion and hair, passed down from their father, Helena had inherited their mother's features: black hair and eyes, olive skin. Jules had transcended generations and appeared to be a copy of her redheaded paternal grandmother.

Paige sipped her wine and blew them kisses. It was good to be out with them, talking and laughing, doing something they all loved. She had looked forward to her theater nights since Jules was a little girl. Whenever she could, she had traveled home from medical school and residency to share dinner and a show with two of her favorite people.

"I know," Jules replied gleefully, a smile spreading across her face as her big blue eyes doubled in size. "I'm so excited. Do you know it's the second longest-running show in Broadway history? Second only to *Phantom*."

"I did know that." Paige took a bite of a shrimp, and the exotic flavors of Asian spices exploded on her tongue. She moaned. They talked about the food for a moment before shifting back to the show. "The dancing is unbelievable."

Jules had danced as a child, giving it up only when the demands of high school forced her to make choices in after-school activities. Jules nodded. "I saw some videos on YouTube."

"Well, Scranton won't compare to Broadway, but it's live, so I think that makes it better than YouTube. And our seats are so good," Paige said. Helena and her husband, Al, had been subscribers of the cultural center's Broadway series for years, and they'd added a ticket for Jules when she was just a little girl. They'd gotten orchestra center, ten rows back. When Paige came home to Scranton, Al was happy to relinquish his seat to her, so now they did this five or six times a year.

"Did anyone from the cast come to the ER this time?" Jules asked with wide-eyed, eighteen-year-old wonder. During the production of *A Chorus Line,* one of the performers had developed a tiny finger abscess after biting a cuticle, and Paige had the unusual experience of watching the man perform on stage in the evening, only to slice open his thumb with a scalpel in the early hours of the next morning.

The ER had been slow that night, and they'd spent time chatting. Then, the next night when she'd returned to work, she received a gift: a program signed by the show's cast. Of course, she had given it to Jules, who'd framed it and hung it on her bedroom wall.

"Not yet, but there's been only one performance so far. The weekend is young."

"But growing older by the minute. We should go," Helena said as she signaled the waiter.

Paige paid the check, since her sister had bought the tickets, and a minute later they were out the door. The cold spell had broken, and it was a comfortable two-block walk to the theater. They passed Paige's Jeep on the road. "That was a bit of good luck," Helena said as she nodded to the car.

Paige nodded. "I'm having a good day." She'd managed to revive a woman in cardiac arrest that morning and was still flying high on the adrenaline of the save. It had been simply amazing—a code that was nearly over when the medics pushed the stretcher through the door, just waiting for her to make the call. But she'd not been ready to give up on the fifty-year-old, and she went through her protocols, hoping something would work. And then, finally, the woman's still heart started quivering, and then beating, and though she was quite critical, she was still alive.

"How's Uncle Will?" Jules asked innocently, and Paige instantly tensed. Will still wasn't home, and she hadn't heard from him—nothing after that brief note telling her he was going to his cabin. It was maddening, but she tried to maintain a neutral tone for Jules's benefit. No use bringing everyone else down, too.

"He's okay. He's at the cabin, having some quiet time."

"Still?" Helena asked, clearly incredulous. "What did you do with all that time off?"

"Oh, I had some quiet time, too." In fact, she had moped around, cleaning and rearranging furniture, watching Netflix and crafting, but mostly feeling sorry for herself. She'd spent hours on the phone with Liza, whose day as a dance instructor began at two. They'd collaborated on photo wreaths, and Paige had nearly completed three of them—one for her, one for her mom, and one for Helena. The photos were of their family—with pictures through the generations—and she planned to gift it to Helena to celebrate her birthday the next month. Her mom would get one simply because Paige loved her.

The project had helped, and talking to Liza always made her happy, but she was having trouble shaking her bad mood. She'd spent hours thinking, and she just didn't understand it all. She was simply unhappy, and no matter what she did—working at a job that challenged and excited her, spending time with people she adored, doing things she enjoyed—the happiness was fleeting, and her mood soon returned to a miserable baseline.

"When's he coming home?" Helena asked as they joined the queue outside the theater. Paige looked up at the elaborate façade of the building and felt a surge of excitement. Going to the theater was a special treat.

"I'm not sure. Do you want to sit on your coat or check it?"

They decided they didn't have time to deal with the coats and headed directly to their seats, and thankfully, Helena dropped the subject of Will as they got caught up in the energy of the theater. The crowd murmured to a disjointed soundtrack of strings and horns warming up in the orchestra pit. The lights were bright, and she glanced around, ignoring the crowd but instead looking at the chandeliers and the peeling paper. The building needed work, but funding to support the arts lagged, and repairs were on the back burner.

Taking her seat, she opened the program and read through the cast as Jules sat beside her and Helena talked with the people in the seats beside them. After patronizing the theater for two decades, she knew her neighbors.

"I'm looking forward to Paris, Jules."

Juliette leaned over and planted a kiss on her cheek. "You're the best aunt, ever."

"Clearly. Do you want to invite your mom? It might be fun if she joined us."

Jules dropped her chin and shot Paige a look. "Fun for who? She'll just dictate everything I do and interrogate me about how my food tastes and what I think of Picasso. I won't have time to have fun because she'll make it into an experience."

Jules was right, and Paige didn't press the issue. In truth, she didn't really want Helena to join them either, but she wanted the choice to be Jules's. And to her credit, Helena hadn't even brought up the subject. Before she could comment, the house lights dimmed, Helena eased into the seat beside her, and the spotlight shone down on the MC onstage.

Carly leaned forward in her seat in the front row and watched the musician as she lost herself in the rhythm, swaying, her hand dancing as it guided the bow across the strings. It was angelic, the sound she created with the violin, and she thought for a moment she was in love. What else could the woman do with those elegant hands? For just a moment, she gazed at the place on the woman's upper thigh where her skirt met her fishnet stocking. Appropriate for *Chicago*, and so sexy. How could she concentrate on the rest of the show, knowing those luscious thighs were just a few feet away?

When the number ended and the house lights came up, she stood and turned to Tasha. "Drink?" she asked, without waiting for a reply. They always enjoyed a drink during the interlude.

Along the way to the bar, she nodded and waved to a dozen people, without stopping to chat with any of them. She was on a mission. In about ten seconds the crowd at the bar would be twenty-deep, and she didn't plan to be at the back of it. In the lobby they headed in that direction. "Do you want to elbow your way through the crowd, or should I?" she asked.

"You do it. I'll secure us a nice stone wall. You'll find me leaning."

She chuckled, left Tasha in the central lobby, and headed for the bar beyond. Her strategy had worked, and she walked right up and ordered, as the patrons behind her began to gather all around and behind her. A minute later she emerged with two glasses of wine. She sipped from each, to prevent spilling, and a moment later was back where she'd left Tasha.

Tasha wasn't alone, though. Holding up the wall beside her she found Paige Waterford and a college-age girl who bore a faint resemblance to Nicole Kidman.

She plastered on a smile and did a quick attitude adjustment. She hadn't planned to talk with anyone except Tasha, but clearly Tasha had other ideas, and she would have to amend hers. Not that she minded. Paige had been on her mind all week, and she'd resisted the urge to call her. This random meeting might give her the chance to gather a little intel.

"Hi, Paige. Enjoying the show?" she asked as she handed Tasha the wineglass. Then she looked at Paige's companion and introduced herself.

As if she'd waved a magic wand, Paige smiled, and her mood shifted from that familiar detachment to interest. "I love this show," Paige said excitedly. "This is my niece, Juliette. Jules. It's her first time seeing it. How about you? Do you like it?"

She thought of the violinist with the fishnet stockings and had to work to suppress her smile. "It's holding my interest. Juliette, what do you think?"

"The dancing is amazing," Jules replied. "Have you seen it before?"

"This is our third time. Fourth, if you count the movie." Tasha answered for her.

"Wow!" Jules replied.

"It's the best movie of a musical ever," Paige said.

Carly sipped her drink as she tilted her head. "Maybe in the modern era. But I think some of the classics are phenomenal. How about that other Fosse—*Cabaret*?"

Paige shook her head immediately. "No way. It's too dark. *Chicago* is fun and light, and the girls win in the end. How can you beat that?"

Tasha raised her glass. "I'll drink to that," she said.

Paige nodded. "I would, too, if I had a drink. My sister's still waiting in line."

"By the time I get my water, I won't have time to drink it," Jules said.

"You can just cap it and take it back to your seat. No one will notice," Tasha said.

"How'd you get served so quickly?" Paige asked Carly.

"I cut through the orchestra pit. There's a secret passage to the bar so the performers can get a drink during the show."

Jules gasped in apparent shock, and Carly chuckled before apologizing for her comment. "Our seats are close to the exit."

Jules nodded. "That makes more sense," she said, her tone stern.

"Do you come to the theater often, or is it just Fosse you admire?" Carly stared at Paige, who explained the situation with Helena's tickets. "How about you guys?"

Carly flashed back to the first musical she'd seen here. They'd still been students then, and she'd won tickets in a raffle. They belonged to one of her professors, and for the cost of a few hours of her time volunteering at the Thanksgiving food pantry, her name had been entered, and she and Tasha had the thrill of seeing *Sweeney Todd*, right here in Scranton. It had been a great first show to see, interesting and funny, with a plot of revenge and murder, and it had hooked Carly right in. The next week, she'd applied for a job as an usher and had been able to see all the shows she wanted. She kept that job for years, until she moved in with Pip, whose trust fund made shows in New York and London the norm.

"So I've been here since college," she said after sharing the story with Paige and Jules. She didn't mention her position on the board of directors for the theater society.

Paige's eyes opened wide. "That sounds like a blast. You got to see everything, huh?"

Carly nodded. "For free."

Suddenly Jules's eyes opened wide, too. "I'm starting at Scranton in the fall. I wonder if I could get a job here. That would be amazing."

Paige nodded. "It certainly would."

Normally Carly wouldn't say anything in a situation like this, but she found something about Jules's enthusiasm, the light in her eyes endearing. Not to mention she'd have Paige on her good side. Pulling a business card from her back pocket, she handed it to her. "Email me, and we'll talk about how I might be able to help with that."

Paige smiled again, while Jules studied the card, apparently so interested in Carly's information she'd been rendered mute. Finally, she spoke, and as she looked at Carly, the joy she felt was clear. "Thank you. So much."

And at that moment Carly knew she'd pull a string or two to get this young woman a job.

Paige bowed her head slightly and mouthed, "Thank you."

"What's your favorite show, Jules?" Carly asked.

"*Phantom*," she said excitedly.

Tasha nodded. "Me, too."

Paige joined in. "It's hard to argue that. Great story, great score. I had the chance to see it in London a few years ago, and I still think of it."

"*Think of me, think of me fondly*," Tasha sang dramatically. "I didn't see it in London. Just New York, five times or so." Tasha laughed. "London must have been wonderful."

"Yeah. It was," Paige said, and the happiness on her face caused Carly to pause. Paige appeared to have that effect on her—and Tasha, too, it seemed. She was a delightful burst of color in what had been a long, bleak winter.

"How about you? What's your favorite?" Carly interrupted their banter, already contemplating how she'd judge Paige based on her reply. Fun-loving or more serious? Classic or modern?

"*Aida.*" Again, Paige didn't hesitate, and Carly liked her decisiveness. Sometimes, that approach could lead to confrontation, but in this case, it only made Carly want to talk more, to learn what it was she liked so much about the show.

Carly listened as the three of them discussed the story of *Aida* and the promise of reincarnation, and once again she pondered why Tasha had never mentioned Paige before. They seemed to get along fabulously, and from the very little she knew of Paige, they seemed to have the important things in common—travel, the arts, medicine, golf. It was a wonder they hadn't already moved in together.

As she stood musing, she sipped her wine, wishing she had something more fulfilling in her hand. Vodka, bourbon. She'd even settle for rum. Something strong enough to break thoughts of Tasha with Paige from the moorings in her mind.

A woman approached and greeted Paige and Jules as she offered a glass of red wine and a bottle of water. "There you are. You're going to have to slug that if you want to finish it before the second act begins."

Carly watched Paige throw back her head, as if she was going to do just that, but instead she laughed as she took a small sip. "Mmm, thanks. Let me introduce you. Tasha and Carly, this is my sister Helena. She's also joined SAW, so you'll be seeing her again, I'm sure."

"Hey, are you guys in SAW?" Jules asked. "I joined, too. This will be great. I didn't realize the people who play golf are so interesting."

Paige shook her head. "Stereotype much? I play golf, and I'm interesting."

"Yeah, but you're my aunt. You don't count."

They all laughed, and Tasha looked at Paige. "That's tomorrow night, right?"

Paige grimaced. "I know it's a lot to ask on a Saturday night, but… the ladies from Brooklyn—Liza and Mal—they can't make it until the evening."

Tasha waved a dismissive hand. "No worries. Tomorrow night is fine. But speaking of seeing each other again—did you hear from Lynn about the golf trip to Myrtle Beach? She said she planned to reach out to you."

Even in the atmosphere of the dimly lit lobby, Paige's face visibly brightened.

"Yes! She was able to add us for the golf, but Liza and Mal and I decided to get our own place on the beach. We're going a day before you guys, so we'll throw the welcome party. We have a huge deck facing the ocean."

What a great idea. Off-season rentals were incredibly reasonable in Myrtle Beach, and it would be so much more scenic to stay someplace near the water. Carly had been emailing Liza and Mal, and she would mention the beach trip. Maybe she and Tasha could crash their place.

She'd enjoyed her time with them and was sure they'd get along if they shared a house. Plus, she'd get to spend more time with Paige. Of course, she could just mention the idea of house-sharing to Paige. Somehow it seemed safer to go through the other two, though. And it would be easier to sell the idea to Tasha if the invitation came from them.

The house lights blinked, and Carly was disappointed. For some reason, she found Paige more appealing than the woman with the fishnet stockings.

"The curtain calls. Nice to see you both," Paige said.

"Yes. You, too. Nice to meet you. See you soon." Tasha, looking like a little kid on Christmas morning, grinned broadly, and once again, Carly felt a pang of jealousy. Clearly, her bestie had a crush, and even though Carly had promised herself she'd steer clear of Paige, Tasha's attraction bothered her.

"Yes. Tomorrow," Carly said, wondering if she should bow out. A woman had never come between them, and Carly wasn't going to let it happen now.

Paige's smile rivaled Tasha's. "I'm so excited. See you then."

Wow, that smile was nice. She'd be there.

"She's so nice," Tasha said, obviously referring to Paige.

"Yes," Carly said as she watched them walk away.

Paige's eyes were glued to the door as she took her seat, between Lena and Jules, and with great difficulty she clung to the threads of conversation with her sister. Where were Tasha and Carly? Then, just when she thought they were skipping the second act, they slipped through the doors and walked to the front row. They seated themselves in the center section, and she lost sight of them.

She exhaled and found that if she shifted just slightly, she could see the top of Tasha's head way down in front. And even though she couldn't see her, she knew Carly was sitting right there beside her.

When she'd seen Tasha in the lobby, she had been drawn to her, and she'd found Tasha to be a wonderful conversationalist. Yet the hope that she was with Carly had really been the draw, and she wasn't disappointed.

She'd spotted Carly approaching with wineglasses in hand and had felt that same zap she'd experienced the week before at the golf expo. Tonight, instead of casual, Carly was dressed in business attire—a designer suit in navy blue, tailored perfectly for her slim frame, and a bright-blue button-down shirt and loafers. A heavy silver necklace peeked out from beneath the shirt, and matching earrings dropped from each lobe.

Her look was an interesting one, Paige thought. Strong. The jewelry and cut of her suit were classic—not too feminine and not too flashy. Understated. Carly owned the look, and Paige swallowed once again at the image of Carly in her mind.

Concentrating on *Chicago* proved difficult as her thoughts drifted again and again to Carly. After a few numbers she stopped trying and simply allowed herself to daydream. She'd felt this sort of…attraction before and knew it was harmless to indulge in it. In the darkness she replayed all the images of Carly she'd stored in her mind…from the golf expo, and the internet, and the lobby of the cultural center. And she couldn't wait for the next twenty-four hours to pass, so she could create a few more images to store.

Chapter Seven

Home Course

Paige awakened the next morning, and as had happened so frequently since meeting Carly, she found her thoughts drifting to her. How would she spend her day? Would she arrive early at Paige's house or, like at the expo, come at the last minute? Would she bother to come at all?

Doing her bed-yoga, she stretched her shoulders and her back, and then stopped suddenly when she heard a noise. She stared at the control panel near the door on the wall. The security system was disarmed. Willing her heartbeat to settle, she thought back to the night before. She'd armed it, hadn't she? Of course she had. It was the first thing she did when she walked into the house. It was a ritual. Disarm the alarm, reset the alarm.

Quietly, she eased herself to a sitting position and opened the door on her bedside table. Removing her handgun, she checked to see the bullet in the chamber and then released the safety. She stood, opened the door and, gun by her side, took a few steps down her hallway toward the stairs. She reached the top and screamed as she saw someone coming up.

It took her a moment to realize it was Will.

"I guess I should have called," he said as he stopped mid-stride.

Bringing her left hand to her eyes, she rubbed them and sighed, letting out her fear and frustration in one breath. "I might have shot you."

"That might have been a good thing."

She stared into his face and saw the hint of a smile, a shadow of the old Will. And then it was gone.

Trying to stabilize her quaking knees, she held the railing. "How was the fishing?"

"I didn't really fish much," he said as he continued up the stairs, his gait slow and stiff. "It was too cold."

She was shocked. He'd been gone for a week. "What did you do?"

"Just hung out with the guys. Watched some videos. Played poker. They fished a little."

Suddenly, her anger and frustration erupted. "Wait a minute. You were with *your buddies* at the cabin? For a whole week? And you didn't tell me?"

"I left you a note."

His steely gaze didn't intimidate her. She was livid.

She remembered the note very clearly. "Yes. You said you were going to the cabin because I was going to the golf expo. You didn't mention anyone else."

"Oh, so it's okay for you to hang out with your *friends,* but it's not okay for me?"

The way he placed the accent on friends was all she needed to know. He'd been very put off by the fact that Liza and Mal were a couple, and he hadn't been shy in making his feelings known. "So this is about Liza and Mallory? Because you don't like them? You've never even met them." She exhaled deliberately, defusing her anger.

"That's not my fault. You're always hopping on a bus to New York to see them or driving to the Poconos. I don't remember any invitations for me to join you."

She considered his words. Was that true? Had she excluded Will from her relationship with her new friends? She probably had. She'd met them through her golf league, and he wasn't involved in that, and she'd just sort of extended the ground rules.

No, that wasn't true.

The truth was, she adored Liza and Mal, and they were a respite from her life with Will—the anger and depression and hopelessness. They were filled with light and energy, and they pulled her from the darkness of her relationship, from real life. Even if it was only for a few minutes, or a few hours, they helped her recharge.

Yes, she had kept these two parts of her world apart. Was that a crime, though? Why should she feel guilty for indulging herself in the simple luxury of a wonderful friendship?

He reached the landing and turned into his room. They'd married during her residency, and with her schedule of night shifts and middle-of-the-night pages, they'd kept separate bedrooms. They still did, and she was glad for that. Her room was a respite, a space he never visited, a place of her own.

Sighing in frustration, she called after him. "Will, what's going on?"

He paused and turned to her, his blond hair falling over his eye in the boyish way she'd always found endearing. Now, though, it was simply annoying. Get a haircut, she thought.

"I think I should be asking you that question."

"What?" She was incredulous. "Nothing is going on." She'd never cheated on him. She'd never even thought of it.

"Okay, if you say so, Paige."

"What does that mean?" she demanded.

"What *does* it mean?" he asked, anger turning his blue eyes dark. "What does it mean when a straight, married woman is suddenly best friends with the Dykes on Spikes?"

Her jaw dropped. "They. Are. My. Friends."

"Why? Why are they your friends? What happened to Leah and Sonya?" he asked, referencing her two best friends from college, now practicing physicians with careers and families that left them little time for her. "And when was the last time we did anything with Keven and Amy, or Tony and Gina?" She stared while he ranted, shocked by his anger. "Aren't my friends good enough for you, now that you're a hotshot ER doctor?"

Considering his words, she leaned against the wall and sighed. It wasn't that she didn't like those people anymore. They were nice, but they were Will's people. Liza and Mal were hers. Will's people liked to do the same things he did—the things he'd always done, like fish and ride his quad, and hang out at his lakeside cabin. And though she enjoyed those activities sometimes, she didn't love them all the time.

During many hours of therapy, she had come to appreciate that she'd given up so many of the things she'd enjoyed before Will, simply to join him doing the things he liked. She'd lost some of her identity. It wasn't that they'd created a new life when they came together. It was more that she'd just become a part of the same old life he'd always had.

That had made sense, for a while. She had a dream, and goals, and had worked hard to make them happen. She had little time for anything apart from her studies. It would have been unfair to expect him to just stop doing his own thing with his people, waiting around for her. And it had been simple, when she had time off, to just join him at the lake or with his friends rather than try to be with her own. Instead of making plans, she'd just gone along because it was easy. But she'd learned a terrible truth—when you just go along for the ride, you can find yourself someplace you don't really want to be. And it's a very bumpy ride back.

For the past year, she'd been trying to find a way to return from that place. She'd spent more time doing things with her sister and her niece, with a few people from work, with friends from golf. And while being with those people had made her happy and given her satisfaction, it had only served to deepen the fissures in her relationship with Will. He definitely preferred the Paige who followed him like a puppy to the one who had her own ideas and plans.

She leaned against the wall, longing to fall through it, into the sanctuary of her bedroom. "I don't know what's wrong with me, Will. Maybe nothing's wrong at all. I just know that I'm happy when I'm with these two women. And I don't know what's so bad about that, about having friends who make me feel good about myself. But if you really want to meet them, tonight's your chance. They're coming over for a golf meeting. I'm ordering Old Forge pizza, and we're going to have dinner before."

He raised a curious eyebrow. "You're having a party tonight? Well, isn't that nice? Too bad I came home to spoil it."

"If you bothered to check your messages, this wouldn't be a surprise."

"So it's my fault?"

She counted to three before answering. "It's no one's fault. But twenty women are going to be here tonight to talk about the new golf league, and two of them will be here a bit earlier than the rest. If you're here, great. You can meet my *friends* and learn all about Swinging

Around the World. And if not..." She shrugged and left the thought out there without finishing it.

"I'll see," he said with a finality that told her the discussion was over. Typical Will. Yet he didn't leave.

"Do you want to do something today? Maybe go to a movie?"

"Nah. I've been watching movies all week. But I'll let you know about the pizza. Give me some time to think about it." He turned and walked into his bedroom, then closed the door behind him, leaving her standing there, wondering what had just happened.

Feeling despair, she went back into her room, took care of the gun, and collapsed onto her bed.

Why did she allow him so much power over her? Why was it always his decision, instead of theirs? Why did he get to *think* about it, instead of them *talking* about it?

She chewed her lip as she contemplated questions she never seemed to be able to answer and changed into workout clothes. In the basement she spent an hour on the elliptical while she watched *Law and Order,* then followed that with some weights, and finally yoga. Back in her kitchen she pulled out her baking box and whipped up a batch of cookies for the ladies to enjoy later. When she was done, she looked at the clock. It wasn't even eleven. What was she going to do with this day?

She opted for a bath and soaked in the bubbles with soft music playing, meditating while she melted in the heat. When she was sufficiently pruned, she called her niece. "Your timing is perfect if you want to buy me lunch," Jules said playfully.

"I was hoping you were hungry."

They discussed restaurant options and agreed on a diner in Pittston, a place they frequented because it was about equidistant between their respective houses. An hour later, they were seated across from each other.

"So, you missed me, huh?" Jules asked.

Paige perused the specials. "How could I not?"

When Jules didn't reply, Paige looked up and found her staring.

"What's wrong?" Jules asked softly.

"Whattaya mean?"

Jules shrugged. "We were together last night, and you didn't mention lunch. Did someone else stand you up, and I'm the fill-in?"

"Yep."

Jules laughed but continued to stare, forcing her to make a decision. Should she clue Jules in on her relationship drama or leave her innocence intact?

Sighing, she tried to smile. "I just needed to get out of the house." She reached into her bag and pulled out a small container. "And I brought cookies."

Jules's face lit up as she grabbed the container and opened it. "Did you bake for tonight?"

She nodded, relieved that Jules seemed to have moved on from questioning the last-minute lunch date.

Jules bit into a chocolate-chip cookie and moaned. "I miss Nana. She spoiled me with cookies."

"That's where I learned," Paige said with a smile. "And it's not too late for you."

Shaking her head, Jules swallowed. "The kitchen is not my place. But about tonight—should I come? I mean, just because my mother can't make it doesn't mean I shouldn't be there."

"It's not necessary. You're eighteen. You should hang out with other eighteen-year-olds on Saturday night."

"I know. I will. I just—what if no one shows? You'll look like a loser with wasted cookies."

She bit her lip to suppress her laughter. "It'll be worse if you're there to witness the humiliation. Better if I face my fate alone."

Jules crossed her arms and leaned back. "So what's really wrong?"

So much for moving the conversation forward. But what would she say if she told her about Will? She truly didn't know what was bothering her. She just knew she wasn't happy. And how could a teenager answer questions that someone twice her age couldn't decipher? Why should she bother Jules with those questions, anyway? It wasn't fair to Jules to be saddled with her troubles.

"I just found myself with no plans, and I hoped you could fill me in on what's happening in the world."

Her eyes lit. "What would you like to know?"

They ordered burgers and fries, and then they made the food slightly less toxic with the addition of side salads, then resumed their conversation.

"I'm thinking about summer school, but I'm torn," Jules said.

"How so?"

"I know you always took summer classes, and you said doing that made your schedule easier during the rest of the year, but I think I'd like to have some fun this summer. Maybe take a road trip out West, or go to the beach with my friends, hike a little. That sort of stuff."

She nodded, but she didn't truly understand. She was a workaholic and never seemed to rest. In high school and college, she'd worked in the ER for spending money, but mostly for the experience. And she'd loved it. She'd met Will there, and when they weren't working, she hung out with him and his friends, talking about work. But she spent most of her free time in the library. Her summers were always a balance of school and work, and when she and her friends had time, they pretended they were just like everyone else—carefree and adventurous, taking the bus to New York or a drive to one of the Jersey beaches for the day— where they talked about school. Those times were rare, though. The demands of the pre-med program at the University of Scranton were overwhelming, and she had to apply herself, all year round, to make good grades and earn her spot in medical school.

Jules was different though. More social. More pampered. She was the only child of two successful professionals, and she'd wanted for nothing in her life. Not that Paige had been deprived—but her parents had been more conservative, saving money for a rainy day and retiring early. Helena and Al enjoyed themselves much more than her parents had, and they took their daughter along for the ride, creating a very worldly young woman in the process.

Jules's life was so much easier than Paige's had been at the same age. She had less pressure—internal and external. If she failed, she could stay home with her parents until she figured it all out. Paige never had that luxury. Her parents had supported her to a degree, but she'd had to work for spending money and to buy gas, so she could go out with her friends or get the shoes she really wanted. As a result, she hadn't had as much time for fun.

It always seemed the fun would come later—after she'd become a doctor, finished her residency, gotten a job. Then she'd slow down and enjoy it. Here she was, though—with more time than she'd had since she was a kid and more unhappy than she'd ever been. She was barely thirty-two and already felt as if her life was off the rails. She'd done everything right, but somehow it had turned out wrong. Who was she to judge her niece if she simply wanted to act her age and have a good time?

"Where do you think you'll go? If you go West, I mean?"

Jules's eyes sparkled as she began to talk about her plans. Clearly, she and her friends had given this idea some thought. Four of them would pool their money and rent a very small RV—a camper van. Jules pulled up a picture of one on her phone and showed her. They'd travel along Interstate 80, stopping first in Pittsburgh to see a Pirates game, then in Ohio to visit the Rock 'n' Roll Hall of Fame. They'd take in a game at Wrigley Field in Chicago and have a picnic on Lake Michigan, then visit parks in Wyoming, Utah, Nevada, and California. On the way home they'd stop at the Grand Canyon, take an authentic *Breaking Bad* RV ride in Albuquerque, stop by Palo Duro Canyon in the Texas Panhandle, and then drive through Oklahoma on their way back north. The trip would take a month and cost Jules her entire life savings, but she was willing to sacrifice the money for the experience. Paige smiled at her innocence. Jules's life savings consisted of all the financial gifts Paige and her parents had deposited in her account over the years.

"Experiences are priceless."

Jules nodded. "Yes! Like the MasterCard commercial."

"Exactly."

"You traveled in school. You love to travel." Jules's tone had changed from confident and exciting to pleading, and suddenly the purpose of their meeting, from Jules's perspective, became clear.

She offered a smile of understanding. "You need me to convince your mother."

Jules sighed. "Will you? You know how stuffy she is. It'll be super safe with the guys along. Plus, we have Triple A."

She had known the two young men Jules referenced since they were all in grade school together, and while she wasn't sure they could change a tire, they were big guys who would make anyone with bad intentions think twice about messing with Jules and her friend Melody. "I think it's a great idea. You need to enjoy the journey. It's that simple. You can count on me. What do you need me to do?"

"Can you tell her?"

Paige laughed. "You want me to tell your mother that you're planning a cross-country trip?"

Jules nodded as if it were a normal request, and she laughed again. "Email me the details."

"I'll do better than that." Pulling a crayon from a cup permanently stationed on the table, she flipped her paper placemat and began to write.

"We start on day one." She looked up and smiled. "Obviously. And we drive to Pittsburgh."

Paige interrupted her. "Actually, I think you should start with the camper-RV thingy. How much does that cost? Where will you rent it? Does it require special insurance? What's the gas mileage? And then your traveling companions. That's easy, because your parents know them. But do they know anything about cars? How to fix a flat? How much money are they willing to contribute? And then print the itinerary from the internet. You've already done that, right? To calculate the mileage?"

Jules nodded.

"That's good, because it'll estimate your fuel costs. And you should get your reservations at places like Yosemite and the Grand Canyon now, because they'll sell out."

Her eyes flew open. "Good idea."

"I'd start with those details and maybe indicate the miles you have to drive each day, and where you'll be staying. The more carefully you plan, and the more methodical your process, the less your mom has to debate." She paused and smiled. "But the truth is, you're eighteen. She can't really stop you."

"If only that were true."

"It is true. She can make your life miserable, though. Maybe you should put it all together and let me review it, then sell it to your father first."

"Another great idea."

She winked, and the arrival of their food interrupted them.

"What's up with Will?"

The question surprised her, but maybe Jules was more perceptive than she realized. She'd deliberately avoided speaking of him because she knew Jules adored him. She had been with Will since Jules was just a little girl, and they'd included her on many of the adventures they'd shared in the early days of their relationship.

"I'm a big girl, Paige. You can tell me."

She tried not to sigh, but she took a deep breath. Just the mention of his name seemed to aggravate her. "I'm not sure what's going on."

"Are you getting a divorce?"

Looking away, she tried to gather her thoughts. She hadn't actually said that word, but wasn't that where it was heading? She wasn't happy, and Will wasn't either, at least not with her. She had no idea if he'd been happy during his week at the cabin with his friends.

"I don't know," she admitted when she finally met Jules's gaze.

"You don't seem happy. But you haven't seemed happy in a long time."

Shocked by Jules's remark, she was about to protest, but Jules was right, and arguing the point was futile. Instead, she tried to remember what happiness felt like. When was the last time feeling happy was normal? Residency, probably. Sure, she'd had moments since then, like the night before, with Jules and Lena at the Cultural Center. Or the week before, with Liza and Mal at the golf expo.

And she wasn't sad, exactly. It was more like she was lost.

"How'd you get so smart?" she asked as she bit into her burger, remembering the conversation she'd had with Jules's mother just a few days before. They'd also been sharing lunch, and she'd been eating a burger then, too. Maybe she needed to watch the red meat.

"You're deflecting."

She chewed before she answered, saying quietly, "It's been hard since the accident."

Jules shook her head, challenging her. "No. It started before that. In residency."

She thought of those long days and nights. Three years of seventy-five-hour work weeks, peppered here and there with a day or two off, or a week of vacation for recovery purposes. Yet even that was a happy time. She'd loved the drama and excitement, the friends she'd made.

"I think I was just busy, Jules."

"Well, every time I saw you, you looked exhausted. Nana was always praying for you."

She laughed at the thought of her mother, rosary beads in hand, offering her name to the saints.

"I can picture that."

She nibbled on her food, her appetite gone. Jules really was a remarkable young lady. Spoiled, yes. Immature at times, of course. But insightful, and thoughtful, and caring. The spoiled and immature parts of her would eventually go away, and the good qualities would grow. She'd be an amazing woman one day.

She told her so.

Jules waved a hand dismissively. "Look at the three women in my life. I take after you and mom and Nana. How could I not be amazing?" They concentrated on their food for a moment before Jules spoke again. "I feel like you don't have enough friends. Now that you have extra time, you don't have anyone to spend it with."

"I have you and your mom. And for the summer, I have Nana and Pop. Plus, I've met some new people."

"Good. You need new friends. Your old friends are gone, and Will's people are rednecks."

Paige feigned offense. "Hey, watch it! I'm a redneck."

"No. You're a very cultured, sophisticated woman who likes guns and spends time in the woods. There's a difference."

She laughed. She was glad Jules thought so, and her comment reminded her of what Jules had said the night before. *"For someone so worldly, you seem to have a narrow opinion of people."*

"What?" Jules asked innocently.

"Last night. You were surprised my golf friends are also theater people."

"I didn't say they were dumb jocks."

Paige leaned back and studied Jules. Sometimes she was so sweet, and insightful, and then she was eighteen again. "I think it was implied."

Jules seemed to pick up the edge in her tone and didn't say anything for a moment. "They seemed really interesting. That's all I meant. I thought it would be boring to play golf with people my mom's age, but then I realized we might have something in common. That's all."

She nodded. "Okay, Jules."

"I emailed Carly," she said after a moment.

The mention of Carly's name caused an uptick in Paige's heart rate, but she covered her reaction by playing with her food. "What did you say?" she asked after a moment.

Jules sat a little taller in her seat. "I told her it was nice to meet her, and I hope she enjoyed the second act, and that I was looking forward to golf, and that I'd like to talk to her some time about working at the theater."

She nodded. "That sounds perfect. Did Carly respond?"

Jules whipped out her phone. "Let me check."

This was interesting, she thought. Carly and Jules as pen pals. And not surprising either that Jules hadn't hesitated to reach out.

"Yes!" Jules said. "She responded. Do you want me to read it to you?"

"Please." She folded her napkin for a distraction as she tried to remain calm.

Jules held up her phone and began to speak.

Hi, Jules. It was nice to meet you last night. My heart is warmed by young people such as you taking an interest in the arts. I'm on the board of directors of the theater league, so I'll reach out to one of my associates and find out what you need to do to get a job at the cultural center. Since there are only a few more events this season, I would suggest you apply for the fall, but we can discuss that further. Will I see you tonight at Paige's? Carly.

So Carly was coming! She tried to focus on her niece. "Very nice, Jules. It sounds like you have a foot in the door."

"What it sounds like is new plans for my Saturday night."

She laughed. An eighteen-year-old who'd spend her Saturday night pursuing a lead on a part-time job couldn't be too bad.

Chapter Eight

A Meeting of the Minds

Will had decided to stay and meet Liza and Mallory, and he answered the doorbell as Paige put the finishing touches on a salad. He escorted them into the kitchen and took drink orders.

She stopped her food prep and gave them both hugs. She'd already set the table and sat beside them while Will delivered a bottle of wine and two bottles of beer. "Do you need a glass, Mal?" she asked.

"Please."

Paige hopped up and returned a minute later with wineglasses for her and Liza, and beer glasses for Mal and Will. She knew he wouldn't use one. He'd drink his beer from the bottle, then peel the label, leaving little crumbs of confetti all over the table.

"So you girls are from Brooklyn, huh? How'd you end up here?" he asked. His tone was neutral, but Paige knew him well enough to detect the thinly veiled sarcasm, as if they were illegal aliens from a third-world country, stealing jobs from hungry Americans.

"Paige invited us," Mal deadpanned.

They all laughed, and Liza answered his question. "We ski. Or at least we did when we were younger. And every year we rented a chalet near the slopes and invited our parents and our brothers to the Poconos for the holidays. It was always a good time. Then we started renting it for two weeks in the summer. About fifteen years ago, we arrived to discover a *For Sale* sign in the yard. I think it was the look on my mother's face that did it. She grew up in Brooklyn, in a high-rise, and never got to enjoy the outdoors. When she came here, she'd sit on the deck for hours, just watching the birds. In winter, she'd snowshoe through the woods. I realized how much that cabin meant to her, and how much I love it here, too. So, we bought the place."

As predicted, Will began peeling his beer bottle. "What kind of work do you do?" he asked, and Paige detected more sarcasm. He was crafty, though. Liza and Mal didn't seem to notice. Liza piped up and told him about the IT company and the dance studio, and he listened with apparent interest.

"How about you? Paige says you're a paramedic *and* a fireman. That seems so ambitious. In Brooklyn I think you have to pick one or the other," Liza said with a smile.

"Well, this isn't Brooklyn," he said and then fell silent.

Paige had told them about Will's accident, and she was grateful they didn't ask about it. Instead, Mallory redirected the conversation. "You're a fisherman, too, we hear."

Will sat a little straighter. "I like to fish. You?"

Mal nodded. "We live on a lake. It's small, just eight houses, no power boats allowed. But we fish from the dock, and I have a duck boat that I take out when I just want some quiet."

Will nodded in seeming understanding. "It's the most peaceful place in the world, isn't it?"

Paige thought she saw a little shift in Will's attitude.

"What do you catch?" he asked.

"A variety. Bass, bluegills, sunnies, shiners. Small catfish."

"Do you eat them?"

Mal shrugged. "Every once in a while. Mostly just catch and release. But the lake is clean, so they're safe to eat. I'm just not that big a fan of fish."

Will shook his head. "Then you're not cooking them the right way. I'll give you a few recipes."

Paige could feel her jaw drop as she tried to remember the last time Will had cooked something more elaborate than cereal. No, that wasn't fair, she realized. He cooked for himself, and his friends, when they were at the lake.

"Do you ice-fish?" he asked.

Mal shrugged. "I would if I had a buddy. But Liza doesn't like the cold anymore, so she won't go out on the ice, and I think it's dangerous to be there alone. So I haven't done it in a few years."

"Well, let's do it. It's the perfect time. The lakes are frozen solid."

"I'm game," Mal replied. "Tomorrow?" she asked as she looked at Liza. "Are we free?"

"Of course. Paige and I can amuse ourselves for a few hours while you two freeze your asses off. Paige, does that work for you?" Liza asked.

Will hadn't bothered to ask, but when he looked at her, Paige saw happiness in his eyes. He was genuinely excited about the idea of fishing with her friends. Maybe this was a light at the end of their tunnel. Maybe Will was going to snap out of his funk. Perhaps she'd snap out of hers.

The doorbell rang, and she grabbed her wallet and went to answer it, returning a moment later with four trays of pizza, an order of wing bites, and a teenage girl. After Jules hugged everyone hello, she hung her coat in the garage closet and joined them at the table.

"Are you feeding the entire SAW?" Liza asked as she stood to help Paige.

"Just the Scranton division. I asked them to cut the pizza into party bites, so people can have an appetizer if they want. And if not, we'll eat it tomorrow." She smiled and shrugged.

They all took plates and dug in. "This is Valley Forge pizza, huh?" Liza asked. "It's rectangular."

"Old Forge, Liza. The Pizza Capital of the World," Jules replied.

"It's really good," Paige added.

"How could we be Pocono snowbirds for twenty years and not know about this?" Mal asked between bites.

Liza pulled her phone from her bag and walked to the counter, where she took a picture of the pizza box. "We have to go here, Mal. This is the best pizza I've ever had."

Paige beamed with pride, happy that her friends were enjoying the local flavors. She eased back into her chair, sipped her wine, and just watched as they talked. She laughed with them, and after a moment, she recognized that feeling again. Happiness. What was it about Liza and Mal that made her feel so good? And to have Jules join in made it even better. Will was a little more distant since Jules's arrival, but he still seemed to be enjoying himself.

After they finished eating, he looked at his watch. "I'm going to head over to Kevin and Amy's while you do your thing. I'll catch you later, okay?" he said to Paige. "And if you want, figure out the plans for tomorrow. I'd love to challenge Mal to an ice-fishing contest."

"He seems nice," Liza said when they heard the garage door close a moment later.

Paige didn't immediately reply. Was he nice? She wasn't so sure anymore. She'd been examining Will and their relationship for months, going all the way back to the first moment she'd met him in the ER. He was cocky and capable, intelligent and talented, but as she examined all the reasons she'd once been attracted to him, nice was nowhere on the list.

"Will's okay," Jules said after a moment, and Paige felt the need to say something.

"He was on his best behavior. I think he just wanted an invitation to ice-fish." Paige winked to soften the edge of her remarks.

"Whatever," Mal said. "But I'll enjoy it, if you guys decide to come."

"Will you come?" Liza asked, the excitement evident in her eyes.

Paige thought back to the morning, of the torture of being in separate parts of the same house. Her escape to the diner with Jules had revived her, and the prospect of a similar experience the next day with Liza seemed like a lifeline. "I'd love to."

They cleaned up the mess, arranged the pizza boxes for the SAW group, and then Paige gave them the tour while Jules played on her phone. They started in the basement, which was really just one large room with unadorned walls and a blanket of cheap carpeting covering the floor. In the middle of it all was Paige's home gym. The first floor had five rooms, as did the second. At the top of the stairs, Paige opened the door on the right. "This is Will's room," she said by way of explanation. Liza stopped at the entrance and stared at Paige. "Wait. What do you mean? Don't you share a bedroom with Will?"

Paige shook her head but avoided Liza's stare. "No. Different schedules and all that. It just makes it easier."

Liza nodded as she peered through the door but didn't enter the room. "Looks big."

She didn't encourage them to explore; she didn't like to venture into Will's private space either. Instead, she turned around and opened her own bedroom door. "This is my room. Rooms, actually."

She ushered them into her sanctuary, and they both sat on the loveseat in the alcove that overlooked the woods. "This is really nice, Paige. I love the colors."

The room was bright, done in purples and greens, with floral throw rugs over the wide floorboard planks. Art and pictures covered every wall, and her white-noise machine filled the room with the sounds of birds. "Thanks."

"And it's huge. Are there two master suites?"

"Yes."

"We did that when we remodeled our house in Brooklyn twenty years ago. So our parents would think we were just friends," Liza said with a wink.

"That's pretty smart," Paige said as she studied Liza. "But sad. You should be able to be comfortable in your own home."

"Oh, believe me, we are," Mal said. "Liza has two master closets instead of just one."

Liza shot her wife a look, and Paige smiled as she glanced at her watch. "C'mon. Let's finish the tour before the ladies arrive."

She showed them the next room, set up for guests. "This is where you guys can sleep if it starts snowing again."

Mal sat on the bed and bounced a few times. "This'll work," she said with a smile.

At the end of the hall, Paige pointed out two empty rooms, side by side. "This is my future son's room," she said as she opened the door to the bedroom painted blue. "And this is my daughter's room," she opened the other door to a room with bright-pink walls.

"There you go with that stereotyping again," Mal said.

She hadn't thought about it before. "The house came this way. But I suppose it would be fine if my son wants the pink room."

"I'll help him decorate it," Liza said. "You have a lovely home, Paige."

"Yes, it's beautiful," Mal said as they headed back the way they came.

The doorbell rang as they were descending the stairs, and she answered with the other two ladies on her tail. "Hi!" Paige greeted Dr. Reese Ryan. Reese, an ER doctor who worked with Paige, had joined SAW at the expo. They worked the same weekends, so they were off at the same time as well. Paige looked forward to golfing with her and her partner, Ella Townes. "C'mon in from the cold."

Reese was pushed aside by her sister, Cass, who came up to Paige and nearly knocked her over with a hug. Cass had Down syndrome, and Reese shared custody of her with her parents, who wintered in Florida. As a result, Paige saw a lot of Cass in the ER, whenever Reese came in for meetings, or if Ella brought Cass by with dinner.

"Hello, friend," Paige said.

"Hi, Paige. I brought my Ella with me, too," she said, looking back through the door expectantly.

"She's here somewhere," Reese said as she turned and peeked.

Ella appeared at the door, and Paige made the introductions.

"I made cupcakes for the party," Cass said as she grabbed them from Ella's hands. "Chocolate."

"Perfect. Can I have one now?" Paige asked.

"Yes, but you have to eat in the kitchen." Cass's stern tone elicited a chuckle from the rest of the group.

"I'll leave you guys to get acquainted," Paige said as she eyed the baked goods. "Cass, do you want to help me in the kitchen?"

Cass loved to cook and bake, so she eagerly agreed. "How do you think we should set everything up?" Paige asked. "Should I leave the pizza in the boxes or serve it on plates?"

"Plates," Cass replied as they entered the kitchen, where Paige introduced Cass and Jules.

Paige pulled platters from the pantry, the two others helping her wipe them down, and then they shared a cupcake while they arranged them on a platter. Paige pulled the plastic wrap from the cookies and brought the cheese board out of the fridge so it could reach room temperature. Next, she retrieved two beverage servers from the fridge and placed them side by side, along with glasses, small plates, and utensils. After burying two bottles of white wine in an ice bucket, she set four bottles of red beside them on the counter. There was more wine, and beer, in the fridge if anyone preferred.

"I think we're set. We can warm the pizza for a few minutes, and then people can come in here and fill their plates."

Liza walked in as they were ready to rejoin the others in the great room. "Anything I can do?" she asked.

Shaking her head, Paige looked around. "No. I don't think so. I did it all before you got here."

"Impeccable timing," she said, and Paige laughed.

"But when we have about ten minutes left in the meeting, you can pop in here and put the pizza in the oven."

"You've got it."

Liza's face suddenly turned serious as she stared at Paige. "What?" Paige asked.

"Your friend Erin just got here. She knows Reese and Ella."

Paige studied Liza. What had her so concerned? She knew about the connection between her friends—Erin, whom she knew from her golf league, had told her she knew Reese. "Yes. Reese and Erin went to college together. They were both pre-med, but Erin went to dental school instead."

Liza tilted her head slightly but looked directly at Paige. Her tone was muted when she spoke. "Paige, you have a lot of gay friends."

She thought for a moment. Reese was her coworker, and she supposed they were friends. They never really did anything outside of work, though. And Erin—they played golf together. Did that make them friends? She liked her, but there was no great connection there. Not like the one with Liza and Mallory.

"I guess I do." The doorbell rang, saving her from further discussion, yet in her mind, she asked another question. Why do I like lesbians so much more than straight women?

She turned toward the living room, and Liza called after her. "Are you sure there's nothing else for me to do?"

"We're all set."

They went together to the great room, where they discovered four more ladies had arrived, including Linda and a woman she didn't recognize. And standing just beside them, coats draped over their arms, she saw Tasha and Carly.

Paige let out the breath she'd been holding all day, wondering if Carly would come. Wondering, and hoping. She couldn't explain her affinity for Carly Becker, but she couldn't deny it, either. And she couldn't deny the happiness she felt just to see her, or the little uptick in her heart rate.

Paige waved and greeted everyone, but she couldn't keep her eyes from Carly. Tonight, she was dressed in jeans and a blood-orange sweater monogrammed with a huge *B* on the front. The date-night casual look was a good one, and Carly couldn't help noticing that Tasha was similarly attired. Had they been on a date? Brushing the thought from her mind, she tried to regain her focus. Once again, the sight of Carly had put her off-kilter. Tonight, though, instead of skirting the force field, she walked directly into it.

"Hi. I'm glad you made it."

Unlike their past encounters, tonight Carly was as warm as the color of her sweater. She smiled, just a half, almost hesitant smile, but it had the power to melt Paige anyway.

"I'm excited to be here. Thank you for hosting tonight, and for organizing all of this. I think we're going to play some great golf."

She nodded. "I hope so."

"Where do you usually play?"

"I'm in the league at Eagle's Nest, so mostly there. Other places sometimes."

Carly nodded. "Did you ever think of joining Mountain Meadows? We have a very active women's group."

Paige sighed. She hated to share that story, so she told the half-truth she'd grown into. Looking around, she shrugged. "I thought of it, but then I bought a house, instead."

"A better investment, for sure. Who was your realtor?" Carly asked, wishing she'd had the chance to work with Paige.

"Linda."

Carly nodded. She'd wondered about the connection between Paige and Linda, her chief competitor in the local real-estate market. Linda's family had been founding members of Mountain Meadows a hundred years ago, and she'd grown up at the club. She'd been junior girl's champion, then women's champion, and her heart and soul were in the soil of the Meadows. Carly had been surprised that Linda was straying into SAW, but now it made some sense. Paige was the link. Not that Carly could blame Linda. Since Carly had won her membership, she'd gone onto the SAW website and read about the organization, and she had to admit, she was excited about playing.

Shifting back to the topic, Carly nodded. "She found you a lovely home." She looked around at the house, a large, modern design with a two-story great room that overlooked the forest in the back. At the edge of the space, a floating staircase led to the second story. The room was minimally furnished, but that sparseness gave focus to the outstanding design elements of the house—the stone fireplace, the glass, the wide planks making up the wooden floor. Pieces of art were tastefully placed all around—prints of famous paintings, metal sculptures, glass. And Paige's use of color was amazing. The background shades on the walls and furniture were neutral, but the rugs and pillows and art were screaming loud colors. Carly loved it. But why, she wondered, did Paige need such a big house?

Paige beamed. "Thanks. I like art, as you can see, but I'm on a budget. So I collect things, one at a time."

"That's the best. Things have more meaning that way."

Paige laughed. "I remember moving to medical school. A widow from my old neighborhood died, and her family had a house sale after the funeral. I literally bought all the contents and moved them to Philly. For years, I felt like she was haunting me for stealing her things."

Carly was amused. "I would have thought she'd be happy to keep her collection of treasures together a while longer."

Paige shook her head, her expression serious. "Perhaps. But she never liked me, so I think the haunting is more plausible."

"Why didn't she like you?"

Paige shrugged. "I may have picked some of the flowers from her garden."

She chuckled. "I would have haunted you, too."

Paige held up her hands in surrender. "I was only about four when it happened, and the dog and I escaped the yard. Come to think of it, it might have been the dog she hated. For the usual reasons."

Again, she laughed, marveling at the effect Paige had on her. Before she could speak again, Jules appeared and wrapped her arms around her.

"Hi, Carly! I'm so happy to see you!" Jules broke off the hug and stepped back a pace. "I'm so excited about working for the theater league."

Carly could only smile. She'd made a few phone calls, and the executive director thought it best if Jules put in an application soon, even though she wouldn't need any new employees until the curtain went up in the fall. "Well, I have some news on that front," she said, then told Jules the plan. The joy on her face made the cost of the favor she now owed seem trivial.

"Thank you so much!" Jules said with arched brows and both hands. And then it occurred to Carly that even though they didn't look alike, Jules was a great deal like Paige. Expressive.

"They may have something over the summer, too. If you're interested."

Jules suddenly looked frightened, then spilled the plans for her RV trip.

"Jules, you're probably not going to believe this, but I did the same thing when I graduated high school. Only there was no RV. We did it in a Toyota Corolla."

Jules's jaw dropped. Carly turned to Paige, who had been silently listening to the exchange, and she wore a similar expression. "Isn't that a really small car?" Jules asked.

"It seems smaller and smaller every year. But four of us and our stuff all crammed in for the cross-country trip of a lifetime."

"So it was amazing?"

"Better than amazing. That job will wait until the fall. You must do this sort of crazy thing when you're young, and this summer is the perfect time."

Jules nodded. "See, Paige? I told you!"

"What? I'm on your side here."

The doorbell rang, and Paige glanced at her watch, then excused herself. Carly and Jules continued to talk about the trip, but Carly watched Paige from the corner of her eye. She welcomed a group of six women from Mountain Meadows, and within a few minutes another four arrived. And then, Paige stood before that grand fireplace, her back to the flames, preparing to speak.

"Jules, why don't we try to have dinner again before the next show? Maybe I can get you backstage or something? Better yet, email me, and perhaps I can give you some advice about the trip. You know—from a veteran." Carly winked for emphasis.

"You rock," Jules said as she hugged Carly again, then ran to the staircase, where she took a seat a few steps up.

Carly couldn't help feel some of Jules's excitement, and she would be happy to help if she could, to make it as great an experience as her own had been. Plus, somewhere in the back of her mind, she didn't mind doing something nice for Paige's niece. It could never hurt to have an ER doctor owe you a favor. Especially one as attractive as Paige.

The couch and chairs sat six, but Paige had scattered a dozen folding chairs around the room. Carly preferred to stand and leaned against the back wall of the room as she scanned the agenda for the evening. Paige could have emailed the document, and everyone could have read it from their phones, but Carly liked that she'd printed it. Having something in her hands, something tangible, grounded her. And around Paige, she needed that.

After welcoming everyone, Paige introduced herself and Liza and Mal, then allowed a moment for her guests to do the same. It seemed unnecessary to Carly, because everyone already knew each other, so she tuned out and studied Paige instead.

Tonight she was dressed much the same as Carly, with a sweater and jeans and UGGs. Her blond hair was pulled back from her forehead by a purple headband, a match to her sweater, an understated feminine look that Carly found extraordinarily sexy. She wore light makeup and probably didn't need any. Her skin was flawless, her cheeks naturally rosy, and her green eyes jumped from her face. Carly could picture them, peeking out from atop a surgical mask as she cared for her patients in the ER. If her eyes were all you could see of Paige, they would be enough.

Paige called attention to the agenda, and Carly glanced at the paper in her hand. She already knew the basics, so she tuned out again as she stared at Paige. Oddly, it had been difficult to covertly learn any information about her. Everyone she called about SAW knew who Paige was, but details were scarce, probably because she had grown up near Wilkes-Barre, and Carly was from the sister city to the north, Scranton. But she'd even called some friends from Paige's hometown, and they didn't know her either. Carly had secretly started thinking of her as *Mysterious Doctor,* and she'd been thinking of her often. Of course, she could have just asked Tasha, but that would be too revealing. And too easy. Carly liked a challenge, and the thought made her smile.

Even though Paige was off-limits.

She found her...interest...in Paige ironic. For a long time, since her life with Pip had ended, Carly had been much too casual about women. She'd put very little effort into relationships, and she'd gotten out even less. Paige intrigued her, though, and for the first time in a long time, she saw possibility. She was at a point in her life where she was willing to be patient, to foster a friendship and see if a romance developed. Paige seemed like she would be worth the effort. Except she worked with Tasha.

The circle she was going in made her dizzy. Shaking her head, she tuned back into the conversation.

"We'll need several volunteers to organize our matches. Someone to oversee handicaps. Someone for hotels, if anyone wants to stay overnight after golf. I understand a lot of people do that. And someone to do the scheduling—basically who plays in each foursome. Remember, only eight of us can play each week. The four best scores—net and gross—will count." She paused, and a wide smile filled her face. "Wow, this is so wonderful. When I first talked to Liza and Mallory about this league, I hoped we'd have enough women to field a team of four. I even recruited my sister and my niece, two of the worst golfers in the world, just in case. And look at this. We're going to do super."

"Hey," Jules said. "I'm not *that* bad!"

After the laughter died down, Erin spoke. "Thanks for organizing it, Paige," she said, as she began to clap. Carly joined in, along with the rest of the room, but she was focused elsewhere. Erin sat a few feet from Paige, staring at her as if she'd just spotted a movie star. Interesting. Carly knew Erin and Paige played in the same league, but Carly hadn't realized that Erin had a thing for Paige. Yet from this angle, it was obvious, and Carly stifled a smile. That would be amusing to watch. Erin—middle-aged, nerdy, obnoxious—often fawned over young, attractive women. Carly was pretty sure she'd never landed one.

"I'll do the scheduling," Carly said. What? Wait. Had she really just said that? And then Paige smiled again, and Carly nodded as she noticed Erin frowning. Linda said she would book the hotels. Then Erin volunteered to coordinate handicaps, and Carly couldn't suppress her own smile. Poor Paige. It was good that Erin hadn't taken on the task of booking hotels, or Paige would have found herself in the same room with her.

Paige explained several more things and answered questions, and a few minutes later, the meeting was over, and Paige directed everyone to her kitchen for pizza and beverages. "Carly, Erin, Linda—I'll reach out to each of you separately, and we'll talk about what we need to do to move forward."

As the crowd began to head out of the great room, Tasha approached her. "I can't believe you volunteered." Tasha studied her suspiciously. "What's up with that?"

She hadn't expected the challenge from Tasha, but she quickly recovered. "Well, you know I've been unhappy. I talked to my therapist this week, and she thought SAW was a good move for me. She told me I needed something to knock me out of my funk, so I volunteered."

"Hmm," Tasha said as they began to walk toward the kitchen.

She wasn't sure Tasha believed her, but at least she wasn't arguing her reasoning. They paused just before the doorway to wait for the congestion to clear, and she glanced at a framed picture hanging on the wall. It was a portrait of a younger Paige and a tall, blond man, probably her brother, standing on a beach. His arm was draped casually across her shoulder, her arm around his waist. They both wore bright smiles on their tanned faces.

"He's too big for her, don't you think?" Tasha asked.

"Hmm?" Carly asked, confused.

"Paige's husband. Will. He's too big for her. He makes her seem so tiny." Tasha lowered her voice and leaned closer to her. "Can you imagine having sex with a man like that? He could kill her."

A flush of heat seared Carly's face as Tasha's words slammed her. Paige was married. She had not seen *that* coming!

But it explained why Tasha hadn't mentioned Paige, why no one knew about her. Not only had she grown up in a different county, but Paige also lived in another universe. The straight one. She was trying to focus as Tasha rambled on. She'd never even considered the possibility that Paige was with a man. She'd instantly pinged Carly's gaydar.

Wow. Talk about disappointing. Carly wasn't sure if she felt sadder for herself or Erin. Refocusing, she leaned toward Tasha, trying to keep her feelings from showing. "Tash, just because *he's* huge doesn't mean *everything* is."

Tasha looked surprised. "Isn't it all proportional?"

She laughed. "I'm no expert here, sweetie, but I don't think so."

Tasha placed her hand over her heart. "Oh, thank Goddess. That would be awful."

"What's awful is that she's straight." The words were out before she could think to stop them, but Tasha didn't seem to read too deeply into the remark.

"It sure is. When she first started working in the ER, I was sure she played on our team. Then I found out she was married. Her husband was—is—a paramedic who used to work for the city. He was badly injured in an accident, and I don't think he's employed anymore. I think he has trouble with his back."

"How tragic," Carly said, and she meant it.

She looked up and saw Paige pouring a glass of wine and quickly turned away. That door was closed. Rule number one—no straight women. Rule number two—no married women. Standing taller, Carly put on her best poker face, smiled pleasantly, and willed herself not to be too disappointed about Paige. She wasn't the first woman who'd slipped through her fingers. Probably not the last, either.

She swallowed and looked ahead at all the women in the room. She'd joined SAW to play golf but also to meet people. Women. Other than Paige and her friends Liza and Mal, Carly had known every woman in the room before she joined. Liza and Mal were a couple, and Paige was straight. The golf might work out, but so far, the objective of meeting women was going nowhere. And she'd just committed to doing the schedule. Fuck. Even if she wanted to, she couldn't quit now.

Chapter Nine

First Date

Two days later, at her therapy session, Carly shared the story about the SAW meeting. Ann Marie's laughter was contagious, and Carly found herself letting go of the angst she'd felt all week. "At least you didn't waste too much time on her before you found out she plays for the other team."

"I don't know how I misread that one, Annie."

"Yes. That's a good question. You've worked very hard in therapy to make better choices, and this would be a disastrous one."

Carly lowered her head to avoid Ann Marie's stare. She still hadn't told her about the night of Erin's party. That had been a series of *very* bad choices, though not as bad as dating a straight, married woman. Carly had no intention of doing that. With confidence, she met Ann Marie's gaze. "Yes, it would. And I won't. Sleep with her."

Ann Marie nodded, and her tone was deep, somber when she replied. "If you do, I will fire you as a client."

Carly was shocked. Ann Marie had been her therapist since Pip. They were more like friends than doctor and patient. And with all they'd talked about, and all Carly had done to sabotage her own happiness, Ann Marie had always stood by her. Never once had she made such a threat, even when Carly drank too much or acted like a jerk to keep women at safe distances from her heart. Not when she'd stayed with Pip a year or two longer than was healthy, and not even when she'd stopped seeing Annie because she didn't want to hear the hard truths.

"Wow," Carly said as she studied her, trying not to show the hurt.

"You know I don't like to fail. And you're not a failure, Carly. You're a great success as a person and as my client. But this—Paige— would be suicide for you. And I'm not going to deal with you gluing the pieces of your shattered heart back together. Because that's what curious, heterosexual women do to lesbians. They destroy us."

Carly suddenly wondered if Ann Marie had personal experience with this type of situation, or if she was simply sharing her professional opinion. She seemed more serious than Carly had ever seen her, and she'd spent many hours in this office. In the last years of her relationship with Pip, Ann Marie had helped her decide to leave and to figure out why she'd stayed so long in the first place. Ann Marie had helped her deal with the buried emotions of her mother's chronic illness and the grief of burying both her parents within a year of each other. Carly had cried in this office, and laughed, and dug deep into herself here. Ann Marie was an integral part of her life, and this declaration scared her. Where would she be without her?

Should she tell her that she was having dinner with Paige that night? Definitely not. It was a business dinner, squeezed in at the end of Carly's workday and before Paige went into the hospital for the night shift. They planned to talk about SAW. Purely professional. Nothing she needed to share with Ann Marie.

"Don't worry, Annie. I'm not that stupid."

"I hope not."

Six hours later, Carly turned the key in her office door and headed to her car. Her office was in Clarks Summit, close to the lake, with the wealthiest zip code in the county, the best properties for her to manage, and consequently, the best restaurants. She'd chosen a new one for her dinner with Paige. She'd heard Hemisphere had an interesting menu, and it was BYOB, so she turned right after she left her office and headed to the liquor store.

A mile later, she pulled into the parking lot and applied lip gloss. Something with color, just a hint of red to bring her mouth back to life after a long day. After all, she might see someone she knew.

She shivered when the cold air hit her and pulled up the collar of her coat as she hurried into the store. Inside the front door she ran into a display of wine, the special selections, all on sale. This was one of her favorite chores, choosing wine from the sale rack. Glancing at the options, she was stopped in place by the sight of a woman. She wore all black—heeled boots, a long wool coat, and a furry headband. Blond hair peeked out from the top, and in profile, she was strikingly beautiful. Like Carly, she was browsing the wine sales, and Carly would have liked nothing more than to spend the rest of her night talking about wine with her, whoever she was.

And then she seemed to sense Carly's stare, and she turned her head and smiled.

"Hi, Carly."

With a flutter in her chest, she smiled back. Carly couldn't believe the coincidence. There were three other places to buy wine in town. What were the odds that she and Paige would choose the same place at the same time?

It took her a second to find her voice. "Hi."

Paige nodded toward the display. "Don't you love this place?" She held out a black bottle for Carly to see. "Devilry Afoot. It's a California red blend. My sister tried it and said it's phenomenal. And—here's the amazing part—it's half price. I'm buying two."

"Hmm." She took the bottle from Paige and studied the label. Then she pulled out her phone and did a little research. "Google says it's from the North Coast and is made of a blend of Shiraz/Syrah, Grenache, zinfandel, and Petite Syrah. It pairs well with beef, lamb, veal or poultry."

Paige winked. "So we can pretty much order everything on the menu."

Was that a flirtatious smile? Paige held out her hand to accept the bottle, but instead of handing it over, Carly turned her head and offered a hint of a smile back at her. "This one's mine."

Paige laughed. "There are only three left. Are you sure you don't want two?"

She didn't hesitate. "Well, it *is* half price, right?"

Cradling the wine, they headed to separate registers and met again at the door. "Brrr. How many days 'til spring? I'll see you in a few minutes," Paige said as she turned left. In spite of the cold, she dawdled, waiting to see what kind of car Paige drove. As she wasted time rearranging things in the back of her Bimmer, Paige honked the horn of a white Grand Cherokee as she drove past.

It suits her, Carly thought. Paige seemed adventurous and playful, much like the Jeep she drove. Carly, on the other hand, preferred more sophisticated women who drove expensive foreign cars. This was proof that she didn't belong with Paige. It was a blessing that Paige was straight.

Five minutes later she arrived at Hemisphere but didn't see the Jeep. Paige had left at least a minute before her, and she couldn't remember passing her on the short drive. Was there a side lot where she might have parked?

She wasn't about to sit in the cold car waiting for Paige to catch up. She hurried inside, the bottle of wine tucked into a tasteful bag, and announced herself to the hostess. "The other party hasn't arrived yet," the woman announced. "Would you care to wait here, or at the bar, or at your table?"

Glancing at her watch, she tried not to let her annoyance show. It was ten minutes before seven. They'd been together five minutes earlier. Paige had to cover a mile, and she'd had a head start. Where the hell was she? Carly wasn't about to go in and sit down. What if Paige didn't show? She'd look like an idiot, eating alone. No, that was not a good plan. Better to wait here. She could always fake a phone call and cancel the reservation if Paige failed to appear.

She hoped she did. Her stomach was rumbling with anticipation from the decadent smells in the air. Two of her colleagues had dined here and had given it positive reviews, and she'd really be disappointed if she missed the chance to try the place for herself.

"I'll just use the restroom and check back with you," she said. She didn't need to use it—she'd gone in the clean, private bathroom at her office half an hour earlier. But she refused to loiter in the lobby like some loser waiting for a blind date.

In front of the mirror, she fluffed her hair and shook it out, then ran her fingers through it. Then she added just a touch more of her favorite, red-tinted gloss. Turning her wrist, she saw that three minutes had passed since she last checked the time.

Very slowly and deliberately, she washed her hands, knowing that she was still five minutes early. If she hadn't run into Paige at the liquor store and assumed they were going to start their dinner early, she would have loitered there, reading labels from exotic countries, imagining drinks made from kiwi vodka or orange liqueur. That would have been a delightful way to waste ten minutes. This—loitering in a public bathroom—this was disgraceful.

Five minutes. She'd give her five minutes. If Paige didn't have the decency to at least be *on time*, she was leaving. No courtesy phone call, no message with the hostess. She was gone.

With her head held high, she marched back to the front of the restaurant, smiling and waving at a few familiar faces seated at the bar but not stopping. She didn't want to have to explain who she was meeting for dinner. And then she turned the corner, and standing before the hostess's dais was Paige, running long, delicate fingers through her hair, her rosy cheeks glowing in the dim light, a fluffy headband dangling from one finger.

Before Carly could berate her, Paige noticed her and smiled. "Sorry to keep you. My husband took my car today and left the gas tank empty, and that gas station where they pump it for you was on the way, so I figured I should stop. Much better than standing in the cold and pumping it myself."

All the anger she'd been building escaped on the breath she'd been holding, and she nodded. "I wondered what happened to you. I thought you were standing me up."

Paige stepped back and began unbuttoning the long coat, then winked. "Never."

Is she flirting with me? The thought was irritating. In one sentence she mentioned her husband, and the next minute she was winking. What was it with this woman? Vowing to make the dinner a short one, she pulled off her coat and hung it as far away from Paige's as the closet would allow. "Have you been here before?" she asked politely.

Shaking her head, she smiled. "No. I don't go out to eat very often, so this is a treat for me. But I've heard great things."

Carly nodded. "Yes. I have as well."

The hostess led them to the corner table Carly had requested. It was a lovely setting. A large circular fireplace in the center of the room shot light and heat in all directions, and faux candles winked from wall sconces around the room. Suddenly Carly wished she were here with a date, rather than this irritating woman from SAW.

"I see you both brought wine," the hostess remarked as she seated them. "Shall I open both bottles, or would you like to start with one?"

Not wishing to be beholden to Paige for anything, even a glass of wine, she offered the waitress her wine bag. "Is the Devilry Afoot okay with you?" she asked Paige.

Paige laughed. "Oh, yes."

"I'll take care of this," the hostess remarked.

Carly leaned back in her chair and studied Paige. Her hair was still a little askew from the headband, but the blush on her cheeks was fading. Her eyes were soft, outlined in brown, and her lips painted with lipstick tinted frosty pink. She wore an absolutely fabulous soft, pink, fuzzy sweater that perfectly matched her lips. Had she worn it on purpose because she knew how much she detested that color? And then she took a sensible breath and realized that Paige probably had paid no attention to the putter incident at the golf expo.

"I know you hate pink, so I wore this sweater on purpose," she said. "To help open your mind to new possibilities."

Carly wasn't sure if she should be annoyed or amused, and her reply was out before her brain had a chance to filter it. "Well, if someone has to wear pink, at least it's someone who looks good in it."

A blush seemed to creep all the way from the top of that pink sweater to Paige's diamond-studded ears, and *that* Carly definitely found amusing. It was Paige's reply that surprised her.

"You seem to like color in your wardrobe."

The opposite was true. Carly liked boring when it came to clothing. Black, brown, gray. A little teal here and there, maybe some blue. "You think so?"

"Well, you've been wearing very vibrant colors every time I've seen you. Except for tonight." Carly looked down to the chocolate, woolen turtleneck sweater she'd chosen that day.

"Would you be surprised if I told you that you've seen every one of the three outfits I own that are not some shade of black?"

Paige studied her for a moment, stared at her with those soft eyes. They seemed to caress her, to hold her—gently, but tightly at the same time. Did Paige even realize she was out to dinner with a lesbian? The thought crossed her mind that if anyone she knew saw them, they would certainly think this was a date. Paige just seemed so focused on her, as if nothing else in the world mattered. It was somewhat unnerving. "No. I don't think I would," she said, and the attention made Carly want to change the subject.

"Your niece is a little firecracker, Paige."

Paige sucked in a breath through clenched teeth. "I'm sorry if she's imposing."

She shooed the thought away. "Not at all. I volunteered, remember? I believe in supporting young women and the arts, so it's a win-win. Plus this trip she has planned—I'm so envious. Aside from the golf outing in Myrtle Beach, I don't have a single item on my travel calendar. It's depressing."

"Why is that?" Paige asked.

Again, the attention, the eyes. She had been surprised at every turn when it came to Paige Waterford, and she wasn't prone to that sort of thing. She was thoughtful, prepared, and usually predicted what was going to happen before it went down. Not so with Paige.

"I'm not sure. I guess I'm sort of in a funk. How about you? Do you travel much?" she asked, trying to divert attention away from herself.

"As much as I can. I did a semester in Ireland in college, and from there it's easy to jump on a train and visit other countries. I made a few friends to travel with, and I've been to Europe about once a year since then." Paige sighed, and Carly detected a bit of hesitation. "I'm going to Paris in the fall, with Jules."

Just the mention of Paris filled Carly with sadness. Disappointment. After Myron's heart attack, she and Pip had spent a week with Viv in Nice, burying him and comforting her. Their plans for Paris had been canceled, and somehow, in the nearly twenty years since, she had never managed to get back there. "Ah, Paris." She sighed, and Paige's face brightened.

"Have you been there?"

Carly shook her head, and though she omitted many important details, she told Paige the essence of the story.

"How awful," Paige said, and she knew by the expression on her face that her sentiment was genuine.

"I missed Paris, too," Paige said after a moment. "The weekend my friends were going, I got sick. Strep throat. I could barely stand, so my housemates set me up with bottles of water and medication and abandoned me for days. I was so sick I hardly noticed they were gone."

She felt a sudden camaraderie with Paige over the opportunity they both missed. "It's funny, sometimes, what fate has in store for us."

"Have you heard the Yiddish saying *Man plans, and God laughs*?"

She smiled, remembering Pip's grandfather. He was a wise man, well-traveled, and a lover of all the arts. She had had the privilege of knowing him well, and together they'd laughed at man's plans, among other things. "I do know it," she said, filled with happy nostalgia. "And I couldn't agree more."

Paige stared at her. "You have to laugh sometimes, right? Or you'd cry."

She knew *that*, too, but she refused to share it with Paige. Sipping her wine, she couldn't help wondering what Paige worried over. She didn't ask. "Tell me about your plans for Paris."

Paige's shoulders dropped about a foot as she groaned. "It's a school trip. Jules was in the French Club in high school, and they had a trip last fall, but I couldn't go. So she's already planning this one. It's kind of her graduation gift."

She nodded. "Is your sister going?"

"No, and that's good. She's sort of a dictator. I only hope some faculty members are coming along. The idea of spending a week with a bunch of drunken college kids is not my idea of fun."

Carly was intrigued. "What is your idea of fun? In Paris, I mean."

"Oh, Carly." Paige moaned. "The museums—the Louvre, the Picasso, The Centre Pompidou, the Orsay. Versailles. Chartres. The Eiffel Tower. Moulin Rouge."

"You sound like a guidebook."

"Perhaps, but who cares? I want to stroll along the Seine and stand on one of the bridges watching tour boats go by. Stand under the Arc de Triomphe and take a picture looking straight up to the sky. Stare at *Mona Lisa* for half an hour and fawn over the artifacts from the first civilizations."

She had to admit that was just what she would do. But it didn't sound like the typical agenda for an eighteen-year-old, and she shared that thought with Paige.

"That's why I'm hoping some people my age are on the trip. I mean, I know it's Jules's trip, but still—how can I be there and miss out on all that culture?"

"There will have to be some compromise, I suppose."

The waiter arrived with the wine and filled their glasses, set the bottle between them, and announced the specials. When he retreated,

Paige leaned forward, and the topic of Paris was forgotten. "I don't want to open the menu. I can't even choose between the specials. They all sound great. I'm just going to get more confused."

She was again surprised. After Paige had confessed that she didn't often visit restaurants, she had assumed she wasn't a foodie. "I had you figured for a meat-and-potatoes kind of girl," she said as she sipped the wine. Heaven. The heat flowed through her, and the stresses of the day began to ease.

Now Paige sat back. "Really? Why?" she asked, as she herself took a sip.

"Because you don't like to eat out. What do you think of the wine?"

"Mmm. The wine is fabulous. And that's a faulty assumption about my diet. I love food."

She would love to have asked more. She too loved food, and her great challenge was finding good restaurants. The places with interesting menus never lasted long, and the ones that lasted endured only because people liked their boring menus. It was why she and Tasha enjoyed going to New York or Philly—to see a show and sample the cuisine.

How delightful it would be to be in a relationship with someone who loved food as much as she did, who loved theater, and golf, and travel. She was really disappointed that Paige was straight, because she did find her interesting. And they seemed to have more in common than she had at first appreciated.

Nope. She couldn't dig too far beneath the surface with this woman. It would only lead to trouble. A change of subject was in order.

"I'm curious about the wine. Didn't you mention you're working tonight?"

Paige nodded. "Yes, but it's just one glass. At my weight, and with a healthy liver that can metabolize alcohol at the normal rate of 0.016 % per hour, by the time I start work in four hours, my alcohol level will be close to zero."

What the fuck? She sat back and stared at Paige. "You made that up."

Paige looked surprised. "What?"

"Whatever you just said."

"No. It's true."

"Why would you even know that?"

Paige spoke to her as if she were addressing a small child. "You'd be surprised how many intoxicated patients I see every day at work. The formula is helpful. For instance, it tells me when a patient should be sober so they can talk to a mental-health worker or be responsible enough for discharge. Or when someone slurring their words should be sobering up. If their brain function doesn't improve as the alcohol wears off, I get worried."

Even though she knew she shouldn't be, she was impressed. After all, that was Paige's job, to know such things. But it was still a credit that she did. She herself could recite half a dozen different mortgage rates, from the top lenders in the industry, and estimate what mortgage payments would be when she figured in the taxes, but other realtors didn't bother with small details like that. That could cause problems, such as learning on the day of the closing that the buyer couldn't afford the mortgage payments. She was sure Paige could just look up the information about blood-alcohol levels, just as she could look up interest rates and payments. The fact that they both had the information memorized told her they had another thing in common. They cared about their jobs.

"So how much of this wine can I drink and still be able to drive?" she asked as she nodded toward the bottle.

"You don't really want to know the answer."

"Why?"

"It's not good."

Carly laughed. "Two glasses? Three?" she asked as she envisioned her second. The first was just to relax her. The second was to enjoy with dinner.

Paige shook her head. "Unless we have a three-hour dinner, you probably should not have more than eight ounces of wine."

She shook her head. "I'm never inviting you again."

The server arrived to take their orders, and they confessed that they hadn't even looked at the menu. "Do you like crab?" Paige asked her.

She nodded.

"Would you like to share the crab mushrooms?"

Her mouth had watered earlier when the waiter described them. "Yes. That would be a nice start," she replied, then asked the server to bring them an order.

Paige grinned. "Maybe we should look at the menu."

She waved dismissively. "Nonsense. Who's taking this table after us? No one. What's the hurry?" She recalled that she'd previously envisioned a brief dinner and an early night, but she'd changed her mind. She was enjoying herself. What did she have at home that couldn't wait? Absolutely nothing.

So they studied their menus, and she played a mental game, testing their compatibility. Would Paige consider ostrich? How did she feel about red meat? Would she prefer cauliflower or sweet potatoes?

They talked about the offerings, and ordered, and then the conversation drifted all over the place, and she found it somewhat disconcerting that she was unable to steer it in any one direction. They seemed to have the ability to talk about anything, and they did, for three hours, until the manager very politely asked if he could get them anything else before the restaurant closed for the night.

"Do you suppose I'm okay to drive?" she asked as they donned their coats in the vestibule. After Paige had recited all that medical mumbo-jumbo, she had started nursing her wine and had only two glasses all evening. To stretch the night, she'd added a cup of decaf coffee and shared dessert, a detail she was sure she'd regret as she tossed and turned later. But she was also sure she'd pass the breathalyzer test if a police officer pulled her over on the way home.

"I believe you're at 0.06% now, so you should be fine."

"What?" She thought she should be at zero. She felt fine.

"It's a simple equation," Paige explained as they walked. "And the factors are the volume of alcohol consumed and time."

"I'm never having drinks with you again," she said as they headed toward their respective cars. Even as she said it, she knew she was lying. Her evening with Paige had been one of the best of her life. They'd laughed, and talked, and tasted each other's food, and it had been delightful. Even though they were destined only to be friends, she would definitely be seeing Paige again.

Chapter Ten

Girls Just Want to Have Fun

Paige adjusted her backpack, then walked up the escalator at the Allentown airport and found Liza and Mal waiting in the departure lounge.

"Hi, ladies," Paige said as she hugged them both.

"How did we beat you here?" Liza asked. "This is your state. You should have been here first to welcome us."

"I think this place is actually closer to Brooklyn than Clarks Summit. The drive took forever."

"We thought of leaving from the Pocono house. But somehow we ran out of time." Liza sighed.

Paige wasn't surprised. Like her, Liza and Mal had been working nonstop for the past week so they could take this little holiday. In her case, she'd finished work at midnight and didn't bother sleeping. Their six thirty a.m. flight necessitated she leave her house at three thirty. What was the point? She'd sleep on the plane and make it an early night.

They chatted until they were buckled into their seats on the plane, and then Paige pulled her sleep mask from her backpack and dozed. She didn't open her eyes until Liza awakened her in South Carolina two hours later. They'd rented a car, and Mal drove them to a diner that promised the best breakfast in town. And even though they arrived at the rental agency hours before check-in, they were given the keys to their house and settled in.

The oceanfront house had five bedrooms, but they'd chosen it because of the deck with the rocking chairs. Before they even emptied the car, Paige settled in to test one. "Ah," she said as she glanced out at the ocean. "This is bliss."

After retrieving her suitcase from the car, she quickly unpacked and was back in her rocking chair a few minutes later, a book in hand and a smile on her face.

The view of the ocean was breathtaking, and even though it was a little chilly in early April, it was warmer than home, and it felt so good to be there. She loved being away from work, and Will, being with her friends, and knowing she'd get a chance to spend time with Carly.

Since their first dinner, she couldn't escape thinking of Carly, and she'd struggled with the effort. She wasn't naive; she understood her feelings. She was attracted to Carly. But what should she do about that attraction? It was hard to avoid her because of SAW, but even if she could, she didn't want to stay away. She didn't want to stop thinking about Carly. Her infatuation was harmless, and it made her happy. And she needed all the happiness she could get.

Yet even if she was inclined to think of something more than a relationship based on their mutual love of golf, she knew Carly had no such thoughts. Carly was friendly and a great conversationalist, but she didn't encourage their friendship. They had seen each other only once since their dinner, and when they talked on the phone, Carly kept their phone conversations brief. She was all business, until she let her guard down and Paige glimpsed her humor and passion. They'd talk for an hour, or two, about nothing, or the news, or golf, and she would hang up feeling energized. And then, boom. Carly wouldn't return her call for days, or, if she did, the shades were drawn again, and she had to deal with the super-organized, successful businesswoman that Carly revealed to the world, instead of the friend she had started to adore.

It was incredibly frustrating, but she didn't know what she could do about it. Carly didn't owe her anything, not even friendship, and the fact that she had these thoughts made her feel like some sort of stalker.

Still, the thought that Carly would be arriving later that night thrilled her. She and Tasha would be staying over at the beach house with her and Liza and Mal instead of at the hotel the group had booked.

Carly and Tasha had taken in a show on Broadway and had spent the night in Brooklyn with Liza and Mal, and after discussing it with Paige, Liza had invited them to stay at the beach house. For her, it was a no-brainer, cutting the cost of the house almost in half. Plus, she'd get to spend time with them. How could she say no?

"Wanna go food shopping with us?" Liza asked twenty minutes later. Paige was still sitting in the same spot, staring at the ocean, her book untouched in her lap.

"Sure."

Like the cost of the house, they were splitting the cost of the food, but Carly and Tasha were renting their own car. "And Carly gave me a list for the liquor store. She promised to make me the best margarita I've ever had."

"Let's go then," Paige said.

A minute later she met them back in the kitchen, and they went exploring. They drove around for a little while, into Myrtle Beach, and spent the afternoon checking out the outlets and the restaurants, then stopped for the alcohol and food. Back at the house, Paige and Liza put away their haul, and then they walked the beach and tossed a Frisbee. Later, while Mal cooked steaks and corn on the grill, Paige and Liza tossed a salad. They ate on the covered porch, listening to the surf during lulls in the conversation. By eight that night, she was having difficulty keeping her eyes open.

"Ladies, I need to get some sleep. I'm going to head upstairs," she said after the cleanup was complete. They hugged good night, and she showered and climbed into her bed half an hour later. They'd had fun driving around, and it had been just the sort of relaxing day they all needed. Tomorrow, they'd play golf and spend more time on the beach. Tomorrow, she'd see Carly.

"Tash, coming down tonight was a great idea," Carly said. "We get an entire extra day out of the trip."

Tasha sighed. "It wasn't easy."

"Quit griping. You get six weeks of vacation. You should use it."

"Blah, blah, blah."

"I'm glad I'm going to have other people on this trip to talk to besides you. You're grumpy."

Tasha let out her breath slowly. "You're right. I'm sorry. I'm going to put work behind me for a few days and enjoy myself."

"Please do," she said, and Tasha swatted her in response.

It was after nine when the plane landed, and by the time they went through the rituals of retrieving their luggage and rental car, it was nearly eleven when they arrived at the beach house. Liza and Mal met them in the driveway. The area was so dark they were concerned Carly and Tasha might not see the place, so Mal had turned on her car's flashers to light the way.

"It was like a beacon, Mal. What a great idea," Tasha said as they made their way into the house.

Carly tried to be subtle as she glanced around for Paige but saw no sign of her. She had to admit, she was looking forward to spending more time with her. Paige had grown on her. No matter how she tried to resist her, she failed. They got along well, and she always seemed to brighten Carly's day when they talked. And they talked often.

At first, it was all SAW business. Paige called her the day after their dinner to thank her for a nice evening. She hadn't responded. A few days later, Paige had left her a message about a meeting with all the league leaders, so she had returned that call because she thought she should. Even though she was at the office, they'd managed to talk for two hours. Then, after the meeting, again at Paige's house, they dallied for an hour after everyone else had gone home. After that it was a follow-up call, then a catch-up call, then a what's-up? call, until they were talking a couple of times a week. And though she always tried to center on SAW, their talks tended to drift to new, exciting topics. She tried to stay neutral and professional, and she let Paige ramble, steering the conversations, until she got swept up in Paige's enthusiasm and had to respond. She'd hang up feeling energized, and then later, she'd berate herself and promise not to answer the phone the next time it rang. And it would ring. Paige would call. Paige always called, never Carly, so that made it okay, didn't it?

It *was* okay. Paige was married, and no matter what her motives for befriending half the lesbians in Lackawanna County—even if Paige was bi, or even gay—Carly did not intend to break the rules.

But there was no rule against friendships, right?

She got her answer about Paige when they were halfway up the stairs. Liza whispered, telling them that Paige had gone to bed early, and a mixture of emotions flooded her. Relief that she wouldn't see her. Sadness that she wouldn't see her. Relief that she was here and okay, rather than home taking care of some emergency that explained why she wasn't standing in the driveway with the other two, welcoming her and Tasha to the beach house. It was pretty typical. When it came to Paige, Carly's thoughts and emotions were all over the place. Why did one of the most attractive women she'd ever met have to be married?

They showered and changed into jammies, then met Liza and Mal back on the porch.

"How's the beach?" she asked as she sat on the chair swing, close to the other two.

"Big. And quiet. Not too many people at this time of year, I guess," Mal said.

"It seemed quiet on the way in, too. Maybe it's just late. Everyone's in bed."

"Not us," Liza said. "We're just getting started."

"You and Tasha. I've never been a night owl. I have a hard time staying up late to watch the Yankees."

Mal sucked in a loud breath. "What's that? Yankees? Liza, did you know this when you invited her?"

"Oh, don't start. I'm on vacation."

"Mets, Carly. They're the team."

They debated baseball for a few moments, with Liza telling her how her grandfather had worked in the office at Ebbets Field back when the Dodgers played in Brooklyn. He'd seen all the great games, known the legends, and left Liza's brother autographed baseball cards that were worth a fortune.

Tasha opened the screen door and came onto the porch. "Don't get her started about the Yankees. She's a blue blood."

"That's a great story about your grandfather. It must be nice to live so close to the action. Not just professional sports, but the arts, too. And restaurants. The major airports," she said.

Mal laughed. "Yes, it does make travel easy. We live in the center of a triangle formed by three of the biggest airports in the world—LaGuardia, JFK, and Newark. Except for today. We drove an hour and a half to fly out of Allentown."

The others laughed and then spent an hour talking about the benefits of their respective homes—New York versus the Poconos. In the end, they decided they all lived where they belonged and called it a night.

Carly settled into the bedroom in front of the house, and although the blackness of the night made it impossible to see anything beyond her window, she knew she had no view. Liza and Mal had one of the back bedrooms, facing the ocean, and Paige had the other. It was an excuse to pay Paige a visit, see how neat and orderly she was. Her home, Carly had noted on both occasions she was there, was immaculate. But maybe her husband was a neat freak. She was curious, though, to know everything about Paige she could.

She drifted off to sleep in her silk pajamas, wondering what Paige was wearing in her oceanfront room down the hall.

Adrenaline woke her the next morning, and she was up before the rest of the house. At least she thought she was. They might have all gone for a walk on the beach without her, but she didn't bother to investigate. Tasha had left the keys to their rental in the kitchen, and after pulling on jeans and a Yankees sweatshirt with her slides, she set out to find coffee. She had to go only a few miles before she found a local place, where she ordered bagels and a variety of pastries to take back to the house, as well as a box of coffee. As much as she would have liked to drive around the island and inspect the real estate, she decided to head back and inspect the beach instead.

A few minutes later, with her coffee in one hand, her bagel in her bag, and a chair over her shoulder, she headed to the beach. It was a little after seven when she sat down, and she wasn't alone. A few beachcombers hunted treasures, a couple power-walked, and some solitary souls seemed to wander, looking for something elusive in the quiet of a lonely beach.

Like her, she thought. Would she ever find what she was looking for?

"It's quite a sight, isn't it?" a voice behind her asked.

It was a deep baritone, unmistakably male, and Carly sighed. Maybe if a woman disturbed the tranquility of her moment, she wouldn't be so annoyed. But what would make anyone think that a woman sitting alone on a beach, with just her coffee and her thoughts, wanted to engage in conversation with a stranger?

He stepped forward and stood next to her, and she remained silent.

"I see you like the Yankees," he said this time.

Leaning into her chair, she closed her eyes and meditated, envisioning him drifting off into the clouds.

"Are you from New York?" he asked.

Without even turning to see what he looked like, she spoke in a calm, steady voice. "Sir, I'm just out here trying to have some quiet time by myself. Would you be so kind to leave me alone and make friends with someone else?"

"Fucking New Yorkers," he mumbled as he turned and began walking away, but his response made her chuckle. She'd have to share that remark with Liza and Mal.

"Everything okay?" another voice asked.

This one was familiar, and even though she had wanted to be alone, this time she was glad for the interruption.

"Perfect, why?" she asked.

"I was just enjoying my coffee from the porch—thanks for breakfast, by the way—and I saw you down here. I didn't want to disturb you, but when I saw that guy approach you, I thought maybe I should join you and save you from the crazies."

"Join me, please," she said and told her about the New York comment.

Paige sat beside her and sipped her coffee, uncharacteristically quiet. And then Carly looked over and saw her staring out at the ocean. She, too, sat quietly and enjoyed her coffee, until Paige broke the trance.

"My butt is sore. How can you stand this chair?"

"Wanna walk?" she asked.

Paige nodded, and they stood and headed down the beach. They found a comfortable, lazy stride and walked in silence for twenty minutes, past multi-million-dollar homes of a variety of architectural designs. She wished she could go through and evaluate their layouts and critique their decor. Instead, she imagined how she'd design them, how she'd market them if she were the listing agent trying to sell them. When they made the turn to walk back, she occupied herself with people-watching, wondering if couples were truly happy or *vacation* happy, deciding which husbands were good partners and which took total advantage of their wives. She shared her musings with Paige.

"Check out the father of the year." Paige nodded toward a man walking across the sand with his face buried in his phone while his wife juggled a baby, a beach bag, and an umbrella.

Carly pointed to another couple, two men, carrying a carload of beach stuff, walking in circles trying to find the perfect spot to settle.

The game was so enjoyable they nearly passed the house and were laughing as they made their way up the boardwalk. Their housemates, all three of them, were seated in rocking chairs, eating the baked goods she'd brought back from the coffee shop, sipping their coffees and talking.

"We were just discussing plans for the day. Would you like to play a round at the par-three course?"

The idea was appealing. Carly had played golf in Florida when she and Tasha visited Pip, but that had been months earlier. She was dying to swing her clubs. "Absolutely. Can we play as a fivesome?"

Tasha spoke up. "I'm going to sit out the golf today. Maybe I'll catch up with you for lunch when you're done, but right now I'd just like to relax and read a little."

Carly was relieved. Sometimes, she and Tasha needed space, and this seemed to be one of those times. She couldn't say that though, without risking Tasha's wrath, so instead, she made a halfhearted attempt at persuasion. "Tash, are you sure?"

"Absolutely sure. You guys go. If I want to do something, I have the car."

Now Carly became a little antsy. She hated being without a car, under someone else's control while they decided when and where to go, what to do. Pleadingly, she looked to Tasha for help, but Tasha was gazing out at the ocean. She had to make a choice. Stay here—which was not a bad sentence at all, considering the view, or go with her new friends—and be at their mercy.

Seeming to sense Carly's hesitancy, Mallory spoke. "I want you to know I'm an excellent driver. Only that one bad accident where I drove off the bridge."

She chuckled. "I'm sure you're well qualified to operate a minivan."

"Listen, if you want to head back here after the golf, or go somewhere else, we'll keep your clubs, and you can always get a Lyft. No hurt feelings."

That was a relief. She didn't want to create tension in the house. "That might be a solution. We'll play golf and then see what happens from there."

"I think we should get ready, especially if we want to have lunch when we're done. How long does it take to play an executive course, anyway?"

Paige had been silently listening while she pulled up the course on her phone. "Are we playing nine, or eighteen?"

Liza stared at her. "Really? Is there a front and back nine, just like in real golf?"

Paige held up her phone as proof. "Yeah. Two or three hours, I'd say."

"Let's go then."

Twenty minutes later they were in the car, with Carly's clubs added to the top of the pile of golf bags in the back. They talked about the new clubs Liza and Mal had gotten the season before, and Carly told them about the very inexpensive clubs she'd had made by a local golf shop. Paige listened, taking mental notes. She was thinking of new clubs herself.

Then she pulled up the course on her phone again. "According to the website, the longest hole is only about a hundred yards. What will we do? Just carry a few clubs?"

"I'm taking my entire bag," Liza said. "What if we run into bugs? I'll have spray. And what if one of them bites you? I'll have my first-aid kit."

"Do you have food, too? In case it's slow and we miss lunch."

"I have peanut-butter crackers in my bag, but I brought four apples. Does anyone want one now?"

Paige laughed and glanced at Carly, who was biting her lip. "You sound like my mom, Liza. Prepared for anything."

"Your mother's a smart lady, Paige."

"Prepared."

"Hey. I know someone who carried around a little broom for the greens. It's very practical," Carly said.

"I bet her bag was heavy, too."

They talked about all the things they'd like to have in their golf bag for emergencies, from medical problems to hunger to weather-related issues. The possibilities were endless.

"I think the entire bag should be redesigned, so it opens up, like an armoire," Liza said.

"I think you're all out of your minds," Mal said as she turned off the car at the course's parking lot.

Carly's bag was on top of the pile, and she lifted it and seemed to study it. Paige's was next. She pulled out a few clubs, stuffed her pockets with tees and balls, and then watched the rest of them. Like her, Mal decisively chose three clubs. Carly and Liza looked at their bags, then at each other, and laughed as they simultaneously shouldered them and began strolling toward the clubhouse.

Mal shook her head, and Paige suppressed a smile as they walked together.

"Look. They have pull carts," Carly said as they approached the clubhouse.

"Thank Goddess," Liza said as she placed her bag on the closest one.

Silently, Paige looked at Mal, and they did a dramatic about-face and went back to the car for their bags.

Carly and Liza said nothing but laughed when they returned with bags in tow.

After paying their fees, they waited in line for several other groups before them, all of them taking advantage of the queue to stretch and swing their clubs. To Paige's amazement, Carly pulled three foam balls from her bag, turned toward the parking lot, and hit one. She must have been using a lofted club, because it didn't travel far, even with a full swing. After she'd hit all three, she retrieved them and did it again.

"What a great idea," Liza said as she watched Carly.

"Would you like to hit some? I have more."

And that fast, all four of them were hitting foam balls beneath the South Carolina sunshine. When the first green was clear, they advanced, and Paige stepped up to the tee box, full of adrenaline and joy. The day was beautiful, she had nothing but fun on her agenda, and she was with three of her favorite people. After a deep breath, she addressed the ball and hit her first golf shot of the season—directly into the tree guarding the left side of the green.

"First swing of the year is always the toughest," Mal said consolingly.

Paige laughed, but it didn't really matter. Yes, she wanted to play well, but she was thrilled just to play at all.

She was the only one with such troubles, as her playing partners all hit high, lofted shots that landed gently on the green. "I'll see you guys on the next hole," she joked as she headed toward her ball. After a nice chip she found herself on the green with everyone else, and after Liza and Mal missed their birdie putts, she calmly sank hers for par. Carly, who was the closest, studied her five-foot putt as if the LPGA championship were on the line. She looked at it from the left, the right, from the other side of the green, and finally, from behind the ball. Then, using a putter cut down to half the normal length, and with a grip twice the regulation size, she gently stroked the ball into the hole.

"Nice putt," Mal said.

"Good bird," Paige added.

With a gentle nod and a hint of a smile, Carly acknowledged their remarks but said nothing as she walked from the green.

On the second hole, they all offered Carly the tee. "Never step on a birdie," Liza said while Carly fussed with her clubs, trying to decide which to hit on the eighty-yard hole.

"No, it's fine. Paige, you led off last time. You can go again."

"Look where it got me. Under a tree."

"You still parred the hole."

"And you birdied it," she retorted.

"I'll go," Liza said, and she promptly landed her ball in the sand trap in front of the green. Everyone else was on, and that was the way the round seemed to go. They all did well, considering they hadn't been on a golf course in months. Carly played like a pro and modestly brushed off the compliments the others paid her.

Paige enjoyed watching her. She was really good, but it was more than that. She was so serious about it. From the foam balls to warm-up, to the little squirt bottle to clean her clubs, she was totally prepared for her round, even on the par-three course. Her swing was peculiar, and she found herself watching as Carly carefully positioned herself, back arched, butt wiggling, and made solid contact each time she hit the ball.

"It looks like you have a really nice golf game," she said on the way back to the car.

"You do, too," Carly replied, but Paige knew she was being polite. Carly had finished the eighteen holes just five over par and had whipped the rest of them by ten strokes.

After they left the golf course, they headed to lunch. Tasha had decided not to join them, so again it was just the four of them, and Paige couldn't help but smile as they sat on the patio of a burger joint and placed their drink orders.

As she looked out over a fountain shooting water high into the afternoon sunshine, she noticed the light reflecting through the mist, creating a rainbow. She pointed it out to the others.

"How is that possible?" Liza asked. "It's not raining."

"It could be called a sunbow," she said. "It's the light that does the magic. It's bent by the water droplets, and the colors separate out."

Carly elbowed her playfully. "Stop it. I'm on vacation."

"I love it that Paige is so…scientific," Liza said.

She eyed Liza. "You were about to say *nerdy.*"

"I wasn't," Liza said defensively. "*Nerdy* never even entered my mind. Brilliant. That's what you are."

"Did you ever play with a crystal and make a rainbow?" Carly asked.

"I did," Liza said.

"Yep," Mal added.

"I think it's the same principle," Carly said with a big smile. "But maybe we should ask the nerd."

She roared. "I believe you're right."

They talked all through lunch, and after they paid the check, Liza and Mal excused themselves and headed to the ladies' room.

"How was your flight?" she asked Carly.

"Easy. I was worried we wouldn't make it though. Tash had to work later than she expected, and then we hit traffic. How about you?"

She told her about the late night and the early flight.

"It seems like you like your job, even with the crazy hours."

"That's actually one of the best parts. I can play golf in the morning, before my shift, or rearrange the schedule to go away for a few days, like now."

"It sounds like you make it work."

"I try my hardest. How about you? Who covers for you when you're gone?"

"It depends. Sometimes I bring things to do on vacation, but I have good people around me, so I can delegate much of my stuff."

"It sounds like you make it work, too."

"It's worth it, isn't it? To put in overtime, so you can escape reality once in a while?"

"Yeah. Have you ever thought of moving someplace warm? Where you can golf all year long?"

"I have…but then I'd have to start over. I'd rather just retire early."

Paige snorted. "I have to pay off my student loans before I can even start saving for retirement. At the rate I'm going, they'll be pushing me around the ER in my wheelchair."

Carly shook her head. "Paige! You have to put money away for retirement. Doesn't the hospital have a plan?"

"They do. I'm just kidding." Actually, with all the expenses she'd incurred, she'd been saving only a fraction of her salary, but she didn't share that fact with Carly.

"Do you want to talk to someone? Sometimes it's hard to keep it all straight, but I know a really good woman who manages my office plan. She's top-notch."

"Who's top-notch?" Liza asked, and Carly told her.

Mal joined the conversation, and Paige listened as they talked about investing. Liza said she was brilliant, but as she listened to the others talking, she felt like a dolt. She definitely planned to take Carly up on that offer for some investment advice. If nothing else, it was an excuse to talk to her.

Chapter Eleven

Beach Party

"I can't believe you were at opening night of *The Producers* on Broadway," Paige said as they walked through the door of the beach house. "I love that musical but have seen only the touring show in Scranton."

Carly nodded as she opened the freezer and deposited the remainder of her ice cream, thinking back to that amazing night in New York. "It was just luck. My friend Pip has connections everywhere, and as it happened, the banker who manages her trust fund had two tickets. We were in New York, so we went."

"And?" Paige asked.

Carly shook her head. "It was amazing. Lane and Broderick are just so good together."

"They were great, I agree. But then I saw them in another show, and it was…eh."

"I want to check on Tash," Carly said as Liza and Paige delved into Broadway. Carly would have loved to talk with them—it amazed her that they'd been together for hours and she wasn't feeling antsy, wasn't trying to escape. Their company was truly enjoyable, and she'd had a great morning. Tasha was on her mind, though. She hadn't answered the phone when Carly called, and in spite of the vacation, Carly knew that as CEO of the hospital, Tasha never really had a day off.

Two steps into the great room, she spotted her on the deck, stretched out in a hammock, staring out at the ocean. She looked so peaceful, Carly hesitated to disturb her.

"I'd crawl in there with you, but I'm afraid we wouldn't be able to get out."

Turning toward her, Tasha smiled. "I'm afraid you're right. How was golf?"

Carly thought about her day. The golf and lunch were fine, but she'd enjoy golf anywhere. It was the company that had made it an amazing day. The foursome played well together, talked about golf and travel and prisms and rainbows, and laughed as much as Carly remembered ever laughing before. "Golf was surprisingly relaxing. They're a fun group."

Tasha nodded. "I can see that."

"How was your day?"

"Just what I needed. Peace and quiet."

Carly understood. While her job was demanding, she had few emergencies, and once she left for the day, her time was her own. Tasha was literally on call every second of the day, and lately that seemed to be a grind. It was a relief to see her relaxing. "Can I get you anything?"

Tasha held up the water bottle in her hand. "I'm good."

"I'll be inside if you need me," she said as she turned and headed back inside. The house had a variety of board games, and she was eager to challenge Paige to a game of something. What, she wasn't sure, but she just knew she wanted to engage her.

The living-room bookshelves were crammed with books and board games, stacked high and wide behind the couch where Paige and Mal sat looking at their phones. Carly stood before the wall and eyed the games, looking for something designed for two players. Liza and Mal might want to join them, but Carly chose Scrabble, because it was perfect for two.

She held the game up and called out to Paige.

Paige's eyes shot up. "It's been a while, but I think I've still got game."

They headed toward the table near the porch, one that looked out over the water, and sat near each other, facing the ocean. As they settled into their seats, they both looked up and sighed, then chuckled at their shared response.

"I could look at this all day," Paige confessed.

"It is an amazing view."

"Are you a water person?" Paige asked as she locked Carly in her gaze. It was crazy, what Paige could do with her eyes.

Carly nodded. She loved the water. Some of her favorite times were at the lake, just sitting on her deck, looking out at it. It could be frozen in the winter or shimmering in the summer sun. It didn't matter. It just seemed to calm her. "I am. You?"

"Oh, yeah."

"I'm going to have you over for a drink one of these days," Carly said before she could stop herself. Stupid idea, she thought, but Paige didn't seem to make too much out of it. '

"That sounds nice," she said.

They set up the board and each picked a tile. Carly drew an *A*, winning the right to start the game, and quickly proceeded to lay down a six-letter word using the *Z* on the double-point space.

"*Snooze.* Double points for the *Z*, that's twenty-five, and double for the word to start the game. Fifty points. Do you want to keep score or shall I?"

Paige looked up at her. "What just happened? I haven't even finished arranging my tiles."

Then she smiled and stared at her with those deep-green eyes, and Carly felt that same imbalance again. "Stop whining. But speaking of wine, would you like a drink?" She didn't need one, but she needed to put some space between them. She'd wanted this one-on-one with Paige, but she hadn't expected it to be so intense. Wow.

Paige looked at her watch, and suddenly Carly felt self-conscious. "Hey, it's five o'clock somewhere, and we're on va-ca-tion!"

"I'll pass," Paige said with a laugh

"On the drink? Or on your turn?"

"On the drink. But these tiles are so bad, I may have to pass on the game, too.

"Well, I'm going to make a pitcher of margaritas, and while I'm gone, you can think about your options on the board."

Paige nodded, but she suspected time wouldn't help in this case. She had a tray of vowels, in addition to an *F* and a *D*. After shuffling the tiles, she looked at the board and smiled, then added the *D* to Carly's word and made *snoozed before* placing an *F* and an *A* above them. *Fad.* With a triple for the *F*, she had thirty-two points.

"Thirty-two?" Carly asked. "Are you sure?"

Paige glared at her, and Carly laughed. "Okay, then. Game on."

"Tile for tile, I actually scored more than you."

"What does that mean?"

"You used six letters and scored fifty points, which is an average of eight point three—three points per letter. I averaged ten point six, six points per tile."

Carly shook her head. "Are you for real? I need a drink," she said as she turned and walked into the house.

"Who leaves in the middle of the game to make drinks?" Paige called after her.

"Women playing against you."

"Fight nice," Tasha called from across the deck. "We have to live together for a few more days."

Paige pulled replacement tiles from her bag, grateful to have three consonants. For a minute she shuffled the letters, forming words that might fit onto the board. When she was satisfied, she stood and walked into the sun, absorbing the heat for a moment. It was a pleasant day, in the low seventies, so the sun's rays weren't overbearing. And to stand where she did, looking out over the ocean, was fabulous.

"I have margaritas, ladies," Carly said as she carried a tray toward Tasha and Mal.

"How nice," Tasha said.

"If I start happy hour now, I'll be Ubering to dinner. Just fill mine halfway," Mal said.

After she poured, they sat back at the table to resume their game, and Paige tasted the drink in front of her. "I didn't figure you for a salt girl," Carly said as she licked it from the rim of her oversized glass.

"You're right. Why do you suppose the glass is shaped this way?" Paige asked.

"I don't care. Just drink the damn thing," Carly said, shaking her head.

Paige took a tentative sip and then put the glass down, but she had to admit it was really good. "This is great. What kind of mix do you use?" she asked.

Carly feigned a dagger to the heart. "Mix? You insult me. I made that masterpiece from scratch."

"It seems strong. Is this going to knock me out?"

Carly shook her head. "No, Paige. Perhaps it'll give you a little buzz, but I believe that would be good for you."

Paige laughed. "Touché."

Carly played her word, and Paige came right back with her own. "Is this your strategy? Dull my senses with spirits so you can whip my butt?"

"I don't need any special tactics to whip your butt. I'm just that good."

"Hmm. We'll see," she said, but she could tell Carly was an excellent player, and the lead went back and forth until the very last tile was played.

"That was ruthless." Paige sighed as she leaned back in the chair.

Carly shrugged but stared into Paige's eyes.

"Who's winning?" Liza asked a moment later as she appeared on the deck.

"Carly just gave me a lesson."

"If you're finished, why don't we all play Pictionary?"

"Not me," Carly said. "Besides, with five of us we won't have even teams."

"C'mon, Carly. We'll rotate," Tasha said, and Carly agreed. Paige found herself laughing hysterically as they tried to draw and guess the appropriate pictures. Several times, she had to wipe tears from her eyes. She was sad to see the game end, but they had to get ready for dinner, so they wrapped it up as the clock chimed six.

They went out for Asian food and were back at the house before eight. Mal lit a fire in the pit on the deck, and not long after, a dozen women from Mountain Meadows descended upon the beach house. Their plane had arrived late, and some of them had gone back to their hotel, but the others—Paige quickly decided they were the party animals—had accepted the invitation to meet for drinks.

The tour guide had stayed with the group at the hotel, so Linda led the rest, but not before a stop at the liquor store for party supplies. Paige mingled, getting to know some of the ladies. Eight from the group had signed up for SAW, and she thought they might get even more. Not that they needed more. They already had twenty.

What she did need was an assistant. She'd been studying the players on her team, and Carly had sent an email asking for scheduling preferences. It didn't seem they would ever have a shortage of players. She even had a big response for the Fourth of July weekend. The people above Paige had planned the SAW schedule, so they played over the holiday weekend in Rehoboth Beach, and most of the single women had signed up and decided to take a few days off to enjoy the beach along with golf. Paige had to work, so she couldn't join in, which was a problem. SAW was every weekend, and her job kept her in Scranton for half of them.

As she watched the women on the deck behaving much like college students at a keg party, Paige wondered whom she could trust with the task. Then Linda appeared, and her answer was obvious.

"I need your help," Paige said, and explained the situation.

"I'd be glad to do it," Linda replied. "But it means we'll never play together. We'll be on opposite weekends, and neither of us is available for the Fourth. Why don't you ask Tasha?"

Paige had thought of her but dismissed the idea for the same reason—since she was such good friends with Carly, and they wanted to play together, giving the job to Tasha would mean Paige would be on the opposite weekend from Carly. Paige would do everything she could to play with Carly, not sabotage their friendship with a scheduling issue.

"How about Erin, the dentist?" Linda suggested when Paige didn't reply. "She seemed quite enthusiastic about SAW. Plus, she knows a lot of people. Her family belongs to the Valley Country Club down in Hazelton, and that connection could add a whole new dimension to this league."

"That's a great idea!" Erin was excited about SAW, and Paige knew she'd do a good job. Her dental practice was solid, and Erin had told Paige she never worked weekends. Unless she had some other conflict outside of work, she could probably do it. "I'll shoot her a text first thing tomorrow morning."

"Good idea. Now stop hiding in the corner and come socialize."

Paige laughed, only because she knew Linda was right. She was uncharacteristically tired and wanted nothing more than to escape the noise and crowd and find someplace quiet to relax. Yet their tee times the next day didn't start until after lunch, so what did she have to worry about?

Suck it up! she told herself and spent the next two hours talking and laughing and getting to know the women from Linda's club. She'd planned to join The Meadows before Will's injury, but after he was hurt, she hadn't spent much of that summer golfing. Most of it was in the hospital—first in Danville, then in rehab, and, of course, at her job in the ER.

Mostly, it didn't bother her that she hadn't joined. She still played golf, and she liked the women she played with. After golf, many of them gathered and enjoyed a bite to eat on the deck overlooking the eighteenth green, and Paige felt like she'd made a few friends there. That was where she'd met Erin, and she and other ladies from the league invited her to play at least once or twice a week. They were all very friendly. Yet here she was, watching these women, all evidently great friends, suddenly feeling sad that she wasn't a member of their club.

She decided to escape the crowd and go for a walk in the moonlight. The night was clear and cloudless, and the stars seemed to beckon her, so she picked her way across the sand to a place where two chairs sat abandoned.

As she approached, she realized they weren't abandoned at all. One of them was occupied.

Carly turned as Paige approached. "It's too noisy up there," she said, and Paige saw her smile as the turn of head brought her face into the path of the moon. Her pulse quickened. Carly had been on the periphery of her vision the entire night, but then she'd disappeared. Now Paige knew why, and nothing could have made her happier than to see her here on the beach. In an instant, her mood changed, and she forgot her sadness.

"You're right. It's crazy up there. May I join you?" Even here, a hundred yards from the house and with the sound of the ocean just a few footsteps away, Paige could hear the party.

Carly had wanted to escape the noise and the crowd, so she could enjoy the magnificent night and spend some time with herself and her thoughts. She'd been content to be alone, but suddenly the idea of Paige's company seemed even better. "Of course." She'd had a great day playing golf and getting to know her new acquaintances, especially talking with Paige during the Scrabble match. No matter what they did, Carly enjoyed her time with Paige.

"So, you've met the butterflies. What do you think?" Carly had watched Paige, and she seemed to fit in with the group. Except Paige didn't even pretend to drink, not even a glass of water in her hand she could pass off as a vodka tonic.

"Butterflies?"

"The Meadows. Social people. Butterflies."

Paige nodded as she seemed to get the reference. "They're very nice."

"Very social," Carly said as she sipped the vodka tonic in her own hand.

"Does that bother you?"

"Not at all. And to you, I'm sure they all seem like very interesting people. But I've known them forever, so they bore me to tears." Carly didn't mention that she'd slept with a few of them, and one or two of the ladies might have been just as happy if she hadn't joined them for the trip.

Paige was quiet for a moment. "Everyone has been friendly. They act like Liza and Mal and I are old friends—telling stories, inviting us to the club. Someone invited us to golf in Scotland! Still, it's hard to tell. They're all a little drunk."

"That doesn't surprise me. How's Tash holding up?"

"She seems to be having a good time."

Paige adjusted in her seat and looked out over the ocean. Even with a nearly full moon, the beach was dark, and only the whitecaps of waves were visible beyond the shoreline. She thought about Carly and Tasha, how intimate they seemed when they were together. Paige had assumed they were a couple, yet she had learned from their SAW applications that they didn't live together. Either they were living separate lives, or her initial impression was wrong.

"You and Tasha are tight, huh?"

"Best friends since college."

"Wow. How long ago was that?"

Carly playfully punched her arm. "Is that a polite way of asking my age?"

"Hmm. You're on to me."

"Twenty-six, twenty-seven years. Something like that. You'll have to ask Tash. She's better at stuff like that. She could tell you the day we met, the time, and what song was playing on the radio."

Paige couldn't help laughing because of Carly's description, but also because Tasha was a very organized and hands-on hospital administrator, known for attention to detail. "I suppose those traits can be helpful in her job."

Carly sighed. "They're a handicap, almost. She's very difficult to handle in large doses."

Paige thought of Tasha's decision to sit out the golf this morning and Carly's feeble attempt to change her mind, but she didn't reply. Instead, she sat quietly, enjoying the moon-kissed waves crashing onto the shore a few feet away. "But you handle her okay."

"We were a couple once. In college." Carly spoke softly, and Paige had difficulty hearing over the sound of the ocean. She leaned in, just a little closer, and could feel Carly shift slightly, too, creating an intimacy Paige hadn't anticipated. For just a second it was there, and her breath caught, and then Carly shifted back and broke the connection.

"She was extremely hard to live with. We're better as friends."

Paige thought of her own relationship. Will had once been easy, when Paige wasn't around much and when she gave him his way. Seeming to sense Paige's thoughts, Carly asked about him.

"College sweethearts, too. Will is older, and after a good deal of therapy, I've realized he's a control freak. I'm trying to figure out what to do about that."

"Father figure?" Carly asked.

"No. My parents are still alive. Just a…I don't know. Let's not talk about him. You know about me. One sister, one niece. Two parents. How about you? Are your parents still alive? Any siblings?"

"No, and I've been in therapy for years trying to process that fact. I'm an only child, and other than one cousin, I really don't have any family. That's why I spend so much time on my relationship with Tasha, and my other dear old pal, Pip."

"What's a Pip?"

"Penelope Irene Perkins. Ella Townes used to live in her house."

"Oh, yes. I've heard of her but never met her. She's the dog mommy."

"Yes. That's actually *my* dog. Pip stole her in the divorce. Ella dog-sat at Pip's house while she went to film school in California a few years ago. That's how she met your colleague, Reese. Now, Reese and Ella live at the lake a few houses over from me."

"Lake Winola?"

"Yes. It's sort of crazy. I bought Pip's family house after her grandfather passed away. I'd spent so much time there, it felt like home. And Ella spent summers there as a child, with her grandparents."

"So you've known Ella her entire life?"

"No. She just came back a few years ago. That's when I met her. I've known Reese a long time, though. Pip is neighbors with her parents. And Ella dog-sat, and they met, and the rest is history."

"It sounds like fate."

"Do you believe in that sort of stuff?" Carly asked, shifting in her chair to face Paige.

"Oh, yes," Paige replied. "You?"

"This is pretty deep water we're heading into."

"You brought it up."

"Touché."

They were quiet again before Carly spoke.

"When we met, I thought you were gay."

Paige cough-gasped. No one had ever said *that* to her before. "Is it my hair?" She'd gotten it cut during residency, because it was easier to manage, and she sometimes thought it was a little too short.

"What?"

"Is that why you think I'm gay?"

"No. Your hair's cute. You pinged my gaydar."

Paige knew about gaydar. "Really?"

"Don't sound so surprised, Paige. You hang out with lesbians. People are bound to make the leap."

Paige understood. Will had a problem with it. He'd been questioning Paige's sexuality for years, even before she began playing golf with a group that consisted of many gay women. She didn't respond to Carly's comment. What could she say?

"Why is that?"

"Why is what?"

"Why do you hang out with my people?"

Lately, mostly since meeting Carly, she'd been asking herself the same question. But it had been in the back of her mind much longer than that, and although she'd ruminated from time to time, she'd been able to push the thought aside. Since that fateful Sunday afternoon in February, when Carly had walked into the exhibit hall at Mohegan Sun, her struggle had become more difficult.

"I'm not really sure." It was the most honest answer she could give.

"Have you ever slept with a woman?"

Paige shrugged, swallowed, tried not to choke on her own discomfort. "Not really." Once, in medical school, she'd fooled around with a female classmate. But they'd both been drunk, and it had been a one-time thing, and they'd barely gotten beyond some sloppy kisses before they both came to their senses. Before that, Paige had thought she might be bisexual, because she knew she was attracted to both men and women. But the best part of her experience with her classmate had been the verbal foreplay. The actual physical contact had been so underwhelming she'd never had the desire to do it again.

And then she'd met Carly, and the cobwebs seemed to fall free of those long-dormant thoughts about bisexuality.

"What does that mean? Either you have or you haven't. There's no room for ambiguity here."

She turned and looked at Carly, the dark eyes just shadows in the moonlight. "Did you ever go to a restaurant for dessert but not dinner? Could you honestly say you've eaten there?"

"What does that even mean?" Carly said through a belly laugh.

She laughed, too. Carly had come out to her, so why couldn't she just tell her? Or was it more her lack of experience that made her hesitate? Would it make her seem more sophisticated—*cooler*—if she lied and told Carly she'd slept with a woman? But then what if Carly wanted details? As lame as it made her seem, she decided the truth was always the best option.

"I kissed a girl in medical school."

"Kissed?" Carly's tone was tinted with sarcasm, and she felt like burying herself in the sand. It seemed the truth didn't meet Carly's expectations.

"Well, we were in her bed, so…maybe it was a little more than that."

"You may not realize it yet, but you're looking for *a lot* more than that."

She sighed. "I don't know what I'm looking for, Carly. I know I'm not happy in my marriage, but I don't know if that's a Will thing or a Paige thing."

"Are you seeing a counselor?"

"I am. He isn't."

"I find counseling very helpful."

"I find it to be hard."

"How so?" Carly edged closer, once again creating that intimate space that Paige found comforting.

"Sometimes your counselor tells you things you don't want to hear," she said, thinking of her last session.

"Like what?" Carly whispered as she turned to her, searched her gaze with her own.

"Like fuck other people—my parents, Will. I'm allowed to be happy."

"What would make you happy?"

You, she thought. You make me happy. But it was entirely inappropriate to speak her mind, to tell Carly the truth about this little crush, so she didn't. "When I figure it out, I'll let you know."

Chapter Twelve

Stars in the Coffee

Carly rang the doorbell of Erin's McMansion on Montage Mountain, just south of Scranton, and said a silent prayer that the discussion had started without her. Since the first SAW meeting, she hadn't been able to have a conversation with Erin that didn't involve Paige. This was typical Erin, the infatuation with an attractive younger woman, and Carly would normally have dismissed it, but she couldn't. She was jealous of Erin's friendship with Paige. Erin's constant babbling about her had become annoying. And though the likelihood of Paige falling for Erin was slim, since she'd confessed to kissing a girl *in bed*, Carly was convinced Paige was gay. And so, just maybe, Erin had a chance. The thought made Carly ill. Even though she wouldn't sleep with a married woman, Erin probably would.

She'd arrived at this SAW meeting purposefully late, prepared to use the excuse of work. She recognized Paige's Jeep in the driveway, as well as Linda's car, so they just might have started. If luck was on her side. If.

"Hey, you made it!" Erin's greeting was a few hundred decibels too high, her hug rib-crushing. "We've started the food already, but it's still hot. Francesco's Pizza. The best," she said as she stepped aside and allowed Carly into the two-story foyer.

The pizza was Carly's favorite, but she rarely made the trip to Old Forge. Maybe this meeting wouldn't be so bad. Old Forge pizza and Paige.

Her friendship with Paige had continued to flourish since they'd returned from Myrtle Beach. And something interesting had happened to Carly. She was working at her friendship with Paige, fostering it. She enjoyed her company more than she had anyone's in a long time. They could talk about anything, and Paige made her laugh. Instead of avoiding Paige's calls as she once had, she couldn't suppress the smile that formed on her face when she saw Paige's name on her phone.

"Hello, ladies." Carly greeted Paige and Linda when she saw them across Erin's massive kitchen. They were seated at the island, surrounded by food—pizza, a large bowl of salad, and two bottles of wine. She even saw a plate of what appeared to be homemade cookies.

"Hey, girl. How's it going?" Linda asked. Paige, who was chewing, blew Carly a kiss.

Oooh, Carly thought. That's dangerous. Ignoring Paige, she turned to Linda. "Good, good. How are you?"

Without asking, Erin poured her a glass of red wine. "It's the Devilry Afoot blend," Erin said as she handed her the glass.

"Oh. That's really good stuff."

"Yes. I agree. Paige told me you both like it, so I grabbed a few bottles to have on hand for SAW meetings."

Of course you did. "Great idea," she said as she helped herself to a slice of pizza.

"Okay, ladies. I have to work the graveyard shift, so do you mind if we talk while we eat?" Paige asked after sipping from a water bottle. No complex mathematical equations about alcohol metabolism tonight.

"That works for me," Carly said, and the others agreed.

Paige took another bite of her pizza, a smaller one this time, so she could still converse with the others while she ate. She wanted to focus on the business of SAW rather than Carly. As much as she loved talking to her, and spending time with her, Carly was on Paige's mind to the point of distraction. She needed to get a handle on her situation, but how?

"I can't believe it's May already!" she said, stuffing cheer into her voice and a smile on her face. "The first SAW tournament is only two weeks away. It's in Hershey. Twenty-one women are in our league. On average, everyone should play twice in five weeks. A few people—like Carly and Tasha—have requested to play together. So we have to do pairings and schedules so people can plan their summers. Also, anyone not 'officially' playing can come along and play 'outside' of the tournament. I think Erin or I should always be there, in case any problems come up."

Erin flashed a broad smile, and they proceeded to work out the schedule. Carly had volunteered to do that, but they were working together, since SAW was new to all of them. When they finished, Carly would distribute it, and if there were any changes, she'd also handle them.

Paige and Erin would both attend the first tournament, so they could see how SAW worked, but after that they'd alternate weekends. They went through each week, forming teams from the women who were available to play, until they finished with the final tournament in September. They agreed on teal for their team shirts, Linda promised to have the handicaps in order, and Erin would send an email about hotels for anyone who wanted to stay over.

"Do any of you want to go the night before?" Paige asked. She thought it would be less stressful if she was there early.

"I probably can," Linda said.

"Me, too," Carly added.

Erin looked at her phone. "I'm booked until six that day. I could maybe leave by eight or so, if you just want to go and crash."

"I wonder if Hersheypark will be open," Paige said. She'd been taking Jules there since she was a toddler, and she loved the park. "We can ride the coasters at night. That's a blast."

Carly cleared her throat. "Or we could do something more suited to our purpose, like play golf."

"Nice courses down there," Linda said.

Paige nodded. She'd ride the roller coasters another time. "Okay. Golf it is. I'll check with Reese and see if they want to go the day before, too."

They talked about a few other trivial items, and Paige glanced at her watch. It was just about seven. If she left now, she could probably take a two-hour nap before her night shift. She wasn't sure she really needed one, though. She'd worked last night, as well, and had slept most of the day, so she felt rested. She just didn't want to linger. Not around Carly. She was trying hard to control her crush, and she'd been doing well. If she lingered, though, she'd probably lose track of time and be late for work.

"I should take off," she told the others. "But this was a great meeting. I'll type up the schedule and send it to Carly so she can get it out to everyone. Hopefully we won't have any complaints."

"Paige, I have you blocked in, so I'm going to head out, too," Carly said.

Linda opted to finish her wine before departing, so only Carly and Paige walked along the sidewalk to Erin's driveway. When they reached the cars, Paige looked at Carly. "Hey, your car's not blocking me."

Carly shrugged. "It was an excuse to get out of there."

"I thought you liked Erin."

"I do. I do. We've been friends for years. She's just been annoying me lately."

Paige got it. Erin could be intense at times. She'd called Paige almost every day since Paige sent her that text a few weeks earlier, asking her to be the co-chair. And while Paige didn't mind talking to her, it seemed the reasons for the calls were often trivial. Paige sometimes had a sinking feeling that Erin was crushing on her, so she was trying to be a little more formal with her. She liked her as a friend and didn't want to give her the wrong impression.

"I get that."

"So you have to work? What will you do now, take a nap?"

"I was thinking of going for a coffee. Would you like to join me?" Oh, man. Had she just said that? What happened to her resolve, her plan to avoid Carly?

Carly studied her for a moment. The sun was very low in the sky, but it was still light enough to see the sparkle in her eyes. If she wanted to sleep at night, it was impossible for Carly to drink caffeine after about ten in the morning. "I'd love to. What do you have in mind?" she asked.

"Beansie's?" Paige asked, referring to a coffee bar that was open late.

That'll work, Carly thought. They had comfy chairs where they could sit and talk. Or Carly could invite Paige to her place. It was definitely out of the way, but if she had time, it was the best place in town. Plus, Carly could have wine instead of coffee. Like Erin, she'd picked up a few more bottles of the blend they liked, and one was already uncorked, waiting for her on her kitchen counter.

"How about my place? It's a nice night. We can sit out on my deck and enjoy the stars."

Paige didn't hesitate. "I'll follow you."

They got into their cars, and Carly watched the headlights in her mirror as Paige trailed her back to her house. What the hell was she doing, inviting Paige over? "Carly, you are an idiot," she said aloud.

For the duration of the forty-minute drive, Carly berated herself for extending the invitation to her place and tried to devise a plan to get rid of Paige early. What if she wanted to stay until she had to leave for work? Damn. What had she been thinking? Remembering the girl she'd brought home after Erin's party, she wondered if she was losing her edge. She'd been a bit out of sorts, but lately that seemed to be changing. Her dour mood had turned, and she was feeling optimistic. Still, this invitation had been stupid. Did she need to take a closer look at her motives when it came to Paige?

Darkness engulfed the lake by the time they arrived. Pulling into her driveway, she parked beside the house and saw Paige's headlights just behind her. Before she'd even gathered her briefcase, Paige was out of her car and waiting beside hers.

Taking a breath to settle her nerves, Carly opened the car door and found Paige looking to the heavens. She followed Paige's gaze. It was an amazing sight, the inky black sky splattered with twinkling stars. Out here, the absence of light made the night sky breathtaking.

"It's something, isn't it?" she asked.

"It sure is."

"I'd apologize about the darkness, but then you wouldn't see these stars so well. I thought I'd be home tonight, so I didn't turn on the lights."

"Have you ever thought about motion detectors?"

"I had them, but the deer constantly triggered them, and it ruined the atmosphere."

Paige looked around, even though she couldn't see past the hand in front of her. It was dark in Carly's part of the world. Really dark.

"How about something just out front here, so you can find your way into the house?"

"It's fine. I've done it a million times. Do you want to hold my hand?" she asked.

"Uh, maybe that's a good idea."

Paige felt Carly's hand on her forearm, and then the fingertips slid down to her own. Carly took Paige's hand and gave it a gentle squeeze. "Follow me," she said softly.

Paige was so focused on the sensation, the tingling, tickly, electric charges coursing through her hand, that she could only grunt a reply. Her feet seemed to work normally, though, and they moved, doing what they were supposed to, without any input from her brain. In thirty seconds, they'd picked their way along the driveway and around the side of the house, and then a gentle light leaking from the window showed stairs leading up to a deck. Carly released her hand, and Paige breathed again.

Trying to compose herself while Carly entered a combination on a keypad, Paige focused on slowing her breathing. The night was warm for May, still in the seventies, yet she shivered so loudly Carly couldn't help but notice.

"Are you cold? I can get you a sweatshirt. I was thinking we'd sit out here. Is that okay?"

"Yes. A sweatshirt would be great. And I'd love to sit out here. The sky is magnificent."

"Okay," Carly said as she stepped aside and motioned her to follow. "Come in while I get you something. I don't want you to freeze to death while you're waiting."

She followed Carly into a room that was essentially a large square, with support beams strategically placed as the only barriers in the open floor plan. She was standing in the kitchen, a bright, modern tile and granite area whose transition into a living room was marked only by the change in floor composition. The entire room was lit by accent lighting that gave it a soft, warm feeling.

The only thing that seemed out of place was the arrangement of plastic containers near the windows. "What's that?" she asked, and Carly smiled excitedly.

"My babies. Seedlings. Would you like to meet them?"

She nodded. "Sure."

Carly led her to a decorative table that now held three small, plastic containers. Each was filled with small dirt pods, and a tiny plant was sprouting from each pod. The smallest were less than an inch tall, while the biggest was about four inches high.

"What are they?" she asked, fascinated.

"Flowers. I have a ton of perennials around the property, but I like to mix in some annuals and put some planters and pots on the deck for color. So I start them from seeds and see what happens."

"So you do this every year?"

"I do. Sometimes they grow, sometimes not. But it's kind of exciting to start a seed and watch what it becomes." Carly met her eyes, and she could feel her joy, her excitement.

"Good for you."

"Do you garden?"

"I do, but it all comes from the garden center. This is amazing."

"Let's hope I don't kill them. Make yourself comfortable," Carly said as she flicked a light switch. "I'm going to change, and I'll bring you down a sweatshirt."

"Okay," she said as she continued to study the plants. Carly had a chart that described what was planted in each row, and she tried to see if she could tell the difference in the plants. To her amazement, she could.

After a moment, she turned and studied the first floor. The layout and decor could have come from a magazine, with white and beige furniture accented with colorful pillows and rugs and art. Much like her own house, she thought with a smile.

Turning toward the back of the house, just a row of windows, really, she stared into the darkness. Across the lake, lights of homes were visible, but they were far off and faint, and the lake really did foster the illusion that they were all alone. Suddenly, being along with Carly didn't seem so innocent. She thought she had her attraction under control, but the touch of Carly's hand in the driveway had been another life-altering experience.

What was she doing? Things with Will hadn't changed, not really, but she felt happier than she'd been in a long while. Since when? She had trouble remembering a time she felt so light, unfettered. Hopeful. But hopeful about what?

Hearing footsteps, she turned to see Carly in a faded, baggy, gray Rehoboth Beach sweatshirt and leggings. In her hand she carried a bright-blue sweatshirt, which she presented her.

"What's P-Town?" she asked as she pulled it over her head.

Carly studied her for a moment. "You've never heard of P-Town?" She shook her head.

"Provincetown," she said. "On Cape Cod."

"Oh." She *had* heard of Provincetown, but she didn't want to elaborate after that unsettling moment when Carly touched her hand. Everything about Carly seemed to be unsettling, and she was thinking more and more about her sexuality.

"I haven't really spent any time in New England. The farthest I've been is Erie."

"Other direction, but okay. Would you like that coffee?"

She nodded. "Please."

"I wish I could offer you something to go with it, but I try not to keep anything delicious around. I'd just eat it," she said as she opened the freezer and pulled out a bag of coffee. She studied Carly's trim figure for a moment. Even in the oversized sweatshirt, her shape was evident. She didn't have anything to worry about.

Rather than stare at Carly, she looked around the place. "Your house is great."

She tried to focus as Carly told her about the place. "Pip's family built it in the thirties, but they really never did anything with it after that. I bought it about fifteen years ago, and since I had to gut the entire house anyway, I decided to transform it from a summer cottage to a year-round residence. Then when Pip and I split, I moved in."

This was the second time Carly had told her she and Pip were once a couple, and she was intrigued. In her world, the straight world where marriage had always been legal, breakups tended to be messy affairs involving lawyers and bloodshed and hard feelings. No one she knew who'd divorced remained friends, even though they were forced to maintain civility because of shared children.

"It's nice that you still hang out," she said.

"Hold that thought. How do you like your coffee?"

"Creamy, not too sweet."

Carly pulled the creamer from the fridge and smiled at Paige. "You got it," she said as she poured. "If I could combine Tasha and Pip, I'd have the perfect partner. Individually, they're amazing friends." She finished the coffee and handed it to Paige, then opened the bench seat beside the kitchen door and pulled a few blankets from a stack inside.

Motioning to Paige, Carly opened the door. "C'mon. Let's enjoy the stars."

"Carly, this is the best coffee I've ever had." Paige moaned as she sipped. "What kind is it?"

"Some Italian blend. I'm not sure. My secretary buys it for the office, and I just bring it home."

"It's so good."

"It's all in the way I prepare it."

"Really? How is that?"

"Oh, I can't give all my secrets out so early in the game."

Paige laughed and followed her onto the deck. She hit the switch on the way outside, so only the accent lights remained on, and the far side of the deck, where she guided Paige, was dark.

Placing two blankets on a chaise lounge, she sat on the other one and quickly pulled her own blankets over her.

Paige watched everything Carly did, letting her eyes adjust to the dark. She could see the outline of an accent table, and she set her mug on that before copying Carly's movement, with one blanket over her lap and legs, and the other wrapped around her torso. When she'd settled in, she grabbed her mug and looked up at the stars.

They were quiet for a while as they sat there in the darkness, before Carly broke the tranquility.

"Is this your last night?"

"Yes. Number three."

"How late did you sleep today?"

Will had been up and about when Paige got home, so she made them both breakfast, and they'd spent a few hours taking the patio furniture out and getting the grill ready for summer. By the time she had showered and headed to bed, it was nearly eleven, and she'd set her alarm for five so she could be at Erin's for their six o'clock meeting. "I got five or six hours of shut-eye. I should be fine with that."

"I don't know how you sleep during the day. I'm usually awake at sunrise," Carly said with a chuckle.

"You'd be surprised how easy it is when you've been up all night."

"It can't be healthy, though. All that shift-switching you do."

"No. It's not."

"So why do you do it?"

That was a good question, one Paige thought about twice a month, when her string of three-night shifts came around. "I like the ER. And I thought it would be a good career choice, because I want kids. I can shift pretty easily into a part-time position and still have time to be a mom."

"When is that going to happen?"

"I'm not so sure it is anymore."

"Really? Why?" Carly sounded surprised and concerned. Or interested, maybe.

"Will."

"Because of his…accident?" Paige had shared the basics about his injury, but she didn't like to discuss the topic. Apparently, Carly understood that attitude, and her gentle tone reflected it.

"Not really. He's never wanted kids. He was married before and has a grown son who lives in Chicago with his mom. They split up when he was a little boy, and Will didn't get to spend much time with him. I don't know if it's just that he doesn't want his heart broken again, or if he's just too spoiled. But we jokingly said we'd stay together until I wanted kids, then split up."

"Why did you ever marry him, if you knew that?" Carly sounded exasperated.

"I don't know. I think I'm codependent." She'd talked about the subject with her therapist, something she realized went back to her childhood. For whatever reason, she had always focused on pleasing everyone else rather than herself, and because of that tendency, she sometimes agreed to things she later regretted.

Carly laughed again. "Self-awareness is a good thing."

"I'm working on it." It was hard work, and she was beginning to feel good about herself.

They were quiet again, and then Carly asked about Jules.

"She graduates soon. It's an exciting time."

"Oh, yes. Especially with her summer travel plans. When do they leave?"

"She opted out of a party, and her parents are just going to give her money for her trip. Trips. Don't forget, our little explorer has Paris in the fall."

Carly sighed.

"But some of the other kids are having graduation parties, so they're not leaving for another month. She'll be able to make the first SAW meet in June."

"Where's that one?"

"Don't laugh. Brooklyn. We're going to stay over and then see a matinee on Broadway on Saturday before we head home."

"That kid has the life," Carly said.

"She certainly does. But she's my sister's only child. And she's my parents' only grandchild, so she's sort of spoiled by default."

"But she's a good kid, Paige. And she wants to be a doctor, like you. That's great."

"I'm not sure it is. You can see all her personality. I'm not so sure medicine is for her. I think medicine is what she thinks I want, and Helena wants, and her father wants, and so on. I'm not sure she knows what she wants."

"It's hard to make that decision when you're eighteen. Were you always pre-med, or did you change at some point?"

"I was pre-med in kindergarten, I think. I worked in the ER my last year of high school and all through college. I loved it. But I'm not as social as my niece, and I'm more serious. Plus, I work harder. So it was easy for me. All the hours in the hospital—that's a drain. I could see it sucking the life out of her."

"But not you?"

"Sometimes it does. But I'm tougher than Jules. I just want her to be happy, and I don't think medicine is the way. But I guess we'll see. Besides, with all her plans, she might flunk out of pre-med, and the decision will be made for her."

"That's true. My major—business—was relatively tame. And I still had to bust my butt at Scranton. They don't just hand out degrees."

"Nope."

"When's Paris?"

"We'll be gone over Halloween."

"That in itself makes the trip worth the money."

"What? You don't like Halloween?"

"I hate it. It's the…I don't even want to talk about it."

"Even when you were a kid?"

"Well, I ate the candy, of course."

"Best part. I'm going to have to treat myself to some French confections to celebrate."

Carly moaned. "The food will be divine."

Paige only wished that were the case, but since her trip was with a college group, she feared a diet of cheap food for the duration. Even though she was paying Jules's way, her palate wasn't very sophisticated, and she suspected they'd have to choose restaurants carefully.

"You've been to France, right? Just not Paris."

"Yeah. Pip and I spent a week on the Cote d'Azur. That's when Myron keeled over. Instead of seeing the Louvre in person, Pip bought me a book. It's not the same."

"You can do a virtual tour."

"That's not the same, either."

Paige understood, and before she could filter, she blurted out her thoughts. "You should think about coming on the trip with us. I mean, Jules thinks you're great, and it would give me someone to talk to beside a bunch of college kids." Oh, fuck. Why had she said that?

"I can't intrude on your trip with Jules. It sounds like it's going to be a special time for you two."

Paige was both relieved and disappointed that Carly had so quickly rejected her suggestion. And she hoped it would be a fun time with Jules, but it wouldn't surprise her at all if she spent half the time in the hotel by herself as Jules ran off exploring with her friends.

"Carly, I couldn't even relate to twenty-year-olds when I was twenty. How am I going to do it now?"

"You'll figure it out," she said.

Paige had set the alarm on her phone to give her an hour's notice before her ER shift started. They were still talking when it went off.

"Time to go to work," she said. "But thanks for the coffee. And the company."

"My pleasure. And I'm even going to turn the lights on, so you don't kill yourself in the driveway."

She relinquished her blankets and was about to take the sweatshirt off, when Carly stopped her. "It's okay. You can get it back to me whenever."

"Well, then, thanks for this, too."

Carly walked her to the car. "Drive carefully. You know the way, right?"

"Yes. I'll be fine."

"There's deer. And the roads are a disaster. Why don't you text me when you get to work, so I'll know you made it."

"Will do," Paige said, warmth suddenly filling her as she realized that Carly cared. Filled with the sudden urge to hug her, she wrapped her arms around herself instead, then hurried to her car, before she did something even more idiotic than spending the night on Carly's deck.

Chapter Thirteen

Tee Time

Paige stood beside the first tee at the Hershey Country Club a few weeks later and watched Tasha's tee shot land far down the fairway. It was the day before their first SAW match, and Carly, Tasha, and Paige had made the two-hour trip from Clarks Summit to play at one of the country's best courses.

Paige had been out to play a few times with Carly, but this was her first time with Tasha, and she was happy for the opportunity. Ever since they'd met at the golf expo, Paige felt Tasha had been going out of her way to be friendly, and she appreciated her effort, on a personal level as well as a professional one. It never hurt to have the hospital CEO on your side.

"Well done, Tash," she said as she took her turn between the tee markers. She hit an awful tee shot and was unable to turn it around until the match was almost over. It was a disaster of a day of golf, but the sun was shining, and it felt great to be out on such a beautiful course. Afterward, they went for a late lunch on the veranda at the hotel.

"So, you're going to the park now?" Tasha asked.

She nodded. "Yeah. Reese and Ella are taking Cass for a few hours, and I promised Cass I'd ride some coasters with her."

"I'd vomit," Tasha confessed.

"Well, truthfully, these new-generation coasters are pretty wild. Hopefully, she'll just want to ride the Comet. That's the old wooden one. It's pretty tame."

"Well, you're a nice person to volunteer."

"Not at all. It'll be fun. What are your plans for the evening?"

Tasha grinned and nodded to Carly, who'd been silently drinking her vodka tonic. "We have a spa date. The Hotel Hershey has a chocolate massage and pedicure. Two hours of bliss await us."

It did sound blissful, and suddenly she was jealous that she was going to the park instead of getting pampered. Maybe she'd schedule a massage when she got home.

The waitress took their order, and a breeze ruffled their hair. "You'd better dress warm. I think the night's going to get cold," Tasha said.

"You're probably right. And speaking of cold weather—Carly, I have your sweatshirt. I'll bring it to your room after the park, okay?"

"Whenever. I hardly missed it."

"What did I miss?" Tasha asked. "Why do you have Carly's sweatshirt?"

"Oh—I went over to her place for coffee after our last meeting, and it got cold when the sun went down. Carly let me wear it, and I forgot to return it."

Carly sipped her drink again, dreading Tasha's reaction, thankful Paige was there to dampen it. Shrugging off the look Tasha gave her, she focused on Paige, knowing there would be hell to pay later. So much for a relaxing evening at the spa. The moment Paige left, Tasha would demand details, and when Carly told her about that night on her deck, Tasha would be pissed. She'd give Carly a piece of her mind, and they probably wouldn't speak for the rest of the weekend.

It was not how Carly hoped their time in Hershey would go, but she was powerless to stop it. And Tasha would be right. She should not have invited Paige over. She should be keeping her distance instead of fostering the friendship they'd been growing. Paige was off-limits, and even though Carly had been on her best behavior regarding Paige, Tasha knew her history of making bad decisions when it came to women. Another one was not totally out of the realm of possibilities.

Carly picked at her food, nervous about what was coming. And sure enough, as soon as Paige left to join the others at the park, Tasha started.

"What the fuck, Carly? You had her over to your house for coffee? You don't even drink coffee after breakfast. This is a really, really bad idea."

Although she knew it would be futile to protest, she tried anyway. "Tash, I know that. We're just friends. I like her."

"Some lesbians can have straight friends. You *are not* one of them."

"That is not fair, or accurate. I've never knowingly slept with a straight woman."

"How about the fact that she's married?"

"You're right, Tash, and believe me, I've thought about all this. I don't typically hang around with straight women. I don't usually feel comfortable being open with them. But you've gotten to know Paige over the past few months. She's so easy to be with. She's a good person."

"Did you hear me say she isn't? Did you?"

When Carly didn't answer, Tasha answered for her. Carly stared at the tracks of the roller coaster in the distance, trying to avoid Tasha's glare. "No, I didn't. I happen to like Paige, which is a good thing, since I work with her. What does it do to my professional relationship with her if you fuck her and ditch her, as you've been known to do? It will make my job very, very difficult."

Carly couldn't imagine the scenario Tasha described, because quite honestly, she thought Paige was the most perfect woman she'd ever met. If she ever slept with Paige, it wouldn't be a one-night stand. But that was never going to happen.

"I'm not going to sleep with her, Tash. And I know what you're going to say, that it starts with a little coffee under the stars and—"

"Under the stars? Really? You couldn't have coffee in the kitchen, or the living room? You had to drink it under the stars? Are you kidding me?"

"It was a nice night," Carly said defensively.

"How nice could it have been if she needed a sweatshirt?" Tasha shook her head in disgust. "I have put up with so much from you, Carly, but if you do this, with a hospital employee, I don't know if I'd forgive you."

When Carly didn't reply, Tasha spoke again. "Is she gay?"

"I don't know."

"Have you asked her?"

Carly hesitated before speaking. Was it right to divulge what Paige had told her in confidence? She'd trust Tasha with her life, but still, it wasn't her secret to tell. And though she didn't know Paige all that well, she suspected she didn't share her tale about kissing a girl freely.

"Carly, really?" Tasha asked when she didn't reply. "I guess your silence answers the question."

"Tash, you're being a jerk. I understand your concern. I really do. And maybe I have no business pursuing a friendship with her. But expecting me to out someone? C'mon. That's just really below you."

Tasha stood. "Are you ready?"

Her tone was icy, and Carly felt the chill, but she didn't budge. "No, actually, I'm not. And if it'll make you happy, Natasha, I'll answer the question. But I'll lose just a little respect for you."

Tasha paused mid-step, then continued toward the door and into the building. Carly weighed her options. She could go for a walk, avoiding Tasha. After her massage, she could hang out in the bar until they forced her out at closing time. Tasha should be asleep by then. Hell, she could Uber all the way back home. She could join Paige and Reese's family at the park. Or she could walk out that door and—what, she didn't know. Tasha was overreacting, and even though her concerns had some validity, she'd gone too far.

"I'm sorry," Tasha said as she walked through the door. "It's not my business."

Carly stopped. Tasha never backed down, and she wasn't sure what to make of it. But she also knew that her friendship with Tasha was one of the best things in her life, and Tasha was fundamentally right about Paige.

She offered Tasha a half smile. "I'm your business. And I understand why you're concerned. I should back off. I have enough friends. What do I need with a straight, married woman?"

Even though the tournament didn't start until noon, Paige was up at eight and had stretched and showered and checked out by nine.

Her room at the Hotel Hershey came with free admission to Hershey Gardens, and she wanted to explore the tulips' display. It was late in the season, but she knew from prior visits that the horticulturists came up with new varieties of bulbs all the time, and they varied the layout every year. She stopped at a diner for breakfast and ate alone while reading the news on her phone. By ten, she was parked and on her way into the gardens.

After exchanging her voucher for an admission ticket, she walked through the welcome center and out the back door, greeted by a cacophony of color. Paige had hoped to see cherry trees in bloom, but what greeted her went far beyond her expectations. In front of her, to the left and right, were patch after patch after patch of tulips, each grouped by color. Beyond, flowering trees in all their pink and white splendor bordered the rear of the garden. Carly would hate this, she thought with a smile, then wondered about her.

Paige had had a great time with Reese and Ella and Cass the night before, riding the coasters and walking the park under the glow of the twinkling lights. Reese tried to win a stuffed animal for Ella, and after she'd spent about twenty bucks in a losing effort, Cass stepped up and heaved a ring right onto the bottle that won her the largest prize. Fortunately, it was at the end of their evening, because Reese had to carry a Minion bigger than herself all the way to the car. They'd eaten ice cream, and the three of them had their portrait taken with a Western backdrop, dressed as outlaws.

Paige was back in the room at nine thirty, and she texted Tasha and Carly to see if they wanted to meet in the lobby for a drink. Tasha told her she was already tucked in for the night, and Carly didn't respond at all. Paige figured she was probably already asleep. Carly told her she was an early bird, and indeed, she'd usually been the first one to bed during their trip to the beach.

Warmed by the sun, Paige pulled off her jacket and put it into her backpack. She stopped to read each flower's name, weaving her way slowly through the left half of the garden, around the pond and the fountain, and through a gazebo placed to direct traffic. There, she looked around, deciding to walk along the left pathway, through the cherry trees.

The sky was bright, and it was warm, yet few people were in the gardens. The hundred or so visitors were spread out over acres and acres, and Paige seemed to have the place to herself. Strolling along the path, reading signs that described the genus and species of every shrub and tree, she lost herself.

Then she looked up and saw Carly, folded into the wings of a huge butterfly-shaped bench along the pathway.

"Why am I not surprised?" Carly said as she opened her eyes and saw Paige standing before her. She and Paige seemed to be of one mind, and she should have guessed that Paige would take advantage of the free admission and explore the gardens this morning. If her evening hadn't gone so badly, she might have called her and suggested they go together.

It had been an awful evening, though. Even though Tasha apologized, she was distant on their long walk to the spa and buried her nose in a magazine during their pedicure. She snubbed all Carly's attempts at conversation, until she finally stopped trying. Afterward, when Tasha pulled out her laptop to catch up on some work, Carly headed to one of the hotel bars and watched the Yankees game.

It wasn't much of a game, and instead of taking her mind off Paige, she only ruminated more as she nursed her drink, wasting enough time that she could simply go back to the room and go to bed. For a woman she hadn't even dated—and didn't plan to—Paige sure caused her a ton of grief.

Tasha was right. Paige could lead her in a bad direction. As much as she denied it, she could already see it happening, simply because she enjoyed her company so damn much. It would be so easy to throw caution aside and explore her feelings. Paige would be easy to love.

Paige sat beside her, their thighs touching. Instantly, Carly felt warm all over, and instead of fighting her response, she allowed herself to feel for a moment. She felt wonderful.

"Good morning, friend."

"It is a good morning," Carly said softly.

"Listen. Do you hear that?" Paige whispered.

"What?" Carly opened her eyes again and looked around.

"Exactly. It's so peaceful."

For a moment, Carly focused on her sense of hearing. Some birds were gossiping, but it was otherwise quiet in the gardens. Exactly as Paige had described it. Peaceful.

"You always surprise me, Paige. I get the impression you thrive on noise and chaos."

"Chaos energizes me," she whispered. "But this...wow. Wouldn't you love to do yoga right now? Right there, under that cherry tree, in a bed of fallen petals?"

Carly sighed. What she had the inclination to do involved them getting into some interesting positions, but it had nothing to do with yoga. Then she imagined Paige's suggestion, of reaching up to the sun and pulling it back down to the soft place beneath the tree. "Yes. That would be something."

Carly closed her eyes again, felt the sun caressing her, Paige's warmth next to her. Content, she sat quietly for a moment before opening her eyes to gaze out at the gardens. The colors were spectacular, with every shade in the rainbow represented, from white to a purple so deep it was almost black. Her favorite tulips were the hybrids, the blends of oranges and pinks and reds that reminded her of the sunsets over the lake.

A family with children approached, their joyful noise pulling her back to the real world. "Wanna walk?"

Paige glanced at her watch. "I have time."

"C'mon," she said as she stood, then offered a hand to pull Paige up out of the butterfly. "I can cross a butterfly chair off the bucket list."

"You're so wild."

"I am actually," she said, feigning offense.

"Uh-huh," Paige said. "I know."

"I am."

"You're not, and that's exactly why we get along so well. We're not like everyone else."

Suddenly the conversation made Carly uncomfortable, but she didn't change the topic. She just sat with it. Paige was right, of course. They weren't like everyone else. But Carly tried to be—she'd been trying her whole life. Yet her eclectic tastes and range of interests were hard to match, and she always found herself compromising and sacrificing, going along with everyone else. She feigned interest, compromised, trying to blend in and not cause too much friction. All the while, though, while she was laughing and seeming to have a great time with her friends, she felt empty inside—as if she was observing the fun, rather than sharing in it.

Tasha and Pip were the exceptions. They got her. And so did Paige.

They began walking toward the back of the gardens, where daffodils in white and pink bobbed their heads in the gentle breeze. Following the path, they came to a giant tree that had grown across the stones. A tunnel had been cut through the branches, and they entered, finding themselves completely closed off from the outside by the draping branches. The leaves were so thick that it seemed dark, even in the early morning, and it was noticeably cooler.

"This is really neat," Paige said.

Carly read the sign. "It's a weeping birch." Looking up, she smiled. "This would have been fun when I was a kid."

"Hmmm," Paige said as she followed her gaze. "That's pretty high."

"That's what makes it so amazing. You could climb up there, and your parents could never reach you."

"Hmmm," Paige said again. "Did you really want to get away from them that badly? Enough to break your neck?"

"Stop thinking like an ER doctor and let loose a little. Didn't you ever climb trees as a kid?"

"Of course. But then I wised up."

Carly smiled at Paige's joke, then turned serious again. "I love trees. I had a treehouse in my backyard when I was young. It was the place to be in my neighborhood. All the girls hung out with me."

"No boys?"

Shaking her head, Carly bit her lip. "Not even as a child."

"So…did you take dates up there?"

Carly winked. "Only the lucky ones. C'mon. Let's see what else they have here."

"How are your flowers?"

Smiling brightly, Carly stopped and reached for her phone, then moved closer to her in the darkness. "Wait until you see how big they've grown," she said as she scrolled, then handed the phone to Paige.

Paige looked at the photos on Carly's phone, excited to see the progress of the seedlings. Carly's tiny green sprouts had morphed into real flowers. "Wow, Carly. You really did it."

"Yes. Isn't it exciting?" She leaned closer as she pointed out the different varieties, but Paige couldn't concentrate on anything but Carly as the citrusy scent of her filled Paige's nostrils.

When Paige didn't answer, Carly pulled back and looked at her, from her eyes to her mouth and back. Paige saw her swallow.

"We should probably go," Carly whispered.

"Yes. I don't want to be late."

They exited into the sunshine, and Paige wondered if Carly had felt what she'd felt in that moment. If she did, she masked it well. She was walking toward the exit, admiring the annuals, talking about her garden, while Paige was having trouble making her legs work.

"There you are!" someone said, and Paige looked to see Tasha approaching. Her gaze was trained on Carly, and she wore an exasperated look. Paige watched as Tasha shook her head, then turned to Paige, seeming to notice her for the first time. "Oh," she said, obviously surprised. "I didn't realize you two were together."

"Mutual love of trees," Paige explained, but the quip didn't seem to amuse Tasha. Instead, she nodded politely and eyed Carly.

"I'll pack the car while you finish up," she said, then abruptly turned and walked away.

"Yikes," Paige said when Tasha was out of earshot. "What's up with her?"

Instead of replying, Carly sighed. "I should head back to the hotel. I'll catch you later."

Paige nodded. "See you," she said as she walked in the opposite direction, wondering what was going on with those two.

In a moment she reached her Jeep. It took only a few minutes to reach the golf course, and then she was busy checking in and greeting people, talking with Liza and Mal and the others from the league. Carly and Tasha were noticeably late and barely acknowledged her when they did arrive, instead offering a wave as they drove past on the way to the practice area.

Carly's demeanor on the course suggested to Paige that she'd had a blowout with Tasha, because instead of the normal banter they shared,

Carly was quiet. Her group was ahead of Paige's, but the course was crowded, so they found themselves waiting on the same tee box a few times. Paige tried her best to engage her, but Carly was all business. The distance she kept between them reminded Paige of the early days of their friendship, and the memory wasn't a happy one.

She had other matters to attend to, though, and pushed Carly to the back of her mind. At dinner after golf, she tried again to talk with her, but Carly had positioned herself between Tasha and Reese, and there was no opportunity. She kept an eye on Carly, though, and she could tell from their body language that something was dramatically wrong between her and Tasha.

The scores were announced, and Paige was delighted their team had finished fourth. Linda raised a glass in toast. "To the ladies of Scranton SAW. Well done!"

That brought a smile to everyone's face, even Carly's, and as Paige raised her glass, she briefly caught Carly's eye. "Good job, Paige," she said, with a smile that made all the work worthwhile.

Then, as if suddenly remembering that it was Paige's effort that had brought them to Hershey today, Erin offered a toast to Paige. Blushing, she raised her glass of water and smiled at the group. It really was a tremendous feeling to know she'd brought these ladies together, that they'd had a chance to play a great course and had well represented their part of the state.

When the awards were over, many women started to head for the exits, and fearing Carly would do the same, Paige debated how to approach her. Then Erin stood, giving her the chance.

Paige slipped into the chair she'd vacated. "How was your golf?"

Carly shrugged. "I played okay."

"It was a great score."

"I hit some lucky putts. That helps."

"Is everything okay? You seem—distracted. Or something."

"Nothing worth troubling you with."

Paige squinted comically. "I'm a doctor. You can tell me anything."

"You're not a psychiatrist, are you?"

"That bad?" she asked gently.

She watched Carly visibly suck in a breath. "I just have a lot on my mind right now. But hey, you did a great job making this happen. We won some points, which gives our group credibility."

"Yes. This was an easy group to manage."

Carly nodded. "Well, it was nice to see you. I think we're going to hit the road," she said as she stood.

"Drive safely," Paige said, and even though Carly smiled, and they'd talked for a few minutes, she couldn't shake the feeling that there was more to the story than Carly had shared.

Carly whispered to Tasha, telling her she'd meet her in the car, and then headed toward the parking lot, hoping Paige wouldn't follow her. She had to put a stop to this friendship, and she had to do it now.

Tasha had been livid after finding them in the gardens and had spent two hours berating, pleading, and counseling her. And all Carly could do was listen, because deep down, she knew Tasha was right. She had no business spending her time with Paige. Not when she found that time so enjoyable, when she found Paige so easy to be with. She was slowly, innocently, falling in love with her, and if she didn't stop it now, they were headed for trouble.

Chapter Fourteen

Making the Cut

Paige's suspicion about Carly was confirmed as she arrived in the ER Saturday morning. It was Memorial Day weekend, and she was assigned to work the string of dayshifts from Saturday to Monday. She was relieving Reese, who worked the overnights.

"How was the night?" she asked a red-eyed Reese.

"I got my ass whipped, and on top of that, I think I'm getting a cold. Or maybe it's just allergies. But I'm sniffling, and my throat is sore, and my head hurts."

She held up a hand and stepped back a foot. "Take some Vitamin C. Fast."

"Is that big bottle still in the closet in the doctors' lounge?"

"I believe so." She hoped it was still there. She'd bought it just for such occasions and hoped no one had taken it.

"I don't know if I'm going to make it to Carly's party tomorrow. I'll see how I feel, but I think sleep is more important than one of those famous margaritas."

She tried to hide her surprise and thought she recovered well. "Yes. The only mixed drink you should have is a Vitamin Water."

"I think you're right."

"I'll see you in twenty-four hours. But listen—if you need me to come in a few hours early tomorrow, let me know. Five to three isn't much harder than seven to three for me, but it might give *you* a little help with whatever you're battling."

Reese visibly brightened. "How about if I call you later? I should know in the next twelve hours which way this is going."

"You got it."

Reese didn't have a single patient to sign out, so Paige went to work on the new ones. Her shift was much like Reese's had been, crazy busy, and she didn't have time to think about her morning conversation with Reese until she was changing in the physicians' lounge afterward.

Carly was having a party, and Paige wasn't invited. Not that she had any expectations—they weren't best friends, after all. But they'd grown close in the three months they'd known each other, close enough that Carly might mention she was hosting a get-together for her college friends, like Reese. Something. Anything other than the silent treatment she'd been dealing with all week and the brush-off the day of the tournament in Hershey.

It was like a light switch had been flipped. One minute they'd been enjoying the tranquility of the Hershey Gardens, spending time as friends do. The next, Carly behaved like she barely knew Paige and couldn't tolerate her. Since the tournament in Hershey, she had texted Carly several times. Finally, after about the fifth no-reply, she'd given up. Apparently, Carly wanted nothing to do with her.

What had happened? Had she somehow angered Carly? She had a little crush on her, but Carly didn't know that. She had kept those feelings so closely guarded she wasn't even sure of them herself. Sometimes she looked at Carly and felt…something. At other times, she was just a great friend, someone she connected with.

And, of course, she was married. When she was with Carly, she had to remind herself of that fact, because it was so easy to forget. Perhaps she just didn't want to think of Will and the way he dominated her life. Maybe she just lost herself with Carly, too preoccupied with laughing and talking to think about her reality. Yet in the end, life with Will was very real, and Carly was certainly not going to disregard it. She knew that, and she understood.

The thought of Will had the usual consequences, and she sighed with frustration. So much of her energy, her alone-time thoughts were devoted to him, to their marriage. Wondering what went wrong. Had it ever been right? She knew she loved him, but not how she should have. Yet she didn't have the courage to leave him. She felt stuck. She'd worked, worked, worked to arrive where she thought she wanted to go, but it wasn't what she'd hoped it would be. That was true of her marriage and of her life in general.

She'd been just puttering along until she met Carly, and then things had seemed exciting again, the future bright. Why? Just because someone thought she was interesting and respected her opinion and her abilities?

If Carly were straight, would she even be questioning their friendship? Would she simply accept it for what it was and enjoy their time together? She had no reference point. She'd never met someone like Carly before.

In Hershey, on one of the first holes, she had hit a shot out of the bunker that hit the flagstick and dropped a few inches from the hole. Later in the round, when she was in another trap, Carly had smiled at her. "That's a gimme."

And even though Carly had seemed distant on the day of the SAW match, she'd congratulated Paige on the success of SAW and for assembling a great team. She saw Paige's abilities, and appreciated them, and made Paige feel good about herself.

That was a really nice feeling.

In the beginning, Will had been like that. She remembered it well. He'd been so successful, the cocky medic coming into the ER with bloodied gloves squeezing an Ambu bag as he breathed for a trauma patient, barking out a report to anyone in earshot. She couldn't help admiring him—his skill, his confidence, his knowledge. The praise he gave her had seemed so incredible because it was coming from him. Yet as she became more successful, he seemed to have difficulty handling the fact that her star was shining more brightly than his.

She sank into the recliner. How had her life gotten here? Most of the people on the other side of that wall, working their shifts in the ER, had no idea what was going on. They knew her. They knew Will. Yet they thought she was happy with him, and with life in general, and that everything was just perfect in her world. She was such a fraud.

Even the people who knew Will had gone to the cabin with his buddies for the holiday weekend thought that was okay. It was normal for them. Will always did that, and why should they question the norm? Why should it suddenly bother her? She was working this weekend, so why would she care if her husband chose to spend time with his friends? She had no time for him anyway.

Yet she did care. Shouldn't her husband want to be with her? Shouldn't he do things that interested her occasionally? Or even talk of things that interested her? He hadn't once asked about Hershey, or how the first SAW match had turned out. Not even about how she'd played, or the weather, or *anything*. If it didn't directly involve him, he didn't care to know about it. The silence that resulted from the lack of give-and-take was eerie.

Yet, if she skipped a round of golf to spend time with him, or avoided her friends and doted on him, he'd come back to life like a freshly watered plant. She had been playing that game for years now, balancing her own needs with Will's demands. It was exhausting.

Will was smothering her, and if she didn't figure out how to breathe again, she would suffocate. She'd begun to understand that she could never thrive with him, that he would never allow it. She'd begun breaking free, without even understanding what she was doing, when she was still a resident, escaping to New York on Wednesday afternoons to see matinees on Broadway. Next, it was a book club. Then a golf league. Time with Helena and Jules. Now SAW. Inch by inch, she was taking her life back—or perhaps more truthfully, she was creating a new one.

Yet she still had work to do, and she was doing it alone. Even in her darkest times, she'd kept these thoughts to herself. Who could she tell? Her friends were gone. Will's friends were his. Only Helena seemed to understand her relationship with Will, and she was the person Paige was most hesitant to open up to. Helena would tell her the truth about the situation, and tell her what to do, and she would seem even more cowardly when she did nothing but continue to wallow in her misery rather than just see a lawyer and get on with her life.

But what was she waiting for? Financially, she was sure she could make it on her own. Will's money paid his own bills—his truck payment and the payments on his ATV and the cabin. Her salary covered the mortgage on the house, her Jeep, all the bills, and her student loans. She loved her house, but it wouldn't kill her to get something smaller and more affordable if she had to. But she might not even need to sell. Even with all her expenses, she'd still been putting money into a retirement plan and for the trip to Paris. Not a lot, but enough to know she made more than she needed to spend. She wouldn't have a fortune in disposable income, but she'd be okay.

Then she thought of kids. At thirty-two, she wasn't getting any younger. She'd drifted apart from her oldest friends mainly because of geography, but they had kids now, too, adding to the difficulties. What time their careers didn't steal, their children did. Even short conversations on the phone were hard. Yet, even knowing that, she wanted some of her own. If not with Will, then who? It was just one more item on her agenda of troubles.

After brooding for half an hour, she finally decided it was time to get out of the hospital. She had dinner plans with Liza and Mal, and she needed a shower before heading to their place.

Two hours later, she pulled into the driveway of their chalet, greeted by two dancing Labs.

"Fred! Ginger!" Liza called from the deck. "Get back here."

The dogs reluctantly turned, and Paige followed them up the stairs to the deck, where Liza gave her a python hug.

"I miss you! We hardly saw each other at SAW. Is that a rhyme?"

Paige laughed and held out two bottles of wine. "Have you been drinking? Should I take this back?"

She'd brought the Devilry Afoot and told Liza the story of how she and Carly had discovered it. Like Erin, Paige had decided to stock up. She'd had to hunt for it, and it wasn't until the third store she tried that she found a supply. She'd purchased several bottles, because when the sale was over, she'd probably never have it again.

"I can't wait to try it. Shall we?"

Glancing around, she replied. "Why not? Where's Mal?"

"At the grocery store. I just don't feel up to cooking, so she went to pick up everything we need."

Paige felt guilty for intruding. "I'm sorry, Liza. I didn't mean to barge in on your downtime."

"Nonsense. We love seeing you. Mal will put the steaks on, and they'll be done in ten minutes. And we'll eat store-potato salad, and store-macaroni, and store-whatever else she brings."

Paige loved these times with Liza and Mal and had never considered the inconvenience of her company. "We're good-enough friends that you could cancel. No hard feelings. I don't have to see you every time you're in the Pocs."

"But you want to, right?" Liza said as she caught Paige's gaze.

Tilting her head, she shrugged. "Yes, of course. I love you guys."

"I thought so. And we love you, too. So that's settled. If we're here, we expect to see you." Liza gave her a stern look, then softened it with a little smile. "Now let me grab a corkscrew and some glasses."

Paige settled into a comfy chair and thought about Carly. And Liza. And Mal. She adored Liza and Mal, and she had much in common with them. She was very fond of Carly, too, for all the same reasons. If she put it all on paper, it would seem they were equals, offering her the same wonderful gift. Friendship. Yet what was different about Carly?

As she thought of her, she considered the friendship Liza and Mal were developing with Carly. It was totally separate from hers. Carly and Tasha had met Liza in the city for a matinee and been invited to stay at Liza and Mal's Brooklyn house the next weekend, when SAW played there. Were Liza and Mal invited to Carly's party? She couldn't help feeling a little hurt that they didn't mention it. Yet they hadn't talked that much in the past week, either.

A moment after she decided she wouldn't ask, Liza brought it up. Emerging from the house to the deck, she offered Paige a wine goblet. "Are you going to Carly's party tomorrow?"

"Well, I'm working all day."

"It doesn't start until three."

She cleared her throat as Liza poured. "Actually, I wasn't invited."

Liza's dramatic jaw-drop elicited the intended chuckle. "Shut the front door."

Paige shrugged.

"She mentioned that it was women only. And I know you're obviously a woman, but I interpreted that to mean the ladies from my church."

"Your church?" she asked, confused.

"The Lesbeterians."

She chuckled and raised her glass to toast. "To you, for making me laugh."

"That's what I'm here for."

"You've been my angel. Mal, too, but mostly you. You've helped me through a rough transition in my life—out of the darkness. I'm seeing the light again."

Liza sat back as both dogs settled onto the deck beside her chair. They sipped their wine and enjoyed the last minutes of sunshine. It was nearly six, and the evening had already begun to turn cooler. They were both wearing jeans, but Paige would need a sweatshirt soon if they stayed outside.

"Can I ask you a question?" Liza asked after a moment.

"Of course."

"Is Will the darkness in your life, or the light?"

Since the beginning of their friendship, Liza had trod softly on the topic of Will. She'd asked questions but had never probed too deeply, somewhat cautious. She'd asked how they met, and who'd proposed, and where they honeymooned—the superficial stuff like that. Nothing too deep. No questions about their age gap, or salary differential, or their sex life.

"I only ask because I watched you with him the two times we've met him. You're here now, relaxed and laughing with me, and enjoying yourself. That's how you were the first day we met. We started talking, and I felt your energy and your light. You're a positive force. You see the good in people and in the world. And that's been evident every time I've spent time with you—except the times we were with Will."

She tried to listen with an open mind and an open heart. Liza was talking, and Liza cared about her. This wasn't a time to get defensive; it was a time to listen and maybe discuss. Unlike with Helena, who just told her what to do, maybe she could talk to Liza.

"How was I different with him?"

Liza sipped her wine and seemed to ponder the question. "If you are truly yourself with him, then you're pretending with me and Mal. But I fear the opposite is true. You're *you* right now. Relaxed, confident, happy. With *him* you're nervous, like you're afraid of what he's going to do or say. I don't want to use the word controlling, because I don't really think that. You're certainly an independent, free-thinking woman. But I sense Will wants to control you, or has in the past, and you're breaking free. And he's not handling that well."

Now it was her turn to sip her wine, but it was more of a gulp. Liza had nailed that.

"You got all that from spending a couple of hours with him?"

"Well, I talked to Mal. She had a lot to say after fishing with him."

"Really? What happened?"

"Oh, nothing happened. They caught fish. But she got the same impression about him and saw the change in you. It's very evident."

Suddenly the dogs sat up and began barking, then ran in circles as they recognized Mal's SUV.

"I have the garage blocked. Let me move my Jeep," Paige said as she rose from the chaise, thankful for the chance to escape. She needed to dissect Liza's observations—and apparently Mal's too—before she could respond. Or maybe other topics would distract them, and she wouldn't have to answer at all.

"Can I take the dogs with me?"

Liza laughed. "They'll insist."

Paige opened the gate, and the dogs darted down the stairs and greeted Mal. "Hey," Mal said to her, then gave her instructions about where to put her car. A moment later she had re-parked, and carrying her hoodie, she helped Mal with the groceries.

In the kitchen, Liza was in motion, pulling out the things they needed for dinner, putting others away. They decided it was too chilly to eat outside, so Paige set the table in the nook while Mal started on the steaks. "You need one of those patio heaters like they have at fancy restaurants," she said.

"Don't give her any ideas," Mal answered from the deck.

They continued talking while the steaks cooked, and Mal poured herself a glass of wine. "Paige, this wine is really good," Mal said as she took her first sip. "Maybe we can take this to Carly's tomorrow. She said BYOB." Mal looked at Paige, and she tried to keep her expression neutral, but she must have failed.

"What's that look?" Mal asked.

"I didn't make the cut. I'm not invited to the party."

Mal swiftly recovered. "Oh. That's not surprising. I think she probably only invited—"

"Lesbeterians?"

Mal nodded. "Exactly. Carly strikes me as a very private person. I think she keeps a few friends, and that's it."

Paige thought the opposite. It seemed that Carly had a million friends. "I thought I'd become one of them," she said before she could stop the words from escaping her lips.

Mal sighed. "It's tough. You're kind of standing on the fringe of our world, and everyone loves you, but they know you're straight. Some people would just like to keep their worlds separate. Family over here. Work over there. Gay life in another place. Less problems that way."

Liza chimed in. "How old is Carly? Our age, I think. Mid-forties. She's been around long enough to remember what it was like when people were afraid for their jobs and families disowned their children. I'd say you're right. Carly is cautious."

She couldn't argue. She'd never walked in Carly's shoes, and even though she'd always lived in a world where many people were out, that didn't mean it was accepted.

"I was just thinking about Carly. What you said."

"Don't let it get to you. Really, it's no big deal. Or is it? Do we have to be worried about next weekend? It's a small house."

Mal was referring to the Brooklyn SAW weekend. Five of them— Carly and Tasha, as well as Paige, Helena, and Jules were planning to stay with them.

"No. It'll be fine."

"Have we figured out where Paige's going to sleep?" Mal asked Liza.

They had three bedrooms and the ability to sleep four. Paige was the fifth houseguest, and they'd talked about taking the air mattress from the Pocono house back to New York for her to sleep on during her stay. Truthfully, it didn't matter to her. She would have been happy in a sleeping bag on the floor. Yet to Liza and Mal it was a big deal, so she was just letting them figure it out.

"Let's take the air mattress, and we'll have it just in case."

"Whatever, guys. No worries. I just hope it's not too hot Friday. I don't want to be all sweaty and disgusting after golf and then head to the theater."

"Hold that thought," Mal instructed her, and she went back outside to check the grill. Paige sat at the table, still musing a little, until Mal returned in a few minutes with the steaks, and they dug in. She was happy to have the conversation turn from Carly and her party this weekend to the upcoming SAW tournament and their night at the theater. It gave her something to think about besides Carly and why she'd suddenly shut her out of her life.

❖

Carly pulled her SUV into the driveway and looked over at Tasha in the passenger seat. "Can you put the ice in the guest-house freezer? And the alcohol in the fridge? Everything else can come inside."

"Okay."

They'd called a truce a few days after the Hershey trip and were nearly back to normal. Tasha seemed like her usual self, anyway. Carly was another story. She'd spent anxious days avoiding Paige, and sleepless nights thinking of her. She missed her. They'd become friends. Good friends. And Carly felt empty without her in her life. It was a little less warm and sunny than it had been, and she wasn't sure what to do about it. It was only the promise that she'd keep her distance from Paige that was salvaging her lifelong friendship with Tasha.

She and Tasha had spent the afternoon shopping for their annual Memorial Day bash, and Tasha planned to spend the night so they could get things ready for the next day. It wasn't a fancy party, by any means, but Tasha loved to entertain, and her attention to detail was famous. The serving bowls were made of crystal, and they used real utensils. Food and condiment arrangements were designed as if the display would be featured in a magazine. It all made Tasha happy, so Carly let it go. This year, especially, she didn't want to piss her off.

She had been planning to invite Paige to the party. Although the guest list was composed of mostly gay women, she always invited the people from her office. They arrived early, ate some food, and politely escaped by late afternoon. And even though Paige didn't know anyone at Becker Realty, she did know some of her friends from SAW and her other golf league. Liza and Mal would be there, as well as Reese and

Ella and Alex and Britain. And besides, Paige could talk to anyone, and Carly had no doubt she would have had a good time.

Except she was blackballed. Because of one little starlit night of coffee and conversation, and a stroll through the Hershey Gardens, Tasha had this crazy idea in her head and had warned Carly *again* about their budding friendship. So, even though Carly knew Tasha was overreacting, she did the prudent thing and spent her week avoiding Paige.

Hoisting a half-dozen Wegman's bags, Carly headed toward the door, deposited them, and went back to reload. When she returned, her phone was ringing. Reese.

"Hi, Reese."

"Hi, there. I bet you're up to your eyeballs in meatballs and such."

"Just about."

"I'm calling to cancel. It looks like I have strep. Cass, too. Ella will probably fall by the morning."

Carly paused so she could pay Reese more attention. "It sounds dreadful. Do you need some food?"

"We probably couldn't swallow it. But I ordered a tray of pretzels for the party. Do you think you can swing by to pick it up? It's already paid for."

"Oh, that was nice of you. I'll figure it out."

"Super. And can you let Tasha know? I called, but she didn't answer. The three o'clock doctor today is going to stay until three a.m., and then Paige's going to come in four hours early for the dayshift tomorrow, so everything is covered at the hospital tonight. After I get some antibiotics in me, I'll probably be okay for tomorrow night."

"Okay, Reese. I'll let Tasha know. And feel better."

Carly met Tasha in the driveway, and they carried in the last of the food as she told her about Reese's illness. "Those two doctors are good eggs. It makes my life easier when they help each other out."

Carly thought about the situation for a moment. Paige *was* a good egg. She was kind and considerate. And Carly had been treating her badly. It was the best way she knew to keep her at the safe distance she needed to make sure the friendly feelings she had didn't morph into something more substantial. Tasha was right about her. She didn't always act prudently when it came to women. And in this case, if she and

Paige misbehaved, the consequence would be great. It could damage Tasha's professional relationship with an important employee. More importantly, it would rob Carly of a friend she had come to treasure.

But she was acting like a jerk. Paige had called and sent a dozen texts during the week, and Carly hadn't had the decency to return them. She'd tried to avoid the situation, hoping it would go away. If Paige didn't know about the party, she wouldn't have to explain why she wasn't invited, right?

Now Paige had to work two consecutive twelve-hour shifts in the ER, and she probably wouldn't have been able to come to the party anyway. Somehow, the thought didn't make her feel any better about blackballing Paige. Not at all.

"Tash," Carly said softly as she stopped to look at her friend. "We have to talk about Paige."

"What?" Tasha said, sounding impatient.

"She's a good person, and I like her. I think you're being unfair to me. To both of us. I think she enjoys spending time with me as much as I do her. But because of this idea you have in your head, you want us to end our friendship. It just doesn't seem right."

Tasha pursed her lips and squinted. "Did you invite her to the party?"

Carly shook her head. "Per your request, I haven't spoken to her since Hershey."

Tasha leaned against the counter and looked at her. "You're in love with her."

Carly shrugged but didn't deny it. She wasn't sure what this was, because she'd never experienced anything like it. But her absence from Paige had made her feel a sadness that she hadn't known since the last time she was in love, so it was quite possible that Tasha was right.

"I thought nothing was going on," Tasha said.

She shook her head again. "Oh, nothing is. For the first time in my life, I'm behaving. But you're asking me to sacrifice something—someone—who's very important to me. And I will do it, because of how important you are. But I shouldn't have to."

"She's married, Carly."

"Yes, but she's not happy. And I think she's gay."

"So you're going to what—show her the ropes? Hold her hand while she cries over her husband? What?"

"I don't know, Tash. Whatever she needs."

"This is fucking crazy."

She swallowed and looked past Tasha, out the window to the lake. The sun was sinking low in the cloudless blue sky, and she knew the sunset would be spectacular. The forecast for tomorrow was as good as she could hope for in May, and their party would be the smash it always was. Even so, she wasn't excited about hosting her friends for what was always a great day. She was sad and knew in her heart that none of her friends could lift her spirits. No amount of alcohol and no hookup would turn this around. The only balm for her aching heart was Paige.

"Tasha, I know I'm imperfect. And I know how strange my relationship with Paige must seem to you. Hell, I don't completely understand it. I just know that I feel good when I'm with her."

"This can't end well."

She dwelled for a moment, thinking about that statement. She'd been searching for something that had eluded her for years, and she'd found it in Paige. Now she was lost again. This was not such a good ending, either.

Tasha looked at her. "You have to give her space, Carly. She has to figure out what she wants. Otherwise, you'll just be the sordid affair that ended her marriage, the one she talks about with the woman she settles down with in a few years."

"I know, Tash," she said. She did know that, but it didn't make it any easier.

CHAPTER FIFTEEN

B & B (BROOKLYN & BROADWAY)

It was almost midnight when Paige walked into the doctors' lounge after her Thursday-afternoon shift in the ER. She'd never expected to get out of work early, but that didn't stop her from hoping she'd at least leave on time. As it stood, she'd have about five hours of sleep before the trip to Brooklyn. According to Liza, Carly and Tasha were planning to drive today, and Paige wished she'd been able to switch things at work so she could have done that. The trip to New York in the morning would be stressful, and if they hit traffic…Paige didn't even want to think about it.

After changing into her street clothes, she threw her backpack over her shoulder and headed toward the security desk in the lobby. Her favorite security guard offered her a big smile, then left his post and escorted her to the parking lot.

It wasn't until she plugged her phone into her car's auxiliary port that she noticed the text from Carly.

Please call me after work. It's important.

The text was sent at ten o'clock, so Paige assumed Carly knew she was working late. Past Carly's normal bedtime. She pressed the call icon and dialed Carly as she navigated the parking garage.

"Hey, Paige." Carly's greeting was casual, as if they'd just spoken a few hours ago, instead of two weeks. As if Carly hadn't spent all that time avoiding her.

Okay, then. "Hi, Carly. How are you?" Paige congratulated herself for not asking about the party, for keeping her tone friendly rather than bitchy.

"Good, thanks. But actually, not good. Here's the situation. Tasha and I were supposed to drive to Brooklyn tonight, but she has some sort of emergency at work. She's not going to be able to make it to SAW. I'm not thrilled about navigating the streets of Brooklyn by myself. Tasha usually drives when we go to New York, but Liza told me you've been there before, so I was hoping I could follow you in the morning."

For an instant, Paige wondered about the emergency at the hospital. She hadn't heard any rumors. But of course, she worked in the ER, not the executive suite, and didn't know everything that was happening. Turning her attention back to Carly, she kept her tone neutral, trying to hide the happiness, the relief she felt that Carly had finally called. "Of course. But you don't have to drive. You can just come with us. Helena's driving, and she has an SUV. We have plenty of room."

"Uh, well." Carly paused for a second. "Here's the thing. I'm a bit of a control freak and don't like being without my car. It would make me nervous. So do you mind if I just follow you?"

"No worries." They agreed on a meeting place, and Paige thought about the call long after they'd disconnected. Once again, Carly had been all business. What had changed? Whatever it was, whatever had happened, she refused to let it bother her. Carly could follow them to Brooklyn, and she'd see her at golf. Was she even coming to Liza and Mal's, or had that plan changed, too? At this point, she really didn't care. As the chairperson of the Scranton SAW, she felt obligated to be cordial, but that was it. She was done with being friendly to Carly.

This weekend was about spending time with her sister and her niece, about playing golf and seeing a show on Broadway with two good friends. She was simply not going to give Carly another thought.

She thought of nothing and no one else for the duration of the trip home and in her kitchen while a slice of bread toasted. Who are you kidding? she finally asked the reflection in her bathroom mirror.

Carly was a part of her now. Her friend. And the sudden withdrawal of that friendship left an ache in her that wouldn't be so easily soothed. She'd try, though, because it was clear that she had no choice.

A few minutes later, freshly showered but overwhelmingly sad, she crawled into bed and fell asleep.

Waiting in the parking lot of the doughnut shop, Carly sipped her coffee and scanned the passing cars, willing herself to relax. The fingers tapping the center console of her car were telling, and she sat on her hand to quiet them.

Why did this woman affect her so? Avoiding Paige hadn't helped, and now Carly feared seeing her. Would Paige be angry? The night before, the conversation had been focused on formalities, with none of the personal interplay they usually shared. Maybe they were both tired, but she was too smart to believe that lie. She had put up roadblocks in their friendship, deliberately shut Paige out and pushed her away, and now she had to face the consequences.

When Tasha had planned to make the trip to Brooklyn, Carly hadn't been so worried. They could have opted out of the gathering at Liza and Mal's house and, instead, stayed in a hotel. They'd done that many times, and it would have been fine. Now Tasha was embroiled in a sexual-harassment claim at the hospital, meeting with employees and lawyers and board members. Now, she had no buffer, no one she could cling to in order to avoid Paige. She was going to have to face her. Her lifelong strategy of avoidance wouldn't work this time.

The ringing phone interrupted her thoughts. Jules.

"Good morning," she answered.

"Hi, Carly. I heard you're following us to New York. I thought I might come with you instead of my mom. To keep you company."

She couldn't help smiling. Like her aunt, Jules just did that to her. Still, Carly had been planning to get some work done on the trip. "I'm a big girl, Jules. I'll be fine. I plan to make some work calls from the car, and I'm sure they would just bore you."

When Jules didn't reply, Carly wondered if the connection had been lost. After a moment, Jules spoke again. "Who are you going to call at seven a.m.?"

"My personal assistant."

"You have a personal assistant? How cool."

"It is pretty cool." Carly thought of Dominica and said a silent prayer of thanks for her mother figure.

"How about if Paige drives with you?"

Carly paused. She wasn't ready to spend time alone with Paige. But what would a little company hurt? Maybe if Jules was with them, it wouldn't be so nerve-racking. "Okay, Jules. Why don't you both come with me?"

"We're pulling in now."

Carly saw a black Lexus arrive, and Paige waved to her from the front seat as the rear passenger door opened, and Jules hopped out. She ran to Carly's car and flopped into the front seat, in a movement that reminded Carly of Paige.

Carly quickly hid her disappointment that Paige had elected to ride with Helena.

"Krispy Kreme?" Carly asked as she pointed to the box on the backseat.

"No, thanks. We ate."

Helena pulled out of the parking lot, and Carly fell in behind her. "So what's new in your life?" she asked.

"Well, I graduate next week, so this is sort of a pre-graduation present. New York, that is. I can't decide which show to see. What do you think?"

She had been thinking of getting out of New York right after golf. As much as she enjoyed Liza and Mal's company, she'd enjoyed it as part of her relationship with Tasha. She didn't want to be a third wheel with them, which was why she hadn't made the trip to Brooklyn last night. And under the circumstances, she certainly didn't want to spend any more time with Paige than she had to. "What have you seen?"

"On Broadway?"

Carly nodded, and Jules rattled off a list of the perennial favorites. *Phantom*, *Lion King*, *Wicked*.

"Why don't you pull up the list of musicals, and we can talk about them. Although I'm not planning to stay tonight." She'd brought an overnight bag, just in case, but she really didn't think she'd need it.

"What? You can't come that close to Broadway and not see a show. It's almost criminal."

She agreed, though her attraction to Paige was even more almost-criminal. "It would be a shame, wouldn't it?" she asked. How had that slipped out?

"It's settled then."

Changing the subject, she asked Jules about her upcoming trip. "When do you leave?"

"Which trip?"

"Oh, that's right. You're quite the cosmopolitan young lady, aren't you? I guess you can tell me about both of them. We're going to be in this car for a long time."

"Well, the big news is about Paris. Have you been there?"

Thinking the story about Myron was a bit heavy for the day, she shook her head. "No. But I've always wanted to go."

"Oh. My. God. This is perfect. Like an omen. You have to come to Paris!"

"I do, do I?"

"Yes. Well, that's my news. My friend Melody, who I've known forever, is also going on the trip. She went last year, too, and she loved it so much she's going again. So she asked if we could room together, which, quite honestly, would probably be more fun than rooming with my aunt. So, I need to find Paige a roommate."

Carly bit her lip, debating her response. It wasn't about going to Paris—that wasn't going to happen, no matter how much she wanted to go. But how could Jules just discard Paige like that? "How does Paige feel about this news?" She couldn't help feeling defensive on Paige's behalf, but she tried to keep her tone neutral.

"Oh, she won't care. We'll still do all the tours and stuff together. Besides—Paige's sort of used to being alone."

"Really?" Carly asked, wanting to know the more private details about Paige that only someone like Jules could tell her. It wasn't as if she had to search hard for information. Jules just seemed to purge data.

"Oh, yes. You know, my mom is so much older, and my grandparents both worked, so she sort of had the run of the house. And Will—that's her husband—he has a fishing cabin in the mountains, and he goes there all the time. So she spends a lot of time by herself. She's fond of her own company."

Carly sighed. "I see," she said, although she really didn't. There was an awful lot about Paige she didn't know. It sounded like Jules had it all figured out though, so who was she to question her?

"Tell me more about the trip," she said after a minute. Not that Carly was thinking of going, because she wasn't. A week in the same hotel room with anyone would be a challenge, but with someone as attractive as Paige, it was impossible. No matter what she'd told Tasha, she was human.

"You'll come?" Jules asked excitedly. "That would be so great. Paige will have someone to hang out with beside those stuffy history-department people."

Carly chuckled. "I didn't say I'd come with you. I just want to know about the trip."

"Well, I don't actually know much. But it's Paris! What else do you need to know?"

Indeed. She knew the most important things. It was *Paris*, one of the few places on the planet she longed to visit and hadn't.

The ringing of her phone interrupted her thoughts. "This is my personal assistant," she informed Jules. "I need to take the call."

"No problem." Jules whipped out her own phone.

"Good morning," Carly said as she pressed the button on the steering wheel and connected Dominica.

"Good morning," she replied. "I see you left me some work. Will you be available for a little while, or should I email you later when I have more information?"

Carly had stopped by the office before the trip and left a list for Dominica. Nothing was pressing, and she told her that. "I'll catch up with you on Monday."

"Are you on your way?" she asked.

"Yes. We left a little while ago."

"Give Tasha my love."

Carly told her about Tasha's change of plans and about her new traveling companion. "She wants an administrative assistant, too, but I told her it's a bad idea, that you're always bossing me around."

"Huh!"

"Really?" Jules said. "Do you boss her around? Tell her she should come to Paris with me!"

"Paris?" Dominica asked. "You're thinking of Paris?"

"No, I'm not," Carly said.

"But she should be," Jules said.

"Yes, she should be."

"Are you two conspiring against me?" Carly asked. "Because, you don't even know each other. And Dominica, there goes your postcard from Brooklyn."

"I'll live. Jules, when's Paris? I'm going to put it on Carly's calendar."

Jules gave her the dates.

"Thank you, Jules. Can you share your email with me, in case I have questions?"

Jules gave her the address, as well as her phone number.

"What just happened?" Carly asked when she disconnected the call.

"I think you just booked a trip to Paris."

"I don't know about that. But it'll amuse Dominica for a little while. She's got two bad knees and hasn't been able to travel for years, so she loves to help me plan my adventures."

"How old is she?"

"Ninety."

"Ninety? No way."

"No. Just kidding. She's almost seventy, though."

Although she enjoyed Jules's company when they'd been together, and she'd talked to her on the phone, Carly was surprised when she began to see signs for New York City. The two-hour trip had seemed like minutes as they discussed everything from their mutual travels to careers to theater to movies. Jules's age was sometimes evident in her viewpoints, but she was surprisingly mature. Delightfully so.

Traffic grew heavier as they approached New York, but Helena seemed mindful of Carly following and stuck to one lane until she had to merge or exit. Before long, they were crossing the Verrazano-Narrows Bridge and zigzagging through Brooklyn to the golf course.

It was Carly's second SAW tournament, so she knew what to expect, yet she was a little jittery as she left her clubs at the bag drop. They were early, so she stretched her legs and enjoyed the view, while Helena and Jules chatted, and Paige took care of business.

Even though she chose to live in the country, Carly loved the city. Where else could she choose from a million different restaurants or live entertainment to suit whatever her mood? The architecture was amazing, and every time she looked at the Empire State Building, she imagined the wonder of constructing it a hundred years ago. Even the noise and the traffic didn't bother her all that much. They were signs of life, the stop-and-go of cars, the pulse beating through the body of land.

As she looked around the Dyker Beach course, marveling at the blend of the two forces she so loved—the magnificent, brilliant architecture of the bridge and the city it represented, to the cocoon of peace in the middle of it—she felt alive. The blood in her veins was suddenly palpable. And then it coursed even more as she noticed Paige, her head tilted just a few degrees as she walked toward her, laughing at something Mallory said.

What an enigma she was. So seemingly comfortable with women yet committed to a man. Friends. They could be friends. Carly liked her—more than she could ever recall liking anyone. Even Tasha and Pip, who she adored, annoyed her at times. The only thing about Paige that annoyed her was the fact that she liked her so much.

Paige and Mal separated with a hug, and Paige looked around, seeming startled when she saw Carly watching her. Another smile lit her face, and Carly wasn't surprised at all when Paige walked her way. "Not much of a course compared to Hershey, huh?"

Carly shrugged. She was the snob, not Paige, but she hadn't held high hopes for Dyker Beach. Other than the name, which she found incredibly amusing, she hadn't read much about the golf course to inspire her. Yet, as she glanced once again at the bridge, she realized at that moment she hadn't come to this particular place just to play golf. She was in New York, and Paige was with her. That fact excited her so much more than the promise of pristine fairways and lightning-quick greens ever could.

It had been a miserable, self-imposed torture, avoiding Paige. Cowardly. She'd spent two weeks at it, just because she didn't want to aggravate Tasha. Instead, she'd aggravated herself, because she missed Paige. The days without her had been somehow less warm and sunny, less light. And Carly had wilted during that time. Now, as Paige stood before her, holding no grudge, she felt alive again.

"How was the drive?" she asked. "Did my niece talk your ear off?"

Carly relaxed as she leaned against her car, so relieved that they were speaking again. It was like nothing had happened. "Let's say I didn't get any work done."

Paige nodded. "She does have that effect on people."

Should she talk to Paige about Paris? Not that she wanted to go—well, she did want to go—but not with Paige. She wanted to go with a lover, to capture the magic she'd been dreaming of for years. When she thought of it, that's why she'd never gone back. In a dozen trips to Europe since her time in Nice, she'd circled Paris, never quite getting there. Now she finally realized she was saving it. Paris was the City of Light, the place of romance and passion. It was not a place to go with a friend like Tasha or a group of college students. It's where you go with your soul mate, so you can wander along the Seine holding hands and stare from her eyes to the Eiffel Tower and back. Nope. Definitely not a trip for friends. Absolutely not a trip she should take with Paige.

But as her friend, shouldn't Carly tell her about Jules's plan? Didn't she have a right to know? Biting her lip, Carly pushed the thought aside. It was a problem for another day.

"I find her adorable."

"So, have you heard from the rest of our group? I tried calling from the road, but no one answered."

"They supposedly came yesterday, so I would hope they'll be here soon. Did you decide on teams yet?"

"I wanted to talk to you. I'd love to play in a foursome with you and Helena and Jules, but they're not good golfers. Would that bother you?"

She shook her head. "Not at all." She would rather play with weaker golfers who were pleasant human beings than the ladies who acted like they'd lost the LPGA Championship with each missed putt.

Paige nodded. "Perfect. I'm going in to deliver the pairings list. And even if the rest of the team doesn't show up, we can still compete."

She didn't care if they won. It didn't matter. "I agree."

The rest of their team did show up, right on time, and she found herself in the cart beside Paige as they drove to the eighth hole, where they started. The course was in better shape than she'd hoped for, and she shared that news with Paige. "Hey. We're not working, we're with nice people, and we're going to Broadway tonight. What's to complain about?"

She'd known the ladies in the group behind them for many years and was certain they'd find plenty to complain about. That was just one more reason she was happy to be playing with Paige. She was just so easy to be with.

The round of golf was fun, and she smiled constantly as she watched Paige play. She wasn't a great golfer and had no ability at all to hit the green from the fairway, but she approached each shot with optimism, measuring distances and choosing clubs carefully. Still, she didn't hold up play, didn't curse or throw clubs when her shots turned out differently than she hoped. Helena and Jules were truly awful golfers but were happy to be out together, and Carly felt all the sadness of the last weeks melt away as she basked in the sunshine and enjoyed their company.

And somehow, during the drive and the golf, Carly made the unconscious decision to stay with the group at Liza and Mal's. The threesome was great fun. Their affection for each other was obvious, but their humor was contagious. She laughed with them and realized she'd never had so much fun on the golf course. She'd deal with Tasha in due time, but today, she planned to enjoy herself. Today, and tonight, she was going to make up for what she'd missed during the two weeks of self-imposed abstinence from Paige.

The clubhouse was surprisingly well appointed, the food excellent. After they learned their team had finished a disappointing fourteenth, they politely left and headed to Liza and Mal's. It was a quick trip to Church Avenue. The weather had been pleasant, partly sunny and seventy degrees, and Carly was thankful it hadn't been blazing hot, because they had no time for a shower before they headed back out. They talked as they walked the few blocks to the train station, mostly about what show they'd see.

Resigned to the fact that the group might choose something she'd already seen, she listened to the discussion rather than adding to it. She took advantage of the moment to study the people, most dressed in office attire, hurrying along balancing briefcases and cell phones as they weaved through the foot traffic.

After a long block, Paige seemed to notice her and eased closer. "Not quite Clarks Summit, is it?"

She had been thinking the same thing. "No, it isn't."

"So what show would you like to see?"

"It doesn't matter. I'm in New York, we're going to see one, and I get to spy on all these fascinating people. It's amazing." She smiled at Paige, thinking of the fun they'd had on the beach playing this same game.

"Who's caught your eye?" Paige asked surreptitiously as she slowly turned her head, scanning the crowd. A few strands of hair fell forward, and she brushed them back before she deposited her finger beneath her chin and made a comical expression.

"Well, how about that lady? She's like a juggler," Carly said as she motioned with her chin toward a woman pushing a stroller and pulling a second child behind her. Somehow, she had a briefcase looped over her arm in the same hand that held a Dunkin' cup, her phone wedged between her ear and her shoulder.

Paige followed Carly's gaze and laughed. She tended to do that a lot with Carly, and it felt so damn good. Why couldn't she feel like this with Will? Shaking off the thought, she shrugged. The woman was indeed a juggler, and Paige only wondered how she pushed the stroller with one hand. Personally, she needed two hands to guide wheelchairs through the halls of the ER toward the X-ray department, and that was under ideal circumstances. This woman's performance was Olympic caliber. "I hope that Dunkin's a double. She looks like she needs it."

Carly chuckled, and her deep, throaty voice gave Paige pause yet again. "Indeed. So what's the verdict on the show?"

"I think we'll see what we can get at the half-price-ticket booth. Then let Jules decide, because she's never really done this before."

"That's a great idea. Some of the best shows are the ones you'd never go to if you had to order the tickets ahead of time."

"Exactly."

They reached the Church Avenue train station and descended into the earth, using Mal and Liza's transit cards to pass through the turnstiles. Once on the platform, they waited only a few minutes for the F train into Manhattan. She and Carly continued people-watching, offering hushed comments about the bizarre clothing and hairstyles they observed.

"I think you'd own that look, Carly," she said as she moved close to Carly's ear and whispered. "On the right. In the red."

Carly looked up to the ceiling of the train, studied a poster of the transit map, and then casually turned her head to the right. The woman in question, a twenty-something with a head full of eighties-ish high hair, wore a clinging, spaghetti-strap dress that started around her nipples and stopped at the upper thigh.

Just as slowly as she'd reconnoitered the woman, Carly turned back toward her. "She's not a genuine blonde. I can tell by the pubic hair."

Before the laugh exploded from her, the train lurched, and she was tossed against Carly. Their eyes met, and then they both laughed as they tried to hold each other upright.

"What's going on?" Liza demanded as she stepped into their space.

Paige met her eyes and saw a few other people looking their way, including the blonde. She smiled at everyone. "We'll tell you later."

They were quiet for the rest of the train ride, and then when they walked out into the late-June night, Paige felt a change in the air. It had been a warm afternoon in Brooklyn, but it was still spring, and she immediately reached for the sweater in her draw-string bag.

Weaving through the crowd, they made their way to Broadway and joined the queue at the ticket booth. Once again, she seemed to gravitate toward Carly, and when they all huddled, talking, Jules called them on it.

"You two seem to have gotten really close."

The comment made her feel uncomfortable. Defensive. She shifted her weight, creating an inch of space between them. "I guess. We've spent a lot of time getting this SAW stuff organized."

She nodded. "It's good. You have a lot in common."

She forced a smile, aware of Carly's sudden silence.

"So, I was thinking that Carly should come to Paris with us. Because, you know, my friend Melody is coming, and that would work out with the roommate situation. I could room with Mel, and you and Carly could stay together."

Paige didn't quite know what to say. Jules tended to make her dizzy with a continuous flow of ideas and thoughts and opinions, but this was totally unexpected. She didn't even really want to go to Paris and was still saving money for the trip. She was going for Jules. And now, Jules was ditching her before they even left US soil. And the idea of rooming with Carly—that made her anxious for all sorts of other reasons.

"Wow. When did this happen?" she asked, trying to buy time while she formulated a more thoughtful response as she looked from Jules to Carly. Carly's expression was neutral, though Jules was wearing a dazzling smile.

"Oh, just last week," Jules said indifferently. "It's no biggie."

"Okay, sure," she responded, nodding and smiling to cover her anxiety and disappointment. "I can see why you might want to room with someone your own age. But Carly?" she asked. "When did you decide to join the tour?"

Shaking her head, Carly reached out and grabbed her above the elbow. "No. I haven't made that decision. In fact, Jules just threw it at me in the car this morning."

Paige tried to hide the sadness that suddenly coursed through her. No, she hadn't wanted to go to Paris. But now that she'd committed to it, she'd begun to enjoy the idea of the trip. She was looking forward to getting away, to experiencing some culture and food and wine, and perhaps even some good company. But if that wasn't what Jules wanted, maybe it would be better if she just bowed out.

"I don't have to go, Jules," she said, careful to maintain a neutral tone, a blank face. "It's okay if you want to be with your friends."

Jules's mouth flew open. "No. That's not it! I want to be with you, Paige. We'll do everything together, I swear. It'll just be different rooms at the hotel."

They reached the marquee, and the group began buzzing about the offerings, but she held back, the rejection from her niece suddenly deflating her mood.

"Teenagers," Carly said as she squeezed her again, in the same ticklish place above her elbow.

Even now, the contact with Carly caused the butterflies to begin their ballet in her stomach, and Paige searched her eyes. This time, the veil slipped, and she saw Carly's concern.

"It'll work out," Carly whispered, still holding on to her arm.

Sucking in a breath, she nodded and stayed close to Carly while the others studied the options. After deciding on *Tootsie*, Liza stayed in line for the tickets while the rest of them stepped aside. "You're not mad, are you?" Jules asked.

She looked down at her niece. Jules eyes were opened wide, as if surprised, but her mouth was pinched closed. Worried. Jules was worried. What should she say? Mad? No. Sad, yes. Disappointed? Ditto. But the trip was about Jules, and Paige was the adult, so maybe she should act like it. "No. It's okay. I'm just switching gears here. I'm sure you'll let me know the plan."

Jules sprang at her and wrapped her arms around her neck, then repeated her reaction with Carly. She smiled as she noticed Carly's hands hovering somewhere between mid-air and Jules, but then Jules was gone again, talking to Mallory and her mother.

"It's going to be fine," Carly said. "Even if you room alone. It's Paris, for Christ's sake. How bad could it be?"

Chapter Sixteen

The Woman in Gold

As Paige came out of the bathroom a few hours later, Carly was waiting on one of the two beds in the spare room. "You should sleep with me," she said, then laughed at her own words. "In this room. There's a bed, which usually beats a couch."

"I don't know. It seems like a comfy couch."

Carly shrugged. "Up to you."

It was after one, and Paige was beat, too tired to feel excited about sleeping in the same room as Carly. Certainly too tired to debate the topic. They'd stopped at a French restaurant for dessert crepes after the show, and the subject of Paris had come up again. Liza was the instigator this time, and neither she nor Carly nor Jules had mentioned the addition of Jules's friend to the traveling party. But the crepes had been delicious and stirred Paige's imagination about a café along the Seine, about all the things she'd been daydreaming of since she'd committed to the trip. Carly seemed to sense her drifting and tapped her fork against Carly's coffee cup.

They were seated across the table from each other, and Carly's dark eyes were twinkling when Paige looked into them. "Wanna switch?" she asked as she pointed to Paige's plate.

"How's yours?" she asked suspiciously.

"Decadent."

"Then why do you want to switch?"

"Yours might be better, but I'll never know unless I try it."

She pushed her plate in Carly's direction. "Yours might be better," she said as she pulled Carly's plate closer.

Cutting a piece of baked apple and caramel, she waited for Carly to do the same. "Ready?" she asked. When Carly nodded, Paige put the fork to her mouth and moaned at the first taste.

"This is better," she said.

Carly shook her head, closed her eyes, and licked her lips. After a moment, she opened her eyes again. "I don't think so. The chocolate and banana flavors are fantastic."

She smiled. "Then I guess everyone is happy."

Afterward, they walked to the train, talking about the show. It wasn't her favorite, but as Liza said, it beat sitting home.

At the moment, sitting home sounded really good to her, or at least collapsing onto that bed Carly mentioned. She had been up for twenty hours and was tired. Jules and Helena were already tucked in, and Liza and Mal had just bid them good night. It was time.

"Okay," she said, unsure why she'd hesitated in the first place. Sleeping on the couch had been her only option when Tasha was on the guest list, but since she'd canceled, it made perfect sense for her to sleep in the spare bedroom with Carly.

With Carly. Normally, that would excite her, but exhaustion had dulled her senses.

She settled into the comfortable bed and sighed.

"Tired?" Carly asked.

"It was a long day."

"It was."

"Do you have to work when you get home?"

Carly stared into the darkness and sighed, too. Thankfully, she didn't. In fact, she'd been contemplating taking a hotel room in Manhattan on Saturday night, maybe seeing another show or going to a museum. "No. Becker has a few open houses this weekend, but none are mine." She thought of the days when she first established her little one-room office, when all the listings were hers. Paige's follow-up question made her laugh as she asked if Carly ever helped out. "I was just thinking about that," she said. "Not very often anymore."

"Why not?" Paige asked, and Carly explained how she'd started the agency while working full-time as a clerk in a doctor's office. The days were long, but as the business grew, she hired associates whom she relied on to do more and more of the work she'd once handled. Although she still loved that part of her job, running the business was a time-consuming endeavor that chewed up hours of every day.

Paige told Carly how she'd decided on the ER for her career, and Carly found herself asking questions, wanting to know more about Paige. Paige told her about her college job and meeting her husband, then moving back after she finished her residency.

"Am I boring you?" Paige asked when Carly yawned.

"Talk of men always bores me."

Paige laughed. "No alarms tomorrow. But will I find you gone in the morning, out watching the sunrise over Manhattan?"

Carly chuckled. "It's tempting. But I think I'd rather sleep."

"Do you watch the sunrise over the lake?"

"All the time. But my sunsets are better." Then she forgot herself and nearly invited Paige to the lake to watch one with her. "Just the angle of my house. It faces more toward the west."

"I want to see one. I'll bet it's beautiful. But now we should go to sleep."

"Yeah, we should. It was a long short week," Carly replied, her voice almost a whisper as well.

"Huh?"

"A *long* short week. Only three days, because of the holiday and this trip. But I still crammed five days of work into it."

"Gotcha. That's what I do when I need a day off in the ER—I just pick up a day someplace else on the schedule. Are you busy at work? Is this a busy time?"

"I always find something to do, even when I'm not busy. But yes, this is a crazy time at work."

"I'm glad you took the time off to come to SAW."

"Yeah, me, too. It was a nice round of golf."

"It was. The show—eh. Just okay."

Carly sighed. "I've seen better."

Paige wanted to keep talking, tried to keep her eyes open, but soon found them too heavy, and when she opened them again it was morning. Late, she guessed, by the brightness of the sun peeking around the blinds. Carly's bed was not only empty, but she'd fixed the blankets as well, and if she hadn't spotted Carly's carpetbag there, she might have thought she'd imagined the night before.

After using the bathroom, Paige headed downstairs. The wonderful smells of bacon and coffee greeted her as she found Liza in the kitchen. "Your timing is perfect. Help me carry this out to the terrace."

"Oh, wow," Paige said as she hoisted a tray with coffee mugs, a pot, and a variety of creamers. Liza carried a similar one, stacked with food.

"Good morning, everyone," Paige said as she pushed through the door and held it for Liza.

"You're alive!" Helena said. "I was debating waking you. I know you like to sleep."

"I guess I needed it."

After pouring her coffee, she accepted a plate from Mal loaded with a French-toast casserole, bacon, and fruit. "It looks great," she said. "Thank you so much."

"Yes. Thanks again for hosting us," Helena chimed in.

"I wish you could stay. We hardly had any time together."

"My husband can't handle more than one night without me," Helena said, and Paige knew she was serious.

"What about you?" Liza asked as she looked at Paige. "You're off from work, and your husband's off killing fish or something. Why don't you stay another day? We'll put you on a bus tomorrow and send you back to the mountains. Or better yet, Carly, you stay, too. You can drive home together."

Paige was about to decline when Carly answered. "I'm thinking about it. I don't want to leave with *Tootsie* on my brain. I have to replace it with a newer, better memory of Broadway."

They all laughed. "It was a pretty lame show. But that's a perfect plan," Liza said.

"Paige, that sounds great. You should stay," Helena said, and she gave Paige a look she couldn't quite read. It was part older, bossy sister and part sympathy, mixed with something else entirely.

Liza was right, of course. She didn't have anything to rush home to. Her parents, home from Florida for the summer, played golf on Sunday mornings, so they'd have their dinner late in the day. Will was gone. Why not stay in New York an extra day? She'd spend some time with her friends, maybe see another show, and drive home with Carly. Yeah. Staying was definitely the better choice.

"Carly?" she asked as she looked at her. "Could I hitch a ride with you tomorrow?"

Carly didn't hesitate. "Absolutely."

After breakfast, they walked Helena and Jules to their car and waved from the sidewalk as they drove away. It took only a few minutes to clear the remains of breakfast, and she helped Liza load the dishwasher while Carly and Mal put things away.

"So, what shall we do with our day?" Liza asked. "Carly, what were you planning?"

"I was thinking of a museum this afternoon, and then a wonderful dinner and a show tonight."

"Which museum?" Paige and Liza asked.

"I'd like to see *The Woman in Gold* at the Neue Galerie."

"Totally worth it," Liza said.

"I've seen it only in the movie," Paige said. But she'd love to see it in person. Ever since she'd watched *The Monuments Men* she'd been interested in the subject of Nazi art theft, and she liked to view the famous repatriated works when she had the chance. Their storied histories made them that much more incredible. She'd had the opportunity to eye a few masterpieces on her travels in Europe, but *The Woman in Gold* would be the first piece she'd view here.

"Well, the two of you should go. And we'll catch up with you for dinner. Then we'll see something on Broadway tonight."

They went back onto the patio and sat, just talking. Today, the topic was IT. Carly said she felt better after Mal told her the monthly maintenance fees she paid were a bargain compared to Brooklyn rates. Paige, who had a severe allergy to electronics, enjoyed the conversation anyway. Then they talked of their plans for the day, deciding the easiest way to reach their destination was to drive, since she and Carly were unfamiliar with the train and bus schedule to the Upper East Side of Manhattan. An hour later they were on their way.

The drive was easy, with Carly's GPS telling them the turns, and Paige plugged in her phone so they could listen to tunes as they drove. The day was lovely, and they decided to park near the theater district and walk uptown through the park. They randomly chose 5th Avenue and window-shopped at the high-end stores as they dodged the New York City foot traffic. Entering Central Park across from The Plaza, they strolled past the pond and crossed 5th Avenue again to reach the museum.

"The last time I was in this neighborhood, I got caught up in some German Day Parade," Carly told her.

"What did you do?"

"I bought bratwurst from a vendor and watched the parade. The woman I was with was really pissed, but what can you do?"

"You have to go with it, right?"

"Absolutely."

"I've gotten caught up in street festivals a few times," she said as she remembered a few of them. A Mexican celebration, a gay-pride celebration, and another whose details escaped her. "As a matter of fact, I believe they hold street festivals in New York City in my honor. Every time I'm here, one happens."

"Have you ever been to The Village?"

"Yes. A few times. I've been to the Halloween Parade and also to gay pride."

Carly turned to her and raised an eyebrow.

"A friend from residency brought me."

"Another gay friend?"

Answering with a shrug, she countered. "Have you ever been to pride here?"

Carly nodded. "I've done all the requisite gay things people from Scranton, Pennsylvania do. Rehoboth, P-Town, The Village."

"You sound so underwhelmed."

"When I was young, those things seemed important. Now, not so much. I'd rather see a Gustav Klimt than two women dancing together in a gay bar."

She started to ponder Carly's comment, but she didn't get past the image of the two women before Carly continued. "Although I suppose if I saw two women admiring the Klimt together—that would be amazing."

"The best of everything, huh?"

"Hey. It's New York City. It could happen."

She laughed. "Maybe even today."

They were quiet for a moment as they walked. "Do you have a girlfriend?" Paige asked.

Carly hesitated. They were entering personal space, and she had to decide how far in she could allow Paige to venture. But she'd already vetted Paige, so why not just open all the doors, and the windows, too. "I don't think so."

Again, a laugh, this time from the belly. "Shouldn't you know?"

Carly sighed. She hadn't wanted to talk about the party with Paige, but perhaps this was the opening she needed. "I'm sure Liza and Mal mentioned the party I hosted last weekend."

Paige nodded. "Yes. They did say something about going to your place."

"Erin brought a friend. I'm sure it was a setup, and we talked for a while, then again on the phone. I just don't know that we have much in common."

"No spark?"

"Oh, there's a spark. She's gorgeous. I could look at her forever. But—and this is usually my problem—I'm bored. Already. We didn't even sleep together yet, and I'm already planning how I'll ditch her. Because I will. It's inevitable."

"That sounds awful."

"I know." She wasn't proud of it, but it was true, and she felt comfortable enough with Paige to be honest. "I don't have a good record when it comes to women. I see so many happy couples like Liza and Mal, who've been together forever, or even Alex and Britain, and I just wonder if all the good women are taken."

"Is that what you want? To settle down like them?"

"Doesn't everybody want that?"

"I don't know. It's not working very well for me."

Carly took advantage of the opening. "How is your husband?"

Paige shrugged. "I'm never sure. We don't talk much."

Unlike with me, Carly thought. "How are you handling that?"

Paige sighed and shrugged and gave Carly a half-smile. "It's hard, but we weren't in a very good place even before the accident. I was busy with residency, and he did his own thing. We grew apart during that time, and he was injured before we ever had a chance to work on us. So it's not us I miss as much as...the possibility of us."

"Your relationship needs some work, Doc."

Paige frowned. "I'm not sure anymore. That I want to work on it."

"You don't want to be with him? Are you thinking of divorce?"

"I don't know. I feel like I've just run this marathon—which was all my work in school and residency—and now I'm at the end, and someone's moved the finish line."

"It's not what you thought it would be, huh?"

"Which *what* are you talking about?"

Carly couldn't help feeling for Paige. "Life."

Paige laughed. "It's funny...I have so many good things. My job, my house, my family. A few good friends." Paige looked at Carly as she said friends, and Carly felt something tangible pass between them as their eyes met. It felt warm and comfortable, just like she always felt with Paige. And it felt dangerous. Clearly, Paige was struggling with her marriage, and quite possibly with her sexuality. Carly could not encourage her. Yet, even though she knew that, she told herself they could just be friends. Because they already were, and already, after literally just a few hours in Paige's company, Carly already felt a connection so rare she could count the times it had happened before. Exactly twice. Once with Tasha, and again with Pip. In the years since there had been no one she felt this happy with, no one who made her feel so excited about the little things...like wandering around New York in search of a painting.

She needed to change the subject.

"Did you date a lot of guys before Will?"

"Oh, yeah. I was a wild one in my younger days."

Carly could see that side of Paige, the energy and restlessness. But then she'd married a much older and, from what Tasha had told her, quite a boring man. "Really? Spill."

"I thought you didn't like to hear about men?"

"Good point. Leave out the filthy details. But—you were the heterosexual version of me, huh? You slept around?"

"I guess I did." She paused, and Carly didn't interrupt the silence. "I suppose I was looking for something. Maybe just to pair off, like everyone else I knew."

"How do you mean?"

"Well, my parents are buddies. My grandparents are still alive and hold hands on their porch swing. Helena has a great marriage. So I looked at all these couples and thought I was missing something."

"And? Did you find it?"

"No. And I looked hard. Guys my own age bored me. In high school, it was all about partying and sports and, of course, sex. I felt like I was speaking Swahili while the guys I dated were chanting some extinct language. And in college, it was no different. Until Will. He was mature. Responsible. I admired him. And I think I kind of confused my feelings with something much greater than they actually are."

"So why the fuck did you marry him?" Carly couldn't stop the question from escaping her mouth, but once it was out, she didn't apologize for it. She wanted to know, and it sounded like Paige wanted to talk about it.

Paige had thought so much about this question, she didn't need to debate the answer for even a second. "He eased my loneliness."

The comment was shocking—Paige seemed so social and outgoing, not someone Carly would ever imagine harboring such a feeling. Yet when she turned to Paige, she saw the pain in her eyes, and they connected once again. Carly looked away after a moment yet still saw Paige even as she looked ahead on the sidewalk on Fifth Avenue. The revelation, and the sudden awareness that this was yet something else they shared, didn't throw Carly off balance. It seemed to steady her.

"That's fucked up," Carly said, because she knew. She'd been there. Yet she feared she sounded judgmental, and she wanted to retract the comment.

"Yeah, I know," Paige admitted with a sigh before Carly could speak.

"No. I'm sorry. I shouldn't have said that. Why were you lonely? You're an intelligent, attractive woman. You're like a people magnet. And you clearly have a doting family."

Paige bit her lip. "I've always felt a little different. Like I didn't quite fit in. I've had lots of friends, but they were all compartmentalized, serving their purpose in my world. Softball friends, when I was young. Now golf friends. Work friends. Study friends. No one who was just there for me no matter what. It's like if you took away that one connection, the relationship would dissolve. Then I met Will. I started playing golf with him, and I worked with him, he helped me study. He broke down all the barriers."

"Huh," Carly said softly. She understood perfectly. "What went wrong?"

Paige sighed. It wasn't really what went wrong—it was wrong from the beginning. She'd just been so excited to finally meet someone she could enjoy being with that she'd overlooked all the problems.

But how had this magnificent day turned dark? Will, and why she'd married him, and what she was going to do with that marriage were the last things she wanted to think about. Or talk about. "That's part two. A story for another day. Let's enjoy the rest of this one."

They were quiet as they paid their admission fees at the Neue, then made their way up a flight of stairs to *The Woman in Gold*. They entered the gallery, a twenty-by-twenty-foot room, and when Paige saw the painting, she suddenly forgot all the sadness and worry she'd felt just moments before.

It was larger than she'd imagined, nearly life-sized, and square. The gold of the woman's dress and the background shimmered, and her tiny smile hinted she might know this portrait would someday be world famous. Her eyes seemed to seduce, to hypnotize. Paige stepped closer into the room but stayed back, taking in the magnificence of the art. Klimt had taken several years to complete this piece, and Paige wanted to take a few minutes to savor it. Finally, she stepped closer, examined the details, the inlaid gold and fine brushstrokes. Wow, she said to herself. This is what $135,000,000 can buy.

Adele Bloch-Bauer had been a wealthy woman, married to one of the richest men in Vienna, and this painting of her reflected it. It was simply opulent.

Paige wasn't sure how long she stood there as other patrons passed before and behind her, but gradually the spell weakened, and her gaze left the painting as she searched for Carly. And she found her, a few feet behind, staring not at Adele, but at her.

When their eyes met, she felt as if Carly were touching her, as if her eyes were caressing her. Her mouth went dry as Carly moved closer.

"Is it what you hoped it would be?"

Paige nodded. "Yes," she whispered reverently. "How about you?"

"She's magnificent," she said as she turned toward the painting. "And I'm glad the Austrians gave her back."

Paige nodded toward the door, then turned to look one last time at *The Woman in Gold*. "Bye," she said to Adele. "It was nice to finally meet you."

Carly leaned in and whispered, "Do you always talk to the artwork?"

"Only special pieces. I can't wait to talk to *Mona Lisa*."

Carly's eyes flew open wide. "If she could only talk back."

Paige nodded. "Do you want to see anything else?"

Shaking her head, Carly puckered her lips. "What could compare to that?"

They exited into the same sunshine they'd left, with a few hours to kill before they met Liza and Mal for dinner. "How about a cocktail?" Carly asked.

"Can we eat something? It's a long gap between breakfast and dinner."

"Sure. You can eat, and I'll have a drink, and we'll both be happy."

In silent, mutual agreement they turned away from the park and then walked downtown. "You'll eat anything, right?" Carly asked. "You're not picky?"

"Not at all."

"We should find something that you like, then. New York has at least five million restaurants."

"I'm hungry for Mexican."

Carly stopped and grabbed Paige's arm. "I know a great place for Mexican." She nodded toward Central Park. But it's that way."

Paige gave a half shrug and pivoted comically.

"C'mon, you clown," Carly said, excited as they began walking in the opposite direction. One of the things she loved even more than discovering new restaurants was sharing her favorites with other people. That was the way to keep them open, by patronizing them and helping them reach new customers.

Looking up at the entrance to the Neue, Carly smiled. "I'm really happy we were able to see Adele. Thanks for coming with me."

"Yes. Me, too. It was fun. Have you seen any other of Klimt's works?"

"Actually, I have. A few years ago, I was in Vienna, and they still have a few pieces. They lost half a dozen due to repatriation. *Kiss* is still there, though, at the Belvedere. A few others, too."

"I've never been to Vienna. How did you like it?" Paige asked.

"It's a great, old, historical, cultured city. I'd like to go back. I had only about two days, and that wasn't enough."

"Why'd you cut it so short?"

"We did a river cruise."

Paige's eyes flew open. "I love the commercials for river cruises. Everything looks so beautiful. Was it great?"

It had been great. "It's breathtaking. But Tasha and I were the only ones on the trip who didn't need a wheelchair."

Paige laughed, and the sound made Carly happy. They talked about that trip, and some others Carly had taken, comparing notes on the cities and countries they'd both visited and discussing famous pieces of art they'd seen.

Before she knew it, they'd passed through the park, and Carly guided Paige in the direction of the Lincoln Center, home of the Metropolitan Opera. Paige nodded toward the sign. "Are you taking me to the opera?"

Carly sighed. "I wish."

"Really? You like opera?" Paige sounded surprised, and Carly understood why. She didn't know many fans.

"I do. How about you?"

"I love it!"

Carly turned to her and shot her a look. The day was sunny and bright, and they both wore sunglasses, but she was sure Paige got the message.

"What?" Paige asked defensively.

"Don't tease me."

Paige sounded surprised. "About opera? Why would I tease you?"

Carly sighed, thinking of the harassment she'd gotten from friends over the years. "Everyone else does."

"Hmm. I guess I can understand that. I've always kind of done my own thing, so I don't really listen to other people. But you seem to have a ton of friends—and unless I'm wrong, none of them are quite as sophisticated as you are."

Carly chuckled. "Don't let Tasha hear you say that."

"Well, she's okay. But—"

Paige stopped, and Carly looked at her again. "What?"

"I shouldn't be so judgmental."

"No, you shouldn't. But you're right. Hence, the teasing."

"At least you have Tasha."

"Yeah, but she only goes to make me happy. Mostly, I go alone."

They talked about the Met HD performances at the local movie theaters and about the operas they'd seen. Paige preferred the HD, but Carly loved the Lincoln Center. "When I retire, I'm going to rent an apartment in New York for a year and become an usher. Have you had the tour?"

When Paige said no, Carly began to explain how they changed performances nightly, and how the sets were stored beneath the stage and brought up with an elevator system.

"Let's walk up and look in the windows. See what's on for today." Paige looked toward the plaza, with its fountain shooting a jet of water high into the air and hundreds of people scurrying about. It had to be close to starting time.

"You seem to know a lot about it," Paige said. "How'd you get into it? Your parents?"

Carly sighed. "Actually, if you can believe it, it was Pip's grandfather. He didn't have anyone to take him, and I thought—why not? He was an interesting guy. He'd fought in World War II and traveled extensively, spoke a few languages. I loved talking with him. So one day, he hired a limo and brought me to New York, and we had dinner and saw *La Boheme.* I was hooked. After that, we came a few times a year, right until he died. How about you?"

"When I was a resident, there was a custodian on the night shift— an old guy named Sal straight off the boat from Italy. They had a little janitors' closet in the ER where everything was stored, and at night, he'd play opera while he was buffing the floors. The most beautiful noise I'd ever heard came out of that little room. One night, I heard "O Silver Moon," and I literally stopped in my tracks and just listened. All this chaos was happening around me, people were bumping into me, until I finally went into the closet to find out the name of the song. And I've been listening to opera ever since."

Carly understood perfectly. The same thing had happened to her. What she didn't understand was why Goddess had dropped Paige Waterford into her life. Paige was the first woman she had met in forever who didn't bore her. Who, in fact, intrigued her. If she was going to meet a woman who liked to golf, and chase famous art around the world, and listen to opera, why the fuck did she have to be married?

When Carly didn't respond, Paige spoke again. "We'll go sometime. To the opera."

"I'd love to," Carly said, but she knew she shouldn't. She should just run, far away from Paige.

"How about now?" Paige said as she waved an arm toward the entrance. "I think it's starting soon."

"We'll never get tickets. And don't you need to eat?"

"We might get tickets, although they won't be good seats. And I have a protein bar in my bag, so I'm good. Are you good? Wanna check it out?"

The smile that erupted on Carly's face filled Paige with joy, and a moment later they had two tickets in hand and were walking side by side up the grand staircase of the Metropolitan Opera House. They stopped at the top, where Carly elbowed her way into the bar and came out with a drink, then continued up another smaller staircase to the Family Circle. Their seats were in the last row, as far away as they could be, yet when Anna Netrebko began singing, it was as if she were singing just for them. They were captivated.

Paige's eyes were in constant motion as they went from the stage, to the translator, to the woman beside her. Carly leaned forward, watching and listening, never even looking at the translator. During the break, Paige asked her about it. "Do you speak German, Fräulein Becker?"

Carly smiled. "*Ein bisschen.*"

"So you're following this?"

She shrugged. "Some of it. But I've seen *The Magic Flute* before, and I know the story, so today I'm really just enjoying the performance."

That was evident, and Paige was pleased that she'd suggested the detour to the Lincoln Center. "Then I'm glad we're here."

Carly nodded and looked like she might say something sage, but instead excused herself. Paige stood and stretched, and gazed around the gilded hall, taking her seat once again only when Carly reappeared just before the second act started.

The opera was short, and when it ended, Carly told her she'd managed to book a table at her favorite restaurant, but they had to hurry to beat the crowd. "Where are we going?" Paige asked as they weaved through the foot traffic.

"You'll see," she said. They turned at the end of the plaza, and from there it was just a few steps to Rosa Mexicana. "Excellent food. Even better margaritas."

"I might have a little of both. But what about the girls?"

"They're on their way."

Carly asked for their table, and they were seated upstairs, where they could look out at the traffic on the street below. Their margaritas came quickly, and they ordered guacamole for the table while they waited for Liza and Mal.

"This was Tom's favorite restaurant," Carly said with a smile.

Paige thought for a moment, and then she understood. "Pip's grandfather?"

Carly nodded, and Paige raised her glass. "To Tom."

They touched glasses, and Paige took a very small sip of her drink. Carly sucked in a mouthful and then another as Paige nibbled on the chips and salsa. She could imagine him there with her, imagine him whispering in her ear. *Life is short, Carly. Live it! Go to Paris.*

"I can't believe you haven't been to Paris, since you're such a fan of art."

Carly looked at Paige for a moment, wondering how she had the ability to read her mind. After another gulp of the margarita, she sighed. "Neither can I."

"You should come on the trip, Carly. You'd love it."

Yes, she would. That wasn't the problem. The problem was her attraction to Paige, but how could she explain that without jeopardizing their friendship?

"I'll think about it," she replied. What? Had she really just said that? Fortunately, Paige moved on and changed the subject, but Carly couldn't get Paris out of her mind. She thought of her own grandfather, a hard-working man whose only time out of the United States was during the war. How proud he'd been to serve his country and to march along the Seine with the men in his unit. And Tom, who'd traveled the world many times and never lost his zest for life, even as he was struggling with his last breaths.

Both men—two of the most important influences in her life—were telling her to go to Paris. She was beginning to think she should listen.

"There you are!" Liza's voice cut into her thoughts, and Carly looked up into the smiling faces of her new friends.

The hostess seated them, and a moment later the server appeared for their drink orders. Carly might have complained that they wanted more time, but she knew they needed to walk to the ticket booth in time to get evening show tickets, so she held her tongue.

"How was the opera?" Liza asked, and Carly caught her breath as she looked at the expression on Paige's face. She was absolutely glowing as she told them about their spontaneous decision to see *The Magic Flute* and Anna Netrebko's spellbinding performance as the Queen of the Night.

Carly sipped her drink again and thought of Tom. He'd said the same thing about her after their first trip to The Met. *You look radiant, Carly.*

I feel radiant now. That's what happens when I'm with her. Feeling as good as she'd felt in ages, she sank into the soft club chair and watched her three friends interacting. She sipped her margarita. I don't really need this drink, she thought. Or maybe I need a whole pitcher.

Chapter Seventeen

Travel Partners

"Y ou have to go."

Carly leaned back in her desk chair and stared at Dominica. It had been more than two weeks since Jules had invited her to Paris, and she'd been thinking of little else since. And she'd just returned from another SAW event, this one near Erie. Not only had she driven with Paige, but she'd roomed with her as well, and they'd had a great time. There was no drama, no fighting, no issues—just interesting conversation, good music, gourmet food, and wonderful golf.

Yet, still, she was unsure about the trip. Dominica had been nagging her, asking daily if she'd sent in her check.

She repeated herself. "She has a husband."

"Are you really so horny that you're going to jump on her, just because you have a few things in common?"

Carly laughed as an image of her humping Paige's leg flashed through her mind. Then she shrugged.

"You've told me the rules," Dominica said. "And you've never broken them, even though you've had chances. Remember that student from the U who crawled into bed with you after one of your parties?"

How could Carly forget the drunken coed half her age? But that had been easy. She was just a child, and nothing about her appealed to Carly. Not that Paige was much older. Yet she seemed older. So mature. She wondered about it sometimes. Paige told her she'd been a little wild in her youth, and Carly saw the fun side of her, but under it all, she was reserved. She talked but never revealed anything important. After all these months, Carly still felt like she hardly knew Paige at all. What she did know, though, she liked, and, of course, that was the problem.

"Carly, you're forty-five years old. People your age die every day. What are you waiting for? You like this woman, you have fun with her, you say she's easy to be with. And you've wanted Paris since I've known you."

Dominica was right, but she was wrong, too. She didn't just want Paris. She wanted Paris with her lover, to have a picnic in Tuileries, and a stroll beside the Seine, and a kiss atop the Eiffel Tower. That's what she wanted, what she'd been dreaming of since she boarded the plane for Nice with Pip twenty years ago. She was a successful woman. If it were just about Paris, she would have already made the trip.

"I'm waiting for *the one*, Dom. For someone to make Paris special. It's the most romantic city in the world, and I want to be in love when I go. Is that so wrong?"

Dominica walked around the desk and wrapped her in her arms, and Carly rested her head against her friend's chest. "It's not wrong at all. You just have to ask yourself if you want to keep saving that dream, or if it's time to let it go. Make a new dream of Paris. Instead of a picnic, have an ice cream."

Carly pulled back. What did that even mean? Dominica's answer made her chuckle.

"That's what I like to do with my friends. We go out for ice cream," Dominica said. "Manning's," she added, referencing the local dairy farm.

"Get out of here and let me get some work done," she said playfully.

After Dom left, Carly turned and stared out her window at the worst view in history. The back of her office faced a mountain, but all she saw was the remnants of the excavation that had leveled the land on which the office sat. Carved into the hill was a railroad bed, so close to her window that if a train ever derailed, it would squish her. Yet the trees were green with life, and the sun was shining, and suddenly she felt excited.

Maybe her friend was right. At her age, perhaps the days of romance were past. Maybe Paris could be about great food, and wine, and history, about art and architecture. All things she loved. And she didn't know anyone as perfectly suited for that sort of trip as Paige.

Before she could change her mind, she dialed the phone. "Dominica talked me into it," she said a moment later when Paige answered.

"Huh?" Paige asked through a yawn, still foggy from sleep. She'd been dreaming when the phone rang. "Who's Dominica? And what did she convince you to do?" She stretched and looked at the clock. Eight thirty. She'd hoped to sleep a little later to prepare for her evening shift in the ER, but she guessed fate had other plans for her.

"My assistant, and not *what*, but *where*. She convinced me I should go to Paris. So if you're still looking for a roommate, I'm in."

Paige couldn't stop the smile that erupted on her face. "I've had quite a few offers, but I've been holding out for you."

"Well, obviously you have good taste. What do I have to do?"

Paige sat up and walked to her desk. The Paris file was in the drawer, carefully tucked into a file marked *Travel*. When Carly assured her she was ready to copy, Paige relayed the contact information for Dr. DeMichelle, the man leading the trip.

"Let me know what happens," she said after Carly repeated the email address and phone number back to her.

"What are your plans for the day?" Carly asked.

"I don't have anything this morning, but I work at three."

"Wanna golf?"

"Hmmm. Maybe. What are you thinking?"

"Hold on. I'm pulling up the Clubster app for the Meadows."

Paige hummed the *Jeopardy* theme while she waited.

"Oh, shucks. There's a tournament at noon. We'd have to go out now."

With a burst of adrenaline, Paige kicked off her pajama bottoms. "I'll meet you there in fifteen minutes."

"What?" Carly asked, sounding shocked.

"What? It was your idea. Let's go. I'm still in bed, and I can make it. You have no excuse."

"I'm at work. I have work."

Suspecting she could talk Carly into it, Paige proceeded to her closet and pulled out a sleeveless golf shirt and a skort. "You're the boss. What's the point of being the boss if you can't golf when you feel like it? Work when it's dark, or when it's raining."

"Good point. See you in fifteen."

Pulling her hair back in a headband, Paige surveyed herself in the mirror. She detected no evidence that she'd just climbed out of bed.

In the kitchen she started the Keurig and popped a frozen waffle into the toaster, then sliced a banana to top it. In ten minutes, she was out the door, and three minutes after that she was in the parking lot of Mountain Meadows Country Club, searching for Carly's BMW. Instead, she drove up in an old Saab convertible.

Wow, did she look great behind the wheel of that car. Windswept, happy. The Carly who Paige loved to see. The one she kept hidden. Except more often now, as their friendship grew, Paige got to spend time with *this* Carly, and it only made their connection stronger.

Shouldering her bag, she met Carly at her car as she slipped on socks and golf shoes, her feet dangling from the door of the car. "Don't ever tell anyone you saw me changing my shoes in the parking lot. I'll get a citation."

"Really?"

"No, but someone from the upper crust will mention it."

"I'll keep my mouth shut."

Carly stood and made a production of taking a deep breath. "Okay, let me change gears here. No work. No contracts. No listings. No inspections. Drives, chips, and putts. That's what I'm going to think about until they kick us off the course in three hours."

"We can get eighteen in."

"Yes. If you don't hold me up."

"Hey," Paige whined, feigning insult.

"Just kidding."

"How much do I owe you for this?" Paige asked.

"Oh, nothing. First time's on me."

"That's really nice," she said. "I'll get you next time."

"I'd expect nothing less."

Laughing, they entered the pro shop, where Alex Dalton stood behind the counter. "Hey, Carly. Hello, mysterious guest."

"It was an oversight," Carly replied as she held up her hands. "I just booked the tee time three minutes ago."

Paige looked from one to the other, confused.

"Actually," Alex said as she smiled at Paige, "I'd like Dr. Waterford to be *my* guest. Thank you for all the help you've given Britain. She's had a great time in the ER, and she's really pumped about starting her rotations."

"That's so nice of you," Paige said. Britain had followed up their dinner at Ruth's Chris with a phone call and had been joining her in the ER when she could—for a few hours after school, on Saturday mornings, times when Alex was at the golf course. Paige could see her excitement and knew she was going to make an excellent physician. And Paige was happy to play a small role in her development.

"The course is deserted, so you ladies have the tee whenever you're ready. You should get through in three hours—and you have to, because the animal-shelter tournament starts at twelve o'clock sharp."

Paige glanced at the large clock on the wall behind Alex. Five minutes to nine. "Not a problem."

Alex nodded. "It's not you I'm worried about."

Carly turned to leave. "See you in two hours and forty minutes."

"Thanks again."

"My pleasure," she said as Paige retraced her steps and picked up her bag outside the pro shop. Following the path, she met Carly near the snack shop, where she'd filled two reusable cups with water and handed one to Paige. It was an insulated tumbler, with the Mountain Meadows Country Club logo.

"The club reuses these?" she asked.

"Yes. They have industrial dishwashers in the kitchen, so why not?"

"And no one steals them, huh?"

"Actually, no. If you lose a club, someone will turn that in, too. I even get lost balls returned," she said as Paige belted her bag to the cart.

Thinking of the time she'd lost a pitching wedge on the course, Paige realized Carly was lucky to play at a private club. "Do you write your name on your balls?" she asked as she slid in beside Carly and they headed toward the first tee.

"I have a very distinct mark," she said dryly.

Curious, Paige pulled Carly's ball out of the holder and examined it. Beneath the word *Titleist,* a purple martini glass was drawn on the ball.

"You're something else," Paige said.

"There are a lot of CBs in the world, but not so many purple martini glasses."

"I'll take your word for it."

Arriving at the first tee, they pulled clubs from their respective bags and began loosening up. "I usually hit a few off the first tee and play the best one," Carly said.

"Sounds like a plan. How do you play this hole?"

"Driver off the tee. It's a par five, little bit of a dogleg at the end, but it won't come into play until the second shot. The best approach is from the left side."

As if she could control her position on the fairway. Paige was happy to just be on the fairway and not in the woods, or the water. She watched as Carly teed a ball, and then another, and a third, and hit them all fair down the fairway, on the left side.

"Like that," she said with a wink.

Paige managed to hit a nice shot on her first ball. "I'll save my mulligan," she said as she walked back to the cart.

"So what was that about in the pro shop? Alex seemed to be on your case about bringing a guest."

Carly waved a dismissive hand toward Paige. "It's a stupid rule. Each guest is allowed to play the course only three times each year. It encourages people to join the club rather than take advantage of their friends. I usually sign people up as *guest*, so then it's hard for the club to keep track."

"So I can come three times as *guest*, and three times as myself?"

"Oh, we can come up with another identity if we want to. No one cares about the rule. It's not enforced. It's just in the bylaws."

Paige could have debated the merits of a rule everyone broke, but they arrived at Carly's ball. They both got out of the cart to assess the shot. "What's the distance?"

"Fucking far," she said dryly as she pulled a wood from her bag and cracked a great shot.

"Nice drive," she said to Paige as they found her ball fifty yards ahead of Carly's. It was also on the fairway, and her second shot was also a good one. By the time they reached the green, the initial jitters she'd felt about her sudden decision to play golf with Carly had subsided. As Carly lined up her putt, Paige closed her eyes and turned her face to the sun, breathing in the fresh morning air. Grass and pine filled her nostrils, and her pulse slowed as a calm came over her.

"Hey, guest—are you going to putt, or what?"

Paige opened her eyes to see Carly walking toward her ball, a few inches from the hole.

"I thought you might give it to me."

"I made my par. You have to make yours."

Paige putted and picked up a gimme, and as they walked back to the cart talking about the beautiful day, Paige marveled that they were there. If not for the invitation from Carly, she would probably have had a more productive day, but it wouldn't have been so much fun.

She thought back to her round here with Will and Linda and realized she'd never had this much fun with Will on the golf course. She'd never had much fun with him period.

It was a lightning-quick round, and Paige was disappointed when they pulled up to the eighteenth green. "Are you hungry?" Carly asked. "We could have lunch."

"I'd love to," she said, and they discussed choices. She didn't have to be at work for three hours, and if they went out for lunch, she could take leftovers for dinner.

She left separately, but they met up again on the patio at the State Street Grill, and before she even sat down, Carly looked up at her and motioned to her phone. "You have yourself a roommate." Carly had emailed Dr. DeMichelle before she left for golf, and even though the university was on break, he'd already responded.

Elated. That was the best way to describe what she felt as Carly's news settled over her, and they spent the first part of lunch talking about the trip. Carly Googled Paris weather in the fall (highs in the high fifties to low sixties), and they began planning what they'd pack. "It's only four months away," she said. "We don't have a moment to waste."

Their conversation gradually shifted to the upcoming SAW match in Rehoboth Beach. Carly and Tasha were both going, part of a large group of women who'd rented a beachfront house for the Fourth of July holiday. "We were so lucky to get this house," Carly informed her, as Paige listened, feigning excitement for Carly's benefit.

In truth, the thought of the holiday saddened her. Of course, Will wanted to spend time at the cabin and was planning to go for the week. He'd invited friends to watch the fireworks display the locals put on from a boat in the middle of the lake. Paige could either stay home or go. It clearly didn't matter to him. But she'd decided to go for a few days, while she was off from work, and enjoy the fireworks and some quiet time. Her Kindle worked at the lake, even without cell-phone service, and she liked to hunt for rocks in the woods and turn them into painted animals like turtles and frogs. She'd take a few old DVDs and chill, something she often told herself she needed to do but very rarely accomplished.

"What are you doing for the holiday?" Carly asked, as if reading her mind.

When Paige shared her plans, Carly said, "Sounds really nice," with sincerity.

She couldn't tell Carly it wasn't, that she didn't want to be with her husband. She wanted to be with Carly and her friends at the beach. Nothing was left of her marriage. The more time she spent with Carly, the more she realized that fact. She couldn't have much with Will when she had so much with Carly.

They hugged at their cars and drove off in separate directions, and Paige spent the next days and weeks doing what she'd been doing for a long time—working and reading and being on her own, while Will did the same.

He left for the cabin a few days before she did, and after an overnight shift on the last day of June, she slept a few hours and then drove south, past Wilkes-Barre, Pennsylvania. It was a peaceful drive, with little traffic in the early afternoon, and Paige envisioned falling asleep on the deck with Kindle in hand. Her fantasies of a quiet time at the lake were shattered when she arrived and found three other cars parked behind Will's in the long driveway. He'd mentioned inviting friends, but she hadn't expected them until the holiday.

Swallowing her disappointment, she adjusted her attitude and carried her bag into the cabin. In spite of the cars, the place was deserted, but from the looks of the cabin's interior, Will's friends had started the celebration early. Paper plates with dried ends of hot-dog buns and chips and pretzels were scattered around the kitchen and on the large coffee table in the great room. At least a few dozen beer cans were lined up along the floor, creating a trail from the same table all the way to the kitchen thirty feet away. She ventured across the great room, to the doors tucked behind the fireplace, and peeked into the guest bedrooms. The queen-size bed in one room was unmade, and a suitcase spilled its contents onto the floor. Some of the clothing leaking out belonged to a woman, while other stuff was clearly meant for a man. In the other room, two of the four bunk beds were messed up, and the luggage of the room's inhabitants obstructed the path beyond the door.

The loft here had once been the master bedroom, but since Will's accident, he'd taken the other bedroom on the main floor, and Paige headed there. It was the only orderly place in the house. The bed was neatly made, and if she didn't know better, she'd think Will wasn't even at his own cabin party. Opening the closet, she pulled clothing from her small suitcase and then hung it on hangers, deposited her toiletries in the bathroom, and then, Kindle in hand, left the room.

Back in the kitchen, she ignored the mess as she opened the sliding-glass doors to the deck. Walking directly to the rail, she peeked through the trees at the water a hundred yards away and thought of another lake house, and the woman who owned it.

Carly had left two days ago for her trip to the beach, and Paige was rather relieved to not have cell-phone service at the cabin. With the possibility of texting or calling Carly off the table, she hoped to get her off her mind as well. She was here to have a good time with Will, and what Carly was doing and with whom was not her concern.

Paige kept telling herself that and kept hoping it would stick.

Drifting back from the railing, she settled into a cozy, padded chaise lounge and soaked up the sun for a few minutes, then turned on her Kindle and began reading. The book, a murder mystery, held her interest until the noise of the group returning from the lake distracted her a few hours later. Once again she walked to the rail and waved as they began heading back from the pontoon boat.

"Paige's here," her friend Amy shouted when she spotted her. The group of four men waved, and Paige watched as they slowly made their way back to the house, carrying a cooler and fishing gear and bags that she guessed contained snacks and towels and trash.

Amy rushed up the steps and hugged her. "It's so good to see you."

Paige thought for a moment. It had probably been winter the last time she and Will had spent any time with Amy and her husband Kevin. "We missed you on Memorial Day," she said. "But I assure you, Will was the perfect host."

Paige nodded as she processed. She'd worked and had a steak with Liza and Mal afterward. Will had been hosting a party and hadn't told her. "I've taught him well," she answered, trying to keep her expression neutral as she processed her feelings. Did she have any right to be angry, considering her own confused feelings? Probably not, she realized as she turned on a smile as the rest of the group arrived, offering hugs.

In addition to Kevin, Paige greeted Todd and Roger, paramedics who'd worked with Will for years. Only Amy, who was a state-police officer, wasn't in health care.

Will was the last to climb the deck stairs, and Paige could tell by the way he moved that he was in pain. Yet when he looked at her, he smiled, and she could tell he was really happy. "I'm glad you made it."

Biting her tongue, she nodded. "Of course." She saw no point in bringing up the fact that she was never invited here. He surprised her yet again when he walked across the deck, wrapped his arms around her, and kissed her. The beer on his breath repulsed her, but she was too surprised to react, and the kiss was over in an instant. "You're just in time for dinner. We're going to do a lobster pot."

"Fancy," Paige said through a forced smile, covering her feelings once again. For as long as she'd known Will's friends, they'd never brought more than beer and potato chips to the cabin. Will stocked the fridge and the cupboards, and they ate whatever he had. Apparently, they ate very well. "Do you need any help?" Might as well stay busy. At least then she wouldn't be bored with shop talk. It was hard to imagine a time when she loved that, back in college when she longed for the experiences Will and all his friends had every day at work. They'd made it all sound so fascinating, so glamorous. And it was, until she gained her own experience and realized much of what they talked about was exaggerated or completely fabricated.

This was not her lucky day, though. "I got it," Will said, and he disappeared through the sliding-glass doors, leaving her with his friends.

Reclaiming the chaise, she spoke to no one in particular. "What's new, guys?"

Amy smiled broadly. "I've been selected for forensics. I'm going to be off the roads and doing murder-scene investigations."

Paige was impressed. Once upon a time, when she'd just joined the PSP, Amy had been an adrenaline junkie who loved chasing danger. This job sounded so much cooler to Paige. "Do you have to go back to the academy for that?"

"Yeah. Some in person, but some's online. Then I'll follow someone around and eventually get certified to do it myself."

"It sounds amazing, Amy. Congrats."

"We worked a case together a couple of weeks ago," Kevin said as he smiled at his wife. "That SUV versus tractor trailer on the interstate. Amy got to direct the traffic while I saved a couple of lives."

Had he always been so cocky? Paige tried to remember. Probably, but he'd been nice to her and taught her things, and she'd tolerated him. Now, he just seemed immature. His wife was doing well. What point was there in putting her down? Had Will been like that? As much as he frustrated her, Paige had to admit he hadn't. He was smart and a great medic. He could thread IV lines into the smallest veins, over the bumpy roads of Scranton on the way to the ER. He diagnosed his patients in the ambulance and shared his opinions with the doctors in the ER. And he was most often right. Thinking of that guy, the girl she'd been, made her smile.

"What's that grin about?" Todd asked.

"I was thinking of Will. How smart he was. How he used to tell the ER docs what was wrong with their patients and what to do about it."

Roger waved a dismissive hand at her. "He thinks he's smart. Did he ever tell you about the sixteen-year-old with the kidney stone?"

Paige thought she'd heard every one of their stories, but that one didn't sound familiar.

"Shut up, Rog," Will yelled from inside. "Or you're going to have boiled bass instead of lobster."

"C'mon. You can't leave me hanging."

"Back when we first went with one medic on the truck, Blondie in there got called out at two a.m. for a young girl with abdominal pain. Intermittent, severe, colicky pain. He called Rinehimer on the radio and told him he had a sixteen-year-old girl with a kidney stone."

He did leave them hanging for a minute, but Paige suspected everyone else knew the ending.

"Yeah?"

"Yeah. Twenty minutes later, Rinhimer delivered a little baby boy. I think they named him Will, didn't they?"

"I was young," Will said from the doorway as he came out on the deck carrying a large pot. Paige could tell he struggled with the weight of it, but no one tried to help.

Watching him out of the corner of her eye, she came to his defense. "Been there."

"Well, I hope you at least examine your patients, Doc. If Einstein here had bothered to touch her, he would have figured it out."

Will set the pot on the burner and adjusted the flame, then joined Paige on the end of the chaise. She tuned them out as she closed her eyes and tried to relax, trying to feel some of the joy they obviously did.

After a few minutes Will checked the food, and when it was to his liking, Kevin helped him spill the pot's contents onto a pile of papers on the center of the table, and the free-for-all began. Paige grabbed a potato and an ear of corn, a few shrimp, and a half a lobster tail, and sat down beside Will. For the first time in forever she drank a beer, and to her surprise, she enjoyed it.

After they cleaned up, the party moved to the fire pit beside the lake, where they watched the flickering flames and popping embers from Adirondack chairs. Paige nursed a glass of cabernet and stared out at the still lake, where the reflection of a fire glowed on the surface. Across the water, others like them sat hidden in the darkness, given away by the orange glow of campfires. The darkness allowed her to hide, and she felt sad as she blended into the night. What was she doing here?

Needing to escape, she stood. "I'm going to head up," she said.

"I'm coming, too," Roger said. "I have to check on Susie before she heads to bed."

"We'll share a flashlight," Paige said as she flicked hers on.

They walked for a few steps in silence. "What a break that they installed that cell-phone tower, huh?" Roger said.

She nearly tripped on a stone when she turned to him. "Huh?"

"The cell-phone tower. I've always loved the lake, but it was a drag not having service. What a difference. And Will told me in the past year, since they installed it, property values have exploded."

"Yeah. It's pretty amazing," she said, although she was no longer paying Roger any attention. Will had been escaping to the cabin for a year, supposedly with no way to communicate. He'd leave for days at a time, and she never knew if he was okay, depressed, suicidal, even. And the entire time he'd been up here with his friends, hosting parties and playing Candy Crush on his iPhone.

She wanted to scream. Or maybe laugh. As much as she'd been trying to break free from Will, it seemed he'd been doing the same. Escaping to the lake without calling. Hosting parties she wasn't invited to and wasn't even aware of. The emotional distancing, the silence.

Wow.

"Night, Rog," she said. After grabbing a glass and some water and a quick shower, she fell into the bed. It wasn't even nine o'clock, but she was exhausted. Even with all those people around, she felt alone. She didn't fit in with them anymore. Had she ever?

And even though she'd listened and talked, and managed to block Carly from her mind, her success was fleeting. As soon as she was alone, her thoughts once again turned to her.

Where was she now? Out with her friends, most likely. Or perhaps, like in Myrtle Beach, she was by herself on the beach, listening to the waves breaking onto the sand.

Wherever she was, Paige wished she were with her. With Carly, she'd escape the crushing sadness that once again weighed on her. As she curled up in the darkness, with a pillow over her head to block the noises of the night, it didn't even bother her that Will had lied to her. She'd been lying to him, too, essentially having an affair, without the sex.

The thought was a sobering one, and she sat up. She had to leave. The cabin and Will. Whatever they'd had was long over, and she couldn't keep torturing herself. Not when she'd just spent the best night she'd had with him in years and was still thinking of someone else.

But this wasn't about Carly. It was about her and Will. Meeting Carly had simply brought her unhappiness into focus and given her a reason to do something about it. Even if she was never brave enough to tell Carly how attractive she was, or how much she wanted to be with her, this was the right thing to do. It was the only thing to do if she wanted to be happy.

Suddenly, the door opened, throwing a painful swath of light into her eyes. She jumped.

"Hey. You're awake."

She hadn't planned to talk to Will now. She'd simply decided to leave, write him a note, perhaps, as he did so often with her. Yet here he was, stumbling into the room, and she was going to have to face him because she simply couldn't stay with him a moment longer.

"Will, I'm leaving."

"What? You just got here."

He sat on the bed, pulling her with him, and despite his drunken clumsiness, he pushed her against the pillow and slid on top of her. His putrid breath was shocking. The entire scene was shocking, and she was momentarily paralyzed as he kissed her. She turned her head, trying to escape, but he was so much bigger than her, and suddenly he didn't seem so drunk at all as he ground his hips against her.

"What the fuck?" she mumbled as she tried to move. "Get off me!"

"C'mon, Paige. It's been forever," he said as he forced his hand into her pajama pants and his tongue in her mouth. She felt his hardness against her thigh, blindly searching for more intimate places as he moved against her. When he lifted off her to adjust himself, she was able to wiggle out from under him.

"What. Are. You. Doing?" she screamed as she backed away from the bed.

He rolled onto his back and laughed. "You used to like it," he slurred.

No, she thought. I never, ever liked anything remotely resembling whatever this is.

Fully awake, she pulled her bag from the closet and jerked on sweats without even bothering to take off her pajamas. She added her toiletries, then slipped on her sneakers.

"What, so you're just going to leave? In the middle of the night?"

"Yep."

"When did you become such a prude?"

"I'm not a prude."

"Are you a lesbian?"

"What?" she asked reflexively, defensively.

"Well, you hang out with enough of them. And I remember you saying once, that maybe…"

"Just because…" She stopped. What could she say? She was about to deny it, but she couldn't, because maybe she really was gay. Maybe. She wasn't ready to talk about it though, especially not with him, in a house full of his friends, and with his head full of beer.

Maybe she was. And when she figured that out, he'd certainly be one of the first people she'd tell. For the moment, though, she didn't feel like she owed him anything.

"I'm going home."

"Go ahead. Run away."

"I want a divorce, Will. I'm not happy, and neither are you. I don't want to pretend anymore."

"You're fucking someone else, aren't you?"

Not bothering with a reply, she walked quietly from the bedroom, and the house, then picked her way across the gravel of the driveway, thankful she'd been the last to arrive and her car was behind the others.

Feeling as sad and lonely as she'd ever remembered feeling, she turned around and pulled out. If Helena had been home, she'd have gone to her house. But Helena was at the beach, and Jules was on her road trip. Her parents were probably home, but arriving at their house at this hour would just raise questions she didn't know how to answer.

Hesitating for just a moment, she finally clicked the phone icon on her Jeep's steering wheel. Carly was at the bottom of her favorites, the last one. The last one she should call right now.

Tears slid down her face as the phone rang.

Chapter Eighteen

Hydrotherapy

Carly had her iPad connected to the house Wi-Fi and was watching a movie in bed when her watch told her she had an incoming call. Paige.

Strange, she thought. She was supposed to be at the cabin, where there was no cell service.

"Hey. What's up?" Carly asked.

"I just needed someone to talk to."

She could hear something in Paige's voice that didn't sound right. Sadness? Fatigue? She paused the movie and sat up in bed. "What's wrong?"

"Carly, why do you think you're the one I call when I'm having a bad day?"

Whoa. "That's a good question."

"Do you think I'm gay?"

What. The. Fuck. As she listened more carefully, she noted the faint sound of Paige's sniffles. "Hey. What happened?"

"I just can't do this anymore. I'm not happy, and I've tried to be. Today I went to the cabin to be with Will, and he was there with some of his friends, and I've never felt so alone in my life."

"Sometimes it's like that, if you're the outsider."

"It's not that. I just don't fit in there anymore. I'm not sure where I fit, where I belong. But I think it's…"

She heard sobs now but no conversation.

"It's what?"

"What? What does it say when I'm miserable—totally, wretchedly miserable with my husband—but the one thing that makes me happy is the thought of driving to Rehoboth and spending a few days with... lesbians?"

If she had a Hershey's kiss for every time she'd pondered Paige's sexuality in the months since they'd met, she'd weigh about eight hundred pounds by now. But this was Paige's problem to solve, so she'd kept her thoughts to herself. Yet something was really wrong. Paige was cool and composed, not prone to hysterics.

"Have you been drinking?"

"A little wine."

"Ah. That explains it."

Suddenly, she sounded clear. "I'm not drunk. I'm upset."

"Where are you?"

"Lake Harmony."

She hesitated for a moment, but then her heart overruled her head. Paige needed someone right now, maybe even group therapy. And she had just the group, gathered together in a fabulous beach house. "It'll take you three hours to get here. Maybe you should wait until morning."

"You want me to come?"

How could she possibly answer that question? She always wanted to be with Paige. But Paige was still married. "It sounds like you need a friend. And Liza, Mal, and I are all here. Plus a few other friends, too. So you should probably get your butt down here."

"I'm glad the cabin isn't in upstate New York."

She chuckled. "See. You're already getting back to normal, looking on the bright side of things."

Afraid Paige might fall asleep at the wheel, she stayed on the phone with her during the entire trip. They talked about the weather, and the patients Paige had seen at work, and the lack of clothing she had in her overnight bag. "You are going to have fun at the outlets tomorrow," she told her.

And when Paige finally made the turn off Route One onto Rehoboth Avenue and announced she'd be arriving in a few minutes, she climbed out of bed, changed into sweats, and went outside to wait for her. As she saw the headlights approaching, she waved her phone light onto the ground and directed Paige into the small parking area. It was almost midnight.

"Are you hungry?" she whispered as they walked into the kitchen.

"No. I'm good."

"Follow me," she said as she guided her up the steps to her room.

"This house is huge," Paige said.

"Eight bedrooms. I have four twin beds in my room, in case you want to invite any friends."

"Maybe tomorrow."

She showed Paige their bathroom and helped her hang the few items of clothing she'd brought. And then she decided she needed to talk to her about what had worried her from the moment she'd told Paige to come to the beach.

"Paige, Tasha is going to be really pissed when she sees you."

"Tasha? Why?"

"It has nothing to do with you. Well, I guess it does. Because Tasha works with you and is concerned that you and I have gotten... too friendly."

Paige's eyebrows rose an inch. "Too friendly?"

"Yes. She knows we're not sleeping together, but she's suspicious about where this is heading."

Paige sat on the bed and rested her chin in her hand. Sighing, Paige looked at her with pleading eyes. "Where is this heading?" she whispered.

She didn't hesitate. If Paige wanted to be around lesbians, to see if this was the life she wanted to live, she was happy to have her. But that was as far as this could go. She'd be Paige's friend, but she was not getting romantically involved. "Absolutely nowhere. We both know there's a...chemistry between us," she said with a swirl of her hand. "But you're married. And I know you're not happy with your husband, but until you make some changes—well, not some changes, actually, just one—nothing will ever happen with us. I just wanted you to be prepared for Tasha." She gave Paige a piercing glance, to show her how serious she was.

Instead of the intended effect, though, her words seemed to crush Paige as she sighed and collapsed against the pillow. "Thanks for the warning."

She didn't know what else to say. Sometimes, the truth was brutal, and painful. Still, it had to be spoken. She changed the subject. "Hey. Get some rest. This will look better in the morning."

"Thanks for letting me crash your beach house."

"I suppose we'll find something else to talk about tomorrow, but until then, let's get some sleep."

Instantly, she heard the soft, rhythmic sounds of Paige's breathing that told her she'd fallen asleep. Even though she was exhausted, she didn't follow her there. Instead, she watched her across the space between their beds, knowing she loved her, knowing she couldn't act on her feelings. Doing the right thing sucks, she told herself as she covered her head with her pillow.

It was one in the afternoon when Paige opened her eyes, and she found a note from Carly in the bathroom when she finally made her way there.

Call me when you're ready to deal with the world.

Only ten words, but they made Paige smile. Was she ready to deal with the world? She could deal with Carly, but how about Tasha? Or the other women from Mountain Meadows? Will? She couldn't even think about that.

Growling in her stomach told her it was time to eat. Was there food in the house? Would Carly like to join her? Picking up the phone, she dialed Carly's number. She answered instantly.

"Are you hungry?" Carly asked. "We just got off the course and are heading to the Big Fish. It's on Route One."

"I know where that is."

She did a quick change of clothes and was out the door in five minutes, and in another ten minutes, she found a parking spot and walked into the restaurant. The day was a hot one, and she was happy to find Carly and her friends inside, where the temperature was much more manageable.

She knew most of the ten women at the table, and Carly introduced the others before telling her she'd ordered her a margarita and a burger.

"I guess I'm predictable, huh?" she asked.

"I wouldn't say that," Carly said as she shook her head. Carly's piercing gaze sent shivers down her spine. She was seated at the end, beside Carly, and was grateful to break away from her stare. Across the table were two women from Mountain Meadows who'd joined SAW with Carly. Tasha sat quietly beside them, her neutral expression making her incredibly nervous. The group talked throughout lunch, discussing everything from the food to the weather to the golf, but no one brought up her sudden appearance at the beach house. They didn't ask when she'd arrived, or when she planned to leave, or just what exactly she was doing there.

As the server brought their checks, the group started talking about the rest of their day. Some wanted to head back to the house, a few wanted to go to the beach, and she wanted to go to the outlets. "May I join you?" Tasha asked.

Feeling a little uneasy after Carly's warning the night before, she sucked in a breath but plastered on a smile. "Of course."

They made a plan to meet Carly for dinner near the outlets, and she and Tasha headed to her Jeep. They hadn't traveled ten feet down the sidewalk before Tasha started talking. "I'm concerned about you. And about my friend Carly. I don't want to see either of you get hurt."

She wanted to defend herself, but she didn't want to lie, either. She had feelings for Carly, and apparently, she was telegraphing them Tasha's way. "I understand your concern," she said instead of making excuses.

"What's your plan? Are you leaving your husband?"

"I already have." Wow, she'd said it out loud, and as happy as she was about it, she had to admit it was a little scary. She hadn't bothered to work out the details. She only knew that she needed to get away from Will. The rest she'd figure out later.

"Do you need a lawyer?"

She hadn't thought that far ahead, but it made sense. "Yeah. It's probably a good idea."

Tasha looked relieved, and when she climbed into the passenger seat of the Jeep, her phone was ringing. It was on speaker, so Paige could hear.

"Glenburn, Newton and Waverly. How may I direct your call?" a male voice asked.

"Hi. This is Natasha Peterson for Amanda Waverly," she said, and a moment later she was connected to a woman with a deep, clear voice.

"Tasha! How are you, dear?"

"I'm at the beach, so how can I complain?" Then she told Amanda Waverly that Paige needed a lawyer, briefly explained why, and made her an appointment for the next week.

"Thanks, Tash," she said when she'd hung up the phone.

They were stopped at a traffic light near the outlets when she felt Tasha's hand on her arm. "Please don't hurt my friend. I know she seems tough, and strong, but she has a soft heart. She hasn't let anyone get close in a long time, and for whatever reason, she's chosen you. Please, please be careful."

Carly chose her? Paige knew how she felt, there was no question. But to realize Carly felt the same way made her head spin.

"I don't know what Carly has told you—"

"She says nothing's going on. And I believe her. But I see you two together, and it's just a matter of time. So please be sure this is what you want and not some mid-life crisis or an experiment, or something like that."

She nodded. "I understand." This was a serious crossroads for her, but it was obviously just as important to Carly.

"Perfect. What stores do you want to go to? I'd like to stop at Nike."

And just like that, they moved the conversation to safer ground. They split up in the parking lot without another word about Carly and met an hour later to deposit packages and move the car. She had picked up three pairs of shoes and a new bathing suit, and she wanted to get some shorts and tops to see her through the week. She was in the mood to spoil herself.

As she was browsing the racks, her watch alerted her to a call. A split-second later, Liza's ringtone sounded. "Hey, friend."

"Hey. I hear you're in Rehoboth. What's going on?"

She chuckled but expected nothing less than a challenge from Liza. "I'm at the outlets, doing a little shopping."

"Is that your final answer?"

She sucked in a breath and then sighed. "I left Will."

"Shut the front door."

"It's true." She abandoned the clothing in her hands and walked out of the store, anxious for some air. Sitting on a bench in the sunshine, she told Liza what had happened.

"I can't say I'm surprised. You don't seem happy with him."

Tears stung her eyes, and suddenly she found herself sobbing. "Is that so much to ask for? Happiness?"

"Where are you?" Liza suddenly demanded, and she told her. "I'll be there in five minutes."

She didn't move, and four minutes later, Liza and Mal flanked her on the bench. After hugging her, they each took a hand. "Whatever you need, Paige, we're here for you."

Tears re-formed, and she blotted them with a shirt sleeve.

"So were you guys stalking me? How'd you get here so fast?"

"Our condo's right across the street," Mal said.

"Convenient."

"It is. We just got off the golf course, and I checked my messages. Carly told me you'd be joining us for dinner."

She nodded. She hadn't called Liza and Mal because she hadn't really had a moment free before Liza called her. But she had also hesitated because she knew Liza would demand answers she wasn't sure she had.

"So why did we learn this from Carly, and not from you?" she asked gently.

"I'm still processing this situation. Twenty-four hours ago, I was at a cabin with my husband and his friends. Today I spoke with a divorce lawyer."

"Wow. That was fast."

She sighed. In fact, it had taken much too long.

"Paige, is something going on between you and Carly?" Mal asked softly.

"Is it really that obvious?" Tasha knew, but she was reading Carly's cues, something she'd been doing for years. If Liza and Mal could tell, she must really be broadcasting.

"You're happy around her," Liza said.

"There's that. And the fact that you left Will and drove three hours to see her," Mal added.

She leaned back and looked up to the bright-blue sky. "I am happy with her. With lesbians in general, it seems."

"Duh. For a doctor, you're not too smart. It took you long enough to notice," Mal said.

She elbowed Mal but laughed.

"So how long has this been going on?" Liza asked gently.

"Nothing's going on. She doesn't even know how I feel."

Liza chuckled. "She's a smart cookie. She knows."

"Maybe. But we haven't talked about it." Carly had mentioned their chemistry in the same sentence in which she said nothing would ever happen between them.

"No rush, I guess."

She felt the same way. Her attraction was undeniable but certainly controllable. Everything about her attraction to Carly was new and tenuous, and she felt certain about only one thing—she needed to take her time and sort through everything. Her feelings, her desires, the new direction her life was taking. Without the stress and fear and sadness of Will, she needed to think about herself. And if she used a thought of Carly to brighten her mood from time to time, was there harm in that?

"No. No rush."

"Do you want to stay with us? To give you some space?"

The thought made her feel panicky. Yes, she needed to give this time, but not space. She wanted to be as close to Carly as she possibly could. After thanking them for the offer, she told them she needed some retail therapy and hugged them both before heading back to the store. She eventually connected with Tasha and spent some time with her, and when they met Carly, Liza, and Mal in the parking lot of the Crab Shack a few hours later, she felt much better than she had in forever.

They were in Mal's car, and she and Tasha joined them while they awaited their table. Carly was seated in the middle, and she was careful as she eased into the seat, avoiding contact with Carly. They hadn't been alone since she arrived—not while she was awake, anyway—and she was suddenly nervous to be near her.

As the others talked about the golf match scheduled for the next day, she tuned out and instead focused on Carly. The inch of creamy leather separating their thighs. The fresh smell of her hair. The darkness of her sun-baked skin.

She wanted nothing more than to run a finger down the arm next to her, from the top where it poked out of a sleeveless golf shirt, to a spot above her elbow Paige knew she favored. Carly would close her eyes at her touch, and she'd lean in and kiss her neck.

Suddenly she was drawn out of her reverie by the actual touch of Carly's hand on hers.

"You okay?" she asked.

"Yeah. Just tired."

"It's emotional fatigue," Liza said. "The absolute worst."

She nodded.

"I asked if you found anything good at the stores."

She told them about her purchases, and a few minutes later, the beeper began to vibrate, letting them know their table was ready. They ordered crab, shattered the legs with mallets, and laughed and talked while they ate. She sat beside Liza and Mal, and across from Tasha and Carly. It was difficult to concentrate on anything but her.

How had she denied her feelings all these months? Why had she continued to torture herself, staying with Will, when her heart wasn't there anymore? They were questions that would sort themselves out, in time, but for now she tried not to think about them. She was concentrating instead on what she felt...relief. And, of course, that happiness she always felt around Carly and Liza and Mal.

After dinner they drove back to Rehoboth Avenue and walked the streets, people-watching. She and Liza got a dessert crepe, Carly and Tasha had ice cream, and they all sat on a bench overlooking the moon-kissed ocean while they ate. It was nearly ten when they split up, and Liza and Mal hugged her good night, promising to see her the next day for lunch. Once again, she drove Tasha, and she bid all the housemates good night and went to bed early. She listened for Carly but drifted off before she came to bed. And even though she woke at seven, Carly had already left the room.

She found Carly on the deck, watching the ocean.

"Good morning," Paige said.

"It's a great morning. Look at that sky. That ocean." Carly turned to her. "How are you?"

"I'm okay." She had spent her time at the outlets thinking, and she was happy Tasha had called the attorney. Her marriage was over, so why delay the inevitable? No matter what happened or didn't happen with Carly, she needed to get away from Will. She needed to find herself again, and she couldn't do that with him.

"Did Tasha harass you?"

She chuckled. "Nothing I couldn't handle."

"Do you want to talk?"

"Not yet," she said. "I'd like to eat, then go down to the beach, read my book, and work on my skin cancer."

"It's a good day for all of that. Mind if I join you?"

She looked at her and felt giddy. "I'd love it. But don't you have golf?"

"Not until this afternoon."

Carly shared her bagels, and then they hauled chairs and an umbrella from beneath the deck and set up camp on the beach. She managed to lose herself in the book, and an hour later, Tasha joined them on the beach with a picnic basket. From within, she produced a plate of cheese and a charcuterie, and a container of crackers.

"No wine?" Carly asked.

"It's a breakfast cheese plate."

"Mimosas?" Carly asked.

Tasha grinned and produced a bottle of champagne and a small carton of orange juice.

Paige got a pleasant buzz from the champagne, and when Tasha wandered down to the water, she sat beside Carly in Tasha's chair. "Tasha and I called a divorce lawyer."

Carly placed her hand over hers and squeezed. "That must have been very hard."

"Not really. Tasha actually made the call."

Carly roared. "She didn't get to be the CEO by being timid."

"Apparently not."

"What are you going to do? Are you going to move out?"

She had thought about it. She'd suggest to Will he stay at the cabin, and she could have the house. They'd put a small down payment on it, and they hadn't owned it long enough to pay down the mortgage. It wouldn't cost her very much to buy him out, just a little more than half of the modest down payment. She asked Carly how she'd do that.

"You'll have to refinance. How's your credit?"

"Good."

They talked about that process, and Carly promised she'd text a friend to help her with a new loan application. "If you need to, you can stay in my guesthouse."

Carly's offer touched and thrilled her at the same time. Still, she didn't want to leave her house. In fact, after moving for college, a few times in medical school, and again in residency, she'd be happy if she never saw another moving van. "That's sweet, but Will's hardly ever home anyway."

"Once you hit him with divorce papers, he probably won't ever leave the house."

"I hope he keeps it a clean fight. I guess I'll know soon."

They spent a pleasant morning on the beach, then shared lunch on their deck before the group left for the golf match. She lost herself in her book, sitting on the deck looking out at the Atlantic Ocean. The novel was mindless, and when she finished, she explored the bookshelf in the great room, in search of another title. Just something to keep her occupied, to keep her mind from her troubles.

She pulled a title from the shelf and read the back and chuckled. Carly had told her the house was owned by two women from Washington, but Paige hadn't really thought much about them. The lesbian romance novel in her hands brought them to mind. Shelving the first, she pulled out a second, and then another and another. Finally, she took *Tipping the Velvet* with her as she went back to the beach. She didn't put it down, not until the fading daylight told her it was time to head back to the house.

After packing up her camp, she made two trips to the house with the beach gear, showered, and once again curled up with the book. Carly and Tasha found her there reading when they got home.

Carly had a difficult day on the golf course. Of course, she'd come to the beach for the tournament, but since Paige arrived, golf didn't seem important anymore. It had taken all her will to leave this afternoon, to abandon Paige with her thoughts and ideas and fears. She could only imagine what was going through her mind. She'd picked up her phone to call a dozen times, but in the end, she'd put it down. Paige was a big girl, and as much as she cared for her, she needed to keep some space between them.

"Whatcha reading?" she asked as she slid into the chair across from Paige. Paige held up the book, and she could feel her eyebrows shoot up two inches. "Great choice," she said simply.

"Behave yourselves," Tasha said as she gave Paige a stern look. "I'm getting a shower."

"I think she hates me," Paige whispered when Tasha was out of sight.

She shook her head. "She just loves me."

"Still?"

"Not in the same way, but a better way. It's friendship. We look out for each other."

"I can see that."

She nodded toward the book in Paige's hand, wondering about her choice. "So, a lesbian novel. Are you...?" She didn't know quite what she wanted to ask. Curious seemed so clichéd, but fitting. Enjoying it? That was probably the right question. They'd not really spoken about the attraction between them, other than Paige acknowledging it, but they both knew it was there. Now Paige had tiptoed a little farther into her world, and she wondered if she found it a comfortable place.

"Fascinated."

"Hmm," she said. Interesting word choice. It was like curiosity on steroids.

"Yes. And this woman in the novel is so relatable. She meets a woman and becomes infatuated with her, leaves home, becomes a lesbian."

She needed a drink. Standing, she nodded at Paige's empty glass. "Do you need more water?"

"Please," Paige replied as she offered her the glass. A moment later, she was in the kitchen, mixing a vodka tonic as she thought of what she should say to Paige. In all her many experiences with women, she'd never been in one quite like this. And of course, she'd never met a woman like Paige, either.

After handing Paige her water, she sat at the other end of the couch, facing Paige, then sipped her drink for courage. "You relate to this character, huh?"

Paige put the book down and stretched out her legs, so they just reached her. "I do." She tried not to focus on Paige's foot, on the place on her own leg where it touched her.

"You think you're really a lesbian?" she asked softly.

"You sound surprised, yet I think you've always thought I was gay."

"I'm not surprised that you're gay. I'm surprised that you've realized it so quickly. Just a few months ago, you were oblivious." She sipped her drink while Paige lay there quietly.

"I guess that's what happens when you meet someone who opens your eyes to new possibilities." Paige turned her head, and she might have been flirting, but she thought it was more like acceptance. Paige seemed at peace.

They sat for a few moments, and finally Paige closed her eyes as she leaned back into the couch. "How was golf?"

"It was a nice course. That's the best thing I can say about the day." She didn't want to talk about her poor performance, or the heat, or the fact that she'd missed Paige.

Paige laughed. "I have my clubs. Want to play in the morning?"

She didn't hesitate. "I'd love to."

They set their alarms for six and fell asleep quietly, in the same room but in different beds. They were out the door by six twenty and were the first players on the course at seven. As always, they had fun together, and they were back at the beach house before lunch. Tasha had declined the invitation to join them, and they met her on the beach, along with most of the other women sharing the house.

It was July third, and Rehoboth had gotten even more crowded as holiday tourists poured into town. Liza and Mal joined their group, and many of the women played games on the beach, tossing Frisbees and footballs and sandbags, but many, like Carly and her group, just enjoyed the company. That night, they cooked out instead of dealing with the crowds at the restaurants and had a quiet night on the deck.

Carly and her housemates had another day in their rental, but Paige was leaving in the morning for her afternoon shift at the hospital. They'd had a great bonding time, and Carly was afraid to go back to reality. She knew she had to let Paige make her choices, but it was hard to give her that freedom, knowing how much she already cared.

Sleep did not come easily, as once again she stared at Paige in her bed. She wanted to slip out of her own and lie beside Paige, just hold her. Not make love, or even kiss—just hold her.

Although Paige was the one going through the difficulty right now, Carly needed the reassurance, the connection. When she finally drifted off, her sleep was choppy, and she awoke feeling hungover.

After Paige ate breakfast, she walked her to the car. "Call me when you get home. I'm worried that he'll be there."

Paige looked hurt. "Does this mean we won't talk on the way?"

She hugged Paige, giving a little squeeze at the end. "I'm so happy you came. And I'm here for you. Don't forget that."

"Like Tasha? A good friend."

"For now." She sighed. It was all she could offer. For now.

Paige pulled the Jeep out of the driveway and into the beach traffic, feeling calmer than she'd felt in a long while. Her time at the beach had been therapeutic, relaxing but also affirming. Spending time with lesbians felt right, and she had been more comfortable with Carly and her friends than she'd ever been in the straight world.

She liked being with women, she'd realized as she surrounded herself with them for three days. She liked all of them, but especially Carly. The more time she spent with her, the better she felt.

What would happen with them? She wasn't sure if they were destined to be friends, or more, but she was grateful to Carly for the few days they'd had at the beach. No matter what happened, she wasn't going back to Will. Her future was with a woman. She was sure of that. She only hoped Will would take the news well.

It turned out that Carly was right about him. He was at the house when she arrived home, hanging out there on the Fourth of July instead of at the lake. Wasting no time, she told him she'd called an attorney and asked him to move into the lake house while they were settling things.

Even though she'd practiced what she wanted to say, her words came out as a jumble of half sentences punctuated with sobs. Emotionally, it was tremendously hard to end her marriage, even though she knew she had to. She wasn't happy anymore. She had been once, when she'd liked Will and he'd liked her. She'd loved him, but her self-analysis and professional analysis had both helped her realize her love had been more hero worship than actual love for another human being. It had been exciting and even good for a while, but for all the wrong reasons. The right thing now—to fix her own life and let Will get back to his—was to separate.

She was kind, choosing her words with care, but Will was not. He'd clearly anticipated this step, because he didn't flinch when she shared her thoughts. She was an emotional wreck, and he was stoic. Mean, but stoic.

With a few malicious words, he told her he didn't plan to leave, and so she tiptoed around for a week, trying to avoid him. The lawyer advised her to stay in the house so Will couldn't claim she'd abandoned it, but finally, after a rather nasty exchange in the kitchen, she decided to accept Carly's offer of her guesthouse. Taking the essentials, just enough to fill her suitcase, she left for work one night and didn't go home afterward.

It was surprisingly easy to drive past her house to Carly's that morning. "I brought you breakfast," she said when Carly opened her door. Handing her a bag from Carly's favorite shop, she followed her into the house.

Carly looked amazing. Dressed for work in tan slacks and a dark peasant shirt, she scooted around the kitchen getting real coffee cups and plates for their food.

"I thought of a problem with you staying here," Carly said, and her heart dropped. She didn't want to abandon her house, and she planned to stop a couple of times a week to dust and collect mail, but after her latest fight with Will, she didn't want to stay there. Not while he was there, anyway.

"What?"

"Do you hear that?"

She listened and detected the faint buzz of a lawnmower. She nodded.

"That'll go on all morning. And then, about eleven, you'll hear the motorboats and Jet Skis. It's not the best place to sleep during the day."

"Is that what you're worried about? The noise?"

Carly nodded.

Relieved, she waved a dismissive hand. "I have a sleep machine. I fall asleep to the sounds of a waterfall, day and night, rain or shine. No worries."

Carly raised her mug and offered a toast. "In that case, welcome to the lake." She showed her to the guesthouse and gave her a key, helping her make up the queen bed with linens still warm from the dryer.

"I'm heading to the office. I'll check on you tonight," Carly said at the door a few minutes later. She lingered for a moment, a worried look on her face. Second thoughts, Paige wondered for a moment, but then Carly spoke again.

"If you need anything, call. If you can't reach me, call Dominica. She can always track me down."

She hugged Carly. "Thank you." She was a jumble of emotions and suddenly started to cry. Carly held her until the sobs subsided, then pulled away.

"You can stay as long as you need to."

She was relieved. She needed to be away from Will, to be someplace peaceful. But she also needed to be with Carly.

She watched Carly drive away, then slipped into her pajamas and crawled into bed. After an amazing sleep, she woke at six that night and wandered outside. It was pleasant, not too hot, but the lake was busy. Carly came out onto her deck.

"I'm grilling chicken. Would you like to join me for dinner?"

"Can I bring anything?"

"Why don't you whip up a chocolate soufflé for dessert?"

"Wiseass."

Half an hour later, freshly showered with wet hair combed straight back, she turned up at Carly's door.

"Love the hair," Carly said as she held open the door in welcome.

"I didn't want to keep you."

"No, seriously. I love it slicked back like that. It gives you a whole new look. Androgynous."

"Hmm," she said. And she thought she was just being practical.

"What can I do?" she asked.

"Set the table, please."

Carly pointed out the appropriate cupboards, and she collected two place settings, then went outside to set the picnic table on the deck. A moment later, Carly came through the door with a bowl of chicken. "How'd you sleep?" she asked as she placed the food on the grill.

"Either that bed is amazing or I was just tired, because I didn't move for nine hours."

Carly stopped and stared at her. "Good. You need to chill."

Their dinner was pleasant, and at least a dozen times she took a deep breath and told herself to relax. Looking around at the comfortable space Carly had created, it was hard not to, but still—her life was a mess.

Yet living at the lake in Carly's guesthouse that summer was just what she needed. Carly entertained often, but it only bothered her when she was trying to sleep on the weekends and her friends got crazy outside the bedroom window. Since Carly worked long hours during the week, or golfed, the disturbances happened only on Saturdays and Sundays, and she managed to sleep early so she could spend time with Carly's friends.

Perhaps her ease with women might have been a clue about her sexuality, if she had been looking for it. She'd simply lived in a heterosexual world and accepted it as her own. Being at the lake, though, and spending time with Carly and all her friends, provided a window into an entirely new universe. To her amazement, she felt at home here, more than she'd ever felt in her life. It was as if she'd been underwater, struggling to breathe, and finally broke the surface and sucked in a chest full of air. She was alive and had never felt so wonderful.

And even though she'd never gone beyond that one experience back in medical school, she knew the next time she kissed a woman, it would be amazing. And with all her heart, she knew there would be a next time.

Her summer was busy. Planning for the divorce, which Will was blocking at every step, she worked extra shifts whenever she could and put away the money for her attorney's fees. She played golf and hiked, spent time with her family, and healed her spirit. And most days, whether it was early before an evening shift or late after her day at the hospital, she spent time with Carly.

They worked in the garden, sat in the sun, splashed around in the lake. Sometimes, Carly cooked for her, and sometimes, she cooked for Carly. The best times, though, were like that first dinner, when they got everything ready together, talking as they prepped food and cleaned up afterward.

At the end of the summer, with Will still refusing to leave the house, and under the advice of her attorney, Paige stopped paying the mortgage and the bills. She might lose her interest in the house, but Amanda Waverly, one sharp barrister, figured the decision would benefit her in the end. They'd always kept their own accounts, so that part of the separation was easy. Even though she had always paid the mortgage, she was going to get only half the house, because they owned it jointly. But Will would get the entire cabin, because his name alone was on the deed. Every dollar she spent on the house was more money lost.

So, with Helena and Al and her parents there for moral—and physical—support, she took what she wanted of her possessions and moved most of them to a storage unit. All the art was hers, as was her bedroom furniture, so that was easy. After that, Will battled her over everything from the blender to their artificial Christmas tree.

She didn't care, though. She lost some things in her war with him, but she won her freedom.

Carly initially refused her offer of rent for the cottage, but after she officially moved out of her house, Carly relented. It was a modest amount, and if she included the bills she'd been paying to keep the other place running, it came out to be about a small fraction of her prior financial obligation. She was saving a fortune, which was good, because at some point, Carly's good will would run out, and she would have to strike out on her own.

Somehow, the ideas she had about a relationship with Carly had morphed into something else. Carly had made it clear that she wasn't interested in a relationship with her, but her attraction to Carly, and her desire to be with her, had helped her understand and accept that she needed to explore her sexuality. Perhaps she'd have a relationship with a woman and decide it wasn't for her. Or perhaps she'd confirm her suspicions. Either way, she planned to follow her heart, and perhaps her lust, and see where it took her.

And if anyone could put her in a strong position to meet women, it was Carly. Members of her large circle of friends congregated at Carly's house almost every weekend. Even at SAW, where Carly had started out knowing only the local ladies, she had already attracted a bunch of people, and at the sleepovers, people seemed to gravitate to her. Paige had met so many women over the course of the summer, she couldn't keep them straight in her mind. Even so, with all those women around, Paige gave only one a second look.

Chapter Nineteen

The City of Light

Luck was on Carly's side when the travel itinerary arrived. The group was flying her favorite airline, and she was able to use her corporate-credit-card miles to upgrade to first class for the flight from Philadelphia to Paris. After debating for a moment, she booked Paige in the seat next to hers. It just made sense. Didn't it?

As payment, Paige offered her free health care for life, for her and Tasha. She had negotiated the deal to include any woman she was dating, and Paige hadn't balked. She suspected she had no idea how much of her soul she'd sold for a first-class ticket to Europe, but she'd figure it out eventually. She only hoped Paige would still talk to her after she did.

Because, even after all these months, she still loved talking to Paige. They'd had a great summer. Living in her guesthouse, Paige was never in her way, but often available when she was in the mood for company. Which, she'd discovered with Paige, was quite often. They'd made a routine of sharing dinner, except when Paige worked. Every week, they had golf outings at the Meadows, and they traveled to SAW events every other weekend. On two rainy Wednesdays, they'd made spontaneous trips to Broadway. They'd even taken a bus trip to a Yankees game.

It was the strangest relationship she had ever had. They were like an old married couple, completely compatible and comfortable, except they didn't have sex. Not that she hadn't thought of it. After Paige had moved to the lake, she was tempted. But then she'd told herself Paige might reconcile with Will, and she'd put on the brakes. When the reunion didn't happen, they'd just sort of gotten into a groove as friends, and even though Paige had told her she thought she was gay, she'd never indicated she was ready to take the next step. And she cared too much about Paige to push her.

So, friends they were, heading off to the most romantic city in the world.

After depositing her suitcase in her car, she walked across the driveway and knocked on Paige's door.

"I'm going to Paris! Wanna come with me?" She felt like a little girl on Christmas morning, running down the stairs to discover what Santa had left beneath the tree. Only this was so much better because this was the gift she'd chosen herself, and after waiting half her life, she was finally getting it.

It wasn't what she'd always dreamed of, but her dear friend Dom was right. Next year, or the year after, or whenever she found herself in a relationship, she might not be able to walk the streets of Paris. She might be too old to climb the Eiffel Tower. And the truth was, if she couldn't take her lover to Paris, at least she could take someone she loved. And she loved Paige.

Strange, indeed. She had been careful, setting boundaries to keep Paige at a safe distance. For instance, they spent the majority of their time outside, or at least outside the house, where she felt more in control. They didn't watch television together, and even when they cooked—an activity she loved doing with Paige—they stayed in the kitchen, stuck to the business of preparing food and cleaning up afterward. The strategy had worked well. Despite the affinity she had for Paige, she had kept the relationship casual—sometimes acting as a landlord, sometimes as a counselor, sometimes as an older sister. And she'd been rewarded with a friend. They talked, and golfed, and laughed, sang the same songs in the car, ate the same foods. Paige wasn't her lover, but she was the next best thing. As Tasha had sarcastically pointed out, Paige had become her new bestie.

"I think I have a suitcase here somewhere," Paige said as she spun, finger on her chin in the classic thinking pose. "Ah, there it is. I'm in."

Dressed in leggings and a baggy sweater, Paige looked relaxed. It was perfect for a long trans-Atlantic flight. Looking down at her very sophisticated ensemble of a blazer, button-down shirt, slacks, and loafers, she rethought her choice. Paige was going to be so much more comfortable. And she'd arrive wrinkle free.

Pulling the door closed, she smiled at Carly and followed her to the back of the car, where Carly helped her load her suitcase.

"Did you weigh this?" Carly asked. "I think you might be over by a hundred pounds or so."

"Forty-five, and that includes a very chic Vera Bradley duffel stuffed in there, so I can bring home souvenirs."

"Good thinking." Another great idea. Paige really was a good traveler.

She got back behind the wheel and turned to her. "Passport?"

"Check."

"Credit card and spare credit card?"

"Double check."

"Then we're off." As she backed out of the driveway, she asked about Paige's overnight shift. "Did you sleep at all today?"

With a deep sigh, she admitted she hadn't. "I had a call from Amanda Waverly first thing. Will wants to reconcile."

Her heart stopped. This is what she'd been dreading. "What?" she asked as she gripped the steering wheel.

"You heard me. He wants to do counseling."

"Paige, that's ridiculous. Why now?" Over the months, Paige had shared much of her marital heartbreak with her, and she knew there was no changing someone like Will. But even if there were, Paige was gay. Carly was more and more sure of it as time went on. Paige hung out with all the girls, golfing and at the lake, and fit right in. She'd read most of Tasha's collection of lesbian fiction. But above those obvious clues was their undeniable mutual attraction. They hadn't acted on their feelings, but that didn't make them less real.

"I think he's beginning to realize he's not going to take me to the cleaners. His cabin isn't very grand, but it's sitting on a big chunk of lakefront land, and since they built a cell tower on the mountain, home prices have skyrocketed. He was hoping to get spousal support, but since he owns that house, I may just walk away with the house in Clarks Summit, and that's that."

"Wow." She stretched it into three syllables. "Good for Will, I guess. He has a nice investment. Can he afford it on his own? Is that why he wants to patch things up?" She bit her lip, wanting to ask more. Even though she knew their relationship would never work out, that didn't mean Paige wouldn't try.

"He can afford it. He has a lawsuit pending because he was hurt at work, and I'm sure he's going to get seven figures for that. Plus, he's collecting his full salary."

"Seven figures?"

"That's what his lawyer says."

"Maybe you *should* wait on this divorce," she said, hoping Paige would shoot the idea down.

"Hmmm." Paige sighed. "Interesting thought. But let's talk about something else. We're on vacation. And thanks for driving," Paige said as she plugged in her phone and chose a playlist.

It seemed that Paige had tried to lighten her tone with the thank-you, but the first part of her comment sounded angry. Worse yet, she hadn't rejected the suggestion that she stay with Will for the money.

Carly took a deep breath. "No worries."

"How long to the airport? I never realized how far out the lake is until I started living here."

"I hear you. The only thing I'm close to is the lake."

They talked about the merits of living in town, and once again her time with Paige flew. Still, she was troubled by how Paige had blown off her *joke* about staying married for the money. And now she was complaining about the lake. Was she going to move back into her old house if she and Will could agree? And what about this marriage counseling? She wanted to probe, but Paige had practically slammed that door in her face. Ouch.

Thinking it wasn't a great way to start the trip, she grew silent. Would they finally run out of things to talk about? Or would they irritate each other and end up not speaking at all? She sighed at the thought. She'd soon know.

She parked, and a minute later they were in the terminal, where Dr. DeMichelle stood with a sign beckoning the group. She recognized him from her stint at the University of Scranton twenty-five years earlier. After introducing themselves, they checked in and made their way up the escalator to the departure lounge.

"So, what happened to Jules?" she asked. Paige had informed her that her niece was meeting them in Philly.

"When she was packing last night, she realized her passport had expired. They drove to Philly last night so she could renew it this morning."

"They do that?"

"I guess they do. She sent me a text a few hours ago and said she was good to go. It could have been much worse. This flight out of Scranton is a charter. If it had been booked through the airline, she wouldn't have been able to cancel it without voiding her entire ticket. In addition to a crazy passport fee, my sister would have had to pay for another flight to Paris."

She shook her head. "Kids."

"Yes. Sometimes Jules makes me want about five of them, and then other times, I think of having an emergency tubal ligation."

"Not a lesbian problem."

Paige laughed so hard she snorted, and she was relieved. They were okay.

After Paige finally caught her breath, they were quiet for a moment before Carly turned to her. "Do you still want kids? After all this with Will?"

"Yes." No hesitation there, except for Carly's heartbeat. Kids had never been in her plan, but Paige had mentioned them several times, and when she entertained the idea of something happening with Paige, that always seemed to bubble to the surface of her daydreams, clouding the image in her mind. Yet she knew it was Paige's dream, and she'd left Will partly because he didn't share it. No way was she going to get in Paige's way on that issue.

"I can see it. You're patient and kind. And very sweet to your niece."

Paige nodded and smiled widely. "Jules is mostly easy. How about you? Have you ever thought of having children?"

"Umm, no. Never. Not for one second."

"Really?"

"Really. I don't possess those good qualities that you have. I'm not patient or even very nice. I'm extremely self-centered, which is perfect because I have no one to worry about except myself."

Paige tried not to laugh. "I guess it worked out well then."

"Extremely well. I mean, look at us. We're on our way to Paris. If either of us had kids, we'd be home sewing Halloween costumes or something, thinking about what to serve at our monster bash."

Carly's phone rang, and Paige turned to her own, answered some emails and caught up on the news while Carly was on her call. She'd been so busy that morning talking to the lawyer, and her therapist, and her parents, and her sister that she hadn't had a moment to spare. This was the first time she'd looked at her phone since the day before. Her plan for a short nap had never materialized, and right now she was running on adrenaline. When she boarded the plane for Paris and pulled her mask on and her blanket up, she'd sleep until they touched down at Charles de Gaulle.

Dr. DeMichelle asked for their attention, and both she and Carly put their phones down while he welcomed the group and gave some basic instructions. And then they were boarding the plane for Philly. Carly assumed the seat beside her that Jules would have occupied, and they talked for the duration of the thirty-minute flight. Once in the airport they found Jules and Melody and spent time talking to them. Carly pulled out her Paris guidebook, but she had downloaded her itinerary.

Jules and Melody wandered around while Carly and she sat at the bar, and she had to call Jules twice when the announcement was made about their impending boarding. Always the protective aunt, she sent Carly ahead with the rest of the first-class passengers and boarded with Jules and the rest of the group, not meeting Carly again until Jules was settled comfortably in her seat.

In first class, she found Carly sipping a glass of champagne. "I didn't get you one. I didn't want it to get warm," Carly said as she looked around. Then, spotting the flight attendant, she pointed a finger to her glass, and he appeared beside Paige with the champagne bottle and a crystal flute. They toasted, and Paige sat on the edge of her seat, inspecting the accommodations. Her own private pod had a reclining seat and footrest, plenty of space for her personal items, and a television screen as big as the one attached to her computer at home.

When the pilot began talking, she settled in and previewed the dinner menu. Options like steak, seafood, cheese plates, and fruit, and a wine list with a dozen selections to choose from told her she'd made the right choice in accepting the first-class ticket from Carly. This was *nice.*

They settled in for takeoff, and after a wine with her dinner, she found it difficult to keep her eyes open. Unbuckling her seat belt, she knelt on her seat and reached over to Carly, who was watching a movie. "I'm going to sleep."

"It's early."

"I'm beat."

"I'll bet. But you'll be ready for the invasion of Paris in a few hours."

She settled back into her seat, pulled up the blanket, and was asleep before she knew it. When Carly tapped her gently on the shoulder to wake her, she wanted to tell her to come back later, to wake her when they landed. But then she looked around and saw the flurry of activity. The crew were getting ready to serve their morning meal. "I figured I'd let you sleep through breakfast, but I don't want you to get a migraine."

She had shared her propensity for hunger-induced headaches and told Carly she always traveled with food for emergencies. Since then, it seemed Carly always had food on hand, too. Carly looked out for her. "Thank you. That was sweet."

She sat up and situated herself, then took the proffered coffee while declining the mimosa. A moment later she dug into a plate of cheese and fruit served with a warm baguette. Heaven. Leaning back in her seat, she closed her eyes and savored the flavors, amazed at her good fortune.

On her prior trips to Europe after red-eye flights, she'd arrived feeling miserable. Sitting upright in an airplane seat wasn't conducive to restful sleep, and she always felt like she'd been partying all night when she arrived at her destination. Not so today. Her batteries were fully charged, and she was ready to conquer Paris.

And it was all thanks to Carly. Paige wouldn't have even considered flying up front, but everything about Carly was first-class. The food she ate and the wine she drank with it, and the tableware she used to serve it. The clothes she wore and the car she drove. She listened to opera and NPR on the radio. She had met a ton of accomplished people in her lifetime, but few of them compared to the woman sitting beside her. Carly did everything the right way.

After landing and collecting their luggage and snaking through the customs and immigration lines, the group of fifty boarded a tour bus. Dr. DeMichelle introduced their guide, an older gentleman named Claude, who promised them a wonderful week in Paris. And, apparently, they weren't wasting any time. It was the middle of the Paris morning, and the tour bus battled traffic and impossibly narrow streets and dropped them beside the Seine, at the foot of Notre Dame.

"Every time I come to Europe, I find myself humbled once again by the architecture," she said as she gazed up at the towering spire of the iconic cathedral.

"Yes. I'm amazed when I list a house that's a hundred years old. And this is seven, eight hundred."

"That last pig was very wise. He knew to build with stone."

Carly looked puzzled for a moment, then laughed. "You're a goof."

"Isn't it amazing?" Jules asked as they waited.

"It truly is."

"Jesus's crown is in there."

"I think it's just a piece of it. And they probably don't bring that out for American tourists. It's like Nana's good china—it's seen only on special occasions."

They would have loved to walk around, to sit and people-watch, but Claude had an agenda, and he was wearing a watch to make sure they stuck to it. Ushering them inside, he handed the group over to another guide, who showed them the nave and the towers, the three rose windows and the statues. When they had a free moment, she and Carly lit candles, and she said a prayer of thanks that they'd arrived safely. Then they were escorted to an exit and back into the bright Paris morning.

"I want to come back," she said. "I feel rushed."

"Don't cross Claude. I think he's special forces," Carly said with a wink.

"You're not kidding," she said as they hurried to keep up with the herd heading back to the bus.

"Now, we eat," Claude announced when all tourists were accounted for. They drove only a few blocks, crossing the river, and stopped before a café overlooking the Seine. From the bus she could see a dozen open tables outside, with plenty of heaters blazing. Even though it was sunny, it was only sixty degrees, and this was an occasion she wouldn't have minded indoor dining. And then she exited the bus, and turned to wait for Carly and Jules and Melody, and saw Notre Dame, and she sat before anyone else could claim the table.

"I think I want to eat inside," Carly said, and then when she pointed, Carly turned.

"Oh." Without another word, she claimed the seat beside her. Jules and Melody, oblivious, sat without interrupting their conversation.

They were quickly served, and she and Carly talked without facing each other. "It's just magnificent," she said after a while. She breathed deeply, wanting to pull Paris inside her as she looked down the narrow, cramped street beside them. It seemed alive, as people rushed in every direction, on foot and in busses and cars, and even in the boats navigating the Seine. And when she looked up and saw the cathedral, she was awed.

Carly followed her gaze. "It is," she said softly.

"You're here. I'm so happy for you. I know you've dreamed of this for a long time."

Leaning closer, Carly whispered, "Thanks for talking me into it." She squeezed Paige's hand and sent her shivering.

She had thought she'd learned to control that reaction to Carly, but maybe not. Because here she was, sitting beside her at a café in Paris, mesmerized by her all over again.

They talked about the flight, and Jules proudly announced she'd stayed awake for nearly the entire crossing. "Since it's six in the morning in Scranton, I've been up almost an entire day."

"It's good practice, Jules. For med school."

Melody's eyes flew open. "It sounds so exciting. Staying up all night, saving lives."

She told Melody a little about her training, both in medical school and residency, and the girl seemed fascinated. Her father, a pediatrician, must have told her these tales, too, but she seemed as if she were hearing the war stories for the first time. Jules knew all about her education, but she listened as well, and to her surprise, when she tried to change the subject, Carly stopped her. "It's very fascinating. I don't mind the topic at all."

"Did you sleep well in your fancy seat?" Jules asked. "You were snoring when I came to check on you."

"*You* checked on *me?*" she asked, amused.

"Yeah. And Carly gave me her extra blanket."

"I'm glad one of us is watching out for you," she said as she looked at Carly.

Carly winked. "Jules is my bud."

She was happy to know that they were friends of sorts. Jules had started her job at the theater, and Carly had reported her to be an outstanding usher. For whatever reason, Jules spontaneously texted Carly and emailed her things about Broadway and other topics she thought might interest her. It was quite odd, but who was she to judge?

Their food was excellent—a pot of stew served family style with a baguette and a carafe of wine, which Jules and Melody eyed with interest. "Don't even think about it," she said before they could ask.

"What?" Jules asked innocently.

She replied only with a stern look.

When lunch was over, they boarded their bus once again and drove a few miles to the Champ de Mars, where Claude dramatically announced their arrival at the Eiffel Tower. Their tickets took them all the way to the top, and after informing them of all the things they might do in the area, he opened the bus doors, and they were off.

"I'm not sure I'm ready for this," Carly said. "I mean, we just got here. What will I have to look forward to if we see this on the first day?"

They stood for a moment, staring down the green space to the tower. People were everywhere—walking, standing, talking, picnicking on the grass—all seemingly oblivious to the marvel of architecture looming just beyond. It seemed small from this distance, but still it dwarfed everything else. Paige felt small, too, but so alive. Paris had energy, and it seemed to seep from the ground and right through her. And there was Carly's energy, too. Seeing her here, how happy she was, filled her with joy.

She patted Carly's shoulder. "We'll come back, right after we see Notre Dame for the second time."

"I could look at this all day."

"Actually, we *can* come here every day. Our hotel is pretty close by. And I brought a Frisbee," Jules announced proudly.

She looked around but didn't see anyone playing. Jules would be the trendsetter.

"Jules, ready to go up?" she asked. "Want to climb the stairs or ride the elevator?"

"Climb!" they all answered at once.

As they walked the length of the park, she longed to explore the side paths and the buildings lining the green space, and she hoped they'd do that at some point. The tower grew more imposing, and when they reached the open area beneath it, she stopped and spun in a circle, taking it in. The structure truly was massive. The concrete supports of the bases were two stories high, the space enormous. "Wow. You could fit a football field under here."

"Yeah," Carly whispered, and she realized that she, too, was in awe.

They climbed to the first floor and walked around, then to the second floor, where they caught the elevator to the top. The bright, clear day afforded them a magnificent view of all of Paris, and she simply stood and stared, looking for familiar buildings. She followed the snaking river with her eye, taking deep breaths as a sense of calm filled her. And then she saw Carly, staring out as well, and she moved to the place beside her.

Tuning out the world, she and Carly stood quietly as they studied the magnificence of the city of Paris. Finally, she heard Carly's voice. "Thank you for this."

When she turned, Carly was smiling at her, and she felt her energy once again. It was the same thing she'd felt the first time she saw Carly, as if a force field were pulling them together. "I'm really happy you came," she said as she nodded toward Jules and Melody. "Otherwise, I'd be the third wheel."

"C'mon," Carly said as she hooked her arm. "Speaking of three, we have three more sides to see."

As they were facing the Seine, Jules interrupted their quiet. "We should head back. It's a long walk to the bus."

"Five minutes," she said as she wondered what it would look like at night, with the lights reflecting off the river.

Carly spoke her thoughts. "I want to come back at night. Can you imagine how beautiful it must be?"

"Let's do it," she said before they turned and caught the elevator down. They had to hunt for Jules and Melody, but after they found them, the walk to the bus was easy. And then, a few minutes later, they were on their way to the hotel.

Dr. DeMichelle passed through the bus, handing out large manila envelopes. She opened theirs. Room keys, an itinerary, safety tips, a list of local restaurants, shopping areas, and museums within walking distance of the hotel.

"There's a welcome dinner at seven tonight," she said. "That's easy. We have three hours to unpack."

They arrived and retrieved their luggage from beneath the bus, and she stood waiting for the others when she heard Jules shriek and literally jump into the open arms of a tall young man wearing jeans and a trim wool jacket. "Luc!" she yelled, and she took a step closer as Melody joined Jules in her assault of the young man.

"I'm so happy you made it to Paris," he was saying as she interrupted.

"Hey," she said. "What's going on?"

"Do you remember Luc? He was an exchange student at my high school last year. He's here to give us the tour of Paris."

She felt her jaw drop. "What?" Why was she just hearing this now?

Jules was oblivious. "We've been in contact since he came back to Europe. He's going to take us out. It's Saturday night!"

Her mouth went dry as her heart pounded. Jules was her baby niece. And she wanted to go off exploring in a foreign country with some boy she barely knew? "Jules, I think we should talk about this."

"Oh, Paige. It's fine. Luc lives here. We'll be safe."

Speechless, she just stared.

"Just let us put our stuff in the room, Luc, and we'll meet you back in the lobby in ten."

"Oui," he replied.

As Jules turned to pull her luggage, Paige caught her arm. "Jules, you can't just take off with a stranger. He could rape you. Or murder you."

Jules dismissed her concerns. "He's a teddy bear. Besides, I'm eighteen now, Paige. I'm in *college*. You can't really stop me."

She looked around and saw Carly watching the unfolding drama but offering no help. "I'm responsible for you."

"I'm responsible for myself," she said. "If I could manage a month traveling the US in an RV with my friends, I can handle one night in Paris. I'll be fine. I'll text you when I get back to the hotel later."

"Will you be back for dinner?" she asked desperately.

"No," she said as the elevator door closed behind her. Then it opened again, and Jules blew her a kiss. "Thanks for understanding. I'll call your room when we get back."

"Huh! What makes you think I'll be here? Maybe *I'll* be out."

"Very funny!" Jules laughed as the door closed again.

She let out her breath and tried to calm her spinning head. "What the fuck just happened?" she asked herself. Should she call Helena or just let it go? There was some merit in what Jules had said, but still. They were in a foreign country, and she was so young.

Carly approached. "What are you going to do?"

"Do you have all your stuff?" she asked, and when she nodded, Paige hit the elevator button.

"I guess I'll call Helena and get her advice."

"That sounds smart."

They rode the elevator in silence, and when they reached their room, she opened the door and pulled out her phone. It was almost four o'clock Paris time, which meant Helena should be up.

"How about that daughter of mine?" Helena said by way of greeting. "She's been in Paris for less than a day, and already she has a date."

"Did you know about this?" she asked.

"No, but she called me from the Eiffel Tower and told me Luc was going to take them out. He's at the Sorbonne now, so he knows his way around."

"You know this boy?" she asked, still feeling off balance.

"Yes. He's very sweet. I'm sure the girls will have a good time with him."

She was relieved. "Okay, good. I can breathe again."

She disconnected the phone and collapsed on the bed nearest the door. Carly had put her bag on the other one. It was a small room, with only a narrow passage around the beds and a tiny desk near the window. It took only a few steps to cross, and she pulled open the drapes and looked out to a view of the next building.

"Apparently, this is the only building in Paris without a view of the Eiffel Tower."

Carly stood beside her. "We're not here to look out the windows."

She didn't reply, and Carly was quiet for a moment before squeezing her just above the elbow. "She'll be fine, Paige. She really is a smart kid."

Sighing, she felt her energy drain, and she stepped back to sit on the edge of Carly's bed. "I just wish I'd seen this coming."

Carly sat beside her. "Think of yourself at her age. Would you want to be hanging around with your aunt—no matter how cool she is—or your friend and a French hunk?"

She nodded and looked around the room. Wood paneling, high ceilings, thick drapes, a hardwood floor. And the bed seemed comfortable, with a thick white comforter and four fluffy pillows. "Nice room."

"It's perfect, but you didn't answer me."

"I know. I have to let it go. Do you want to nap or go exploring again?"

"I slept on the plane," Carly said. "Let's go explore."

Carly was in Paris, and she didn't care if she missed an entire week's worth of sleep. She wanted to see it all. Since the moment the pilot announced their approach into Charles de Gaulle that morning, her pulse had been pounding. She'd finally arrived in Paris, and she was ready to explore. Notre Dame was as beautiful as she'd expected, the Eiffel Tower even taller than she'd thought it would be. And it was only the beginning! They had so much to see and do, and she was so eager, she pulled Paige's hand. "C'mon!"

"We need to be back by seven for dinner. And we should unpack. And what if Jules calls and we're not here?"

Paige was so adorable. She wanted to smack Juliette, right on the bottom, and ground her for what she'd done to Paige, but on the other hand, she had Paige to herself. And she loved that idea. She'd been putting up with people all day, when the only one she really wanted to be with was right here in the room.

Suddenly, she thought they should get out of the room and go someplace very public, where the thought of kissing Paige would be pushed to the back of her mind.

CHAPTER TWENTY

WHEN IN PARIS

They took a few minutes to unpack, and then were out the door again, turning left and right, looking in shop windows and wandering aimlessly. They laughed at the fashions, and when Carly saw a tiny dress on a mannequin in a shop window, she thought back to the train in New York, and they giggled like little girls as they remembered the moment. Paige stopped at a confectioner's and bought some chocolate for the room, and Carly picked up a few bottles of wine. The afternoon was pleasant, and Carly found herself happier than she'd been in forever.

But had coming to Paris been a mistake? Looking at Paige in the confectioner's, grinning broadly, simply melted her. It was a bad idea to get involved with her, now that she was considering a reconciliation with her husband, but the pull was almost impossible to resist. And why do that? Paige had separated from Will. What more was Carly waiting for? It wasn't as if she'd left yesterday and was emotionally fragile. They'd separated months ago, and if Paige was upset then, she'd healed. Emotionally, she was strong and happy.

And, quite honestly, so was Carly. Depression had plagued her since her parents' deaths, and she'd worked hard with Annie in therapy, learning to deal with her loss and to squeeze some joy out of the little things. That hadn't been easy. Her relationship with Pip had been crumbling when her mom got sick, and she'd just left Pip when her father suffered a heart attack. Three major relationships gone in just fifteen months.

Now, with Paige, it wasn't hard at all. She was full of joy and excitement again. Sometimes she felt like a teenager, discovering the world in tiny segments. A waterfall Paige took her to, or a golf course. A new restaurant or new recipe. It was amazing, the effect this one woman had on her. Maybe it would amount to something more, and maybe it wouldn't. But here they were, with an opportunity, and unless she had really lost her ability to read women, they both wanted that something more.

All she needed was the courage to make the first move.

At dinner, they sat beside each other at a long table, and even though they were surrounded by other people, talking with some faculty from the university who were on the trip, she was tuned in to Paige. She'd changed to a lightweight turtleneck sweater and had a diamond pendant hanging from her neck, with earrings that matched. The sweater was teal, and her eyes darkened to match it. Paige smelled of something sweet, and she wanted to dive into her right there at the table.

Sighing, she sipped her wine and felt Paige's hand on her thigh. *Oh, wow.*

"You okay?" she asked.

Carly nodded. "I'm great. How about you?"

Paige nodded in return. She couldn't remember being so happy. But, of course, being with Carly always had that effect on her.

"Fantastic," she said. She sipped her wine but then discreetly put her glass back on the table. This was her second glass, and she felt a little tipsy already. In just a while, she'd be alone with Carly, and on this particular night in this very romantic city, she needed to keep her wits about her. Obviously, her attraction to Carly wasn't as dead as she'd thought, and that could only complicate things for her. Not only could she lose their friendship if she did something stupid, like make a drunken pass at her, but she could find herself homeless, too.

Once again, the food was served family style, with fresh bread and good conversation. When they finished, Dr. DeMichelle gave them directions back to the hotel. Some went with him, and some went off on their own.

"What are you thinking?" Paige asked.

"Oh, let's walk," Carly replied.

Instinctively, they turned toward the Eiffel Tower, and after walking a few blocks, following Paige's phone, they turned left, and right, and stopped at the Champ de Mars.

"Let's do it," Paige said when it came into view.

The walk through the park at night was magical, and Carly weaved her arm through hers as they strolled down the promenade. Hundreds of people were walking about, but the muted lighting gave the park a romantic ambience, one that set her on edge. Having Carly so close, in this place, after so many months of wanting her, was like her own dream come true.

As if reading her mind, Carly leaned closer, whispering in her ear. "I still can't believe I'm here. Look at it," she said as she nodded toward the tower. "Look there," she said, as she nodded left. "And there," nodding right. "It's Paris."

"It is," she said, buoyed by the magic of the night. It was perfect—the weather, the food, the wine, but mostly the company.

Their tickets from earlier in the day were no longer valid, so they purchased new ones and rode the elevator alone to the top. The crowd had mostly disappeared. "Wow," she said as she first saw the twinkling lights over the city. Then she was simply silent. A few others were enjoying the view, but compared to the daytime crowd, the human population was sparse.

The bird population was not. "I didn't notice all these pigeons before," she said.

Carly squinted and pointed. "Paige, look. That pigeon has only one leg."

She tried to get closer, but the bird in question hopped away. "Maybe it's just tucked under him. Don't they stand on only one?"

"This is not at all how I imagined my nighttime trip to the top of the Eiffel Tower."

They leaned on the railing and looked out over the river. Carly sounded disappointed, but Paige was in awe. "What did you imagine?" she whispered after a moment, hugging herself to chase the chill. Her light jacket had been fine when the sun warmed Paris, but now, it was cold. And atop the tower was a breeze she hadn't noticed from the ground.

"I imagined being here with someone I loved. Kissing her up here."

Paige swallowed as she looked out over the city again and then back to Carly. The tower seemed to sway in the breeze, or perhaps it was the effect of the wine. Even in the dim light, Carly was gorgeous, her dark hair dancing around her face. She thought of kissing her and then pondered how ridiculous that idea was. How inappropriate. And then, before she could think any more, she closed the space between them and took Carly's face in her hands. Her lips were on Carly's in an instant, and Carly tried to pull back, but then she felt Carly relax, and she was kissing her back.

She felt so many things at once that nothing seemed to make sense. Then Carly's arms were around her, pulling her close, sharing her warmth. And her mouth was so soft and wet as their tongues met in the middle. The kiss had started out strong, challenging, but it quickly morphed into something tender that left her panting, suddenly breathless and wetter than she'd ever been.

Carly broke the kiss and mated their foreheads. "I was not expecting that," she whispered. "I need to regroup."

She kissed Carly's cheek, and her nose, then found her mouth once again. And once again, the kiss was all-consuming. She wanted to crawl inside Carly's jacket, to wrap around her. She couldn't get close enough. Her need for Carly had exploded.

"Paige, what are you doing?" Carly panted.

She pulled back, looked out at Paris once again, her eyes unfocused. Those had been the two most amazing kisses of her life. She didn't want to think about what it meant to have kissed Carly, or that it had been phenomenal. She'd spent too much of her life thinking, and all it did was confuse her. At this moment, she didn't want to think. She just wanted to feel.

"Kissing my favorite person in the world, atop the Eiffel Tower."

Carly's fingers gently turned her chin, and their eyes met. Then Carly wrapped her arms around her and pulled her close again. The kiss was deep and sultry, but when she felt her center meet the corner of Carly's hip, her lust exploded.

"Let's go back to the hotel," she whispered into Carly's neck.

Carly pulled back. "It'll take half an hour to get back. I'm hoping this fizzles out by then."

Grabbing her hand, she pulled Carly toward the elevator. "I don't. Let's take a cab."

They found one near the Seine, and her hand trembled as she opened the door for Carly. They kissed all the way back to the hotel, soft sensual touches of their lips and tongues that seemed to electrify the air around them. They managed to pull apart to pay the driver and traverse the lobby, but then they were in each other's arms as soon as the elevator door closed behind them. They stumbled into their room and onto her bed, because it was closest to the door.

Carly's hands were up her shirt, and hers were in Carly's hair, and their tongues tangled as they wrapped around each other, moving apart to remove single pieces of clothing before rejoining at the mouth and hips. As she frantically tried to slip out of her leggings, Carly put her hand inside them, slid them over her hips, and pushed her back onto the pillows as she devoured her with her mouth. Flinging her legs about, she managed to free one, and Carly had free access to all of her, but suddenly she stopped.

She looked up and met Carly's eyes, and Carly smiled at her, then closed them, and much more slowly, tenderly, Carly took her sex into her mouth. She gasped at the light touch and then again as Carly's fingers found her opening and slid inside her. She was as wet as she'd ever been, the throbbing in her center almost painful. Defying her need, she was able to keep still as Carly licked and sucked, but then she just couldn't contain it any longer. She lifted her hips to meet Carly, writhed against her, and exploded.

"Ohhhh!" she groaned as the orgasm hit her, and then she shuddered a few more times as the sensations died down. Aware of Carly between her legs, she tried to lift her hand to Carly's head, but found it difficult to defy gravity. In fact, nothing seemed to be working properly. It was partly the wine, she knew, but Carly literally made the room spin, and she giggled as she told Carly she couldn't focus her eyes. Carly crawled up the length of her body and put her head on her shoulder. "Is that a complaint?"

She moaned. She'd had sex before, on quite a few occasions, and with more than a few men. But nothing like this. It was like she'd been searching for this all those other times, looking for this connection. Maybe it was simply that she'd been with men, or maybe it was something special about Carly. Thinking back over the last months, of the friendship they'd been building, she suspected it had everything to do with this woman. In her fuzzy brain, she knew something monumental had just happened and that she'd have to figure out what came next for her. But she knew, without a doubt, she wanted Carly with her as she worked the puzzle.

"It's a compliment."

In response, Carly nibbled her ear, and her neck, and worked her way down to her breasts, clearly savoring each square inch of her flesh, with her hands and her eyes and her mouth. She tingled everywhere, in the places Carly touched and the places she left wet with kisses. Impossibly, her desire grew as if she hadn't just had that explosive release, and she found herself moving, panting with lust.

Carly's lips met hers as she slid a finger inside her again and made small, gentle circles. Carly's thumb was busy, too, caressing her clit. Paige's hips moved on their own, seeking contact, aching for release. After a few moments like that, Carly pulled back, searched her eyes.

"Would you like my mouth again?"

"Oh, yes."

Carly chuckled and moved back to the spot between her legs, and once again Carly found her clit with her tongue. She moaned, a sound that seemed to push Carly to move her hands and mouth more eagerly. Mere seconds later, she came again, and the orgasm seemed to turn her inside out, as it started between her legs and traveled down them and up her spine at the same time, so her entire body shook with the force of it.

The sounds she made were incomprehensible, but Carly seemed to understand. She grew still, with her head on her belly until her breathing grew quiet.

Then she slid beside Paige and kissed her softly. "Welcome to Paris."

"We should have come here months ago."

Carly traced a nipple with one finger. "Our timing is perfect."

"That orgasm was perfect."

"Hmm. Which one?"

"Touché."

"I need a glass of wine," Carly said as she kissed her and sat up. "Or should we have champagne?"

"Do you have champagne?"

"I believe it's on the room-service menu."

"Carly, I'm already drunk."

"Okay. I'll just order one bottle."

To her amazement, Carly reached over and picked up the phone, and placed an order with room service. "Fifteen minutes," Carly whispered into her ear. "Whatever can we do to keep busy for fifteen minutes?"

She moaned as she grew wet again, and she spread her legs as Carly stretched out on top of her, kissing and touching, her hands relentless as they sought her skin. This time, Carly was in no hurry, and when Carly finally slid a finger inside her, she came almost instantly.

As the pounding in her ears faded, she heard the pounding on the door and watched Carly slip into the robe from the closet and retrieve the small cart from the attendant. Back beside her on the bed, Carly twisted the cork free and poured them each a glass. Carly still wore the robe as she slid beside her and offered her a flute. When she took it from her, Carly retrieved hers from the table and touched it to hers.

"To a night of passion in Paris."

Without awaiting a response, Carly sipped, and she did, too.

"Just one night?" she asked, suddenly feeling panicked. She hadn't wanted to think about what she was doing, but she definitely wanted more than a one-night stand.

"I don't want to think, Paige. I just want to feel. I want to feel your hands and your mouth all over me. Is that okay?"

Smiling, she handed Carly her flute, then planted kisses from Carly's neck to her navel, and then lower, to that hot, wet place between Carly's legs.

Everything about the past hour had been unbelievable. She'd kissed Carly and made out with her in the backseat of a taxi in Paris, and again in the elevator of their hotel. Carly had made love to her, and in the span of half an hour, she'd had three earth-shattering orgasms. And now she was making love to Carly, this woman who made her laugh and made her think. A woman who loved Broadway and opera and golf. A woman she loved.

Carly's lips and her skin were so soft, and she touched every part of Carly with the tips of her fingers and her mouth. The noises Carly made—moans and groans and murmurs—only excited her more. But none of the excitement prepared her for the moment when she put her own mouth on Carly's sex and tasted her sweetness, smelled the musky scent of her. She had never done this before, but she instinctively knew where to kiss and just how much pressure to use, when to slip a finger inside Carly, and when to add a second. As Carly's hips rose from the bed, she got to her knees and followed, wrapping her arms around Carly's waist so she wouldn't slip away, wouldn't deny her this great pleasure of tasting her, of making love to her, of giving her the pleasure of an orgasm.

A loud yelp and a shudder a moment later made her smile, and she gently eased Carly back to the bed, where she rested with her head on Carly's thigh as she tenderly fingered the folds of her sex. A minute passed, maybe two, and Carly gently arched her hips toward her. "Please, Paige, put your fingers inside me again."

She complied and found a place that Carly seemed to like, then stroked the spot with her finger while sucking on Carly's sex. "Oh!" Carly screamed as she came again, so quickly it seemed the orgasm surprised her.

After a moment Carly reached for her champagne and sipped it, and Paige found a spot on the pillow beside her.

Carly handed Paige her glass and smiled. "Okay. Maybe more than *one* night."

CHAPTER TWENTY-ONE

PARIS RULES

Carly hovered just above Paige, kissing her breast, her fingers buried inside her when the alarm began beeping the next morning.

"It's time to wake up," Paige said.

"Should I stop?"

"Please, no."

"This is your last orgasm. At least until later. We have to be on the bus in an hour."

"Plenty of time." She sighed as she arched into Carly's hand, holding pressure, then exploded for about the tenth time. Never before had she made love all night. Until this night, she hadn't known it was physically possible. But it was, and she had, and now the only question was whether her legs would hold her for the trip to the Musée d'Orsay.

Carly kissed her lips softly. "I'm going to hop in the shower. Can you call and get us breakfast? Coffee for me, and a spinach omelet. And maybe you should check on your niece."

Still trying to catch her breath, she nodded. "Okay."

Room service promised delivery in half an hour, and then she called Jules.

"We're going down to breakfast now. Do you want me to come by your room and pick you up?" Jules asked.

Panicked, she pulled the blankets over her naked body. "No. I'm just hopping in the shower now. I'll see you in the lobby at five of nine."

Rolling onto her side, she disconnected the phone and stared in the direction of the bathroom, where she heard the water running.

Wow. What had happened to her? She had seduced a woman and had a sexual experience beyond her imagination. She hadn't slept since arriving in Paris more than twenty-four hours earlier, yet she'd never felt more alive. Being with Carly had been like an infusion of iron, bringing her to life, and she marveled. For a long time, she'd wondered if she might be gay, and now it seemed she didn't have to ask that question anymore. Her connection with Carly was the most perfect thing she'd ever experienced—first as her friend, and now as her lover.

For a second, she thought of Will. Poor Will. He'd never had a chance. Then she pushed him from her mind.

Carly peeked through the bathroom door, her hair wrapped in a towel and a smile on her beautiful face. "I left the water on for you. What did room service say?"

Swallowing the emotion she felt at the sight of Carly made her take a second to answer. "Breakfast is on the way," she said as she slid from bed and met Carly at the bathroom door. The kiss took her breath away. "I wasn't sure my legs would work."

"Yeah. I hear you. My tender flesh is a little tender this morning."

"Oh, God. Did I hurt you? I'm so sorry."

Carly smiled, a sly little sexy lift of the corners of her mouth that made Paige wet again. "Oh, no. It's a good pain."

Wearing her own smile, she hopped into the shower while Carly dried her hair. When she pulled open the curtain a few minutes later, she found Carly standing there with a towel and a bathrobe, waiting for her.

After sliding into the robe, Carly gently pushed her into a chair and ran a brush through her hair before towel-drying it. Then she gently kissed her on the nose.

"You look happy," she said.

"Yes. Incredible sex does that to me. I may be in a good mood until Christmas."

"How many orgasms did you have last night?" Between her own, and Carly's, they hadn't stopped all night. They'd slowed down though, and talked, and cuddled, and kissed, which inevitably led to more sex.

"It felt like about fifteen."

"Seriously?"

Carly shrugged. "Who's counting?"

"Me."

Carly laughed. "Then you're going to have to do a better job, because I lost track after about ten."

"It was an amazing night."

Carly bent over, tilting Paige's chin toward her, and kissed her softly. "Yes, it was." Pulling away, she smiled. "Thank you for a wonderful introduction to Paris. Now dry your hair. We have to eat and explore the Musée d'Orsay."

Carly's pulse pounded again as Paige pulled her down for another kiss, and Carly lingered there for a moment before breaking free. As much as she'd like to take Paige back to bed, they had to get dressed and eat and be on the bus in half an hour.

As she was slipping on a light sweater to match black jeans, she heard a knock on the door. This time, she allowed the attendant to bring the tray into the room, and after signing the chit, she poured two coffees and bit into a forkful of omelet. She'd eaten half her breakfast before Paige emerged from the bathroom.

Glancing at the clock, she felt a hint of anxiety. She hated being late. "We have to leave this room in fifteen minutes."

"No worries," Paige said.

She sat and pulled on flat ankle boots and finished her food as she watched with pleasure as Paige moved about the room. A bite of food, a sip of coffee, a walk to the dresser. Another bite, another sip, a trip to the closet. She didn't hesitate as she reached in and pulled out what she'd wear—an outfit similar to Carly's, she quickly realized. Bite, sip, bra and panties on. Bite, sip, sweater and black jeans.

Damn, she was sexy. Carly sipped her coffee and reflected on this new reality. She and Paige were lovers. And she'd hit the jackpot. Paige was the total package, everything she had ever hoped for in a woman, in and out of bed. She'd still been trying to gather the courage to kiss Paige when Paige had pounced on her. And every second since then had been just amazing.

Whoa. She needed to regain some control. It seemed she'd lost it somewhere during the night.

She raised her coffee cup. "To discovering the wonders of Paris."

Paige stopped and looked at her, and again she wanted nothing more than to take her back to bed. "Yes," Paige murmured as she slowly walked toward her and kissed her gently. "It's already the best trip ever."

"Get dressed, would you please?" Carly said as she shooed her away.

Turning her mind to the day's itinerary, Carly closed her eyes for a moment. Wow, was she in trouble. Here she was, minutes away from some of the greatest art in the world, and all she could think about was sex.

"I can't wait to see the museum," she said, hoping to distract herself.

"Yes. The Orsay has some real treasures."

Well aware, Carly nodded. Before coming, she had hardly been able to wait to see the works of Renoir, Cezanne, and Monet, and, of course, van Gogh. She had to refocus.

She glanced at the clock. To her surprise, only seven minutes had passed since she had issued her warning. Paige slipped on black walking shoes, stood, pulled both their jackets from the closet, and asked Carly if she was ready.

Paige was always surprising her, she realized as she slipped into her jacket. And it was always good.

They found Jules and Melody in the lobby, and finally she forced her mind away from Paige's body as the girls regaled them with details of their Saturday night with Luc. "And if it's okay with you, he wants to meet us at the museum. He's going to take us to the Sorbonne and show us around, in case we want to do a year abroad."

"That sounds like a wonderful experience for you. Are we invited, or is it just you two?" Paige asked.

Jules's eyebrows shot up. "Oh my God. Do you want to come? I can totally ask him. That would be great!"

Paige patted Jules on the shoulder. "It's okay, Jules. We're in Paris. Carly and I won't be bored."

Paige's eyes met Carly's, and she felt weak in the knees. What an effect this woman had on her. Yes, they were in Paris, with so many things to do and see, but she had no doubt that if Paige asked, she would jump into the first taxi back to the hotel the minute Jules left for the Sorbonne.

Jules looked relieved. "You're the best. And you are too," she said as she looked at Carly. "I'm so glad you two have each other."

Carly bit her lip. If Jules only knew.

On the bus, Jules and Melody sat together, leaving Carly and Paige side by side. "So, the Sorbonne," Carly said.

"I feel like such a bad person. I came to Paris to be with Jules, and I'm so happy she ditched me yesterday. And I'm happy she's ditching me again today."

Carly felt her mouth go dry. "You are?"

"Yes."

"So what do you want to do this afternoon?"

"I just figured I'd be doing what Jules wanted, so I didn't really plan anything other than what's included in the tour. How about you? Any thoughts?"

Carly felt a surge of excitement. "Well, the museum is just across the Seine from the Tuileries Garden. I've always wanted to have a picnic in the garden. It's very French. And then, if you're feeling adventurous…" she tilted her head and drew out the word, "we can stroll down the Champs-Élysées to the Arc de Triomphe. My grandfather marched through it when he liberated Paris."

Paige stared at her, and she felt her gaze pierce her. "That sounds like an amazing plan."

So they wandered through the Orsay, gazing at some of the great works of French art, with a few other masterpieces as well. Vincent van Gogh's self-portrait was haunting in its monochromatic blue scheme, and Carly thought he had done a fabulous job of capturing his own insanity. They spent nearly three hours viewing the art before escaping to another magnificent Parisian afternoon. They found a café that would serve them takeout and bought food and a bottle of wine with a screw-off cap, then headed across the Pont Royal to the Tuileries.

They strolled like locals, enjoying the sunshine and finally sitting beneath a tree near the Grand Basin Rond. There they feasted on a sandwich, ate brie and raspberries on a baguette, and washed it all down with wine sipped from paper cups. "If we were home, I would have brought my picnic basket with the china and stemware."

"Really?"

Carly nodded. "It's very heavy, so I take it out only on special occasions."

Paige looked around before meeting her eyes. "This is special. No china necessary."

"It's chilly, though. Let's walk."

After discarding their litter, they circled the fountain, then headed back the way they'd come, but this time on a smaller, tree-lined path. The leaves were changing, and all the colors of fall surrounded them, reminding Carly of their accidental meeting at the gardens in Hershey. "I bet this would be magnificent in the spring."

"I was thinking that, too. But the foliage is spectacular now."

Glancing at her phone, Carly oriented herself. "The Arc de Triomphe is just ahead."

"Do you know which way your grandfather walked when he came through?"

"I'm not sure. I would guess he was coming from the north."

Paige pulled out her phone and typed as they walked. "It says France's Unknown Soldier from World War I is buried under the Arc, and out of respect, no one has marched through the Arc since 1919."

"My Pop lied?"

"I think they just march around the side of it."

Carly stopped and stared at Paige. "Damn."

They walked in silence after that and crossed under the street before the Arc, then climbed the stairs, emerging on the street level inside a traffic circle. Before them stood the massive structure, 164 feet of stone. It was nearly as wide as it was tall, carved with emblems of war and the names of France's fallen soldiers.

"Shall we go up?" Paige asked, and she nodded.

They paid a fee and climbed the stairs, then looked out over the seven roads that intersected here. Even if he didn't walk through the Arc, her grandfather had still made an amazing journey. If he were still alive, she would have told him how proud of him she was. Instead, she said a little prayer to him as she imagined the Allied troops flooding Paris all those years ago, liberating this beautiful city from the horrors of war. She felt peaceful.

"Wanna walk some more?" Carly really wanted to take Paige back to the hotel and make love to her again, but there was no hurry. Jules didn't plan to be back until bedtime, so they had hours and hours.

"Sure."

Without discussion, they strolled back the way they came, window-shopping along the Champs-Élysées as they made their way toward the gardens. The shops sold high-end purses and scarves, clothing and jewelry. They bought cheese in a shop that sold only that and more wine from a store beside it. And then Carly stopped when she saw the contents of the store beyond a millinery. *Sex Shop.* The rest of the store's name was written in French, and Carly couldn't read a word, but *Sex Shop* probably meant the same thing in all languages.

Turning, she saw Paige eyeing hats in the window, and her breath came short. Oh, what they could do with a toy or two.

Her mind made up, she stepped closer, into Paige's space. "We have rules about lesbian relationships, Paige. They make the world keep turning in the right direction, make the sun come up every morning. Prevent murder and mayhem. The biggest rule is never, ever sleep with a married woman."

Paige swallowed but didn't reply.

"However, we are in Paris. We're clearly attracted to each other. And we seem to have an amazing sexual chemistry. So I'd like to propose a new set of rules—Paris rules. We live by the Paris rules until we get on that plane, and then we go back to being friends. What do you think?"

Paige studied her without speaking, and Carly didn't realize she was holding her breath until she quietly let it go.

"Are you suggesting a fling? Just a little crazy week-long, one-night stand? Then what happens? We pretend it never happened?"

Carly knew that would be hard, but it was better than letting Paige break her heart if she chose to go back to Will and his pending million-dollar injury settlement. Crushing, in fact. And there was the issue of the moral right and wrong of sleeping with someone else's wife, even if they'd been separated for four months. Carly wasn't a saint, but Paige's situation still caused her angst.

But here she was, finally, in Paris. And with a woman she adored. She could operate under Paris rules for a week, but then, it was over, because she wasn't a gambler, and she wasn't going to bet her heart on Paige's whim. "Yes. Back to being friends."

Paige looked torn, but then she nodded and smiled. "Okay."

"Okay, it is. How'd you like to go toy shopping?"

At first Paige looked puzzled, and then her eyes opened ever so slightly, and she looked around. A blush turned her cheeks pink, but she smiled when her eyes found Carly's.

"Ooh, la, la."

"Now let's not get carried away," she said as they walked through the door, but then she simply watched Paige. She knew without asking that this was her first time in a store like this, because her head was practically spinning as she rushed from one display to the next—strap-ons and vibrators and dildos, lubricants and massage creams, fetish and fantasy clothing. The store had it all, arranged and displayed with flair and sophistication.

"I've never been in a place like this," Paige confessed. "What do you want to get?"

"A small vibrator, but something with punch. And maybe a double-header."

She watched Paige's face closely, and she could tell the moment Paige understood her meaning. Her eyes twinkled. "Oh, Goddess."

They picked out one of each, a package of batteries, and a bottle of lube and some cleanser, and a moment later they were back on the street, walking toward the gardens. Paige stopped and turned to Carly. "I think we should get a taxi."

Paige's smile, the softness of her voice, the heated way she looked at her took her breath away, so all she could do was nod. They spotted a queue of cabs just ahead in a circle and silently walked that way. When they were seated, she gave the driver the hotel's address and then reached for Paige's hand as she sat back and enjoyed the scenery. The ride couldn't have been more different from the previous night's, but for her it was even more exciting. Last night she'd been fueled by lust and hope. This time, something much more was going on. She knew what would happen in that hotel room, and she knew it would be incredible. Yet this little bit of buildup, the anticipation, would make it even better.

This time, when they entered the elevator, they stood slightly apart, but with eyes locked. They were silent during their few steps to their hotel-room door, and even after Paige opened it and pulled her into her arms, they didn't speak. Instead, they sought each other hungrily with their mouths, and when they pulled away, they were both breathless.

"Can you get ice? I bought a bottle of champagne for us."

Paige looked flushed as she pulled away, but she nodded and grabbed the ice bucket, then planted a sloppy kiss on her lips before heading out the door. As she watched Paige leave, she pulled scissors from her toiletry bag and went to work on the thick plastic encasing their new toys. It was difficult to control her smile as she pulled them free. A moment later she'd washed them both and wrapped them in a clean towel, which she tucked under the pillow just as she heard the door opening.

Paige walked in and smiled. "Did you miss me?"

"Terribly," she said as she took the ice bucket, then went into the bathroom and spilled the ice into the sink, where she added some cold water and the bottle of champagne.

When she was done, she found Paige sitting on the side of the bed, a serious look on her face.

"Are you okay?" she asked, suddenly worried. She'd taken for granted that Paige was as eager as she was to get back into bed, but maybe she was wrong.

Paige shrugged. "I'm thinking about our...purchase."

She sat next to Paige and tried to lighten things up. "The brie?"

Paige dropped her chin and raised her eyebrows. "Don't make fun of me."

She kissed Paige's chin, wanting so much to ease her fears. "You're adorable. But—I'm sorry if I made you feel uncomfortable. I was feeling bold. Please forgive me. We've already demonstrated that we don't need toys, and I'm perfectly happy with just you."

Paige turned to her, and what she saw in her eyes made her tremble. They simply smoldered.

Paige touched Carly's cheek, then closed the small gap between them and kissed her softly. Although the night before had been amazing, spending the day with Carly had only cemented her feelings. They'd been friends, and she'd been crushing on Carly since they met. She knew she loved Carly, yet it had been a chaste love. But making love with her had changed something. They had connected in a way she hadn't known was possible. But could she really fall in love with someone just because of great sex?

"You excite me so much," she whispered into Carly's neck. Ever so gently, she pulled Carly with her down onto the bed, kissing her the entire time, touching her as her passion grew with every passing second. She pulled Carly's shirt up, Carly eased it off, and then they shed the rest of their clothes and came together again, touching, kissing, fingering. She slid down Carly, found her wet sex with her mouth, and licked slowly around Carly's clit, around her opening, circling, teasing, as Carly levitated above the bed, trying to get closer to her. And then Paige slipped a finger inside, and another, as she finally took Carly's clit in her mouth. Carly's motion grew frantic, her moaning louder, until finally she cried out and fell back onto the bed.

Paige rested her head and chuckled. "That was amazing."

"You've done this before," Carly said. "You have to."

"All night long, as a matter of fact," she said as she eased onto the pillow beside Carly and wrapped her arms around her.

Carly rolled and faced her. "Seriously? You've never made love with a woman?"

She shook her head, and then Carly did as well.

"Well, you have natural talents, Paige."

"And we didn't even have the champagne yet."

Carly seemed to debate. "I thought we might spend an hour or two in bed, have a little bubbly, then go out for a nice dinner. But now, I think we should order room service and spend the rest of the evening right here in this room."

Her mouth grew dry. "That's a great plan."

"Then let's pop the cork."

Carly had saved the champagne glasses from the night before and pulled them from the top drawer in the dresser, then retrieved the champagne from the bathroom. Sitting beside Paige on the bed, she uncorked the bottle and poured a glass for each of them, before proposing another toast.

"Pip once told me you must have sex in Paris. Wow. She was right. Paris sex is amazing."

Paige suspected it had more to do with the woman sitting beside her, but she didn't debate the point. "It is."

"To the Paris rules," Carly said.

Paige clinked glasses and sipped, realizing already that one week wouldn't be enough. She'd never known she could have so many orgasms or feel so good just being with another human being. It had been a blissful day—seeing the masterpieces in the Orsay and the magnificence of the Tuileries, but she would have been just as happy at the Everhart Museum or at Nay Aug Park in Scranton. As long as she was with Carly, location didn't matter at all.

"Hear! Hear!"

She sipped her wine and leaned back against the pillow, then felt something against her back. Reaching behind her, she grasped the hard, cool plastic of the vibrator. She didn't have to see it to know what it was, but just touching it made her dizzy.

Pulling it from beneath the pillow, she held it in her upturned palm, then returned her wineglass to the table. With her free hand, she clicked the knob at the bottom and felt it come alive in her hand. From a few feet away, Carly's gaze bored into hers, and Paige watched as it followed her hand and the vibrator it held from her neck, down her chest wall to her left breast. She stopped at the nipple and felt a jolt of pleasure shoot through her as the sensations caused by the vibrator triggered a shocking orgasm.

"Oh!" she exclaimed, then laughed as her hand fell to the bed beside her.

Carly's eyes shot open. "Did you just come?"

"Oh, yeah."

"That was so hot."

She watched Carly set her glass on the table, then pick up the vibrator from the place it had fallen on the bed. Sliding next to Paige, she kissed her, while the hand holding the vibrator ventured lower, across her belly, past her hip bone, to the wetness of her sex. Arching her back just a little, Paige spread her legs, giving Carly full access. Then Carly slid her hand farther, tickling Paige's sex. The overwhelming stimulation of the vibrator left Paige panting, gasping for breath as she teetered on the edge of another orgasm.

She wanted to protest when Carly pulled her mouth away, but she knew where she was going, knew what plans she had for that mouth. A second later Paige felt Carly's tongue on one side of her clit as the vibrator massaged the other. With so much sensation, so overpowering, she couldn't do anything but let go, and she did, as another colossal orgasm wracked her.

She was aware that Carly had turned off the vibrator, could feel herself move against her, felt the softness of the blankets that Carly pulled over them. Yet every sensation was muted, dull in comparison to the tingling inside her.

Her eyelids felt too heavy to open, so she simply rested them, trying to control her breathing as her mouth found Carly resting beside her. She kissed Carly's hair and had to swallow several times before she could speak.

"I love you."

Carly kissed her and laughed. "You're high on hormones."

"I don't think so. I love you. It took me a long time to figure it out, but this is how love should be."

Carly's voice was soft. "If this were how love was, the world would stop turning. No one would play golf or go to the movies. Or work. Garbage would pile up, and the electricity would shut off, and grass would grow wild because no one would cut it. No one would ever get out of bed."

She tried to suppress her smile. Carly had just blown her off, discounted her declaration of love, but that didn't change anything. She felt it. She thought Carly did, too. But it was a new and scary thing, quite complicated. Paris rules. They'd figure it out when they got home. "I can imagine tourists missing out on Paris, just so they could stay in the hotel room."

"Hmm. I've waited half my life for Paris, Paige, but I definitely don't want to leave this room any time soon."

"We have tomorrow."

"Yes. The Louvre. I can't wait. *Mona Lisa*. But tonight, I just want to be with you."

"Should we order dinner?" she asked. "To sustain us?"

Carly laughed. "We probably should."

They huddled together, looking over the menu, and then she called room service while Carly poured more champagne.

After placing the order, she hung up the phone. "I guess other hotel guests are staying in as well. The food won't be ready for an hour."

"That's perfect," Carly said as she began kissing her again. They didn't stop until the food arrived, and then after they ate, they were right back in bed, making love again. When they were cuddled together, after pausing to catch their breath, she kissed Carly's neck.

"This has to be some sort of world record. In the last twenty-four hours, we've been in this bed like twenty," she said.

They were lying beside each other on the bed, but Carly had somehow spun around, so her head was near Paige's belly, her feet resting on the headboard. "Hmm. So, there's room for improvement."

"I don't know. Tomorrow's the Louvre. We probably won't want to skip out early. Even for fabulous sex."

"It is pretty fabulous, isn't it?"

"Oh, yeah."

"I find that an issue, sometimes," Carly said as she traced a finger along Paige's palm. "I've been attracted to a few women, but the sex was awful."

"Is that a deal-breaker?"

"Yes. I think sexual compatibility is on the top of the list."

"You didn't mention that last time."

Carly shrugged, and she didn't press the point, but instead said aloud what she'd known for so long. "When you told me your list, it was so hard to keep quiet about my feelings. You know you were describing me, right?"

"You were married. You still are."

She rolled onto her side and propped her head in her hand. "Do you believe in 'love at first sight'?"

"No."

She laughed. "Of course you don't. You're too practical. I didn't either. But from the moment I saw you, I was gaga. I didn't necessarily recognize it for what it was, but it was there. An—obsession, almost."

"But you've never slept with a woman."

"Is that a trick question?" She stared at Carly.

"No. It's a statement. So—when did you, I don't know—figure it out?"

"That I'm attracted to you? Right away. But I dismissed it as harmless. Don't forget, I had that kiss, so I wasn't oblivious to my feelings. I'd just never acted on them. But each time we were together, whether it was a meeting for SAW or a round of golf, they grew just a little bit. I realized I had a crush on you, but I thought it wouldn't amount to anything, and I was okay with that."

"Have you ever crushed on a girl before? Besides the one you made out with."

She sighed. "Yes. A police officer named Amy, who's married to one of Will's best friends."

"Ah. A woman in uniform."

"I don't think I ever saw her in uniform. I just…click with her, you know? I click so well, in fact, that Will figured it out. He's thought I'm gay since then."

Carly pulled away, and Paige opened her eyes. "Really?"

She stared at Carly for a moment, then shrugged. What could she say? It was true—she'd adored Amy. After Will had expressed his concerns, Paige had to make a tremendous effort to avoid her, because she knew deep down that he was right. And she probably also knew that would have been a disaster. Amy was definitely straight, and the attraction was totally one-sided. One-sided, but real. But nothing compared to what she felt now.

Carly sat up, then leaned close to her. "I think he's right," she said as she kissed Paige softly. "And I am so happy he is."

Chapter Twenty-two

The Movie Scene

Carly awoke before the alarm, but she didn't move from her spot. She and Paige were a tangle of arms and legs, with their heads at the foot of the bed, resting on the same pillow. Paige had crazy bedhead, and Carly resisted the temptation to comb it with her fingers.

What the fuck was she doing? Earth-shattering orgasms were one thing, and she'd walked away from great sex partners the morning after without ever looking back. With Paige, it was different. The night before, Paige had revealed so much. The instant attraction, which Carly had tried to deny as well. The sexual confusion she'd felt. Her love.

When she'd said the words, Carly had expertly deflected, but she knew Paige wasn't confused. Carly knew, because she felt the same way. She'd been falling in love with Paige since she first saw her, from across the exhibit hall at the golf expo. And just as Paige had suggested, each dinner, every phone call and golf match, had fed and watered that seed.

So why was she fighting Paige and the feelings she had for her? Why not just have a good time? That's what she'd asked herself, for the brief second her mind had functioned, before the kiss atop the Eiffel Tower diminished her ability to reason. Now, she knew why it had been a good idea to resist Paige and the feelings she had for her. Because this was so good. They were so compatible. Everything on the list, every quality she'd looked for in a woman, she found in Paige. And when they went home, it was going to be so hard to play by Scranton rules.

And they had to. Paige was married, and even though they shared this attraction and sexual chemistry, that didn't mean Paige would abandon the safety of the heterosexual world and move in with her. Paige could easily have a change of heart, and when she did, Carly didn't want hers broken.

It was tempting to just end it now. Get another room, in a different hotel, and try to change her flight back to the States. Hell, she'd even fly coach. Then she could stop this before it grew any more consuming.

Looking at Paige, still sleeping so peacefully, she knew she had to walk away. But she wouldn't. What difference would it make if her heart broke now or in five days? At least if she waited, if they had the time of their lives in Paris, she'd have some great memories, a remarkable story to tell, someday, after she healed.

Glancing at the clock, she began to extricate herself from Paige's arms. A moment later, she was standing beneath the shower, and a moment after that she was all lathered up with a delicious-smelling French soap.

"Do you have room in there for one more?" Paige asked with a knock on the glass door.

"Only if you wash my back."

"I want to wash everything."

And she did, and before they left the shower, Paige gave Carly another orgasm.

Half an hour later, they were at breakfast, where Jules and Mel joined them and regaled them with their exploits from the day before. They'd toured all of Paris, it seemed, as well as the Sorbonne, and had been the guests of honor at a party at Luc's apartment near campus. And, Jules was excited to report, they'd met two *really* nice guys, who were taking them to dinner that night.

"Jules, you don't even know these guys. They could be rapists."

"Paige," she said sweetly, "you have to think of what I'd be doing if I was here without you. It would be the same things, only this way, I get to see you in the mornings and start my day off the right way."

Carly bit her lip as Paige seemed to contemplate a response, then smiled at the girls. "I wish I had your energy. All I'm up for today is staring at a few paintings and statues."

"See?" Jules said, looking at Paige. "You two are great together. You like nerdy stuff like that, too."

"It's not nerdy. It's culture."

Carly was silent as Jules rolled her eyes and forked a potato into her mouth while Paige sipped her coffee. In just a little while, they were on the bus to the Louvre.

"You watch," Paige said to her, leaning so close that Carly could smell the citrus scent of Paige's hair. "They're going to ditch us the moment we get through the doors."

Carly leaned closer still and elbowed her gently, confessing what she'd known for months. "I don't mind. I like having you all to myself."

Paige looked straight ahead, to the front of the bus, but Carly could see the corners of her mouth turn up in a small smile.

Due to traffic congestion, their walk to the Louvre from the bus was a long one. As they turned a corner and the pyramid at the entrance came into view, Carly stopped. She had to. After all this time, there it was, dominating the landscape, the modern glass and steel structure looking so obviously out of place in front of the classical stone architecture of the Louvre Palace. It was almost the reverse of Rome, where the ancient Colosseum sat in the midst of a modern city, but equally striking.

"Ladies," Dr. DeMichelle called to them, "please keep up."

"Sorry," Carly said as they joined the tail end of the group to hear the tour guide tell them they could either stick together or separate once they were inside.

Sure enough, Jules said immediately, "Mel and I are going to do our own thing and then meet the guys for a burger or something later."

Paige nodded, and Carly couldn't read her mood as they entered the queue ahead of the crowd and descended the escalator into the subterranean lobby. "Do you want to stay with the guide or venture off on our own?"

"Let's see what she says," Paige suggested, as Jules and Mel walked off.

"It would take days and days to see all of the Louvre's treasures," the guide said. "Over 35,000 pieces of art are on display on any given day, spread in eight different departments, along nine miles of corridors. So today, we're going to just focus on the big items such as *Mona Lisa*, *Venus de Milo*, *Winged Victory of Samothrace*, and other famous pieces on display as we journey between those three. Our tour will be about three hours in duration, and then you will be free to wander the galleries on your own or enjoy something else in the beautiful city of Paris."

"Well?" Carly asked. "Should we stay with the group?"

She really just wanted to go off on her own and take her time, rather than rush to finish a three-day tour in three hours. Yet it was Paige's trip, too, and she didn't want to be too bossy. To her relief, Paige didn't have a strong opinion.

"It's up to you. We might learn something from the guide that we won't get on the headphone tour, but she's going to rush us."

"I agree. Let's take our time and make it a day. We'll explore for a few hours, stop for lunch, then explore some more. Let them kick us out when they close up tonight."

"Sounds like a plan."

Quietly, they slipped away from the group and down a random corridor. Carly had no idea where they were, but she figured that would be fun, just seeing where their feet took them. And if they didn't see the big pieces the guide had mentioned, they'd hunt them down later.

"Do you know where you're going?" Paige asked after a moment.

"I have no idea. But how can we screw this up? Everything here is a treasure."

"Do you want to know what my phone says?" Paige asked.

"No," she said as she pushed away Paige's hand and the phone it held. "Let's just be free and spontaneous."

So they walked away from the central area, saw ancient artifacts used by cavemen and women every day of their lives. She smiled at the thought that someone would one day marvel at her own cereal bowl or the pottery vase on the table in her living room. Sharing her musings with Paige, they laughed at the idea.

"I still have my little plate and cup from when I was a kid. It has jungle animals painted on it. Think of how that would confuse someone thousands of years from now. Would they think elephants roamed the hills of Clarks Summit?" Paige asked.

"It could be misleading," she admitted, humored by Paige's always interesting point of view. "How about everything we have in America that was made in China? Will our descendants think Scranton is in China?"

Paige shook her head. "They'll think Scranton is in Ireland, because of all the beer bottles they find."

She bit her lip. "That is really bad. True, but bad."

They wandered, stopping to read about interesting pieces and listen to the headphone tour. "There is so much stuff," Paige said as they examined a sculpture a while later.

"A lot to process."

"Is it what you'd hoped?" Paige asked as she studied her.

What a question, she thought. She'd come on this trip with Paige just so she could see Paris, see this. Yet sleeping with her had changed everything. Now it wasn't just about the *Mona Lisa* ; it was about seeing it with Paige by her side. The kiss at the top of the Eiffel Tower hadn't been what she was hoping for when she got here, but everything since that moment had been what she'd wanted all along. She was in this city, with an amazing woman, having the trip of a lifetime.

"It has exceeded my expectations," she said as she looked into Paige's eyes.

In response, Paige simply took her hand and gave it a gentle squeeze.

They explored each gallery, stopping for a light lunch when they were hungry. They accidentally discovered the towering statue of Nike at the top of a tall stairwell, then saw artists copying the works of masters in a great hall of paintings. Venus was on her pedestal, the center of attention in one of the museum's great halls. Two works of Vermeer—*The Astronomer* and *The Lacemaker*—were hanging close to each other in another hall, as if positioned so the artist could gaze upon both of his creations. Finally, they followed a sign that directed them to *Mona Lisa*.

Entering a great room, they saw a crowd of hundreds at the far end and could just glimpse the top of the painting on the wall beyond them.

Disappointment rose like bile in Carly's throat. "That's it? It can't be. It's too small."

"It's not that small. It's bigger than *The Lacemaker*."

"That's not saying much."

"They say it's all in her eyes. They're supposed to pull you in and make you feel like she's smiling at you. So we have to reserve judgment until you see her up close."

"I don't get it," Carly said as they waited in line. "*The Last Supper* takes up an entire wall. Was this a destitute nobleman who commissioned *Mona Lisa*? Was Leo short on paint?"

Paige bit her lip, and Carly shook her head. She'd waited half her lifetime for this moment, and it was such a disappointment. They finally reached the front of the line, and Carly stared into the famous woman's eyes, just as she was supposed to, but nothing happened. She found no magic. After a minute she turned away.

"If I ever have cancer, I'm going to name the tumor Mona Lisa, in honor of this painting."

Paige's jaw dropped. "Carly, that's horrible."

"That's how I feel about that painting. Horrible. Let's get out of here."

"Are you sure you're done?"

Carly sighed. "Yeah. Let's go get a few minutes of sunshine before the day is through."

Out on the concourse, the day had turned cooler, but the sun was still shining. Before they could speak, a man approached them. "Hop-on, hop-off?"

"No, thanks," Paige said reflexively. "It's too late in the day."

"Wait, lady," he said as Paige moved on. "I'll make you a deal. Two-day ticket, pay for one day."

Paige stopped, and Carly looked at her. "What do we have tomorrow?"

"A tour to Chartres, I think. That's probably a good part of the day. Thanks anyway," Carly said.

"Wait, wait," he said again and began walking with them. "I have a two-day ticket. And today free."

Carly shook her head. "I don't want to do that. We're not going to be able to really use it tomorrow."

"Okay, I tell you what. I give you today, tomorrow, and next day. Three days, pay for one."

"How much?" Paige asked.

"Forty."

"Two for forty?" Carly asked.

"Deal," he said.

Carly handed him forty Euros, and he handed them a receipt for the bus and a brochure showing the stops.

"You should have asked for a foot massage, too," Paige said as they walked toward the bus stop.

"I couldn't have a man touch my feet. Yuck."

They stood in the crowd under the bus sign and opened the map with the description of the stops on the tour. It was red, with a squiggly white line giving a rough outline of Paris and large numbers and caricatures of famous Parisian landmarks indicating their general location.

"Where do you want to go?" Carly asked.

Paige looked up to the sky. It was still bright, and the day was warm. "Why don't we just sit on top and ride around Paris? Then we can decide where we want to stop tomorrow afternoon. And we can get off close to the hotel, find some place for dinner, and walk back when we're done."

"Do you think we can find the way?"

"We have our phones," she said, and shook the paper in her hand. "And this detailed map."

"Sounds like a plan," Carly said through a chuckle.

They boarded the bus and climbed to the top, where they found seats up front. Sitting quietly, they watched the traffic and the sights, and then Paige touched Carly's arm as Notre Dame appeared ahead of them. They passed the Orsay and the Opera House, the Grand Palais. They got off at Trocadero and found an Italian restaurant, where they talked for two hours over dinner.

Back at the hotel they checked on Jules and Mel, who weren't back yet, then fell into bed yet again. Hours later, Jules texted that she was back, and she and Carly finally fell asleep, wrapped around each other.

The next morning the tour bus took them to Chartres, where they toured the ancient cathedral, and afterward, they explored Paris with their bus passes. The day was perfect, with great weather and time with Paige. Their chemistry amazed Carly. Never before—not with her family, not with Pip, not with Tasha—had she felt so in sync with another human being. She could hardly believe they'd spent four days in France. The trip was more than half over, and she began to dread going home, knowing her time with Paige was going to end.

The rest of their days were a blur, and on Friday, when Jules and Mel finally decided to spend some time with them, they enjoyed the afternoon at the Picasso Museum, posing comically in front of paintings and statues, and laughing the day away. They walked for miles along the Seine, had dinner in a small café near the Eiffel Tower, and talked about their trip. It really had been two separate vacations. Jules and Mel had spent a great part of their time with Luc and his friends, and Jules had decided to study for a semester at the Sorbonne.

"Good for you," Carly said. "It will be the experience of a lifetime."

"You just have to get your pre-med requirements in," Paige said cautiously. "That means summer school."

"I'm sure it'll be fine," Jules answered dismissively. "Carly, was Paris everything you hoped?"

"It will be, if we can just go to the top of the Eiffel Tower at night."

"Didn't you already do that?"

"Yeah, but it was the first night we were here. I was exhausted. I want to go back."

The girls agreed, and Paige bought them all dinner. Then they walked back to the Champ de Mars and rode all the way to the top of the tower. Carly breathed deeply when they exited the elevator, breaths to calm her as the girls rushed to the railing so they could look out. She and Paige followed, in no hurry. They simply stood beside each other, looking out at the lights.

"In so many ways, this trip was not what I expected," Carly said.

Paige turned around backward and leaned against the rail, looking at her. "How so?"

"Well, this tower, for one. Who knew you can climb only two stories?"

"Even with an elevator, it's a pretty nice view."

"Agreed. But I wanted to *climb* it. And the Arc de Triomphe—we didn't march through it."

"No."

"And I don't even want to talk about *Mona Lisa*."

Paige sighed and spoke softly. "I guess Paris has not lived up to the billing."

The girls approached, and Jules spoke. "We're going down. See you at the bottom," she said as they headed toward the elevator.

"I'm glad they ditched us again," Carly said as she inched closer to Paige.

Paige turned to her once more, and Carly leaned in and gave her a soft kiss on the lips. She lingered there, feeling such peace. Paige excited her, but she grounded her, too. That was an even better feeling. Pulling away, she gently rubbed her thumb across Paige's cheek. "I'm glad they ditched us," she repeated, "because I wanted to do that."

"*That* was nice. Can we do it again?" Paige whispered.

Instead of kissing, they hugged, and Carly kissed Paige's hair as she held her close. "Thank you, Paige. You've made one of my dreams come true," Carly said as tears stung her eyes.

Paige brushed away the tears with her fingertips. "You got to see *Mona Lisa*," she said softly.

Carly took Paige's hand and kissed the fingertips as her heart pounded. Suddenly her mouth was dry and her knees weak. Meeting Paige's eyes once again, she gathered her courage. Paige had been brave enough to admit her feelings, to take what she wanted. Why couldn't she? Having a future with Paige was worth the risk.

Stop thinking, she told herself.

"I've always wanted to kiss the woman I love at the top of the Eiffel Tower. Now I have." Carly looked at her expectantly, waiting for her reaction.

Paige sighed. She'd never heard words so welcome, or so sweet. "I love you, too." Even in the muted light, she could see Carly's eyes. Questions, pain, love. All of it.

She leaned back but held both of Carly's hands in hers and brought them to her heart. "How can you just walk away from this? From me?"

"Paige, we've had a great week. But this was a fantasy, not the real world. Do you actually think we could live under Paris rules at home? The magic would wear off, and all we'd have is bitterness. At least this way—we have a hell of a story to tell."

She shook her head. "No. I don't want a story. I want you. Since the moment I saw you at the golf expo, I've had this attraction. This isn't about Paris. It's about Myrtle Beach and Hershey and New York and Rehoboth. And Lake Winola. It's about cooking dinner together and cleaning up afterward. It's everything we've done together for eight months, every conversation where you made me think. And made me laugh. It's about the little things—like how you make sure I have food, so I won't get a migraine."

"We *are* food-compatible."

"We are compatible in every way."

"This is crazy."

"What's crazy is throwing this away. I've known I was attracted to women for a long time. And I was attracted to you from day one. But for whatever reason—call me dense, maybe—I never thought I was gay. Bi, maybe. But not gay. And then I made love with you, and it was like the lights came on, and I could see myself for the first time. I'm not bi, Carly. I've slept with a dozen guys, and I've never connected with any of them. Not really. But with you—it's like an electromagnet. You'll never get me off you."

Carly chuckled. "That's an interesting visual." She paused and looked out at the lights of Paris. "Are you really getting a divorce?"

"I've been getting a divorce since Tasha called the lawyer from my car in Rehoboth." Paige stared, not at the city before them, but at Carly—the woman who had done so much to help her finally realize who she really was. Carly was beautiful, and strong, and funny, and kind, and smart. She was amazing, and Paige loved her. She was already divorced and had been since the moment she met Carly. Maybe not on paper, but in her heart.

Carly looked out over the lights, avoiding Paige. This was so damn scary! She was always in control, she needed to be in control, and in this situation, she had none. If this woman beside her chose to break her heart, she was powerless to stop her.

Yet, she thought with a sigh, her heart already belonged to Paige. She'd needed to stop it right in this very spot, the last time they'd been atop the Eiffel Tower at night. Perhaps then, she could have protected herself. Not now, though. Not after what they'd shared this past week.

This trip hadn't been the one she'd planned in her mind, but it couldn't have been better. Even if she'd made it to Paris with Pip all those years ago, she doubted it would have been as magnificent a week as this one. She and Pip would have stayed in a nicer hotel, and every meal would have been a five-star production. Yet that wouldn't have made it better. This week—wandering and seeing what was around the next corner, and window-shopping, and studying art, eating crepes and baguettes from vendors along the sidewalks—all that had made the trip fun. Being with Paige had made it amazing.

She knew her heart was with Paige, and this trip proved they were compatible in every way. But could they really transport this magic back to Scranton?

Paige interrupted her thoughts. "Remember your list? The perfect woman? You should just put my picture right at the top of it."

"Perfect, you say?" she asked as she finally turned toward Paige, looking at the beautiful woman she loved.

Paige shook her head as she gazed into the distance. "No, not even close. But perfect for you. And you are perfect for me. Not because of a list of qualifications—we clearly have all that. Just because we have magic together. We had it all along. It just took us a while to figure it out." Paige met her eyes, and Carly saw her love there.

"I guess Paris enlightened us," Carly said as she stepped closer and kissed Paige softly on the cheek.

"It *is* the City of Light. And as you said, we'll have a hell of a story to tell our grandchildren."

That was a big one. The only thing, really, that suggested they might be incompatible. Children. They were not on Carly's bucket list. "Would you settle for a dog?"

Paige roared. "We can talk about it. Kids, I mean. And we can certainly get a dog."

It had never been her dream, but she knew it was Paige's. And Carly didn't hate kids. She kept a stash of candy in her office for Dominica's grandchildren. That was something, right? They'd figure it out.

Paige stepped closer into Carly's space, wrapped her arms around her, and kissed her cheek where it joined her ear.

"Please, Carly, have faith in me. In us. I can stay in the guesthouse. It won't be much different. I'll come for dinner and a movie, and we'll have sleepovers."

"I never have women in my bed. I use the guesthouse for that."

Paige pulled back and stared, wide-eyed. "In my bed? It's scandalous."

"Yes. You really put a damper on my summer frolicking." Carly paused. "But truthfully, somewhere I lost the desire for frolicking. I'd rather sit on my deck with you at night than have some random woman in the sack."

"See?"

Carly looked at her. She knew just what Paige meant. And Paige was right, about so many things. What was the worst thing that could happen? Paige would break her heart some day? If they went home and ended their relationship, it would break Carly's heart now. Did she really have anything to lose? She didn't think so.

Maybe, though, there would be no heartbreak this time. Maybe they really had what it took to make it last.

Carly sucked in a breath. "We'll need new rules."

"Scranton rules?"

"Yes."

"You tend to be a little bossy," Paige said with a wink. "Can we write them together?"

She could tone down the bossy. "Our relationship. Our life. Our rules."

Leaning in, Paige kissed her, softly, gently, then mated their foreheads.

"I love you."

Carly felt it. "I love you, too."

"This is sort of like a movie scene, don't you think?" Paige asked.

Carly turned and looked at the twinkling lights over the city. "It's not a classic romance, that's for sure."

"We're more like a rom-com."

"You do make me laugh," Carly said as she bumped her shoulder into Paige's.

"It's the best medicine."

"C'mon, Doc. Let's go home."

About the Author

Jaime Maddox is the author of seven novels with Bold Strokes Books and was awarded the Alice B. Lavender Certificate for her debut novel, *Agnes*. She has co-authored a book on bullying with her son, Jamison, and written an unpublished children's book about her kids' uncanny ability to knock out their teeth. A native of Northeastern Pennsylvania, she still lives there with her partner and twin sons. Her best times are spent with them, hanging out, baking cookies, and rebounding baskets in the driveway. When her back allows it, she hits golf balls, and when it doesn't, she does yoga. On her best days, she writes fiction.

Books Available from Bold Strokes Books

#shedeservedit by Greg Herren. When his gay best friend, and high school football star, is murdered, Alex Wheeler is a suspect and must find the truth to clear himself. (978-1-63555-996-5)

Always by Kris Bryant. When a pushy American private investigator shows up demanding to meet the woman in Camila's artwork, instead of introducing her to her great-grandmother, Camila decides to lead her on a wild goose chase all over Italy. (978-1-63679-027-5)

Exes and O's by Joy Argento. Ali and Madison really only have one thing in common. The girl who broke their heart may be the only one who can put it back together. (978-1-63679-017-6)

One Verse Multi by Sander Santiago. Life was good: promotion, friends, falling in love, discovering that the multi-verse is on a fast track to collision—wait, what? Good thing Martin King works for a company that can fix the problem, right…um…right? (978-1-63679-069-5)

Paris Rules by Jaime Maddox. Carly Becker has been searching for the perfect woman all her life, but no one ever seems to be just right until Paige Waterford checks all her boxes, except the most important one—she's married. (978-1-63679-077-0)

Shadow Dancers by Suzie Clarke. In this third and final book in the Moon Shadow series, Rachel must find a way to become the hunter and not the hunted, and this time she will meet Ehsee Yumiko head-on. (978-1-63555-829-6)

The Kiss by C.A. Popovich. When her wife refuses their divorce and begins to stalk her, threatening her life, Kate realizes to protect her new love, Leslie, she has to let her go, even if it breaks her heart. (978-1-63679-079-4)

The Wedding Setup by Charlotte Greene. When Ryann, a big-time New York executive, goes to Colorado to help out with her best friend's wedding, she never expects to fall for the maid of honor. (978-1-63679-033-6)

Velocity by Gun Brooke. Holly and Claire work toward an uncertain future preparing for an alien space mission, and only one thing is for certain, they will have to risk their lives, and their hearts, to discover the truth. (978-1-63555-983-5)

Wildflower Words by Sam Ledel. Lida Jones treks West with her father in search of a better life on the rapidly developing American frontier, but finds home when she meets Hazel Thompson. (978-1-63679-055-8)

A Fairer Tomorrow by Kathleen Knowles. For Maddie Weeks and Gerry Stern, the Second World War brought them together, but the end of the war might rip them apart. (978-1-63555-874-6)

Holiday Hearts by Diana Day-Admire and Lyn Cole. Opposites attract during Christmastime chaos in Kansas City. (978-1-63679-128-9)

Changing Majors by Ana Hartnett Reichardt. Beyond a love, beyond a coming-out, Bailey Sullivan discovers what lies beyond the shame and self-doubt imposed on her by traditional Southern ideals. (978-1-63679-081-7)

Fresh Grave in Grand Canyon by Lee Patton. The age-old Grand Canyon becomes more and more ominous as a group of volunteers fight to survive alone in nature and uncover a murderer among them. (978-1-63679-047-3)

Highland Whirl by Anna Larner. Opposites attract in the Scottish Highlands, when feisty Alice Campbell falls for city-girl-about-town Roxanne Barns. (978-1-63555-892-0)

Humbug by Amanda Radley. With the corporate Christmas party in jeopardy, CEO Rosalind Caldwell hires Christmas Girl Ellie Pearce as her personal assistant. The only problem is, Ellie isn't a PA, has never planned a party, and develops a ridiculous crush on her totally intimidating new boss. (978-1-63555-965-1)

On the Rocks by Georgia Beers. Schoolteacher Vanessa Martini makes no apologies for her dating checklist, and newly single mom Grace Chapman ticks all Vanessa's Do Not Date boxes. Of course, they're never going to fall in love. (978-1-63555-989-7)

Song of Serenity by Brey Willows. Arguing with the Muse of music and justice is complicated, falling in love with her even more so. (978-1-63679-015-2)

The Christmas Proposal by Lisa Moreau. Stranded together in a Christmas village on a snowy mountain, Grace and Bridget face their past and question their dreams for the future. (978-1-63555-648-3)

The Infinite Summer by Morgan Lee Miller. While spending the summer with her dad in a small beach town, Remi Brenner falls for Harper Hebert and accidentally finds herself tangled up in an intense restaurant rivalry between her famous stepmom and her first love. (978-1-63555-969-9)

Wisdom by Jesse J. Thoma. When Sophia and Reggie are chosen for the governor's new community design team and tasked with tackling substance abuse and mental health issues, battle lines are drawn even as sparks fly. (978-1-63555-886-9)

A Convenient Arrangement by Aurora Rey and Jaime Clevenger. Cuffing season has come for lesbians, and for Jess Archer and Cody Dawson, their convenient arrangement becomes anything but. (978-1-63555-818-0)

An Alaskan Wedding by Nance Sparks. The last thing either Andrea or Riley expects is to bump into the one who broke her heart fifteen years ago, but when they meet at the welcome party, their feelings come rushing back. (978-1-63679-053-4)

Beulah Lodge by Cathy Dunnell. It's 1874, and newly engaged Ruth Mallowes is set on marriage and life as a missionary...until she falls in love with the housemaid at Beulah Lodge. (978-1-63679-007-7)

Gia's Gems by Toni Logan. When Lindsey Speyer discovers that popular travel columnist Gia Williams is a complete fake and threatens to expose her, blackmail has never been so sexy. (978-1-63555-917-0)

Holiday Wishes & Mistletoe Kisses by M. Ullrich. Four holidays, four couples, four chances to make their wishes come true. (978-1-63555-760-2)

Love By Proxy by Dena Blake. Tess has a secret crush on her best friend, Sophie, so the last thing she wants is to help Sophie fall in love with someone else, but how can she stand in the way of her happiness? (978-1-63555-973-6)

Loyalty, Love, & Vermouth by Eric Peterson. A comic valentine to a gay man's family of choice, including the ones with cold noses and four paws. (978-1-63555-997-2)

Marry Me by Melissa Brayden. Allison Hale attempts to plan the wedding of the century to a man who could save her family's business, if only she wasn't falling for her wedding planner, Megan Kinkaid. (978-1-63555-932-3)

Pathway to Love by Radclyffe. Courtney Valentine is looking for a woman exactly like Ben—smart, sexy, and not in the market for anything serious. All she has to do is convince Ben that sex-without-strings is the perfect pathway to pleasure. (978-1-63679-110-4)

Sweet Surprise by Jenny Frame. Flora and Mac never thought they'd ever see each other again, but when Mac opens up her barber shop right next to Flora's sweet shop, their connection comes roaring back. (978-1-63679-001-5)

The Edge of Yesterday by CJ Birch. Easton Gray is sent from the future to save humanity from technological disaster. When she's forced to target the woman she's falling in love with, can Easton do what's needed to save humanity? (978-1-63679-025-1)

The Scout and the Scoundrel by Barbara Ann Wright. With unexpected danger surrounding them, Zara and Roni are stuck between duty and survival, with little room for exploring their feelings, especially love. (978-1-63555-978-1)

Bury Me in Shadows by Greg Herren. College student Jake Chapman is forced to spend the summer at his dying grandmother's home and soon finds danger from long-buried family secrets. (978-1-63555-993-4)

Can't Leave Love by Kimberly Cooper Griffin. Sophia and Pru have no intention of falling in love, but sometimes love happens when and where you least expect it. (978-1-636790041-1)

Free Fall at Angel Creek by Julie Tizard. Detective Dee Rawlings and aircraft accident investigator Dr. River Dawson use conflicting methods to find answers when a plane goes missing, while overcoming surprising threats, and discovering an unlikely chance at love. (978-1-63555-884-5)

Love's Compromise by Cass Sellars. For Piper Holthaus and Brook Myers, will professional dreams and past baggage stop two hearts from realizing they are meant for each other? (978-1-63555-942-2)

Not All a Dream by Sophia Kell Hagin. Hester has lost the woman she loved and the world has descended into relentless dark and cold. But giving up will have to wait when she stumbles upon people who help her survive. (978-1-63679-067-1)

Protecting the Lady by Amanda Radley. If Eve Webb had known she'd be protecting royalty, she'd never have taken the job as bodyguard, but as the threat to Lady Katherine's life draws closer, she'll do whatever it takes to save her, and may just lose her heart in the process. (978-1-63679-003-9)

The Secrets of Willowra by Kadyan. A family saga of three women, their homestead called Willowra in the Australian outback, and the secrets that link them all. (978-1-63679-064-0)

Trial by Fire by Carsen Taite. When prosecutor Lennox Roy and public defender Wren Bishop become fierce adversaries in a headline-grabbing arson case, their attraction ignites a passion that leads them both to question their assumptions about the law, the truth, and each other. (978-1-63555-860-9)

Turbulent Waves by Ali Vali. Kai Merlin and Vivien Palmer plan their future together as hostile forces make their own plans to destroy what they have, as well as all those they love. (978-1-63679-011-4)

Unbreakable by Cari Hunter. When Dr. Grace Kendal is forced at gunpoint to help an injured woman, she is dragged into a nightmare where nothing is quite as it seems, and their lives aren't the only ones on the line. (978-1-63555-961-3)

Veterinary Surgeon by Nancy Wheelton. When dangerous drugs are stolen from the veterinary clinic, Mitch investigates and Kay becomes a suspect. As pride and professions clash, love seems impossible. (978-1-63679-043-5)

A Different Man by Andrew L. Huerta. This diverse collection of stories chronicling the challenges of gay life at various ages shines a light on the progress made and the progress still to come. (978-1-63555-977-4)

All That Remains by Sheri Lewis Wohl. Johnnie and Shantel might have to risk their lives—and their love—to stop a werewolf intent on killing. (978-1-63555-949-1)

Beginner's Bet by Fiona Riley. Phenom luxury Realtor Ellison Gamble has everything, except a family to share it with, so when a mix-up brings youthful Katie Crawford into her life, she bets the house on love. (978-1-63555-733-6)

Dangerous Without You by Lexus Grey. Throughout their senior year in high school, Aspen, Remington, Denna, and Raleigh face challenges in life and romance that they never expect. (978-1-63555-947-7)

Desiring More by Raven Sky. In this collection of steamy stories, a rich variety of lovers find themselves desiring more, more from a lover, more from themselves, and more from life. (978-1-63679-037-4)

Jordan's Kiss by Nanisi Barrett D'Arnuck. After losing everything in a fire, Jordan Phelps joins a small lounge band and meets pianist Morgan Sparks, who lights another blaze, this time in Jordan's heart. (978-1-63555-980-4)

Late City Summer by Jeanette Bears. Forced together for her wedding, Emily Stanton and Kate Alessi navigate their lingering passion for one another against the backdrop of New York City and World War II, and a summer romance they left behind. (978-1-63555-968-2)

Love and Lotus Blossoms by Anne Shade. On her path to self-acceptance and true passion, Janesse will risk everything—and possibly everyone—she loves. (978-1-63555-985-9)

Love in the Limelight by Ashley Moore. Marion Hargreaves, the finest actress of her generation, and Jessica Carmichael, the world's biggest pop star, rediscover each other twenty years after an ill-fated affair. (978-1-63679-051-0)

Suspecting Her by Mary P. Burns. Complications ensue when Erin O'Connor falls for top real estate saleswoman Catherine Williams while investigating racism in the real estate industry; the fallout could end their chance at happiness. (978-1-63555-960-6)

Two Winters by Lauren Emily Whalen. A modern YA retelling of Shakespeare's *The Winter's Tale* about birth, death, Catholic school, improv comedy, and the healing nature of time. (978-1-63679-019-0)